PENGUIN
CITY OF REEDS

City of Reeds is Tina Shaw's third novel. *Birdie* was published in 1996, followed in 1997 by *Dreams of America*, which was serialised and broadcast on National Radio. Her short stories have been published in anthologies and literary journals. Stories and articles have also appeared in *Metro* and other magazines. In 1998 Tina was editor of a collection of travel essays by New Zealand writers called *A Passion for Travel*. She was a recipient of the Buddle Findlay Sargeson Fellowship in 1999. Tina lives in Auckland.

City of Reeds

Tina Shaw

PENGUIN BOOKS

PENGUIN BOOKS

Penguin Books (NZ) Ltd, cnr Airborne and Rosedale Roads, Albany,
Auckland 1310, New Zealand
Penguin Books Ltd, 27 Wrights Lane, London W8 5TZ, England
Penguin Putnam Inc, 375 Hudson Street, New York, NY 10014, United States
Penguin Books Australia Ltd, 487 Maroondah Highway,
Ringwood, Australia 3134
Penguin Books Canada Ltd, 10 Alcorn Avenue, Toronto,
Ontario, Canada M4V 3B2
Penguin Books (South Africa) Pty Ltd, 5 Watkins Street,
Denver Ext 4, 2094, South Africa
Penguin Books India (P) Ltd, 11, Community Centre, Panchsheel Park,
New Delhi 110 017, India
Penguin Books Ltd, Registered Offices: Harmondsworth, Middlesex, England

First published by Penguin Books (NZ) Ltd, 2000

1 3 5 7 9 10 8 6 4 2

Copyright © Tina Shaw, 2000

The right of Tina Shaw to be identified as the author of this work in terms
of section 96 of the Copyright Act 1994 is hereby asserted.

Quote from 'God's Dice', from the collection
Einstein's Monsters by Martin Amis reproduced
by kind permission of Jonathon Cape.

Designed by Mary Egan
Typeset by Egan-Reid Ltd, Auckland
Printed in Australia by Australian Print Group, Maryborough

All rights reserved. Without limiting the rights under copyright reserved above,
no part of this publication may be reproduced, stored in or introduced
into a retrieval system, or transmitted, in any form or by any means
(electronic, mechanical, photocopying, recording or otherwise), without
the prior written permission of both the copyright owner and
the above publisher of this book.

ISBN 0 14 029791X

The assistance of Creative New Zealand towards the production of this book is gratefully
acknowledged by the Publisher.

ACKNOWLEDGEMENTS

I am very grateful to Creative New Zealand for an arts grant that carried this novel through its early stages, and to the Buddle Findlay Sargeson Fellowship, which I held in 1999, for giving me the time to finish it.

I wish to thank Dr Dave Hopcroft for his advice, and Dr Paul Silvester of Thames Hospital, who kindly talked to me about surgery. Thanks also to Bernice Beachman for her support and belief in the book, John Shaw for his inspiration, Graeme Lay for his wisdom, and Jane Parkin for her excellent editing.

Two books, among many, were particularly useful in my research: *The Wisdom of the Body* by Dr Sherwin Nuland, and *The Wind Blows Away Our Words* by Doris Lessing. The folk story on page 159 was originally from *Oral Narrative in Afghanistan* by Margaret Mills.

The town in my novel, although based upon a real New Zealand town, is nevertheless my own fictional version. The characters are also fictional.

Bujak was right. In the city now there are loose components, accelerated particles – something has come loose, something is wriggling, lassoing, spinning towards the edge of its groove. Something must give and it isn't safe. You ought to be terribly careful. Because safety has left our lives.

– 'God's Dice', Martin Amis

PART ONE

Firth and Frith

ONE

Her father's house is just the same: white weatherboards and yellow trim, small fishing gnome bullied by marguerite daisies in the front garden, white picket gate and concrete path leading to the front door. The yellow banksia rose over the trellis archway threatens to knock them about. It is a house that Clare always thought would better suit Mrs Kray, and suspects her hand in its choosing.

She lays out her things in the spare room, while Lou crashes about in the kitchen fixing something. Food, Clare hopes suddenly – though the pop of a champagne bottle belies it. Marty was up when they arrived, but has since gone back to bed. Mrs Kray has only just left. Neighbours have been ringing. Somebody has left a bag of tomatoes, and a pile of fishing magazines.

There are two flutes of champagne on the Formica bench when she comes out. Lou, thin in black skirt and poloneck, leans against the bench, eating a grape – a bunch is sprawled on a plate at her elbow, along with a round of brie.

'Do you think the old man'd like a glass?'

'No,' says Clare, 'that's the last thing he needs.'

'All the more for us then.' Lou takes a long mouthful of her own champagne, then squeezes the bridge of her nose. 'Lovely.' She takes her glass over to Marty's armchair and seats herself as if she's travelling first class. 'Just as well I brought the glasses – all he has in there are old jam jars.' She laughs at her joke. Clare, taking her seriously, peers in the cupboard (well stocked with an assortment of glasses, none of them jam). She takes the plate of grapes and cheese, and sits in the other armchair. Her father's needs, she remembers, are simple.

'It's very noble of you, rushing back like this,' Lou says after a while. 'But then I suppose this must be like a holiday for you – or a, um, sabbatical.'

'That's one way of putting it.' Though Clare wouldn't have. 'I was thinking about coming back, anyway.'

'So what are you going to do now?'

'I haven't decided yet. I left San Fran in such a hurry that I hadn't organised everything.'

Lou studies the bubbles in her flute. 'Well, if it were me, I'd be heading straight back to America.' She meets Clare's look, then smiles, as if to say, Another joke.

'I daresay I will,' says Clare, feeling dizzy from jetlag and the champagne. She has been back in her hometown for approximately two hours, and everything seems out of whack. She cuts a piece of cheese, remembering the day she left five years ago. She'd got her skirt caught in the escalator at the airport and it had ripped, showing too much pale leg, and her father had blushed in attempting to extricate her, while Louise had rushed off on the pretext of getting help but really to escape the embarrassing sight of her older sister making a fool of herself in public.

'You're not running away from anything, are you, Clare?'

Clare looks up, startled more by the rudeness of her tone than the question itself. 'Of course not.' Though she can't help sneaking a glance at Lou, to read her expression. They never did confide very much. But Louise is already moving on.

'So how bad is Marty anyway?'

She realises that this is the first time Lou has asked after Marty since they met at the airport. She'd had plenty of time to ask in the car, but hadn't. After they had arrived at the house, and while Clare was talking to their father, Lou had buggered off to the shops.

'All the signs are good,' she said. 'It wasn't a huge heart attack. Probably not too much damage done. But I want to have a chat with the Registrar at Middlemore yet.'

Despite her immaculate make-up, Lou looks tired. She refills her glass, giving a laugh. 'I had a funny thought, that day I rang you – I thought, I must ring Beth next, and tell her about Marty too.'

'Where would you have rung, I wonder.'

'That's the thing,' says Lou, 'I was thinking she was still in that dreary third world country she went to.'

'Afghanistan.' Clare tucks her feet beneath her. 'I sometimes think she's still there, too. I like to follow the news from there, on the Internet.'

'Yeah? What's happening over there?'

'Oh, the usual thing. Fighting, destruction.'

'Good for them.'

'I think I'll check Marty.' Clare pads out of the room, and pokes her head round her father's door. His eyes are shut, though Clare doesn't think he's sleeping. By the bed is a black and white photograph of the three of them, the Purefoy girls, in shorts and blouses. Clare notices there's something a little askew about the photograph, but then dismisses the thought. She quietly closes her father's door.

'I get so claustrophobic in this house,' sighs Lou, pacing the lounge. 'Let's take a drive.'

Mainstreet, with its goldrush-era shop-poles and forlorn line of shop fronts, is desolate in the early evening. Clare holds her hands carefully in her lap. 'Where is everybody?'

Louise, behind the wheel, barely gives it a glance. 'How should I know?' she says languidly. 'It's always like this.'

Litter is blowing along the gutters, asphalt gleaming metal-grey in the light, and several of the shops have 'For Lease' signs in empty windows. A man in an army overcoat is standing outside the Four Square eating a meat pie, yellow-stained beard over his chest. Have all the people fled? Clare is reminded of medical horror movies that feature viruses which threaten to wipe out whole populations. Old cold war scenarios pale beside nightmares such as ebola. Medical plagues offer more dramatic scope than a nuclear explosion.

Louise, who has been talking nearly non-stop since leaving the house, has grown silent now, which only reinforces Clare's fantasies. They will return to their father's house only to find it empty – a pile of slime where once there was a living man.

They drive up to the War Memorial, its pale stony finger pointing at the clouds. Lou takes the corners like a pro. When they pull into the carpark, gravel flying, Lou is first out. Clare follows more slowly. The air smells nice. 'I used to come up here on a Friday night, and hang out.'

Lou glances back at her sister with disbelief. 'I don't remember you coming up here on Friday nights.' That was the kind of thing she used to do herself, when Clare was at home studying.

'Well, maybe just the once,' she adds, laughing at herself now. 'I did come up here with Beth though.' That time she and Bethie had cycled up the sharply winding road.

'Oh yes?' A few strands of Lou's ashen hair blow across her mouth.

'It nearly killed me,' says Clare, 'that bike ride. But you should've seen Beth. It was like she was still on the flat – not even puffing!'

Louise takes out a cigarette and lights it with a match. 'Well, she was very fit.'

'Yes,' says Clare.

They walk up the concrete steps to the pillar engraved with names of the dead. Lou sits with her back to it, smoking, while Clare walks over to look at the view, a breeze smelling of mudflats fingering her fine blonde hair. Spreading out to her right is the firth, so brown and wide you might think of the Nile, and in the far distance the rest of the mainland rolling greens and browns. Straight ahead is the snaking Waihou River. The amount of greenery is staggering.

Down below, practically at the foot of the hill, lies the town, neat as a pin. The familiar grid with its straight grey streets, dominated by mainstreet running from north to south; a small flat town that is a puzzle of creams and reds. It all looks so small from this modest height: was it always so small, and flat? Or has it shrunk since she's been away? Like Marty. With all the trauma she's seen in her working life, Clare realises that deep down she still thought of him as untouchable. That he'd live on for ever, despite the evidence of medical science.

The town below is indolent in the twilight; a blue jeep glides along Mary Street. Clare would like to wrap the town around her like a woolly blanket. She'd like to nestle in its folds and secret corners, until she feels completely safe again.

Louise joins her, dropping the cigarette butt on the gravel and grinding it down with her toe. 'Nothing but the dead and the dying, eh . . . Gives me the willies.'

Clare wakes panting and disoriented. There's a man creeping about the apartment – she's convinced of it. Creeping, a creep, in her . . . where's the streetlight that beams into her bedroom all night, regardless of curtains? Where's the traffic noise? She is sweating now, panic-stricken. It's so dark, and silent. Like being on another planet. Where the hell is she? She lies very still, eyes searching for clues.

Her father's house – New Zealand.

Clare gets up, disturbed, and goes out into the short hallway. Marty's door is open, and he is sitting on the side of his bed, like a soldier contemplating his hands. What a pair, she thinks.

'All right, Dad?'

He looks up, but she can't make out his expression. 'Can't sleep. No big deal.'

'Want a cup of tea?'

'Sure.'

She leaves him sitting in the dark, and flicks on the kitchen light. Bland red Formica, a stainless steel sink, scratched with age, a battalion of mugs hanging on a row of hooks. She'd forgotten about Lou sleeping on the couch, but there is no break in the measured breathing coming from the darkness.

What am I doing here? Suddenly Clare's panic returns tenfold. She can't just walk out on her work, her life, like that. She must be going nuts. Loco. Wiseman's voice ricochets inside her head: *Go home for a while, take care of your father, rediscover your roots.* Who was he kidding? She'd tried for a joke, *pure Californian corn* – but their faint laughter was still self-conscious. Maybe she was just being paranoid.

And here she is, thousands of miles from life as she knew it. Clare leans her forehead against a cupboard door, and groans.

'All right, Doctor Purefoy?' Marty stands there in his striped pyjamas and dressing gown, grinning.

Touché, thinks Clare.

'How's that tea coming along?'

When she wakes the next morning Clare lies listening to the shower running. Silence from Marty's room: he will be exhausted. She hopes he's still sleeping. Clare gets up and wanders into the kitchen. The empty champagne bottle is on the floor.

The house seems flooded with sunlight. She stands at the kitchen bench blinking, unaccustomed to so much light, pale in the white cotton boxer shorts and T-shirt she slept in. Through the kitchen window she can see the familiar dark shape of the mountains that seem to herd the town towards the sea. They loom maternally, just at the end of the street. There is some mist clinging to the tops – the sun is not yet high enough to burn it off – and the highest point, the Pinnacles, is obscured.

Clare takes her mug of coffee outside, breathing in the clean air, still amazed by the emptiness and the silence. Do people actually live here? The house fronts could be plywood, a movie set. Then a small truck trundles past, and the driver wolf-whistles at her, his red elbow pointing out the window.

Lou comes out of the house. She is wearing a pink lycra miniskirt, heels, a white shirt, Ray-Bans. She throws her overnight bag into the back seat of her BMW, and gives a desultory wave.

'Keep in touch –'

Clare watches as the car makes a three-point turn in the narrow street, then zooms off dramatically down the hill. 'Can't get out of here fast enough,' their mother once said, about an acquaintance who had moved to Auckland. And later, after Pat had gone, there was Bethie with her nose pushed against a window, staring out at the empty street and hissing into the glass, *Can't get out of here fast enough.*

Why is it that Clare suddenly feels bereft? As if she has just been told bad news. There's a heaviness in her body that seems unrelated to the jetlag.

I could do anything now, go anywhere. Clare shivers against the sun, and holds the warm coffee mug closer to her chest. So much possibility is dizzying, she thinks, and goes back into the dim house to escape the intensity of the light.

TWO

THEY WERE the Purefoy girls.

There was a time when they used to laugh a lot. She and Lou and Bethie. The Purefoy sisters. They'd get up to pranks. The time they put salt in the sugar bowl and their father, who always had three spoonfuls in his breakfast cup of tea, made a face. 'Who's been putting salt in the sugar bowl again?' he boomed. But it was always funny. They would run giggling through the house and hide in all the cupboards. There was a short wooden banister to slide down, and an angled cupboard beneath the short flight of stairs to the attic room, but you had to make sure you didn't hide in there with Lou because she always farted and you had to burst out again only to be caught. For there was much hide-and-seek played on rainy days, much clattering up and down the wooden boards of the hallway. There was the time they dressed up, in wigs and swinging handbags, and walked down mainstreet playing Goldrush Ladies. Boys had shouted with laughter and just shouted, and they'd shouted back, and somehow it ended in handbags being swung, colliding with red faces, and mother's dresses getting dirty. Running back up the hill, and barely able to because of the heaving laughter that was dragging them along, grabbing glances over shoulders only to find – with some relief – that the boys couldn't be bothered following after all. They would get their own back later, those boys: it was a small town. Everybody knew the Purefoy girls.

Mainstreet was deserted on a Monday evening, on an early Sunday morning. Like gunslinging cowgirls they would walk down the middle of the road to the bakery, its window redolent with fancy goods. *Rustle us up a custard square, buddy.* Taking freshly baked bread back for mum, but making a hole at the end, pulling out fragments of soft white innards from a mousehole and somehow reminiscent of the White Cliffs of Dover that their mother longed to visit.

'Who's been at the bread?' mother said reproachfully, looking at all three of them in turn. But nobody owned up. It was the wind, said Lou, the youngest, and the most whimsical back then. It was a dog, said Clare, the pragmatic; a large blue dog – though she could run to a little embellishment. But Bethie always had to outdo everybody: 'Just as we were walking back home a man rushed up to us and tried to steal the bread, *right* out of our hands, but I *fought* for the bread, he at one end, I holding onto the other – for dear life' – an expression adults often liked to use, and having the proper sense of drama to it – 'and I started screaming at the top of my voice, we were struggling so *hard*, Mum, that you should've seen it, the end broke off in the man's hands, and he ran away . . . faster than you can say Jack Spratt.'

Bethie and their mother drew breath. Clare and Lou were wide-eyed with admiration. Beth looked about proudly for applause. But the bread had still been desecrated.

'Thank you, girls,' said Pat, 'but next time, please leave the bread alone till you get home.' And she walked away, with that certain measured swing to her skirt.

Bethie looked at the others. 'Well,' she said, 'it might have happened that way. Don't you think?' She was unsure for a moment.

Clare and Lou both thought that it could easily have happened that way.

'When I grow up,' she added enigmatically, 'I am going to be a baker.'

Mrs Kray, who goes back a long way with the Purefoys (though she eludes easy description beyond 'family friend') turns up on the doorstep one morning. She doesn't bother knocking, but scrapes her feet and enters the house with a 'Hal-loo there –'

Clare looks up from the carrot salad she's making at the bench. Mrs Kray is solid in a dress that appears to be made out of pink tapestry, and is carrying two plastic shopping bags filled with the shiny leaves of silverbeet.

'I thought Marty could do with these' – she plonks the bags onto the bench at Clare's elbow – 'he hasn't got any in his garden.' Then, after a few nervous steps about the kitchen, her voice drops to a hiss, her lichen-like hair aquiver. 'How is he?'

Clare smiles at her apprehension. 'He's fine, really. You can see for yourself, when he gets out of the shower.'

Mrs Kray does a double-take. 'He's in the shower?'

'Where did you expect him to be?'

'That's safe?' Mrs Kray's eyebrows are scrunched together anxiously. 'I mean, after all he's been through?' Clare wipes her hands on a teatowel and leans against the bench. Mrs Kray moves closer. 'It's just that, I wouldn't like him to have another, er, attack.'

'Neither would I,' says Clare firmly, 'but we can't keep him wrapped up in cottonwool. Rest assured, he is out of danger.'

'Ah,' sighs Mrs Kray, rubbing her right hand over the left. 'Well, you would know, you're the doctor.'

To keep busy she springcleans Marty's house, while he lies on the couch, slowly turning the pages of *Fishing New Zealand*. The house is extraordinarily clean, which makes Clare wonder if Mrs Kray isn't still playing an active part in Marty's life. She checks out the basement last. Tools are hanging on the wall, their painted shadows behind them. Everything is in place. The workbench with its vise at one end is immaculate. Used, dated cans of paint are stacked up against the wall, and his house-painting ladders hang from hooks below the ceiling. Under the bench are cardboard boxes labelled: *Clare, Louise, Beth*. Most of the boxes seem to be Clare's old things, left with Marty when she went overseas. Tucked into a corner is even Beth's old backpack.

Clare pulls out one of the Bethie boxes, and opens it up. It's full of school books, and hard-cover diaries – she'd forgotten that Beth kept diaries – all neatly labelled and packed in order. Clare takes out a blue diary with *Afghanistan* printed on the cover.

February 1983
Our first day in Peshawar is hairy . . .

She takes it up to the bedroom and puts it quickly into her pack, as if somebody might catch her.

Beth Purefoy lay on her bed in the hotel and listened to the sounds coming from above. It was early in the morning, though still dark, and the ceiling fan was clunking away, sending uneven waves of stuffy air over her now-cold arms. Terry slept on oblivious in the other bed, her slippery dark hair hanging over the side and touching the floor with every breath she exhaled.

As in a myth, Bethie's journey to Kabul turned out to be time-consuming and circuitous. First there had been the flight from Heathrow to Islamabad, then the smaller plane that had brought them to Peshawar, the centre in Pakistan for the eastern side of Afghanistan. There were several nights spent at Dean's Hotel, that seedy conglomerate of buildings which acted as a base for foreign journalists (the ones who were brave enough or crazy enough to report on a forgotten war), aid workers, bedraggled hippy travellers, and the spooks. Most of the staff were said to be Russian spies; there were spies from the KHAD, the Afghan secret service which was actually run by the Russians. 'Have you been *in* yet?' was a common refrain. The coolest way to get into Afghanistan was with a group of the local resistance fighters, the mujahedin. They walked the city streets like proud bandits from another age, wearing turbans or Afghan caps, often with a blanket draped over one shoulder (in the mountains, this constituted their bedding), bearded, black-eyed men who were fighting the Soviet invasion with little more than ground-to-air missiles, Kalashnikovs and an intense belief in the justice of Allah. To the Afghans it was a holy war, *jihad*; Western journalists tagged it the 'Soviet Vietnam'.

Another bang from the ceiling. It sounded like possums having a wrestling match. Scratches followed, a scattering, as if of paws running on boards. Thuds. A muted cry. Perhaps there were more rooms up there, though she didn't think so.

Bethie pushed her legs out from beneath the covers. She turned off the fan, then sat cross-legged on the floor at Terry's head. She lifted the hair between her hands, and started gently to plait it. When it was a braid, she laid it along the covers beside Terry, smoothing it with her fingers. She felt filled up with happiness. As if she had only just discovered what it meant.

From outside came a sudden jarring of bells; then a voice wailed, raised as in a war cry. Terry stirred, opened her eyes. 'What's that?' she muttered.

Bethie had her head to one side, listening. 'It must be the call to the faithful.'

A temporary surgeon is needed at the local hospital – a Dr Brightly wants to take three months' leave – and Clare finds herself accepting the position. Details are surprisingly easy to arrange. It takes only a few phone calls back to San Francisco.

'Where are you going to live?' wonders Lou, over the phone. 'With Marty?' Her aversion is palpable.

Clare grins. 'I'm going to housesit the Brightlys' place.'

His job, his house – what else is there to a life? Would she eventually take on his persona as well, use his name, meet his friends? It all seems rather funny and absurd. The hospital as well. 'I bet the emergency room here only handles one gunshot incident a year,' Clare says on her first day. Alex Mather, the other full-time surgeon who is now her colleague, reinforces this impression.

'There's hardly any tonsillectomies; all those uncomfortable anal procedures like haemorrhoids – gone; forget varicose veins – in fact the government has specifically excluded them, they have to go private, used to do about 200 a year, now we're down to two – no grommets, negligible ENT surgery in general; there's still a fracture clinic but most of it goes to Waikato first – all the little old ladies, we ship 'em. To sum up, we work with the notion of unnecessary surgery.'

Clare Purefoy looks down into her cup of milky instant coffee, then looks back up at Mather, concentrates on her breathing. They are standing in the ground-floor staffroom; the walls are a putrid shade of tan. Clare is aware of the brittle sound of children's laughter coming from the grassed area out the front.

'You're joking, right?'

Mather gives an emaciated grin. 'Already regretting you took the job?'

Clare too smiles, politely, thinking him unnecessarily cynical. 'Not at all,' she says.

'Think you can find your way around?'

'Of course.'

So Clare takes on Brightly's duties, and moves into his house with its shingle roof and dormer windows, halfway up a long set of concrete steps called 'Jacob's Ladder'. The Brightlys have packed away the valuables, stripped the place of anything too personal; there is the odd gap on the wall where a painting had hung. The pictures that remain are bland landscape prints that would do nicely in a motel unit. There is a framed cross-stitch in the kitchen that says 'Bless this mess'.

Clare wishes she could work a night shift, as she often did in San Fran, but the local hospital doesn't run to that. So she must put up with the yawning dark spaces within the house, the creaking of timbers, the constant rustlings and knockings from the oak trees that surround the garden, and occasional rusty screams of possums. It's like being a kind of prisoner. There are so many trees and plants – Clare can only recognise the oak trees – that it's a relief to be able to turn her back on all that and look west, down over the town, and to the sea.

As if to prove her commitment to this new life she buys herself a secondhand VW. When the house becomes too unbearable she gets into the car and drives up around the hill and down to mainstreet, to sit in Harry's Bar with an Irish whisky between her hands.

It is on the way back from one of these desperate excursions – on a rain-battering night – that she discovers part of Parawai Road, near the white church, has flooded. She was driving slowly anyway, or she wouldn't have seen the water spewing across the road until she was upon it. Instead she pauses, the car idling, while she decides whether it is safe enough to drive through. Then she sees something in the water. Half wading, sinking: a squashed-up face with distressed eyes goggling. *Oh God.* She jumps out of the car, and wades into the filthy water – it comes only partly up her leg, not even to the knee – and hauls out what turns out to be a dog, a pug.

She holds the animal up to the light of the headlamps. 'A rat dog.' The pug, gratefully and with little grunts, starts to lick her face.

Back at the house – lights blazing, just the way she had left it – she fixes herself a whisky and pours a measure into a bowl of milk for the dog. Then she gets the fire going, wraps the dog in a towel and puts him in front of the fire.

'You better hope somebody comes forward to claim you,' she tells the dog, 'because I am not going to keep you.'

The dog, who is very ugly, gives her foot a lick, then falls asleep with his chin resting on her toes.

Only a few blocks away from Brightly's is the house that their father had built on the Terrace, where Clare grew up. A few doors along from that house, on the corner of Hape Street that runs both up towards the hills and back down towards the flat, was the Mansion. Not that it actually was a mansion – it was a large two-storeyed villa that would once have sat solitary among the scrub and eyed a goldrush town at its feet – but they all liked the sound of 'mansion'.

'Those people up at the Mansion,' said their mother, 'don't know how lucky they are.'

There were the mosquitoes for one thing. Their own house was low, in a dip in the road, and with the creek burbling along beside the house, which was all very well to play in, but it gave off cold in the winter, bred mosquitoes in the summer, and brought in the rats. The foxie caught three in one week – a record – and the Mansion wouldn't have that problem either, said their mother. There was even the rat that eluded the dog: their mother found it preening itself on top of the laundry basket. Her scream was heard all the way down the street, and old Mrs Barrow next door thought somebody had been murdered.

Their mother planted bushes to conceal the sight of the creek, but it was impossible to hide its constant burbling, even if she did have the radio playing all day, then the television at night – at some stage of the day the sound of the creek would slip in. You could never truly escape it.

But for the girls the creek was a friend. There were paper boats, and plywood creations, there was paddling and the occasional unsuccessful hunt for eels. The creek gave, and the creek also took away. There was the flood of '72 when the water rose silently in the night, creeping over the lawn to lap at the back door, filled the sandpit and stole the plastic buckets and spades and one of Lou's Barbies, and their mother's gumboots, and turned the back lawn into a quagmire for days afterwards.

Their mother set her mouth and turned away from the sight: her lovely back lawn, shaved every Saturday. 'This wouldn't happen up at the Mansion,' she was heard to say, beneath her breath. And the unspoken criticism: that this wouldn't have happened if the house had been built on higher ground. Higher ground, their mother knew, was the secret to successfully living in this one-horse town: you were safe from floods and rats and you would have a View. The Mansion, of course, had a grand view. 'You'd never get sick of that view,' declared their mother.

Grunt is still so nervous that the telephone startles him, especially when it rings at odd hours, as Louise seems to like doing.

12.09 a.m., Saturday. 'So how's Marty?'

Clare, who was asleep in bed, rolls onto an elbow, relieved that at least it's not Marty himself, or the hospital. 'He's fine. But why don't you ask him yourself.'

'Yes, I must.' Yet Lou betrays no interest in doing so. 'So, tell me about that hunk you were seeing in San Fran. I want to hear all the juicy details. Won't he be missing you?'

Clare rubs her face. She has forgotten that she'd mentioned Marcus in a letter. 'We broke up, ages ago.' Was it, ages ago? It feels like a long time, but it was probably only a few weeks before Marty's heart attack. The timing, to come back home for a short period, couldn't have been better. 'I'll tell you all about it, next time we meet.'

'Right,' Lou says sharply, 'I get the hint.' And rings off. Clare replaces the receiver, feeling as if she's done something wrong.

Every night, after Marcus's arrest, Clare was visited by a dream in which objects of beauty were falling down a deep mine shaft, reminiscent of the well in *Alice in Wonderland*; she would struggle to catch them, but they smashed at the bottom anyway.

And small, stupid incidents got to her. The clown, for instance, on Mission Street. One morning, on her way to the hospital, there was a clown sitting on top of a rubbish bin and eating a kebab, a dribble of red chilli sauce on his chin. He screwed up the paper kebab-wrapping and threw it down on the sidewalk at his feet. 'Is it such an effort,' said Clare, stopping, 'to just turn around and put that in the bin –?' He looked up in surprise. 'Now that you mention it, yes, it is,' he said, and ambled off. She picked it up herself, put it in the bin. '*You useless piece of shit*,' she shouted after him. Clare drew breath, shaking. Look at you, she muttered, you're screaming at a clown.

When she wasn't working, she took to drinking in bars by herself. She discovered a bar where Kiwis liked to hang out. Sitting on one of the stools, a glass of cold Budweiser between her hands, Clare listened from the periphery to the familiar accent, the talk about baches and cabbage trees and Marmite. One evening, while the Sharks played Montreal on the big screen in the corner, she got talking to a couple, dancers who were training at the local school; the dark, lean woman came from Wellington, the man from Napier. It was a delight to hear the familiar place names again. They even discovered a mutual acquaintance, a friend of a friend who was in Clare's class at med school and who was now in melanoma research and struggling to get funding – ironic for a country with such a high rate of skin cancer, the man commented.

'The country's gone to shit,' the man continued. 'It's a country of philistines and rugby players who get paid megabucks – just like it's always been really, only now it's worse.' He poured more beer into his glass, his long legs twisted round the barstool. 'You're way better off here.'

'I don't know,' said the woman, 'I can't get the hang of it sometimes, this city. It's like there's too much of a buzz.' She pushed her shoulders up to her ears. 'Where's all the normal people?'

'You're looking at them,' joked Clare. They all laughed, although the woman's words had left her feeling hollowed out. The stories she could tell this shining couple, she brooded.

The night before a boy had come to the hospital with a fake leg wound – fake blood, a rag tied around his thigh – and when the attending doctor had entered his cubicle, the boy had held a gun to the doctor's head and demanded drugs. That kind of thing was a common occurrence in the Emergency Room; they even had a security guard at the door. That wouldn't happen back home, thought Clare. And Marcus . . . what he did, that would be unthinkable in New Zealand. The longer she was away, the more idealised and innocent the country seemed – despite the newspaper clippings Marty sent her, indulging his interest in home invasions and medical misadventure. Clare used to laugh over them. After the things she saw on a daily basis, they just didn't seem real.

March 1983
A bomb went off in the bazaar yesterday. A man was thrown into the sky! Jeez, eh.

Through the office window Beth was aware of the mountains of the Hindu Kush looming in the distance, violet through the haze of afternoon smog. There was a dull, aching drone in the front of her head that she attributed to jetlag, and drips of sweat were running down her side. Both she and Terry were dressed in long-sleeved shirts and long skirts, and their hair was covered, though the men on the other side of the desk still wouldn't meet their gaze. An antique desk fan was moving hot air around the room in a way more irritating than relieving. A donkey started braying in the street below.

Rob was arguing with the Pakistani men about their permits. It is too dangerous to go into Afghanistan at the moment, they were saying, much fighting. But we're aid workers, Rob was saying. 'The journalists are still going in,' said Beth. The men ignored her. Finally one of them made a telephone call. All right, he said, putting down the receiver and shaking his head sadly, they could have permits. 'But safer to stay in Pakistan.'

Outside on the street a group of men were leaning against a battered truck, staring at them as they walked past. Bethie was aware of her blonde hair, even beneath the flimsy scarf, and withered under such an intense gaze. Their dark eyes seemed hard and unforgiving. Foreign women. Were they being blamed, excoriated, stripped naked? There was no way of telling.

'Get a load of them,' hissed Terry. 'What d'you think's passing through their heads?'

'I don't wanna know.'

'Hey,' Terry called back over her shoulder, 'have a nice day.'

A quiver seemed collectively to jerk through the men. Then one of them grinned, and called back, 'Merry Christmas!' Hilarity followed them down the street.

THREE

Tupulo has a large mouth. He likes to widen his mouth to its full capacity and take a bite of a tall hamburger; he likes to order the tallest hamburger the takeaway bar can make, explicitly to perform this small feat. 'I could have been a great opera singer,' he boasts between mouthfuls, 'along the lines of Carreras.'

He and Clare are sitting in the Forest & Bird duck hide among the mangroves: the firth is well-known for its bird life, although tonight there is not a bird in sight. The tide is well out – for miles it seems – leaving toffee-coloured corrugated sands and pools of ensnared sky. Mangroves rustle their fingers together beneath mantles of dull foliage.

'I've certainly got the mouth for it. I really could have been, except you can't do medicine and opera, it's impossible to do both of them at the same time with any kind of proficiency. Either the medicine suffers, or the opera suffers. But I could've been a pro, if I'd gone that way.'

'Why didn't you then?'

'In the long run, medicine is more secure. Opera is great, but there's always the risk, isn't there?'

Clare doesn't know very much about that kind of risk. She has really only given herself the one career option.

Nevertheless Tupulo likes to sing with amateur groups. The town has a small light opera group that does three productions a year, all poorly attended, and Tupulo is rehearsing *The Pirate King* with them, in the role of the pirate king himself. He is doing a six-month stint at the hospital as an intern. 'Sampling the country's endangered rural hospitals,' he had joked over coffee, then added, 'Six months in hell,' the corners of his mouth turning down.

'It could be worse,' said Clare.

'How?'

But she didn't know, after all; this is her hometown, and she couldn't even defend it.

They met over the arm of a young man who'd been in a motorcycle accident. He had sustained a large gash in the forearm, and Clare was busy syringing lidocaine into the wound, to reduce the pain when the patient later came round. A soft voice began to sing over her shoulder: *La donna è mobile.* There was Tupulo, looming largely. Clare felt her neck going hot: she doesn't like an audience. She proceeded to stitch the wound loosely – it was the best thing she could do with such an injury – with the singing as an accompaniment. The nurse, giggling, daubed the jagged line with a cloth where blood was easing out.

'All right,' said Clare, 'let's bind it up.'

'May I?' Tupulo was already handling the bandages. 'Nice job,' he added beneath his breath, flicking her a look.

'Don't be fresh,' Clare muttered, just as quietly.

He was large, like a rugby prop, and Clare thought the nurse would do a better job; yet his hands were deft – he bound the arm even more neatly than she would have. '*Voilà*,' he whispered. He was, she discovered later, always quiet around patients, whether they were conscious or not. Away from the hospital, as if having to let out his energy somehow, he was loud in an exaggerated, theatrical way.

In the duck hide, he leans over and hisses into her shoulder: '*Room 17.*'

It is still early days.

'Excuse me?'

'*Room 17.*'

(He is staying at the hotel, Clare recalls, flushing.)

'We are dead for millions of years,' he says, to add a touch of drama to the proposal.

It isn't very convincing. Clare goes straight home, to the Brightlys' house. She has no intention of visiting him at the hotel. 'How sleazy,' she mutters, banging two dirty pots into the sink. 'Room 17, for Christsake. One hamburger and what does he think I am?' There is *no way* she is going to sleep with him – he's a house surgeon, for goodness sake, even if he is a few years older than the others.

But then there comes a night of darkness and wind, sound and fury. Grunt has wiggled underneath the duvet – Brightly's: a pattern of astringent watermelon slices – and is quivering. Every time that branch bangs against the laundry window, he yelps.

Bugger this, thinks Clare, starting up the computer, a bottle of red wine at her elbow. Going into the Internet, she finds the *Dawn Karachi Weekly Digest*. Foreign aid groups that were expelled from Kabul have been told that they are welcome to return to the city, but only under strict terms set out by the militia. Tens of thousands of residents are without running water, and desperate for food and medicine. The expulsion marked the culmination of two years of rising tension between the Taliban and the international aid community, which is particularly focused on helping women. The Taliban have banned women from working, and girls from attending school.

The branch bangs obstinately on the side of the house. It will have to be fixed, it's becoming unbearable. Clare finishes her glass of wine, and pours another. Room 17, she mulls . . . *no*.

Then the security light at the rear of the house flicks on. Clare goes into the back bedroom to peer outside. The lawn – preternaturally yellow – is awash with leaves and small branches, and as she stares a child's plastic bucket somersaults forlornly across the lawn. She leans her forehead against the cold clammy window. Suddenly she has to get out of this house, or go mad.

At the old hotel Clare slips through the glass doors and up the carpeted stairs without anybody noticing her. The musty-smelling hotel, in fact, seems empty. 'I am weak,' she mutters, knocking on his door and frantically hoping he won't have another woman in there. *I had no idea just how weak*.

But he is alone, and pulls her unceremoniously into the dark narrow room as if she has been entirely expected. There is a frantic tussle with zips and buttons. Clare hauls off her jumper, then skivvy, throwing them away like extinguished memories. She can't get naked fast enough. His chest, in the dark, seems covered in fur, his erection huge.

'Life is a stage,' declaims Tupulo, hauling Clare onto his barrelly chest, 'and we are but actors upon it!' Whereupon he stretches his mouth wide and sucks in one of her breasts.

The boy who comes to mow the lawns arrives on a bicycle painted matt black, and makes a casual arc on the gravel driveway at the front of the house. He gets off the bike, and simply lets it fall to the ground, as if it has fulfilled its purpose and he now has no other interest in it. Clare has come out with a handsaw to ask if he'll cut off the offending branch.

'Do you mind?' she says. 'I'd do it myself, except I've got to get to work.'

He stands side on to her, a wave of hair falling down across his forehead and covering his right eye. He seems to be meditating on some matter in the distance. She follows his gaze, but there is nothing more exciting than a bed of scrawny plants. Perhaps he only ever does the lawns; perhaps he's a little slow. She is about to repeat her request, but then he takes the saw from her, silently, without even a glance, as if negating her very existence, and slouches off around the side of the house, spitting carefully into the grass.

Clare stands about on the gravel driveway. *What a rude boy.* If it were up to her she would get rid of him, but he's a friend of the Brightlys, apparently; he comes with the house. She doesn't even know what the arrangement is with his money. At least he is reliable, and comes every fortnight to mow the lawns, usually when she's at the hospital. Which is just as well. Clare isn't very tolerant of morose teenagers. She can't even be bothered remembering his name, but thinks of him as 'the Marshall boy'.

Later, when she gets home, she walks around to the back of the house to check the tree. It seems a little excessive, but the entire branch has been amputated. Only a pale oval in the trunk shows what had been there before. Good job, thinks Clare, and forgets all about it.

Clare doesn't like to admit that the real reason for her prolonged stay in the town has less to do with Marty than with escaping the aftermath of a disastrous love affair. It is too humiliating. I should be beyond that kind of thing, she tells herself, trying to be stern – after all, it's only human to slip up; everybody fails, at one time or another. She had left New Zealand for America, the land of promise and medical advances, in a subdued flame of success, yet she has returned with not much more than a bag full of wretched stones.

Clare and Marcus, outwardly the perfect couple. Sometimes she is haunted by the sound of lifting weights – clank clank – in the dark stillness of night, and is back there again, in that high-ceilinged room of his, with Marcus pumping iron. And what a curious phrase that is, as if heavy metal could somehow be flexible.

Their first meeting was in the San Francisco hospital staffroom, at the narrow kitchen bench.

'What would you give,' he wondered, stirring sugar into his black coffee, 'for one night of pure passion?' Clare was painfully aware of his fingers, the fine black hairs between the joints. His voice was even, pitched low, though not as low as a whisper, and the tone was pragmatic; it might have been an exercise in linguistics. 'Would you, for example, for one night of pure passion, relinquish that blouse you're wearing right now –' Hidden beneath the white coat, it was mauve satin with pearl buttons, a recent extravagance. 'Or, perhaps, would you give away your ability to thread a needle? Or,' he imagined, his eyes growing darker, 'would you give up all memory of former lovers, friends, family even, anybody of any importance in your past . . . simply for one perfect, all-encompassing, astounding night of fucking?'

This was the kind of thing you might expect at a crowded bar – not at work. He was obviously trying to shock her. Though she couldn't think why he would bother: she had seen him around on occasion, but nothing had happened to merit this attention now. Clare stirred her own coffee, the cream running into swirls.

'That's a clever line,' she said finally. 'Does it usually work?' She could sound quite priggish at times.

His adam's apple flicked up and down, then he gave a thin smile.

'Obviously not.' And walked off.

Clare, left at the bench with a cup of coffee that she didn't feel like any more, wondered if he hadn't just been trying to be friendly. No, she decided, he's a prat. Best avoided.

Only, later, she found herself wondering about what she *would* give for a fleeting taste of passion. Would she, or wouldn't she? What was so great about passion, anyway? She had no idea.

They are standing out the front of the hospital, on the shaved grass beneath a plane tree.

'I don't think we should see each other,' says Clare, 'socially, I mean.'

Tupulo digests this information. 'Are you saying that we should only see each other sexually?'

Clare bites her lip. Nothing is straightforward with Tupulo. 'Not at all,' she hisses; then she says more calmly, 'I'm talking about not seeing each other at all.'

'But what am I supposed to do in my spare time?'

'I am not here to provide you with entertainment in your spare time.'

He looks sheepish. 'It was a joke. A joke.' Then he regroups, exposing his large hands to her. 'But we have to see each other, you know.'

'Whatever for?'

Tupulo plants his feet and juts one hip forward: he could be on stage, about to deliver a telling line. 'Because I have seen the future,' he announces, 'and I can see that, one day, you and I will be inseparable.'

Clare inhales slowly, but then can't help smiling, though she tries to hide it behind her hand. What has impressed her is that there is no talk of love, or passion for that matter.

And so, like Pandora opening the box of tricks, she lets him into her life.

A problem with living in the town again is having to see the old water tower.

They used to go there for impromptu picnics, the three girls and their mother, during the interminable summer holidays. As far back as Clare can remember, it had never been used; in fact nobody seems to know why it was even called a water tower. It was always just there, placed in the empty paddock beyond puriri trees, a brooding brick finger with little wooden-edged windows and a door at the side. They'd thought of it as the witches' tower. Witches breed in there, said Bethie mysteriously, and Lou wanted to know why they never saw them. *'Because you need to come here at midnight.'*

Their mother would lay out the tartan rug, and they'd eat scotch eggs in the shade of the trees, the paddock ticking in the heat, air drugged with cicada noise. When they could get away they'd run across the grass, their mother's warning echoing impotently behind them – 'Don't go near the tower' – and, skirting it, they would play on the bank of the sluggish river among the reeds. The entire world seemed encapsulated in an afternoon.

Eventually the heat would send them back to the shady rug and to their mother lying on her back, ankles crossed, cigarette smoke spiralling lazily into the still air.

'I don't know what you find so interesting in that old river,' she said.

'The reeds wave,' cried Lou, 'like hands saying goodbye out a window.'

Their mother looked sideways at Louise, as if wondering what she had brought into the world, then she smiled. 'You ought to look out for babies. Like Moses, he was found in the reeds, in a little cot that had floated along the river.'

Lou was delighted. 'This river?'

'No, silly,' said Beth. 'A long-ago river.'

'What was he doing in the river?'

Mother rolled onto her front, and crushed the cigarette into the grass. 'I don't know, maybe nobody wanted him.'

'They were trying to save him from the Egyptians,' said Bethie, frowning.

Pat smiled. 'Of course, that's it.'

Louise too lay next to her mother, and followed the pattern on her dress with a fingertip. 'How romantic,' she sighed.

The water tower is often on the edge of Clare's peripheral vision. Try as she might to avoid it, when she moves about the town – jogging, driving – she sees it; and occasionally she must go down the gravel road where the tower is situated and pass it. Though it's set well back from the road and is partly masked by trees, its shape still intrudes on her consciousness.

Clare has a dream where the tower is a huge pin and she a moth, caught by it, pinned down. In the dream she can even feel her dusky wings fluttering helplessly.

Then she forgets about it for a while – until the next time. It's not until she relegates the tower itself to dream status that she can dismiss it more easily.

Clare calls round to visit their father on a Saturday afternoon. Marty's house in Karaka Street is quite different from the house Clare grew up in; it is higher, for one thing, perched in a street up behind the hospital; and where the old house was dim with trees, the Karaka Street house seems to draw light into it.

She lets herself in the front door and finds Louise sitting in Marty's favourite armchair, reading a magazine and sipping a beer. Their father morosely watches golf on TV. He looks pale and drawn. Lou starts, as if Clare has caught her out.

'I was just about to ring you.'

'I'm sure you were.'

'Clare,' their father sighs, looking relieved. 'How's it going?'

'More to the point,' says Clare, 'how are you?'

He shrugs. 'Me, I'm okay.' He glances at Lou as if for confirmation. 'Beer?'

Clare shakes her head and sits on the sofa.

Louise, wearing black, a colour which sharpens her face like a pencil, studies Clare with interest. 'I've had a postcard from Mum.' she says. There is a barely perceptible flicker in Lou's eyes. 'Dunk

Island. I'm tempted to visit . . . Dunk Island, that is. It's supposed to be nice.'

'Don't,' says Clare. 'The water is full of deadly creatures. Sharks, stingers, and suchlike. I had a case when I was –'

'That's decided it then.' Lou laughs brightly. 'I shall go.' She looks over at Marty, who is watching Tiger Woods teeing off. 'Why don't we go for a walk, Clare –' She stands, stretching languorously. 'I could do with some fresh air.'

They stroll up the hill, turning into a deadend street that overlooks the town and firth. A black and white pig grazes in the overgrown front garden of a miner's cottage. Lou wrinkles her nose in disgust. 'Sometimes I don't know why I bother coming back to this dump.'

Louise is the entrepreneur of the family. She gets her hair done every fortnight at an uptown salon, and eats only organic meats and vegetables. This is expensive, she has admitted, but it's worth it to make up for her other, less healthy habits. She works out at a women's gym for the same reason. Clare remembers how Lou used to claim she wanted to be healthy and making money even when she was 100. Like Tupulo, she doesn't believe she will ever degenerate. The reason for living, she is fond of saying, is to achieve – and money is her religion.

Clare shoves her hands in her jeans pockets.

'. . . is there something going on with you and Marty?'

Lou looks surprised, then laughs. 'Me and Marty? No, why?'

'Oh, I don't know. You both seem a little tense with each other.'

'It's his ticker,' says Lou, 'he's worried about it. That he's going to have another attack. I've told him, You'll be fine, *and* you've got Clare handy. But it doesn't seem to make much difference what I say. Maybe if you have a talk with him.'

'Sure, I will.'

They walk back down the hill, past weatherboard bungalows and tidy front gardens, dahlias and roses.

After a while Lou says, 'I was putting something away in the basement, and I noticed that Bethie's box is gone.'

'Yes, I've got it at the Brightlys' place.'

'Whatever for?'

'Well,' says Clare, 'I'm not too sure. Curiosity, I suppose. It gives me something to do in the evenings.'

Lou snorts. 'I can certainly understand that, in a place like this. Though personally I would've found something a little more stimulating to do.'

'It's interesting,' she smiles. 'I'm reading about Afghanistan at the moment. You don't suppose she'd mind, do you?'

'Course not,' says Lou abruptly, squinting up at the sky. 'I've got a barbecue to go to tonight. D'you think it's going to rain?'

The road to Kabul was potholed, the journey tortuous for the small group in the Landrover. The driver, their guide, was a young Afghan called Anis. 'People travel this way all the time,' he explained, shouting back to them above the noise of the engine. 'Many people coming, going. But travel by day, that way mujahedin don't shoot us in the dark.'

Terry grimaced at Beth. Already the wind had blown off her scarf, and her long dark hair was flicking about unrestrained. Beth gathered it carefully between her hands, and began to make a plait. They weren't in New Zealand any more, where it didn't matter about showing your hair. 'We'll have to get you a burqa,' she said. Beth had already acquired one of the tent-like dresses from a Red Cross woman based in Pakistan. Looking out through the eye grille, Beth was surprised at how the world seemed transformed. There was a sense not so much of being caged, but of being protected, as if she was looking out from a cloistered room.

'There's no way I'm wearing one of those things,' exclaimed Terry. 'And by the way, you look weird.'

'Thanks a bunch. These things were originally designed to ward off the evil eye. You might find that comes in useful one day.'

'Evil eye?' She laughed. 'You must be joking.'

They passed the ruins of many small villages. Some were by the road, others away in the crotches of the dusty hills, like piles of rubble in the distance. Occasionally there were burnt-out tanks by the side of the road. At one bombed village a man had set up a teahouse in the body of a helicopter. A group of nomads appeared in the distance with a herd of thin goats; the women shimmered in turquoise veils. Often whole groups of people, families, walked along the road, heading back towards Pakistan. She thought of the Afghan women they'd met in the refugee camps outside Peshawar, their stories of escape. 'We left our village, when the Shurovee came. Much bombs, shooting, many killed. We left in the night. We travelled through the mountains. It was so cold that this woman here, her feet froze. Then coming out of the pass, so very cold, I look down at my baby, very still in my arms, and see that he is dead. Three years ago, we come down out of the mountains.'

Beth stared, from behind the grille of her burqa, and the people stared back, as flinty as the surrounding landscape. It was a relief to catch sight of a field of yellow flowers, shiny as strewn buttons. Near the remains of a village Rob pointed out an abandoned orchard, apples trees bright with white flowers.

'There'll be butterfly mines in there,' he shouted. 'The Soviets drop them from the air, thousands of them.'

Then the Landrover broke down. Anis jumped out and looked under the hood. 'No worries,' he claimed, 'I can fix.' He pointed them in the direction of a cluster of buildings by a thin, ochre-coloured river. 'Over there, you can buy tea.'

And sure enough there was a teahouse. A gaggle of small children appeared out of nowhere and stood at a distance to stare at the foreigners; an emaciated dog skulked along behind them.

That night they were to sleep on mats in a domed mud hut. For dinner they were each given a scoop of rice, some naan, and a plum. Bethie didn't have much appetite. Cradling the plum in her hand, she went outside to look at the mountains. The sun was an orange globe burning above a grey ridgeline. A little boy carrying a Kalashnikov appeared from around the corner of the hut. He pointed the gun at her. 'Bang bang!'

Her heart gave a thump. 'Shit.'

The boy, laughing, was about to run away. 'Hey,' she called, and held out her plum.

He hesitated. The gun that looked so huge in his hands sagged.

Beth thought of the Koran that she'd started reading each night. *And the shades of the Garden will come low over them, and the bunches of fruit there, will hang low in humility.*

Stepping forward with sudden shyness, the boy reached out and took the plum from her. Giggling then, he rushed away.

FOUR

There is comfort, or there is passion – and there are accidental, shifting positions in between.

Clare wonders if, on some instinctual level, one must choose between passion and comfort. The cynic might say that passion is merely the catalyst which propels the organism to reproduce. Clare, who does not particularly belong to the biological school of thought, is undecided on this point. All she knows is that she has had passion, and it didn't work out. She and passion are unsuited to each other.

She didn't know how lonely she was until she met Marcus. After the 'incident' in the staffroom, she next saw him outside the Emergency Room, hands in pockets, shuffling in the night air, almost skulking. It was easy to think of the hospital as being an epicentre. Beyond the hospital, the city was shifting about like some gigantic beast, moving and snuffling in its sleep. A kind of guard dog. Clare, trying to look for stars in the muffled city sky, saw it sometimes in her dreams, that monolithic beast, its coat of dark short hairs revealing the pale skin beneath, its stunted snout equally ready to snarl or to grin.

'You won't see anything up there,' he drawled, quite close, smoking – rather nervously, she thought, on first impression. He was holding the cigarette close to his side, his face thin and, in profile, reminding her of rock art. 'Only idealists look for stars in this city,' he said.

'Where should I look for stars then?'

He gave an amused grimace. 'Maybe in Union Square.'

She paused. Neither of them mentioned the previous conversation, although Clare had thought of little else in the intervening days. What did he know about passion that she had so obviously missed?

They walked through the city as the sun began to colour a street of Victorian houses a uniform shade of rose, and they talked about the people inside who would still be sleeping in their beds. A man pedalled past on a bicycle, sitting back with his arms folded across his chest.

'I can do that,' said Marcus. 'I was going to be a cyclist when I was a kid.' It seemed obvious, once he'd said it, his arms so wiry and taut.

'What happened?'

'Nothing,' he shrugged. 'I got beaten one time too many –' And he gave a self-deprecating smile, showing small white teeth.

They seemed to walk for miles, through Soma and the Financial District, until finally they came to the waterfront. At Fisherman's Wharf an early commuter ferry was leaving for Sausalito, so they hopped on board. Ahead a thick mist lay over the water, yet standing at the rail and looking back at the city, the skyscrapers towered into a silvery sky. The boat jolted against a wave and Clare gripped Marcus's wrist. He seemed to glare back at her.

'Sorry,' she said.

'It turns me on when a woman grabs me,' he said.

She laughed, thinking he'd made a joke, though his face remained deadpan. In the distance Alcatraz Island loomed out of the mist. Clare was aware of the sun caressing the back of her head, and the buildings lit up from within; and it was as if she had only just arrived in San Francisco, it was that new and heady. It made her laugh, again.

'What?' He turned his sharp features to her.

'Nothing,' she gasped, 'just, being on a boat so early in the morning, it's great.' Might have uttered the word 'joy' except that it was too trite. Clare was so taken up with everything – the glittering silvery water, the fiery buildings, the throb of the engines, the man's proximity – that she missed his flickering look of suspicion. If he had said, 'Are you kidding me?' it might have shifted the day into a different course altogether. He pressed his body into her back, however, and the moment was sealed.

The town often makes Clare think of a nonsensical holiday camp. Mrs Kray, for example, is waging war with her neighbours. It has got to the stage where the man has come over in the dead of night and cut down one of her trees, the dark cigar-shaped yew, that he complained was blocking out their light.

Clare sits on Mrs Kray's back veranda, drinking Earl Grey tea and eating pineapple cake.

'Why don't you just make up?'

Mrs Kray is shocked. 'Those kind of people,' she says, very loudly, 'don't know how to be civilised neighbours. If there was an award for worst neighbour of the year, they would get it.' She leans back smugly, folding her arms across her red checked dress that is reminiscent of a tablecloth. 'Have some more cake, Clare, I made it specially.'

Clare cuts another slice. They have a symbiotic relationship: she likes to be spoiled occasionally, and Mrs Kray likes to do the spoiling.

'How did it start, anyway?'

'Well,' breathes Mrs Kray, leaning forward, 'first of all there were the fireworks –'

'Sorry? Whose fireworks?'

'Mine, of course,' frowns Mrs Kray, suspecting Clare of not paying attention. 'You were there, Clare. Guy Fawkes 1994.'

'It's been going that long?' Clare is trying to keep a straight face. No wonder their father and Mrs Kray went their separate ways.

'That's when I got the first letter of complaint. Honestly,' wheezes Mrs Kray, 'as if I, of all people, could possibly be any sort of a nuisance. And then, well I admit it, I was annoyed, I can't stand prissy letters at the best of times, so I –' Mrs Kray breaks off with coy reticence.

'Yes?'

'So then I let off firecrackers every night for a solid week. And the sky rockets, I pointed them in that direction.'

Clare coughs into her cup of tea.

'They called Noise Control. And after that, I guess you could say it became a bit of a vendetta. Like the Mafioso!'

Clare can't hold it back, and bursts into loud peals of laughter.

Mrs Kray is piqued. 'It's not that funny, Clare. It has its serious side, you know, girl. I could've been killed. They left banana skins lying all over my driveway. I mean, there were masses of them. What do those people do all night? Eat bananas? By jimminy, no wonder I can hear them farting!' Mrs Kray covers her mouth: she has yet to determine whether 'fart' is a swear word or not. Clare would know, being a doctor, only she doesn't like to ask.

Clare is laughing again, and her face has turned red. 'How could banana skins possibly kill you?' She can barely get it out. This is one of those moments when she loves Mrs Kray.

'But Clare.' Mrs Kray is amazed. 'You of all people should know that!' She stands up, throwing down a paper napkin to demonstrate. 'You're walking along, minding your own business – which is more than some people are capable of –' she shouts over her shoulder – 'you're walking along, when you suddenly step on a banana skin, and whoosh –' she mimes falling down, though carefully, as her hip is a bit dicky – 'you've hit the ground running, split the back of your head open, and you're dead as a doornail.' Mrs Kray resumes her seat. 'You understand? My life was in peril the moment those banana skins landed on my concrete driveway. What if I had gone out in the middle of the night to put out the rubbish?' Mrs Kray's eyebrows are twitching with deadly seriousness; she snaps her fingers at Clare. 'Phit,' she says, 'that's where I'd be,' and she leans back in the plastic chair with satisfaction. 'And no pineapple cake today, I can tell you, darling girl.'

Clare controls herself, only just. 'So what did you do with all those banana skins?'

'I put them in the compost, of course – what else? Banana skins are brilliant for compost! Those crazy neighbours of mine, they were doing me a favour, I tell you.' And finally, Mrs Kray allows herself a long snickering laugh. 'Thank God you're back, Clare, it brightens my day, that's for sure.'

The past, too, could seem innocent. The Purefoy girls went on a camping trip into the valley that ran up between the arms of the bush-clad hills. Even though Bethie was seventeen, the girls weren't allowed to go by themselves, so their father, who refused to go camping ever again, got Constable Harold and Mrs Harold to go with them.

Out the front of the house, Bethie had everything spread out on the concrete driveway. Clare was doodling on the checklist. Their father, hands in pockets, watched from the doorstep as Bethie packed the car. He couldn't have done a better job himself. Lou stood swaying under the boughs of the pepper tree, holding a Barbie behind her back.

'I don't know what people see in camping,' he said loudly. 'It always rains.'

Bethie was stowing the picnic basket in the front seat – thermos and sandwiches, a packet of chocolate biscuits: everything planned.

'Watch out for wetas,' said their father, grimacing. Lou's skinny frame shuddered beneath the tree.

'*Dad*,' warned Bethie.

But he was not to be put off so easily. 'You'll be back early, I'll guarantee.' For there was the thumb, or rather, the lack of thumb, that bothered him. He wanted to say to the girls, 'Camping is dangerous!'

It was Harold and Mrs Harold, revving along the street in their muddy Landrover, who saved them. The girls bundled into Bethie's car, tooting and waving goodbye as if they couldn't get away fast enough. A falsetto echo of their singing – 'Staying Alive' – reached back to their father as he stood and watched the vehicles disappear around the corner.

The DOC camping areas, enveloped in bush, offered concrete barbecues, toilet blocks, and not much else. Clare got to choose a place for the tent – a flat area between an oak tree and the creek. Harold and Mrs Harold, set up in the next clearing, sat in deck-chairs beneath a tree. She leafed through the *Woman's Weekly*; he alternately dozed and sipped at a bottle of beer.

Bethie had everything organised. There was firewood to be gathered, Clare would be in charge of the sausages; Lou could stir the baked beans and fetch a pot of water to make tea. There was a certain feeling of bliss.

With the rattling of the creek noisy in the night, they lay on their foam mats and tried to sleep. About midnight a possum came squawking around looking for food; Bethie had already thought of this, and put all their supplies in the chillybin. Lou wanted to leave out a piece of fruit, but Bethie said No, you wouldn't want to encourage a dirty possum, would you? It was disconcerting how she could sound like their mother. Lou was worried then, thinking that the possum would come into the tent.

'It'll storm the tent,' cried Clare, 'it's a military possum, on a suicide mission –'

'Mission Impossible,' cried Lou, no longer anxious now they could laugh about it.

There had been rain, and the river was high. At one of the low concrete bridges that spanned the rock-strewn river, Bethie had had to drive the car through gushing water. Later they walked back along the gravel road and lay on the concrete bridge, clinging on with their fingertips, screaming while the water rushed over them. It was cold, even though it was summer. Lou had jumped up and down and shouted. There were blackberries by the sides of the road, leaves washed clean by the rain. Their fingers and tongues were stained purple.

'Let's pretend we're living in the bush,' said Bethie, 'that we've left home and we're living here, all the time, with no parents, no school, just the three of us, surviving on berries and fern roots and sleeping rough –'

'Let's make a bivouac,' cried Lou, 'with ferns.'

'Let's do some bush crashing,' said Bethie.

'Yeah. Which way will we go?' Clare asked, pale and lanky in her shorts and sandshoes.

'But what about telling the Harolds?' Lou was saying. The other two hadn't heard her: they were already running along the road, Bethie out front, Clare at her heels like a faithful dog. Lou didn't want to crash about in the bush – it was creepy, and there might be spiders – so she hung back. Any moment, she thought, they'd come racing back to get her, and then they could all sit down by the fire and cook sausages, like their mother used to do, with the happy sound of fat spitting in the pan.

Lou waited and waited, but nobody came back. Eventually she wandered along the dusty road as well, the bush all around her ticking like a big clock. Where would they have gone? And didn't their father tell them to keep together? There was a path, leading away from the road. Lou stood peering, deliberating. All right, if they could go in there, so could she. They were probably just hiding behind some bushes anyway, waiting for her to come, so they could jump out and surprise her.

They were up ahead: she could hear them. Bethie's instructions, and Clare's excited squeals. Lou trudged stolidly forward, in what she thought was their wake. It seemed easy at first, following the broken twigs and occasional footprint. But then there were stunted tree ferns that she had to push through like pushing herself through swing doors, and then a short time of following meandering paths through the trees, and then she found her way completely blocked by fallen debris; and as she stood gazing and wondering what to do next, she realised her sisters' voices had gone.

Lou pulled at her T-shirt and wiped her sweaty face. Longing for a dunk in the cold mountain water, she wiggled her hot toes in her sandshoes. Then Lou thought she could hear running water, and set off again, in another direction.

Twenty minutes later she stumbled back out onto the road, red in the face and weeping inconsolably. Her legs were bleeding from many small scratches. At the camping ground the others were lolling about on a rug under the tree.

'Lou,' said Clare, 'we thought you were hiding.'

'Hadn't you even missed me?'

'I thought it had got quiet round here,' quipped Bethie. They laughed, two older sisters, but the day seemed to soak up their laughter and toss it away. 'Hey, what's up?'

Lou was running for the tent, bawling, her face scrunched into a fist. It took Mrs Harold an hour to calm her down and tease out the story. The result was that Beth and Clare were in trouble, especially when Marty got to hear about how they nearly lost Lou in the bush. That night, their last in the camp, Beth brought Lou a bar of chocolate she'd had hidden in her pack, as a peace offering.

Sitting cross-legged on her sleeping bag, Lou looked up with round eyes. 'I wouldn't have got lost if our mother had been here. She would've been watching over me –'

Beth could easily have argued that point, but bit her tongue. 'I'm sorry about that, kid.' Though she couldn't help adding, 'Except she'd never have let us go camping in the first place, either.'

Louise was not so easily placated. Tight-lipped, she climbed out of the tent, and went and sat with the Harolds. She kept the chocolate bar though.

'I'm falling into another relationship,' Clare realises when Tupulo, who had been living at the old hotel, edges his way into her house.

And why shouldn't he move in, considers Clare. She has more room than she needs, and it will only be temporary. A sense of recklessness has invaded her, as if she can be a different kind of person here, back home; or, more simply, as if she doesn't care any more. But she warns him that he will have to fit in with her routine. She and Grunt want as little disturbance as possible. Tupulo agrees, then promptly sets about changing Clare's routine to suit himself. Instead of an early jog on a Saturday morning, there are now waffles, followed by sex, coffee and the paper. Instead of reading journals in bed at night with a cup of herb tea, there are hot whisky toddies, sex and *Nightline* (Tupulo has moved his small TV set into the bedroom). Instead of showering alone, Clare might be surprised by Tupulo, a naked intruder trembling largely.

Tupulo has come complete with appliances: there is the waffle machine, the coffee-bean grinder, the pasta maker and the espresso machine. The house is becoming an electrical highway. Clare comes to wonder how she has ever lived without such equipment before.

Then she comes home to find the Brightlys' furniture has been moved about. Another day he rearranges the kitchen cupboards, and announces that he will be the chef: there will be creamy fettuccines, creamy lasagnes, creamy seafood soups and wontons – wontons? wonders Clare. Then he promptly forgets about any promise of cooking, so Clare returns with relief to her salads and tomato-based pasta combos – if only she could just find the grater! And as for the Brightlys, it is Tupulo who seeds the idea that they never existed in the first place: they become 'the mysterious Brightlys'.

To Lou, Clare jokes that she has taken in a 'toyboy'. Except that later she regrets this petty betrayal – though she thinks of Tupulo on the flatmate level, sort of. (He even contributes to this idea by taking over the spare room, although he rarely sleeps in the single bed.) And, after all, they are both just passing through.

Still, it's a little like being in a whirlwind. Clare, surprising herself, is secretly enjoying it. She stretches her arms above her head on a sunny Saturday morning, the smell of waffles beginning to percolate through the house, and wonders how she ever managed to live *without* Tupulo.

Everything between them seems so easy. Almost *too* easy. She can't help but make comparisons. For she hasn't been very good at choosing men in the past, and wishes that relationships were as straightforward as work.

Despite that, there are only brief moments when she looks sideways at Tupulo, and wonders if you can be struck twice by lightning.

She could barely wait to see him, yet sometimes whole days, sheets of day, would drag by before they could meet. And during those times she would watch out for him: was that Marcus getting onto a cable car? And if it was, what was he doing on the Powell Street line? Was he going to meet another woman? At the hospital, hearing a woman's laugh as she passed a room – that rising scale – she had to backtrack and check. But it was only two nurses sharing a joke.

She was calm only when they were together; had no idea that you could become so obsessed with a man. One moment that obsession seemed natural – *this must be love* (and Marcus himself talked often of love); the next moment she plunged herself into longer shifts than necessary, to free herself from his spell, for surely he had cast some kind of gossamer net over her. Then a spray of red rosebuds would appear at her apartment and she would immediately have to ring him, to hear his voice.

At the hospital he kept his distance, and they often worked different shifts. But there were times when inevitably they coincided. One night, a group of them were in the staffroom getting coffee, and Marcus, thin in his white coat, was holding forth to two other doctors about fly-fishing, a subject he loathed. All she could do was linger nearby, pretending to check the staff noticeboard. He didn't get on well with the others, yet still she was jealous.

'I don't want people to know about us,' he had told her, 'I don't like gossip.'

That seemed reasonable. Or did it? Sometimes she wanted everybody to know; at others it didn't seem to matter. Or was he hiding something? She wasn't used to being buffetted about by her emotions. She found herself listening in on other women's conversations, hoping to pick up some sort of clue; she even bought women's magazines, and pored over advice about keeping your man interested, how to tell if he's cheating on you, how to transform yourself into a supermodel just by using a different foundation. It was like studying a partly known foreign language.

He talked about their taking a trip together into the rural hinterlands where he was raised. Clare was keen – it was a commitment of sorts; they had had a vaguely similar upbringing in common – but there was never enough time.

Clare is in the backyard at the rotary clothesline, feeling up the washing – running her hands up a pair of trackpants, squeezing the arms of a sweatshirt – as if searching for limbs. Over by the oleander bushes there is still a blush of frost. No wonder it was so cold last night. Clare shivers now, remembering how she had had to get up in the night and fetch a blanket in which to cocoon herself before getting back into bed. Clare likes to be as warm as possible at all times; she misses the Californian summers. Underneath the clothesline there are a few patches of grass which the Marshall boy has neglected: his lawn-mowing has become rather haphazard.

The kitchen window is pushed open and Tupulo pokes his head

out. 'I need a little action,' he booms. 'I shall go crazy, pretty soon, if I don't get out of this boring burg. Baby, let's hit the road.'

Clare gets suspicious when Tupulo calls her 'baby': it is his role-play mode.

'That Tupulo,' says Sheila who runs the reception desk at the hospital, 'he's such a dag. What a card.' They all admire Tupulo, and that admiration rubs off on Clare, who has him.

They are on the coast road.

'Where are we going?' Clare shouts above the noise of the VW, into which Tupulo has only just managed to squeeze himself – and even then he must drive with his shoulders hunched over the wheel.

He is driving her car fast and cutting the corners like a local hoon. At least it's not wet, thinks Clare, hanging onto the passenger door. There is a cyclist, whom Tupulo adroitly misses, slashing out into the road.

'Surprise,' he says shortly. His eyes are on the road, his hands grip the steering wheel. There is no sense in talking to him at this moment, though Clare plans to take control of the car when she gets a chance.

And then they are pulling over in a flash of dust.

Clare gets out of the car, a little shaky. They have stopped at a gravel layby beside a pohutukawa tree that leans precariously over a bank towards the sea. Its roots are a study in ancient history. 'This way,' cries Tupulo, clambering down a rough path to the shingly apron that is washed by small waves. There are rocks that go out into the water, a natural promontory, and Tupulo, with surprising dexterity, is trotting over them now. Clare follows more sedately. A pair of oystercatchers fly overhead, their black wings scritching the air like scissors. By the time she reaches the large flat rock, Tupulo has laid out a rug and is opening a bottle of champagne.

'Heaven,' he sighs, producing two glasses like magic from his pockets, and pouring. There is a pottle of caviar as well, and a packet of pretzels. 'For dipping,' he explains.

There is a chill on the air, but they are both wearing jackets, and the rocks are dry. The sea heaves all around them: the water steel-blue, the surface jagged and choppy. They are on a promontory, and Clare hugs herself at the illusion of safety.

'I can't swim, you know.' Unusually, for a New Zealand girl, Clare somehow missed all those swimming lessons in the school pool stinking of chlorine. 'Well, not properly. Though I suppose I could save myself if I had to.'

Tupulo looks at her in mock horror.

'You're right,' she smiles, 'swimming is for other people.'

Tupulo shrugs with an uncanny modesty. 'You see,' he boasts, 'you can already read my mind –'

'For all that's worth,' laughs Clare.

Tupulo decides then and there – at the age of thirty-one – that he will live on, as he is now, for ever. There will be no growing old for him, no getting sick either. There is no wheelchair or mobility cart in Tupulo's future. He will always be boyishly good-looking and exuberant. This is a fact of life, he decides, and nothing is going to change that. That's why he gives in to his cravings, and why he likes to treat Clare – at least once a day. Because this is *it*, baby.

'Call me old-fashioned,' sighs Tupulo, 'but it doesn't get any better than this.'

The sun, beyond his head, drifts winking above the malachite mountains, an orange ball.

April 1983
Happy Birthday, me! A silver plastic key from Clare (a joke) – which got broken in the post – and chocolate.

Clare can tell it is the middle of the night by the absence of sound. There isn't even a morepork to break the silence. Everything is asleep, she thinks, except me, and I have a dreadful pain in my abdomen. If it was low it would be appendicitis, it's that sharp; but it's high, just below the ribs. At least not the heart. All the things that can go wrong, she thinks – *knowing* about all the things that can go wrong. Somebody once asked her at a party, how do you live with that kind of knowledge? Well, you do, of course: it's a job, you don't take it personally. You could ask the same question of lots of other professions – law, psychiatry, school caretaking. You live with it. You're not always scaring yourself with the possibilities. A zookeeper isn't lying in his bed at night imagining runaway lions bursting into the house to maul him.

Clare, however, with the pain in her abdomen, is rapidly running through the possibilities. The pain is so bad she can't move. She can't even get up to take a painkiller. She would like to sit up – to ease the congestion, for she's decided it's a temporary blockage, wind – but cannot. So she lies very still, and takes shallow breaths.

She hopes she never gets really sick, because she would make a terrible patient. A patient must have patience; it is an enforced patience, giving yourself up to a higher power. It is what she expects of her own patients – 'Put yourself in my hands', literally – but to be in that situation herself would be humiliating. If I get sick, thinks Clare, I will treat myself. Or I will go off into the wilderness and curl into a ball. Of course I won't. I will submit. Whatever it takes, to get better. Dear God, just relieve me of this pain in my gut.

Breathing, the house ticking, the pain starts to ease. *Thank God.* So, she is fallible after all. Won't Tupulo be pleased to hear.

FIVE

The TURKOMAN was sleeping. Pale light, unhindered by the luxury of blinds, poured into the infirmary and fell across the man's dark, aquiline features. The only patient, he lay as if on a stone tomb, his breathing for the first time undisturbed and even.

Usually the small ward would be full. There must be a lull in the fighting, thought Bethie. They sometimes got a space of days, like in the eye of a storm, when there weren't any casualties. At such times local women might come in to speak to one of the nurses. They wouldn't see Rob or Franco, no matter how bad their complaint. They could be dying, but if there was only a male doctor at the clinic they would not see him. Bethie saw many kinds of conditions; often they were the product of depression, of living in a war zone, of malnutrition. Sometimes she knew how to help them, and sometimes not. Occasionally an American doctor, a woman, came to Kabul – she had a clinic in the mountains but would travel the country from time to time, specifically to treat women – and then the women would come out, in twos and threes, in their flowing turquoise robes or dark burqas, children hanging off them like jewels, and line up at the clinic door. It always surprised Bethie that they knew, the way they would just appear. If the American doctor was delayed for some reason, then they stayed away.

Beth crossed the room and sat on the bed next to the Turkoman, listening to his breathing. She looked at her fingers, linked on her lap, blunt and chapped. The city too seemed very quiet. It was as if everything was holding its breath, waiting. In the distance, a tank rumbled along the street.

She picked up the copy of the Koran that a visitor had left on the Turkoman's bedside table. *O true believers, if ye assist God, by fighting for his religion, he will assist you against your enemies, and will set your feet fast.* Beth wonders about the Koran, how much to believe, how much to take with the proverbial grain of salt.

The Turkoman stirred a little in his sleep. Three days earlier he was brought in with wounds that had made even Franco blanch. There were days, Beth found, when you simply didn't want to look any more.

It is the spring of flash floods. The area is prone to flooding, owing to the usually unremarkable river that snakes through part of the town to the sea. Yet people decide that you can't rely on the weather these days (as if you ever could). El Nino is blamed, and then La Nina. Everything's up the spout, says Marty.

After several days of rain, their father's basement has been flooded by the creek at the back of his section swelling over the boundary late one night like an intruder. He is on the phone to Clare at 7 a.m. 'I got up, just like usual, and not suspecting anything, went down the basement stairs to get a screwdriver – I was fixing that old radio of mine – and what should I see but water. Two feet of water!' He sounds excited: something has happened.

When Clare arrives half an hour later there is a green frog sitting on top of the letterbox, and the lawn is awash with speckled, muddy water. The house has become an island or boat and their father, standing on the front veranda, the captain. He even gives a kind of salute through the rain, and talks to her across the watery gulf of his front lawn.

'My neighbour has been evacuated!'

Clare gives a shiver, and is thankful to be living on high ground, away from any rivers, tributaries or treacherous creeks. Those foresightful Brightlys – if I were trapped by floodwaters, thinks Clare, what would I do? How would I save myself? With stilts? I must take some swimming lessons, she decides.

'Dad,' she calls back to him from the gate, water washing around her feet, 'pack a few things and come stay at my place till the water goes down.'

He shakes his head and grins. 'No thanks, I'm fine here. Besides, the rain'll stop tonight, you'll see. I'll be fine.'

Later that day, back at the house, she looks down over the town and discovers a changed geography. There is a grey lake-like area down to the left, on the flat, where normally there is pasture. Ah, and there's the church – it, too, has become marooned on an island, its little red steeple pointing bravely into the rain. She is anxious about Marty, who really ought to come and stay with her. How can he be so sure he's safe, Clare wonders. How can anyone know how long the rain will continue? Such determination with regard to the weather is dangerous.

At 1 a.m. she is woken by the sudden absence of rain.

Tupulo is eating donuts. He may be a doctor, but he has scant regard for his own health. He would smoke as well, except that he doesn't like the taste. He sticks to chocolate instead. This morning it is chocolate-coated donuts, still warm from the bakery, that he eats out of a paper bag.

Life is short, thinks Tupulo, you've got to get some enjoyment out of it, or what's the point. You're buggered, either way.

He takes a large bite, and masticates thoughtfully: he's sitting on a wooden bench and watching Clare working out. He likes to watch her exercise. She's running round the school playing field, even though there are still swathes of frost on the grass beneath the far trees; from a distance, in her lycra leggings and baggy sweatshirt, she looks quite delectable. I could go for that chickie, thinks Tupulo, except that she's already pink in the face and sweating – she's run past him twice now, so he's had a close-up – and Tupulo is turned off by sweating women. So he thinks about his lunch. Lunch, he decides, will be one of those delicious kebabs from the new place that's opened on mainstreet to cash in on the summer crowd. He shivers: if summer ever comes. Thank God for civilisation. When his six-month internship at this dump is over, Tupulo intends to have a little holiday, possibly to Malaysia, and eat a lot of delicious exotic food that he can't get in this one-horse town. In fact, broods Tupulo, he might just have a weekend in Auckland instead; there's a good Malaysian restaurant he discovered on his last trip.

'Clare!' His voice booms across the playing field, startling Clare, who veers sharply and trots towards him, looking anxious. 'Clare,' he shouts when she is five metres away, 'we're going to the big smoke.'

'We are?' She's puffing. She's done three laps, and doesn't think she can do another. Running is torture, but she forces herself to do it anyway, to keep fit.

'Yes. This weekend. We are going to eat Malaysian food and sit in a sleazy sauna.'

She picks up her towel and buries her face in it. 'Not the sleazy saunas again.'

'What did you say?'

'I'm on call this weekend. Let's go next weekend.'

'No no, not possible.' He hands over her jacket solicitously. 'I have a craving. It can't wait.'

Clare smiles: she has been learning about Tupulo's cravings. 'Well, I'll come if I can swap with Mather.'

'Excellent, Clare. You're a gem.'

'By the way, Tupulo, have you ever thought of getting some regular exercise?'

'Me?' He looks shocked. 'No, never. Exercise is for other people.'

Tupulo is so attached to his Viking's helmet that he wears it in the car on the way to Auckland.

'I knew there was a good reason you got a convertible,' he says, throwing a bag in the back.

They are going to stay two nights at the Sheraton and indulge several of Tupulo's weaknesses, and perhaps one or two of Clare's as well. This is the benefit of not having children, thinks Clare; you can take off for impulsive weekends and stay at flash hotels. It's not a convincing argument, but at least she feels glad about getting away.

Getting away. You would think there was something that needed escaping from.

They drive off in a flurry of dust and cross the swollen muddy river outside town; there is fresh-looking countryside ahead, and it is a relief to be bucketing over hills. The wind is cool and damp, but they have thick jackets and Clare wears gloves. Paddock animals take no notice as they go past, though Tupulo is attracting a lot of attention with his helmet. It has horns, and is furry around his forehead. Cars toot, and women smile secretly. Tupulo, the natural performer, bathes in the attention. A colleague from the hospital roars past, on his way back to the town in his Volvo, and leans his wrist on the horn. That crazy kid, they'll all be thinking.

Once they get onto the motorway, however, and are among the anonymous traffic, Tupulo wearies of the helmet and levers it off, throwing it onto the back seat. He has to concentrate, he says.

'Goggles,' he exclaims, and Clare gets out the pair of Biggles-style goggles from the glove compartment and hands them to him. They are especially for this part of the journey. There is a pair for her too, which usually she doesn't wear, but she dons them now. Tupulo, behind his goggles, looks pleased. 'This,' he cries into the wind and traffic fumes, 'is going to be a weekend to remember!'

Tupulo acts as if he is in self-imposed exile, a lion in the wilderness. He misses everything about cities, even noise and pollution. Clare often tells him how much he would like San Francisco. She catches herself imagining them both there, Tupulo in the place of Marcus – and yet, if that had been the case, she would never have come back home. She is undecided yet whether that might be a good thing or bad.

Tupulo is certainly far too unusual for a small country town between a firth and the mountains; but Clare suspects she is probably the only one to have realised this fact. Other people, nurses, patients, their fellow doctors, even the baker, are seduced by his boyish charm and his jokes – even Lou calls him the Michelin man – without seeing that he doesn't belong here. He is a tourist; his time in this town is finite.

As too is Clare's.

Perhaps that is Tupulo's gift, she thinks, that he can be at home almost anywhere. He is at home with himself in a way that most people are not.

Clare has also come to realise that she has started to depend upon Tupulo's presence. There are nights when she wakes and puts out a hand for him, thinking him gone. When she finds him there – breathing heavily, his hairy chest heaving – she feels ridiculous but is nonetheless relieved.

San Francisco was Clare's own exile.

She had an apartment in the heart of the city, in an older building that had a black- and white-tiled foyer at street level. She had her name – Purefoy – above her bell outside, even though her neighbour Mrs Dillon advised her to leave it blank. Bugger the psychos, she thought; it was her small claim on the city.

Mrs Dillon had a hairy chihuahua that she carried about in a shoulder bag. Inside the apartment she carried the dog around on her shoulder. Clare would examine the dog from time to time while Mrs Dillon made fresh coffee and cut slices of freshly baked seed cake. She enjoyed her tiny patient – hearing its rapid-fire sparrow heartbeat through her stethoscope, peering into its brown eyes with the light, feeling its fragile limbs – for she didn't often get the chance to touch animals in the city.

'You should get yourself a Jewish man,' Mrs Dillon always told her. 'I could introduce you to a nice boy. Mixed marriages are all the rage these days.'

On Clare's free weekends there was breakfast at her local deli. Steaming hot espresso, crunchy rolls with peppered pastrami and cream cheese. When Neville, the deli owner, discovered she was a doctor he would give her treats to take away. A bag of tiny cookies, some freshly sliced salami, a packet of ground coffee.

One day he asked a favour of her. 'Will you look in at my wife?' Clare sometimes caught glimpses of the wife out the back, a dark-haired woman, possibly Italian, who spent her days baking, making salads and quiches, washing dishes. Neville looked at Clare anxiously across the high glass counter. 'She's not talking. It's called being a selective mute, or some such bullshit. I don't know what to do any more.'

There were jellied ox tongues in the display cabinet. Clare stared at them – grey, lumpish – with a kind of numb disbelief. He would have no idea, of course. *Why don't you talk? What's the madder with you? Talk, go on, I dare you to.* But she eased back into her professional role and stammered out the most obvious question first: 'So she's seen a doctor?'

Neville shrugged. 'Sure. They gave her some pills, but it didn't work. I've taken her to a shrink, to an acupuncturist, you name it, I've tried it. Nothing has worked.' They both looked at the back doorway, where the wife was chopping onions at the kitchen bench. 'She seems happy enough, but how am I really to know?' *It's like an island hideaway with palm trees and flour for sand, a sea of silence.*

'What pills?'

'Prozac.'

'Do you think she's depressed?'

Another shrug. 'Hell no . . . I think, well, maybe she just doesn't feel like talking. We're having a break from the doctors for a while.'

So Clare went in and said hello to Marta. 'How're you doing?' The woman glanced up with dark eyes, smiled, and returned to her chopping. It could have been a kind of meditation. Clare picked up a carrot, and twiddled it awkwardly between her fingers. Was this what she herself was like as a child? This intense, mesmeric quality. Marta took the carrot from Clare's fingers, smiled again, and started rapidly to slice the vegetable into thin slivers.

It was difficult, at first, talking to somebody who didn't respond, but she would do it only in small bursts – as if popping in to visit a friend – and it became easier the more she did it. One day she hoisted herself up onto the table opposite where Marta was working at the bench, cutting bacon. Neville was out front, serving customers. He had a girl, too, who helped with the morning rush. She was tiny, with closely shaved blonde hair, and darted about like some kind of exotic rodent. Clare was telling one of her stories. 'I was walking along the street, on my way to work, when this old man who was coming towards me suddenly swung out his cane and whacked me on the leg. I cried out, but he ran off, laughing. Can you believe that? Why would an old guy do such a thing? Anyway, later, after I'd been at work for a while, the nurse buzzed me to say there was an emergency – remarkably, it was the old man, he'd been hit by a car, just outside the hospital and somebody had carried him in, he had a broken leg and was bleeding from his arm. He took one look at me, his eyes rolled up into his head, and he died.'

Clare was silent for a moment. Marta carried on slicing her bacon, quite slowly. There were times when it seemed that she was just on the verge of saying something. Perhaps Marta was some kind of savant, and one day she would reveal the secrets of the universe.

'Sorry,' said Clare, 'that's probably not a very nice story to tell you. It was just so . . .'

'– *Bizarre*,' whispered Marta.

Clare looked up. 'Yes, thank you.'

Marta glanced over her shoulder, and put a finger to her lips, then went back to her chopping.

Jesus, thought Clare, this city. As she left the deli, Neville gave her a large jar of stuffed olives. Behind him the blonde girl stared impassively. Perhaps it would be enough to be a friend to Marta, and not solve her problem for her, Clare thought. And she was hardly a patient; this was on the good-deed level. But then, maybe Marta didn't have a problem at all.

The town's hospital seems to be up against it – there have been staff cuts, there's no money for new equipment, and it is closed on the weekends. It makes Clare wonder how it will all end.

She is watching the protest from a window on the second floor, where she has been doing her ward rounds. There is a group of about 1000 people on the lawn below, chanting, waving placards; many are holding white bits of paper (song sheets?). She can see Mrs Kray, in an obviously symbolic red dress. The protesters have already walked down mainstreet, and have gathered out the front of the hospital for the speeches. There is a press photographer hanging about on the periphery. She spots Tupulo, simply attired in a white coat: Clare had persuaded him to leave the Viking's helmet at home.

They are being addressed by the mayor, who is speaking from a flatbed truck about the need for the town to stand behind its hospital, or lose it – just like the Toyota factory, which is also an endangered species. The place will end up being a ghost town, claims the mayor, if people don't fight to keep what they have. The community must band together.

'I thought you might've been down there too,' a voice mutters at her shoulder.

Clare is surprised to discover Robeson, the hospital manager, who very rarely comes up to the wards. She turns back to the window. Across the street, and seemingly oblivious to the protesters, four children are tossing a yellow ball to each other.

'I would be,' she says, 'except I'm the only doctor left in the building.'

'We are very lucky to have you here – Clare.'

Robeson smells of stale cigarette smoke. It came as a surprise, on her return from San Fran, to find that New Zealand hospitals were now run by people who knew nothing about medicine. The state of coffee had improved in her absence, but as far as the public system was concerned, it was like coming back to a Third World country.

'For the record, I too must protest, about the loss of the nurses' – twenty-three so far, and it is rumoured that more will go – 'and, Jerry, I understand you have to make these cuts, but can't you do something about getting another surgeon? How are we supposed to cope with only two? The situation is becoming ridiculous. It's already ridiculous, in fact, having an A&E that shuts on the weekends. What are people supposed to do – save their trauma for the working week?'

She looks over her shoulder for an answer, but Robeson is no longer there. Has she been talking to herself all this time? Clare leans her forehead against the window and huffs, fogging the glass. *Honestly*.

Down below, the protesters are all starting to hold hands and spread out around the hospital, singing. Clare knows from Mrs Kray that the intention is to encircle the hospital in a symbolic gesture.

She wonders if they will have enough supporters to stretch that far.

Tupulo looks over her shoulder as she sits at her computer. There is a song playing on the radio in the kitchen, a candyfloss song by the latest British pop phenomenon, and an image flashes through Clare's mind of the group freefalling off the Cliffs of Dover.

Tupulo is fidgeting around the back of her chair. 'What are you doing?'

Clare scrolls down the screen. Drinking water in north-west Kabul had broken down one day after the last aid workers left. Piped water was being supplied by the French aid agency Solidarité, which paid for fuel and spare parts for the pump.

She exits the page, has read enough Pakistan reportage for one day.

'My sister went to Kabul,' Clare explains briefly.

Bethie was more of a mother than their mother had been. When Clare or Lou had bad dreams in the night, she would sit on the side of the bed and make soothing noises. She baked peanut brownies and fly cemeteries. She would read bedtime stories, even though they all thought themselves too old for it. 'Never mind,' said Bethie, 'one more won't hurt.' She brushed their hair, over and over, strokes that made hair shiny, made hair lift and crackle with electricity. She made their lunches each school morning. She made sure there were carrots planted in the vege garden when their father forgot. She read their school reports, and laid wet flannels on their foreheads when they had a fever. She saved them the kids' page from the newspaper and the card from the Weet-Bix packet.

'What do you want to be when you're grown up?' Bethie asked Lou, brushing the thin golden hair.

'Exactly what I am now,' said Louise.

'Something else.'

'Well,' said Lou, begrudgingly, 'perhaps an air hostess.'

'Excellent career choice,' said Bethie. 'Then if you want to go to Fiji or Bali, you won't need to pay for it, you can just go to work.'

Lou had to laugh. '*Yes*,' she shrieked, 'and you get to wear a cute little hat.'

'*Exactly*,' agreed Bethie, brushing and brushing, till hair shone and everything was right in the world.

She discovered rowing by accident, when she was fifteen. Her best friend, Smith, wanted to row but was too shy to do it by herself, so Beth said she'd join too. Smith soon gave it up for less strenuous activities, while Beth was rowing four, five times a week. Early mornings before school, with the mist hanging low over the flat depressing dairy farms, washing limp on clotheslines, and the Waihou as calm as a bowl of seaweed soup, their father would drive her over to the river and watch the training, a thermos of coffee on the dashboard. Bethie adored the smooth glide of the land beyond her elbow, and the sense of hard work that achieved speed; but most of all she loved the teamwork.

Saturday morning and climbing into Clare's bed, her legs cold against Clare's hot skin: 'Get out,' she moaned, barely awake, trying to push her sister away.

'I've made you bacon and eggs, can't you smell it?' Shoving her cold hands into Clare's side to wake her up.

'Stop it, I tell you!'

Then both of them lying on their backs staring at the ceiling. 'What is it, about the rowing?' Clare, still finding her own way through a morass of uncertainties, wanted to know. Bethie seemed to have a gift for finding exactly what she needed to do at any given time. 'What d'you like about it?'

'I belong,' whispered Beth, as if it might be snatched away if she said it too loudly. 'It's mine.'

Clare finds a card in the box among the diaries. It was obviously printed in more peaceful times, the photograph of a many-towered mosque, its exterior decorated with thousands of mosaic tiles. *Great mosque of Herat*, reads the caption in English, German and French. There is no address, no addressee.

May 1983
Moments of bliss. Like a window opening. A 'city' among reeds, he tells me. Just when you think there's no hope for them here, that they're fighting a losing battle, there's something to remind you that it's not all hopeless. Working here – our flimsy haven in the middle of a war.

Clare traces her forefinger over the skyline of the mosque. It is different from Turkish mosques with their single breast-like dome; and the design is far more complicated than the English stone churches that sit solidly in their own sense of eternity. This building is prickling with towers that are rounded at the top, like a primeval fungus.

She presses the card onto the side of her computer screen with a piece of Blutack. It could be her talisman. The country may still be in turmoil, but Clare is relieved to know that Bethie found her own peace in Afghanistan – though she doesn't literally understand what she meant by a city among reeds. She did read once about the Marsh Arabs, the Ma'dan, of lower Iraq. For at least 5000 years these people had lived in the marshes, building reed houses on artificial islands made from layers of mud and reeds. These days their lifestyle is threatened by industrial development. Would Bethie's reed city have been like that?

Clare thinks, too, about safe havens.

Eventually there was a day when Clare Purefoy came out of theatre feeling completely at ease. Feeling very much, well, *herself*.

It was nine in the evening; she had been working for most of the day, and the fluorescent lights had become blinding. She had just spent two hours taking bullets out of a young man who had got in the way of a gunman who opened fire inside a corner liquor store. Fortunately only two people had been injured; no fatalities. Clare had probed about for bullets and then done damage control, putting in small swift sutures, working on the upper body while Brown was on the other side of the gurney working on the left leg. One bullet was lodged in the chest, miraculously missing the heart.

'It's not called theatre for nothing,' Clare muttered in the corridor. She was lingering about, not sure what to do next – get changed, get a cup of coffee – but nevertheless she paused, wanting to prolong the moment.

Brown, and Wiseman the anaesthetist, crashed out of the doors behind her, slapping her on the back as they passed. 'Good work, Clare,' said Wiseman, giving her a black-eyed wink. Brown was blood-spattered. Clare looked down at the front of her own gown, and the gloves that were rusty with the young man's blood. These hands, she thought – allowing herself a little tingle, nearly giggling – have been ferreting about inside a body, fixing things. If I were a man, thought Clare, I suppose I would feel God-like, omniscient. Except it wasn't that, not exactly. There was a feeling of being *above*, somehow, yet more than that.

It was true, there was a sense of mystery about the body, but mostly there was the known, the predictable – all the organs, as they always were, the veins, those interior rivers of blood: she could picture it all in her mind's eye, like a tree fanning out within the body. There was a high degree of certainty. *My profession has offered me shelter. Hurrah.* As long as she kept going (and there was no reason why she should not), then her job would sustain and protect her. *I am the antithesis of Jonah, no whale will swallow me!* She wiggled her blood-stained fingers. If only Bethie could see her now. It was like discovering, all over again, one's childhood safety net.

'Dr Purefoy,' mizzled a nurse, pushing past with arms full of bloody laundry and raised eyebrows and what is the Kiwi doctor up to now? 'You're dripping, dear.'

Clare obediently took herself off to strip down.

Through the half-open doors of the male scrub room she saw Wiseman with his hairless gleaming chest already exposed, soaping his long thin arms, white suds on black skin.

'So Dr Purefoy,' he called out, rather formally, considering Clare had been some time at the hospital already, 'this little trio of ours is now free for the time being, and Brown and I are going off for some Ugandan snacks –'

She might have thought him to be making some kind of elaborate joke – as if Ugandan was a code for something more louche – except that he was from that country himself. She had also heard them talking about a new African restaurant that had opened in the Castro, the gay area, and taking bets on how long it would last.

'Are you coming?' They had never asked her to go out with them before, though the three of them were often teamed up together. Wiseman & Brown generally liked to remain a couple.

Inexplicably – for after all, there had already been plenty of surgery, plenty of legs arms stomachs spleens kidneys saved sutured or removed with only one or two in the not-so-lucky basket – her heart, or perhaps she should say her soul, sang. If it hadn't sounded so foolish she might have said proudly, 'I'm a grown-up now, I have come into my own.'

Instead: 'Thanks, Wiseman, it would be a pleasure.' Adding, from her girlhood, 'I'm hungry enough to eat a horse.'

'Or perhaps antelope?' added Brown from the vicinity of lockers.

The insides of Clare's ears were humming. 'I'll eat anything that's not moving.'

The Turkoman was getting restless.

'Why can't I get up? Walk around a little, what harm?'

Bethie grinned. 'D'you think you're Superman, or something?'

'Who is this super man?'

'A comic book character. He used to fly through the sky and help people.'

It was the Turkoman's turn to laugh. 'We could use such a man here.'

'You could use several.'

'Tell me,' he said, 'what brought you to this country?'

Beth shrugged. 'I like to keep busy.'

The Turkoman shook his head. 'You come here, to this place, when you could stay in your Garden of Eden.'

'You've got your own kind of paradise in Turkistan, by the sounds of it. Tell me again, about the city.'

The Turkoman gestured for her to sit on the side of the bed. Then he began to draw on the coverlet with a nicotine-stained forefinger. 'Paths,' he said, 'here, here, here, we follow – reeds very high, at night they sound like hundreds of people talking – have many supplies, and houses for our army. Men who get hurt, they can come here –' and he made a cross. 'We have a doctor who has trained in America,' he said proudly, 'and along this path, house for guns, bullets, very dry, safe, everything is built up with water in between – further, this way –' sketching with his finger and glancing up to see if she was watching – 'here even places to grow food, potatoes, room here with small oven –'

He closed his eyes then, exhausted.

'We will move this headquarters soon, maybe even when I get back it will be gone. If you stay too long in one place the Russians might find you. The best thing is to keep moving.'

SIX

Inside the body it is like a treasure trove, thinks Clare; always the same treasures, yet always precious. She pauses for a moment, breathing leisurely and calmly, then starts to remove the gall-bladder from the liver bed. Behind her the machines are articulate, measuring this patient's life flow, and the operative field is white with light.

The first time Clare looked inside a live, anaesthetised body she experienced a feeling of such intense awe that she thought her hand would slip and she'd wedge the scalpel into bone or tissue. This body was *alive* for Christsake – not a model, not a cadaver stinking of formalin. *Oh my God what if I –*

'Keep breathing, Purefoy,' drawled Dr Sangster at her side, 'now hold back the abdominal incision with the retractors –' Clare did as she was told. And still remembers every detail of that operation.

In twenty years, thinks Clare, making her incisions over the neck of the gall-bladder, we won't be cutting these great big holes in the stomach, clamping back the sides, and plunging in our hands ... Yesterday she had shown Tupulo the article in *Discover* about the latest in laparoscopic surgery: the robotic finger that would act like a hand, a kind of joystick, with the surgeon using one in the left and right hands, the tiny movements translated via a computer screen to complete surgery that at present requires the body to be cut open, wrenched apart – Clare proceeds to dissect until the gallbladder bed is displayed – all that would be needed would be a smallish cut. Way less trauma, shorter recovery time.

'But I like getting my hands in there,' said Tupulo, 'I like to palpate those organs –' He was palpating her breast at the time, as if it were a spleen, a heart. Clare, rather disgusted, pushed him away firmly. 'Where's the fun,' he continued in a huff, 'if you can't get your hands inside, eh? You may as well hand over surgery to the scientists, for Christsake, and their little machines.'

But Clare is intrigued: it would be like surgery through a peephole. Really she ought to go back to the States where she'd have more chance of using such technology; already in California they are doing abdominal procedures on pigs with the new instruments. Twenty years, she thinks, and people will look back to what she is doing today and be appalled. But then, you can only do your best in any given moment, with the limited knowledge available to you at the time. Such is the human conundrum; it is like a symptom of our own mortality.

Later, closing up, she stitches deftly and carefully, imagining a time when there will be only a scar here, and the patient able to look in a mirror and trace a finger along the line that she has cut and stitched back together again. There are signatures of her work all over the country, the world; visible reminders that we are really just bodies of water, but tough, too. She stands back to admire for a moment, while behind her people move about, tidying up. For after all, look at what she has just done to this body – and it is still functioning, and will continue to function.

The body seems fragile – and it is – yet it is also elastic; its elasticity is its saving grace, like a city hidden among reeds. Clare starts whistling behind her surgical mask. Daily miracles, she thinks.

Bad luck is said to come in threes. Appliances too seem linked to such superstition.

When the first of the Brightlys' appliances refuses to function, Clare just goes out and buys a new one. Nothing is made to last, she thinks in disgust.

This first traitor is the toaster. Clare finds that there are three models to choose from: the cheapest, which will break down in about a year; the middle-of-the-range, which comes with a one-year guarantee and will probably last about five years, or so the saleswoman assures her. This middle model, however, is designed for a family: there is space to cook eight pieces of toast simultaneously. Clare doesn't like the idea of this – though it would be useful, given Tupulo's appetite – and has only ever had toasters capable of cooking just the two pieces at the same time. Eight seems extravagant. No no, she tells the saleswoman, that's far too big for us. So there is the deluxe model, with a flash silver handle and bits which, when you depress the handle, clutch in and hold the piece of bread with precision, no matter what width, whether crumpet or panini. Tupulo will enjoy playing with it. It can sit on the bench next to his Italian espresso machine.

'I'll take it,' sighs Clare. At least it might last longer than a year, or five.

Her American kettle packs in next – as if, transplanted from its native environment, it has decided to give up the ghost. One evening when Clare goes to make her usual cup of green tea – Clare depends on that cup of tea – it refuses to boil water.

'But it's a good-quality kettle,' rants Clare uselessly in front of the thing. Its convex silver belly distorts her reflection and turns her into a tiny stamping dwarf. 'I only bought it a year ago and it cost a bundle. It ought to last for ever.'

Tupulo is strangely silent on the subject, and merely puts on a pot of water to boil.

'What does this *mean*?'

Tupulo scratches his nose. 'It doesn't mean anything.'

The woman at the appliance shop frowns when she sees Clare coming through the door: has Dr Purefoy changed her mind and brought back the toaster? But then she moves into professional mode. Again there are three different price levels when it comes to kettles. This time Clare, disillusioned and in small revenge against the old kettle, buys the cheapest model. When it craps out in a year's time, she will simply go out and buy a new one. And after all, it is not the most vital piece of equipment in the house: they only use the thing to make tea.

And then, in the middle of Satie's piano works, the CD player dies. This time Clare puts her head in her hands and screams. Tupulo and Grunt come running from different directions, although Grunt is running to hide beneath the couch. Then the phone starts bleating: it is Ken Gillman from next door wanting to know if everything is all right. Clare's beeper goes off. She is needed at the hospital. *Jesus.* She leaves the disk in the player and storms out of the house, hair uncombed, trailing her jacket behind her.

Tupulo looks at the black wall of dials, then leans forward and whispers: 'You are a very naughty machine.' By some kink in the wiring Satie starts up again. Tupulo jumps back, and Grunt runs out of the room, whimpering. Tupulo will definitely not tell Clare about *this*.

They bought the kettle together. Holding hands, she and Marcus wandering through the Haight, the neighbourhood that hippies made famous in the early 60s and where Janis Joplin and the Grateful Dead had once hung out. Now it was mostly dominated by punks, vintage clothing stores, and bars. A mild sun was shining, people were wearing fresh colours, a florist's shop had buckets of daffodils on the pavement, and a feeling of optimism was ripe in the air. For no reason, Clare recalled the 'naked ladies' that flowered in the autumn back in her hometown, and the heavy scent of their blooms.

She might have been homesick, but instead put her arm round Marcus's slim waist. (The boxed kettle in its plastic bag banged between them.) Clare felt a wave of pure contentment. She was in love. His smooth hair was slicked back off his forehead, like a gangster's, and catching the light. He could be an angel, she thought, a modern-day angel. She wanted nothing more than to be filled up with him. Could drown in the sight of him.

'Any old day,' he said suddenly, looking around, 'all of this could be dust.'

She laughed. 'That's a pleasant thought.'

'A stray meteor could hit – *pow* – and it'd be over – if you believe the scientists.'

'And do you?'

'I like to think our time here is temporary.'

Clare shivered.

He glanced over her with a lazy smile. 'Don't you like the idea of going out in a big bang?'

'Not especially.'

Up ahead she noticed a man in a red miniskirt and red high heels, staggering across the road. He had very hairy legs, bare, and was lurching, zig-zagging, as if drunk. At 10.30 a.m.? Perhaps he was on his way home. Several cars had to swerve to avoid him, tooted their horns. One man pushed his elbow out the car window and shouted, 'Hey Josephine, wanna lift?'

Red Heels made it across to the other side, then leaned against a lamp-post.

'We should go over,' she said, though Brown & Wiseman had warned her about helping people on the street. ('You just keep walking,' they advised.)

Marcus was already moving; as she got closer to the man it was obvious he was very drunk. 'Do you need help?' she said, bending to get a closer look at him.

Marcus stood behind her, watching. 'Just a drunk,' he muttered, as if disappointed.

Red Heels gave Clare a bleary glance, then sank down onto the pavement like a squashed can and started snoring. Clare looked round helplessly. Passersby didn't even bother to look. So she crossed the street to a café, and asked them to call the police. At least they would put Red Heels in a bed for the day. But when she went back outside, he was gone. *Oh, God.*

Then a shout made her look up. Red Heels was halfway up the side of an apartment building, scaling the fire escape. There were seven floors, and he was already up to the third. A small crowd had gathered on the pavement below, anticipating a show. 'A jumper,' somebody said.

Marcus stood with his arms crossed, a crooked grin on his face, watching too.

'Maybe he lives up there,' considered Clare. But no, she knew he wouldn't, he would probably have a basement room in the Castro. 'I should go after him.'

'Leave him,' said Marcus.

But Clare dropped the kettle and took off after him, climbing up the metal steps. 'Hey,' she called, 'wait for me.'

Red Heels looked back briefly – he was on the verge of the fifth-floor landing. 'The end of another perfect night,' he declaimed, and then jumped.

Oh Jesus, no. Clare huddled gasping against the wall.

But then there came the sound of ragged laughter, applause. She pushed herself out onto her own landing, and peered over. Red Heels had landed on a shop canopy. He was on his back, spreadeagled, bouncing as if on a trampoline; the red-faced shopkeeper below was jumping up and down, shaking his fist.

'You crazy idiot, you lunatic. This time, I call the police!'

The shopkeeper disappeared into his shop, still shouting over his shoulder. Red Heels, laughing gleefully, chucked his shoes down, grabbed the end of the canopy and slid himself back to the pavement, his skirt ruched up around his thighs. He put on the shoes, and gave his admirers a bow, before tottering off at a surprising speed along the street, followed by wolf whistles.

Clare climbed back down the fire escape with jelly legs. Marcus was waiting for her, coolly lighting a cigarette as if nothing had happened. He handed her the bag containing the kettle.

'What did you mean, leave him?' said Clare, barely able to contain her anger. 'He could have been a real jumper. You were just going to watch?'

Marcus was watching Red Heels disappear up the street. He put out his hand as if to take hers – a natural enough gesture, and one she was used to, this seeking out of her hand – but instead his fingers closed tightly around her wrist.

'So I'm the *bad* guy here –?'

Clare opened her mouth, then shut it again. The day had taken on a stinging grey edge. She was aware of his fingers pressing against her pulse. In one part of her mind she knew she ought to move, run off, something silly like that. Make a move. But she didn't. Clouds had moved in front of the sun. Clare inhaled, then blinked; again the light shifted, as if a pane of glass had been turned. An ending could be that subtle.

'No, of course not,' she said evenly. 'No,' she said.

Marcus released her wrist. 'Good.'

Clare comes back from the supermarket one morning to find Tupulo still fast asleep and snoring, and Louise sitting on the end of the bed watching him. She's wearing a pair of red heels and, legs crossed, is jigging one of them in the air.

'Lou,' says Clare. 'Lou, how are you?'

Louise stands up and carefully smooths her linen pants. 'Clare, you oughtn't to leave the house open like you do. Anybody could just walk in from the street. Anybody.'

Anybody just has, thinks Clare, noting that the alarm clock will go off in three minutes and she needs to get round to that side of the bed to turn it off. She doesn't want Tupulo's first waking sight to be Louise: they have met only once, but Tupulo has developed a full-blown antipathy for her. ('But why?' Clare asked him once. 'What's she ever done to you?' Tupulo had merely narrowed his eyes and muttered something about instinct. When it comes to people, Tupulo obeys his instincts. God knows what kind of surgeon he will make, thinks Clare.)

Lou is carrying on with her train of thought: 'Somebody could just walk in and take, ah, the stereo –' It is visible through the open bedroom door, a mini system. 'Or the video. I hope the Brightlys are insured.'

'I'd be surprised if they weren't,' mutters Clare.

'Or, even –' Louise drops her voice to a hiss, 'some strange person – and the world is full of them these days – could come in here, just like I did, and hurt Tupulo.' Both of them gaze down at the sleeping man. 'Tupulo is such an innocent.'

Her eyes are gleaming in the half-light. Clare is reminded of a time when they were girls and one of them had broken a window – Lou, probably – and they were hiding in Clare's wardrobe. They were poised, barely breathing, while they listened for sound of their father coming to punish them. 'He'll hit us with his belt,' said Lou. 'Rubbish,' said Clare, 'he wouldn't do that, we're girls.' But because Lou had said it, she wasn't so sure any more. 'He'll take his belt off, and *slap* our legs,' Lou hissed. And in the semi-darkness her face seemed transformed – drained of all colour, the whites of her eyes shining unnaturally. She looked frightening. That was before children were constantly thinking about aliens, or Clare would have seriously wondered about Lou's origins.

'He's a buffoon,' pronounces Lou.

'That's exactly what I like about him.' Clare knows it sounds defensive; and is glad she's resisted the urge to tell Lou the real story about Marcus.

Then the alarm goes off. Tupulo sits bolt upright, opens his eyes and sees the two women standing at the foot of his bed. He slumps back again, obviously thinking he is still in a dream. Clare goes around the bed and switches off the alarm – it is actually programmed to go off three times, because of his difficulty in waking.

'Would you excuse us, Lou?'

Lou, who has been riveted by the sight of Tupulo's awakening like a modern-day Lazarus, mutters, 'All right,' and goes into the sitting room. Clare shuts the door behind her.

'Tupulo,' she hisses into his ear. He opens his eyes again, grins, and gathers her largely against his chest. 'Not now, Tupulo. My sister is here.'

'What?'

'My sister is here, in the house. And you have to get up.'

He is jolted awake for a second time. 'Am I late? Am I late?' White Rabbit-like, he leaps out of bed. Then stops, swaying in his red boxer shorts in front of the wardrobe. 'Your sister is here?' he mutters.

'Yes.'

'Call the witch busters.' Tupulo is fully awake, and despairing.

Lou's overnight bag sits by the back door. It is the first thing Clare sees when she comes out of the bedroom, intending to make some coffee. Louise, wandering about the lounge and looking at things, calls out: 'I've bought three frozen Indian dinners.'

'All is forgiven.' Tupulo's muffled voice comes from the bedroom.

Lou frowns. 'What did he say?'

'I didn't catch it either. Coffee?'

'No thanks. I'm on the liver diet. No coffee, booze or dairy products for eight weeks. It's the latest thing.'

Tupulo emerges from the bedroom in his bathrobe, chest pushed out defiantly. 'That's exactly what the world needs,' he exclaims loudly, 'another bloody diet.'

'And hello to you too, Tupulo,' says Lou drily. 'The liver diet would do wonders for you, y'know. I've got the book with me. You could have a look at it while I'm here.'

'Thank you, but no thanks, Louise. My liver is perfectly happy with its present imperfect diet.' He strides for the bathroom, and Clare listens as the shower goes on. She pours a cup of coffee and takes it to him, squeezing the door shut behind her.

'Hey, coffee,' she whispers.

He peers out from behind the plastic curtain – Aphrodite standing on a clam shell. 'You don't need to whisper,' he whispers darkly, 'this is your place.'

'Thanks for reminding me,' she says.

'Get rid of her,' he hisses.

'I can't do that.'

'Of course you can.' The shower curtain swishes back to hide his bulky form.

'You're acting like we're married: stop it. You can always go back to the hotel –'

Tupulo sticks his nose out from behind the curtain. 'Is this what it boils down to – me or your sister?'

'I *have* known my sister longer than I've known you.'

'That's hardly a ringing recommendation,' he hisses.

'Your coffee,' says Clare firmly.

A hairy hand emerges, and the cup disappears into the shower.

They were going to the pond. Lou was in front: when it was just the two of them, Lou liked to lead, as if to compensate for her usual more passive role. Clare followed warily behind in her black gumboots. For first they must cross the cow paddock. Clare was afraid of cattle, sharp-horned, eyeballing beasts that were capable of lunging at you at any moment; Lou merely picked up a stick and proceeded boldly forward.

Then they were slip-sliding down the bank. Clare also disliked this part, as she was afraid of hurting herself. But she would overcome nearly any fear to get to the river. This was one of their special spots: a bend in the river where the water lay shallow and muddy. They had come to get tadpoles. Clare clasped the net tightly in her hand; a screw-top jar was in her oilskin pocket and banging against her leg.

'Come on, slowcoach,' yelled Lou from the small strip of sand. They could have gone the other way, except Lou enjoyed the challenge of going down the bank. She watched with satisfaction as Clare, clumsy as always, slipped on the last bit and ended on her bum. 'Now look what you've done.' But she was pleased. Lou liked to see Clare fail.

Now that she was down the bank, Clare was quite happy. She got out her jar, and plodded into the water, started to delve about in the muddy water with her net. But now that Lou had achieved what she set out to do, a certain boredom was taking over.

'I bet I can run faster than you in my gumboots.'

Busy, Clare gave no response.

'I bet I could race you home even.' Lou stood defiantly with hands on hips and appraised her sister scathingly. Why couldn't God have given her an interesting sister? A teen model, for example, or a child actor. The whole point of coming to the river was to go across the cow paddock and down the steep bank, not to search for disgusting creatures in the water. The school holidays dragged out before her like a prison sentence.

'Well, you stay here, see if I care, I'm going back home.' Lou began stomping away across the lumpy paddock.

Clare looked up, to make sure she had really gone – Lou had a tendency to backtrack and play tricks on the unsuspecting – but there she was, small and dark at the fenceline. Clare could happily catch tadpoles without a lot of distraction going on in the background. She intended, when she got back to the house, to make an aquarium in the old fish tank, and raise a family of frogs. She would also raise maggots for them to feed on. It would be a watery world of her own invention.

Many pleasant hours were spent dissecting rabbit carcasses, thanks mainly to the air of indolence that had entered the house after their mother's departure. Pat would never have tolerated dead rabbits near the house. Now their father had taken up shooting again, and after he showed Clare how to skin and gut them, she took on the job permanently. He would go into the kitchen and drink coffee until she was finished, secretly relieved that he didn't have to do it any more.

The trick was to use a sharp knife. One slit down the belly, slits down the legs, then you peeled off the skin. The rabbit lay exposed, a different kind of creature altogether, as if its true self was now revealed. So this is what animals are like without their fur, thought Clare. Yet somehow it was perfect. You could clearly see the long leg muscles for running, and also the muscles up the back. Then you slit the belly, and the guts tumbled out: tiny heart, lungs, kidneys. Clare would separate them and lay them out on a sheet of glass to study. You had to take care not to pierce the intestines.

'Hurry up, Clare,' her father called from the kitchen. 'If we're to have any stew tonight –'

Usually, Bethie would cook. But rabbits were Marty's domain. Clare cut the carcass into pieces – slicing carefully through tendons and cartilage – and carried in the meat from the garage on a tray, neatly laid out: it was meat now, no longer the rabbit. All her father had to do was sprinkle flour and pepper and put them in the pot. He would have the carrots and onion ready, chopped and waiting on the board, and the pot of water on to boil.

'Nothing like rabbit stew,' he'd sigh. The best thing was that it was cheap.

There were also fish from the river, but Clare found fish slimy, somehow repulsive. 'What's wrong?' Lou would tease. 'Fish have intestines too, you know.' But she didn't do the fish. Their father gutted them outside and threw the bits to the cat.

That was all later, after Clare had stopped being a kid. After their mother had run away to Queensland with the Accountant, taking the family savings with her. She had sent a postcard, of Surfers' Paradise – a stretch of yellow sand cluttered with bikini girls, the foreshore cluttered with apartment towers – promising to pay back the money. And eventually it came, in uneven instalments. Her departure, however, was less easily dealt with; no parcelled explanations were offered. And it created a gaping hole.

Although with hindsight Clare remembers signals, some visual clues. The day, for instance, when their mother was banging about the house and knocked a glass onto the floor by accident. She threw up her hands and cried out, 'I'm going *stir*-crazy!' She went out, the car roaring out of the garage; and hours later, it seemed, she returned with packages. She'd been to Auckland. From a brown paper carrybag she pulled a thin red dress with shoestring shoulder straps: 'Voilà,' she said, grinning. Clare was confused. It was beautiful, that dress, but where would their mother wear it?

'This *town*,' said their mother, sighing it at times, at other times railing bitterly against her prison, 'the town'. What about this town, wondered Clare, though only briefly, for the town seemed perfectly all right to her. 'This town stinks,' whispered Bethie behind their mother's back: their private joke. 'It stinks of eels,' she giggled, 'and little boys, and nasty seaweed.'

And then there was that long summer which had driven them over the hills and into the valley, camping. Their mother had a headache from the car trip and was lying inside the tent, limbs sprawled, with Clare curled up dozing against her side. The weather had broken and it had started raining. The patter of rain on canvas was syncopated by their father's chopping just outside the tent, digging a ditch in case the rain got heavier and the camping area flooded; he was fixing everything into place as if a hurricane was forecast. 'There's always something, isn't there,' their mother said, sighing and stretching her fingers to touch canvas. He was using a spade that his mate Barry, the DOC ranger, had loaned him. A radio sang in the distance, from another tent: Jefferson Airplane's 'Afternoon Delight'. His mind was back in 'Nam when his reverie was broken by a scream. Clare jumped up in fright, then screamed too. Their mother drew herself in like a hurt starfish, blood spurting. He had chopped off her thumb.

Later, at the hospital, it was obvious in their mother's eyes that he had committed the cardinal mistake, the unforgivable.

June 1983
There's a universe contained in this kind of work. Well, nearly. Soul-satisfying.

Everything changes. Where once – and not all that long ago – she got excited about her work, now Clare wonders, What else is there? She wonders if she shouldn't follow Bethie's example; there is always work for a doctor with the aid agencies overseas. She could give Red Cross a call. Only, she hesitates. She doodles, sitting at her desk in Outpatients, waiting for the next patient – endoscopy, late. Sunlight is coming in from the big windows, the examining bed behind her white-sheeted, in readiness; and she is aware of the muted sound of traffic humming along the main road. Only, she likes it here, she likes the quiet, and how everybody knows each other. She doesn't want to sacrifice herself to a war zone, to the endless hurt and wounded. *Call me selfish, but it's not my thing.* She sucks the end of her pen, puts her feet up on the edge of the desk. She also likes her creature comforts. '*Bombing today,*' reads Beth's diary, '*no electricity, again – cold showers tonight.*' Clare doesn't think she could cope without hot showers.

Instead of her next patient, Peter Lincoln pops his head round the door. 'Gidday. Run off your feet as usual, Doc –'

Clare puts her feet down, pleased. Peter can always cheer her up. She met Peter Lincoln in A&E. He had cut off all the fingers on his left hand with a Skilsaw. His mate from the building site had the severed fingers – still joined together – in a plastic bag. Deadpan, he put them on the desk, like some Hallowe'en practical joke. 'Here, you'd better have these,' he said to the nurse on duty. The nurse put the severed fingers in a chillybin, while Clare staunched the bleeding and put a line into Peter's arm. Then they put him in an ambulance bound for Auckland and plastic surgeons.

'Hi Peter, how's the hand?'

For answer he holds it up: still bandaged. He manages a wiggle. 'The wonders of modern technology, eh.' Though he could be being facetious, as Auckland only managed to reattach two of the fingers. 'Hey Doc, I've got a little trick to show you –' Coming over to the desk, he puts his hand on the wood and sidles the two-fingered hand along its edge. '*Incy wincy spider crawled up the doctor's desk –*'

In one of Clare's moments of weakness, while waiting for the ambulance, she had admitted to Peter Lincoln that she had arachnophobia. Their mutual weaknesses, although mismatched, make a friendly bond.

Yet after he has gone, she lapses back into her pensive mood. I am already in a kind of war zone, thinks Clare, the suburban warfare of Skilsaws, poorly placed ladders and drunk drivers.

In the old bazaar there was a one-legged man, wearing a turban, sitting on a moth-eaten rug and selling war souvenirs. Beth wouldn't have seen him, except that Terry had stopped at a large stall next to him, festooned with hundreds of coloured beads and long silk scarves. Spread out on his rug were fur hats, Red Star badges, belts, brass buttons, handguns, spent bullets.

'From Shurovee,' he said, opening his palms to her. His bare and calloused foot was propped up on the thigh of his amputated leg, as in a yoga position, and he peered up at her with a look that was both ingratiating and calculated. 'Dead Soviets,' he explained, 'you buy for *souvenir*.' He pronounced the word as if it was the French, to remember. His look continued to probe her. 'Deutsch? Inglistan?'

Bethie fingered a cotton cap. There was a circle of yellow inside the brim. She felt repulsed by the man's display, yet drawn to it as well. The Soviets were so militantly atheist that to the Afghans they appeared to be monsters. They told stories about how the Soviets ate babies, how they laughed while they raped and slaughtered women, and called them 'the invader who believes in nothing'.

She picked out a compass for Marty.

'I'm from New Zealand,' she said, handing over some coins.

'May Allah favour your path,' he replied, using the standard greeting. He had probably never heard of the place.

SEVEN

The first patient of the morning is a woman who has a lump in her breast. Clare asks a few questions, establishes that there is no history, although the woman is a smoker. She has long lank hair, wears a fake-leather jacket and glitter earrings. Her eyes dart around the surgery suspiciously: it could simply be nervousness. Plenty of people, thinks Clare, are nervous about being examined. She checks the name on the file.

'Well, Marise, just slip off your top and bra, and lie down on the table. We'll have a look and see what we've got.'

Clare remains seated at her desk while the woman undresses behind her.

The surname is different, but now that she has thought of it, Clare is seeing similarities. The nape of her neck feels hot, a sure sign of recognition. But still, it's unlikely: Marise Walker would've left the town years ago – she was a Bright Lights sort of girl; there wouldn't be enough action in this place for her. And there's no way she would ever come to Clare if she needed a doctor. There are other women doctors in town; she could even take a trip to Auckland and see somebody there. It is easy enough to avoid a person; it's what Clare herself would do. But then, thinks Clare, perhaps she isn't the one who feels the need to avoid anything.

A throat is cleared behind her, rather like a sheep coughing. Clare forces herself to get up and be professional. Even if this is Marise Walker, what happened was years ago, ancient history, and should not affect Clare's role as doctor. Besides, she has treated all sorts of objectionable people before, and survived: this is no different.

The woman is lying on her back; she hasn't even put the sheet over herself. Clare pulls it up, as she likes to do with all her patients, for modesty and a modicum of warmth. But the patient makes an irritated noise. 'Don't worry about that, Doc, we're all girls here.' Even the voice . . . Clare gives her hands a quick chafe, then starts to massage in a circular motion around the right breast, her eyes on the ceiling. The sound of their breathing fills the room. There are cysts, but she doesn't feel anything out of the ordinary. She thinks about the new dummies that the medical school now has for the students to practise on: there are breasts with lumps apparently. Clare didn't have such benefits when she was at med school. The breast is warm and clammy, as if the patient has a fever, and Clare swallows a slight feeling of revulsion. When she glances down she finds the woman's eyes on her. It is an odd expression, as if she has discovered herself in a place she would rather not be, but Clare doesn't take it personally.

The other breast is slightly smaller, and on the anterior side there is a lump. Clare feels around, just to be sure. Yep, bingo.

The woman has tensed. 'My boyfriend found it. He's good that way.' That look again.

'You can get up now.'

The woman – Marise – sighs. 'I was right, wasn't I. It's cancer, isn't it –'

Clare pauses, turns to wash her hands at the sink. The look in the woman's eyes was fear, of course. 'We can't assume that,' she says with conviction. 'There are many options. It could well be benign –'

But the patient obviously doesn't believe her. 'Yeah, right.' She is sitting on the table, thick fingers slowly doing up the tiny white buttons of her blouse.

Clare finds herself surprised, yet again: this isn't what she expected at all. She considers asking the woman a few pertinent questions about herself: school? parents? any accountants in the family? But she realises it's not necessary, after all.

'I'll do anything except get it cut off. I've heard about women getting them cut off and they end up like men. I don't want anything like that happening to me.'

Clare sits at her desk. She could almost laugh, the woman's so backward; surely that would be a small price to pay, to live. On the other hand, that's what they're all afraid of. 'Well, Marise –' there, she has said the dreaded name – 'you really don't need to worry about that yet. The next step is to get a biopsy done, and then we'll know what we're dealing with –'

On the way out the woman turns. 'By the way, welcome home, Dr Purefoy,' she says, and gives Clare a sharp, pebbled look. But Clare is beyond bullying now.

This is her surgery, she thinks; and what strange twists life or fate, if you can believe in such an ephemeral thing, dishes up.

'Thanks,' she says, 'it's good to be back,' and firmly shuts the door.

There was a girl at school who hated Clare's guts. Marise Walker. It was hard to understand such hatred when you didn't seem to have done anything to earn it.

It began after their mother left and somehow word had spread around the town – for no matter how careful you try to be, somebody always finds out, and no matter how well-intentioned that person is they must tell somebody else, and that next person happens to tell several other people. So there came a day when Clare was hurrying down the school corridor, late for class and hating being late, when Marise Walker stepped out from behind the long island of dark wooden lockers and banged heavily into her. Books went flying: her maths text was splayed open, face down, under the lockers.

'Oh, *sorry*.'

Marise didn't look very sorry, but leaned against the lockers, watching as Clare crawled about the shiny lino collecting her things. Her pencil was missing – it had been propped behind her ear – she heard it tinkling across the floor; but she'd have to leave it, she had to keep moving. At face level were the girl's legs: the socks hanging down and the shaved legs which were a little smeared with clay. Normally Clare didn't notice much about other people. Then, Marise was walking away, swinging her hips jauntily.

Days passed and it still seemed like a coincidence when Clare found the bag of rotten cheese in her locker. She had to hold her nose to get it out, take it to the bin. Kids giggled, peering, eyebrows raised. 'What's *that*?' Clare couldn't say a thing, even to explain. Locked within her own silence, she had become a 'dark horse'. People muttered this phrase when they thought she wasn't listening; even her teacher had said it, though adding 'poor kid' at the end, like she was a kind of fixture. *There is nothing worth talking about any more.* Somehow, seemingly overnight, she had become the class joke; it seemed almost natural that she should be the target of another's malice. Her locker stank. She stood about wondering what to do.

Marise Walker strolled past – socks tidy today, but her tie awry – folder held against her chest. She barely glanced in Clare's direction. Marise Walker and Clare's muteness had become intertwined; after a while it seemed as if one had caused the other.

There were other incidents – accidents and unpleasant surprises – until the day of the fire drill. The fire drills were considered pointless, but nevertheless a welcome break from class routine. That day it was sunny outside; the air smelt of humus. When they filed back indoors, Clare stopped off at the toilets. She had no idea that anyone was behind her, until she was slammed into the cubicle, a sweaty hand shoved over her mouth. Two bodies in a narrow compartment. Marise Walker was remarkably strong. With Clare's arm up her back, she easily had her pinned against the wall. The hand tasted of charcoal and butter. Tears pricked out of Clare's eyes. She had never been manhandled before, and was terrified. Would Marise push her head into the toilet bowl? Alan Piggot had been suspended for doing just that to Chris Black, a small boy, thin and pale; and here she was, one of the 'wankers', for that's what they called kids like that, kids who got their heads pushed into toilet bowls. Clare didn't think she'd survive that kind of ordeal: she would drown, for sure.

Yet still she didn't speak, couldn't speak. It was like a test for the true mute.

A voice hissed into her ear, a voice so venomous it burned. '*I hate you, Purefoy.*' Time stood still, tortuously. 'If you ever tell anybody –'

But no threat came. No punch to the kidneys, either. Just a

lessening of the pain, and Marise was letting her go. Still, she gave one more shove in the back, for good measure, before leaving the cubicle.

Clare sat on the toilet seat, shivering, her face pink and mottled, rubbing her arm. They'd be wondering where she'd got to; but she couldn't go out, not just yet. She couldn't face going to class and having everybody looking at her, wondering why she was late. She wanted her mother, she wanted . . . nothing made sense.

Eventually, taking in the quiet hum of kids in classes, Clare left the toilets and walked out of the school. It felt strange, just leaving, not telling anybody, walking through the deserted playground. And the streets themselves seemed strange – empty and hot – like being inside a movie. *So this is what it's like out here while I'm at school.* She walked past the school pool on the opposite side of the road, heard the sounds of splashing; an old lady pulling a trundler passed her without even a glance; cicadas sang innocently.

It wasn't far to get back to their house – just down the road in fact – and there was Bethie, at home with the flu, lying on the couch watching soap operas.

'Jeez Clare, you gave me a fright! I thought you were a bloody ghost.'

Clare sat on the floor and laid her head on Bethie's stomach. It felt nice, being home – home, being with Bethie – so that somehow she found her voice again, it was that urgent, the necessity to speak.

'You won't ever leave, will you Bethie?'

Beth sat up abruptly; they had got used to a silent Clare. 'Course not,' she said brusquely. She was capable of sympathy, but didn't believe in being soppy. 'Now get up, kid, and tell me what's been happening.'

It was difficult to tell the story, but she forced it out like so much mincemeat – it was her or Marise, now.

'A girl,' she whispered, surprised that her voice still worked, 'a girl, hurt me –'

'What girl?'

Clare couldn't bring herself to say the name, but instead wrote it on the cover of the *Woman's Weekly*, in tight capitals, with an exclamation mark at the end.

Bethie shook her head slowly, bleached hair shifting around her cheeks. 'You know, don't you, who that is –'

'That girl?'

'It's the Accountant's daughter.'

'Do you think our mother will ever come back?'

Lou was sitting up in bed, her hair in plaits because she liked it crinkly in the morning, and glowing in a white nightie, the only kind of night attire she wore – and did she have a Victorian vision of herself, wondered Clare. There were two Barbies in the bed with her, hard thin lumps like frozen stoat corpses beneath the covers, which Clare had inadvertently sat on before realising what they were. Lou was a kind of Barbie herself, with her pale blonde hair and her thin legs.

'She'll come back, won't she, for me –'

'Mother?' Clare ruminated, painting her fingernails in Tropical Delight, a funny shade of orange. 'I don't know.'

She was always truthful with Lou, even to her own detriment. Like when Lou had slipped in the bath and splashed water everywhere; Clare had told their mother truthfully what had happened, and had been punished a) by their mother for not cleaning up after Louise, and b) by Lou for being a tittle-tattle. And Clare had thought she was doing the right thing, by telling it the way it was. She still runs into difficulties with this instinct at work, too. Mr Harvey hadn't wanted to be told he had a rotten liver; he had wanted to be told he could take a few tablets and carry on with his life of singular self-debauchery with no ill effect whatsoever. There are times when Clare has to hold herself back from screaming out the obvious: *You are sick, you are going to die, you are a fool to smoke cigarettes, to drink, to drive too fast* ... She has a puritanical streak, which is exacerbated by her profession; every day she sees the evidence that we reap what we sow.

But their mother? They had had a third postcard in the mail

recently from Surfers' Paradise. Pat must have bought a whole bundle at once, because the postcards were the same. Louise found it confusing. Bethie just laughed bitterly, and didn't bother reading them. Their father would glance over the cards, as if not caring, but then later, over a whisky, would repeat the words verbatim, over and over, beneath his breath. Had he photographic memory, wondered Clare. No, Bethie told her later: he took the cards into the toilet with him, and read them over and over till he had memorised them. She had even heard him muttering the words in his sleep: 'Hope you're all well . . . the weather here is superb . . .' And there was always the word 'sorry' thrown in as if it was a magic spell. Clare wondered how much apology she could handle.

While they were cooking tea one night – bangers and mash (Home Economics had finally realised a purpose) – Bethie said that he was probably planning to go over there one day and kill them both in their sleep.

'In their sleep?' repeated Clare.

'Of course. That's how lovers are always killed. Or at least in bed together. But I think, because it's Dad, he'll wait till they're asleep.'

The word 'lovers' was disturbing, and Clare quickly tried to think of something else. 'How will he do it?'

'He'll blow their brains out, of course, with the .22.'

This sounded entirely natural, but it was a puzzle how their father would get the shotgun onto the plane to Queensland without it being confiscated and himself arrested. Even Bethie had no answer for that one.

'I don't know.' She was getting sick of the subject. 'Maybe he'll buy one when he gets over there.'

'Maybe he'll hire a hitman,' said Lou.

Clare and Beth both looked at her. They had forgotten about Lou, who was sitting on the kitchen bench, watching.

'What did you say?' asked Bethie.

'A hitman. I heard about it on the TV. The six o'clock news.'

Beth sent a scathing look to Clare. 'This child,' she said heavily, 'is watching way too much television.'

There was a pause, while Bethie poured boiling water and sliced carrots into the colander in the sink, and then they all burst into laughter.

Bethie and Terry shared a room that was attached to the clinic. The mud-brick walls were whitewashed, and the room was relatively cool during the hot weather, a place to retreat. The praying at dawn probably started, thought Bethie, because of the nightmares. Terry would start mumbling in the early hours, long before the sun was due to rise, waking Beth. A pale arm would be flung sideways, a sudden shaking of dark hair on the pillow; a leg would be thrust from beneath the sheet.

'What were you dreaming of?' Beth asked her one morning.

But Terry shook her head, and walked out to the bathroom to wash the shadows of sleep from her face. Did she not know, or was she not telling? When she came back to their room, she was her old self again, as if the restlessness of the early hours belonged to somebody else altogether. 'Get up, sleepyhead, we've got work, remember?' And already the sun too was belying that other reality that played itself out in the night.

So Beth would get up when Terry was beginning to stir in her sleep. She'd roll out a prayer mat and kneel in the direction she had seen men at the clinic kneel, facing towards an imaginary Mecca. The mat hurt her knees, she wasn't even sure what she was supposed to say, and she felt a little silly, but Bethie persisted. *All praise belongs to God, Lord of all worlds, the Compassionate, the Merciful, Ruler of Judgement Day. It is You that we worship, and to You we appeal for help. Show us the straight way, the way of those You have graced, not of those on whom is Your wrath, nor of those who wander astray.*

By the time Terry actually woke, Beth was dressed and sitting on her bed brushing her hair.

'So, smartalec, was I talking in my sleep again?'

'No,' she lied.

It took a long time for Clare to feel as if she belonged in any significant way in San Francisco. It helped to go out regularly with Brown & Wiseman, who seemed to take it upon themselves to introduce her to San Fran cuisine. There was The Golden Turtle, a Vietnamese restaurant in Van Ness Ave; and Kasbah Moroccan style in San Rafael, complete with belly dancer and eating food with one's hands. Even an Afghani restaurant, Helmand at North Beach. At Harris's they ate mesquite steaks, grilled dry-aged beef with pepper sauce, potato salad on the side, Caesar salad, and debated the likelihood of another huge earthquake. Brown & Wiseman were telling Clare about the big one of '89.

Wiseman said, 'There was an apartment building in Marina District that was thrown off its foundations and crushed a car. And fires – they were everywhere, from the broken gas lines.'

'Forget about gas lines,' said Brown, 'my mother was caught in that quake. She was in her house – not that she would've left it anyway; the street was splitting down the middle like a peach. She went down to the basement and crouched under the pool table she's got there, for the grandkids. They found her like that, surrounded by rubble.'

'Was she badly injured?' Clare is struggling with her steak.

Wiseman gave her a scathing look, his skin nearly dark purple in the light of the country-style glass lamp over their table. 'She was dead, Brown's mother. They found her two days after the quake.'

'Oh God, sorry.'

Brown was slicing his steak as methodically as if he was working on the operating table, seemingly unmoved by his mother's death. 'But the thing that always gets me – the pool table was still intact. Everything round it was rubble. I mean, that wasn't exactly a high-grade pool table, it was just, hell, chipboard. I bought it for her myself, for the grandkids.' He laid his serrated knife carefully to one side of his plate, shaking his head. 'Chipboard.'

Clare tried again. 'The ground really opened up?'

'Of course,' stated Wiseman drily. They had lost interest in the actual earthquake.

'So what I did,' continued Brown, 'I bought myself one of those pool tables and I put it in my laundry, for the next one.'

'You need to put it in your basement,' said Wiseman.

Brown picked up his side plate of salad and examined it. 'You know very well that I don't have a basement. The basement flat in my building is tenanted by a man who breeds ferrets, God bless him.'

'Isn't that illegal?' asked Clare.

'You could move.'

'I don't want to move.'

'You should move,' repeated Wiseman, pushing a piece of steak into his mouth.

'You could just as well get under your dining table,' said Clare suddenly, and they both looked at her. 'It's not the pool table, but the idea of the pool table. If you think you're safe, then you feel better. It's not the pool table that's going to save you, but your instinct for safety.'

There was a pause, during which Wiseman blinked languidly, once, and then both men broke into laughter.

'What?'

Brown returned to his steak, grinning. 'You're right, Clare. I could just hang an Indian mandala over my bed, and when the next quake comes *I will be safe.*'

Unexpectedly, Wiseman sided with Clare. 'She's right, man. You're being superstitious. Come another big one, there's no way a chipboard pool table is going to save your ass. Just like it didn't save your mother – sorry,' he added. They exchanged a look across the table that excluded Clare, then Wiseman continued his bantering. 'You're treating this like it's an hereditary disease. You're behaving like a hypochondriac.'

'You say that every time we talk about my pool table. Couldn't you think of something more original to say.'

'Personally, I think we should all move to New York.'

Brown gave a derisory snort. 'And get shot at walking along the street.'

'At least I'd sleep in peace.'

'That quake isn't waiting till you're asleep, Wiseman. It could just as well come while you're sitting on the toilet.'

'Then at least I won't shat my pants.'

'Wiseman,' said Brown, 'if there's one thing I hate about you, it's that you don't take anything seriously. At heart you're just a dilettante.'

Wiseman quoted Flaubert. 'Is it splendid, or stupid, to take life seriously?'

'I suspect it's a bit of both,' said Clare, muttering over her potato salad.

Clare is lying in bed and has pulled back the duvet to watch Tupulo sleeping nude. She is reminded vaguely of Holbein's painting of the dead Christ, except that Tupulo isn't a bit emaciated. It is more the attitude of repose, decides Clare. His stomach is hairy, though less so than his chest, and he's already a little paunchy – comfortable, he calls it; he has solid thighs; he sleeps with his left arm lying along his side while the right is folded across his chest, the hand over his left breast. His hands are not delicate, nor his fingers tapered, as some people expect of a surgeon. Clare holds up her own hands: neither are hers. The fingers are longish and thin, but the palms are square as bricks. She traces a finger over Tupulo's hand, the one lying across his heart.

There are obvious comparisons. She once did the same to Marcus's hand, following the blue vein and down the middle finger – his hands were fine, the wrists delicate and thin, his skin olive and smooth. Except for his fingers he was practically hairless, like an Asian. He had a ring through his right nipple, wore only Levis, clipped his toenails onto a sheet of newspaper, which he'd wrap up and throw away, as if suspecting some voodoo foul play. 'Where did you say you came from again?' she asked him, thinking of Louisiana, New Orleans. But he refused to say, after the first time – had he said too much, that time? Both of them drunk on bourbon and not expecting anything much to come of the encounter. 'You can tell anything to a stranger,' he said that night, 'there's no such things as secrets.' Clare couldn't agree. 'Secrets are what make us human,' she'd said, quite drunk and thinking herself philosophical. But he'd liked that.

She could trace a finger along his arm and feel the tension in his muscles, as if he was always on edge. He was fit, she told herself, he worked out. She liked to watch him work out: he had weights at his house and an exercycle in a room with a bare wooden floor and no furniture. She would sit cross-legged against the wall and watch sweat gathering at the base of his neck and the vein in his forehead swelling like a worm.

One time he stopped lifting his weights – not so much because she was there, but because he had reached his goal – and she went over and kissed him on the mouth. He tasted like sulphur, heat rising off his skin. She had an image of the steaming mud pools at Rotorua. His fingers dug into the back of her neck. *I have discovered true passion.*

Sometimes she would open her eyes while they were kissing, to find him watching her. It felt odd, and she couldn't help but think, *He is looking at me as if I am just anybody, a stranger, a lamp-post.* She pulled back once, as if singed.

'Why don't you close your eyes when we kiss?' she asked.

'Does that worry you?' he said.

'No,' she lied.

'I keep my eyes open because I don't want to miss anything,' he said.

And then, when he pulled her in close, she thought, how paranoid you could get, reading things which weren't there: it was just his focus that gave him that look, the focus of his passion. She liked to hold his arms, up high, and feel the muscles tighten; his face might remain expressionless but his body betrayed emotion. Or at least, that's what she told herself. All she had to do, when they kissed, was to keep her eyes shut.

'A penny for them –'

Clare smiles. The old phrase, used by their mother, now belongs to Louise. 'I was thinking about Bethie's accident. I was just wondering, if it hadn't happened . . .'

'Would we all be sitting here playing Happy Families?' Lou lights a cigarette, then thinks better of it, and stubs it out. There is a brittle energy about her today. She tops up her glass of chardonnay, and squints at the Brightlys' framed photograph of a sunflower hanging behind Clare's head. 'Grow up, Clare. You're as bad as the old man.'

Clare, recalling the empty wine bottle on the kitchen bench, realises that Lou is drunk.

'Crap,' Lou exclaims, 'he is so full of *crap* I feel like throttling him, the old coot.'

'Tupulo will hear you,' Clare says.

'I don't care.' Lou leans forward, hissing drunk and venomous across the arm of the sofa that divides them. 'My therapist says I've got to get it out, all those buried feelings. She says I have to deal with it, face up to it, all that buried shit, then I can move on –'

'You have a therapist?' (A therapist would make good sense, thinks Clare.)

'She agrees with me, that it was all Marty's fault.'

'What?'

Lou leans back in the armchair, sipping wine, her shoulders slumped. 'Boundaries,' she mutters ominously, 'all those broken boundaries – bloody dysfunctional family –'

'Excuse me?'

'Our mother leaving!' She is nearly shouting, and Clare glances at the closed kitchen door, wondering if Tupulo is standing statue-like behind it. 'It was all his fault. My therapist, she said it's got to be out in the open – so I confronted him with it.'

Clare has a cool feeling at the base of her throat. 'Really – when?'

'You wouldn't believe what he told me.' She waggles the glass of wine at Clare. 'He told me that he was impotent, when he came back from Vietnam. Can you fucking believe that?' Lou laughs hysterically, though Clare can't see anything funny in it. 'A changed man, he said, that's why she left. As if it was her fault. What a fucking load of . . .'

'When did you confront him, Lou?'

Lou closes her eyes, as if she has already finished with the conversation. 'Oh,' she waves her hand, 'sometime before you came back.'

'Before his heart attack?'

'Don't know – probably.'

Clare controls her growing fury like shutting a wasp in a jar. 'Was any of this upsetting to Marty?'

'I dunno, how should I know . . .' Lou seems to be going to sleep. Clare reaches over and retrieves the wine glass from between her fingers. 'You and Bethie,' Lou murmurs, 'you always had each other . . .'

Yes, thinks Clare, we did.

Bethie was the oldest. As far as their father was concerned, as far as the town was concerned, she was the Golden Girl. At seventeen she was a champion rower, spending weekends over at Lake Karapiro, competing. At eighteen she was at nursing college in Hamilton and training for the Commonwealth Games.

'Hi, Shrimp,' she called, coming through the kitchen from the garage where she'd parked her hatchback. Clare was sitting at the table doing her homework.

'Hi, Amazon Woman.'

Bethie plonked down on a chair opposite Clare. Behind her head was the half of the sliding door that had the stag – its head lifted eternally to catch a breeze – etched white and ghosty onto the glass; it must once have been considered a feature of the house. 'Whatcha doing?'

'Er, maths.' Lifting a cover, to show her.

'Easy stuff.'

'Well –' Maths was the one subject she had to struggle with to get Bs.

'You're a swot, you know that. How about after tea I do your fingernails? I've got some new polish, Violent Desire.' She giggled. Bethie loved the names; it was the only reason she bought nail polish. She always gave it away to her friends, or to Lou. Clare liked painted nails, but found them too distracting – she might find herself staring into their shiny surfaces in the middle of a class, and the shades reminded her of strange things, her nightmares, for example.

'I had a dream last night,' she told Bethie – she always told Bethie; Lou wasn't interested in anything as unrewarding as dreams.

'Hm?'

'I was digging under a bath, a big old bath with claws for feet, except it was outside, and I'd dug this big hole, when there was an earthworm –' there had been an earthworm dissection in biology, but that was interesting, hardly the stuff of nightmares – 'but it was humungous, the size of a python, only fatter, squishier –' Clare looked at Bethie, a tiny line appearing between her eyebrows. 'What do you think that means, Bethie?'

Bethie, to put herself to sleep at night, often read from a paperback book of dream interpretations that she found in Trash to Treasure. She and Clare would pore over it, in hysterics: 'If you dream about falling in water . . . it means you married the wrong woman!' Now, Bethie put her long tanned legs up on the table, crossed them at the ankle, so Clare could study the cracked strong soles (Bethie walked nearly everywhere barefoot), and folded her arms across her stomach. Clare was starting to grow anxious. Maybe Bethie would say something serious, like, You really dug up your mum in your dream.

'What I reckon is that you need pizza for tea.'

Clare laughed in her surprise. 'Oh, Bethie!'

'Am I right, or am I right?'

Clare had to admit it. 'You're right. About the pizza anyway.'

Bethie was already on her feet. 'I'm always right about pizza. Come on, get your coat. We're walking.'

When Clare thinks back – as she is prone to do – she can't remember exactly how it happened: the picture's a little fudged, too rushed. The sliding door was obviously closed: mostly they left it open, to hide that revolting stag. Clare was sure it had been open when they left the house, the doors fully pushed back. They must have been playing a silly game on their way back with the pizza. Bethie, who was always hungry because of her training, would have been in a hurry to get home. So they were running, and possibly shouting. And surely the lino in the kitchen had something on it; perhaps someone had spilt some oil, or water, and not wiped it up.

For Bethie went through the plate glass door, the proud stag splintering down around her. The pizza box discovered a graceful arc, covering most of the living room, landing humbly, appropriately even, on the coffee table in front of the TV. Bethie sat up, in a pile of broken glass, and looked at her arm. There was a gaping cut in the forearm, as long as the body of a small fish. The skin was white, but inside it was a dark red secret cave; there was no blood, yet. Time held its breath. (Even back then, one part of Clare wanted to step forward and examine the wound.) Bethie looked over her shoulder at Clare, her face splotched with pale leaves.

'Clare,' she whispered, 'I think I'm going to –'

Clare hopped forward, feet crunching over glass, and just managed to catch the heavy weight of her sister as she fainted backwards.

'*Dad* –' she screamed.

PART TWO

The Invader who Believes in Nothing

EIGHT

A MAN IS walking down the corridor wearing an ancient gas mask. His rubber-gloved hands are homicidally outstretched towards her, as if aiming for her neck.

'Not that way, Clare.'

'Alex?'

'Some *idiot* is venting glutaraldehyde into my surgery!'

She watches as he hurries away along the corridor of Outpatients.

Glutaraldehyde? Of course, the stuff used in the Clinical Services Unit, to sterilise equipment. Builders have been renovating, and it looks as if there's been some sort of mistake. Clare had been planning to catch up on paperwork in her own surgery slash office right next to Alex's. She decides to go and get a cup of coffee instead. It might be safer.

As Clare goes back out through the entrance foyer, gleaming with morning sunlight, a bevy of men in overalls rushes past her and disappears into the bowels of Outpatients. My God, she grins, what catastrophe will befall us next?

Bethie came out of hospital with a wired sling and joking that they should have given her a cast so at least she'd have people signing it with silly messages, like 'We're all rooting for you Bethie – signed, the 1st XV.' She and Clare made them up in the car on the way home: 'You're our blood and guts hero – from the team at the fish factory.' 'Call home soon – ET.' 'Open that glass door – Bethie's coming through.' And inexplicably from Lou, 'Don't throw stones in glasshouses.'

But then Bethie liked to quip. The day their mum left, when they found the note on the kitchen bench – *'Sorry, girls, I hope you'll understand. I'll be in touch'* – Bethie had said, 'Is she talking about touchy-feely touch, or touch football?'

Marty, driving, cleared his throat. So far he had been silent, as if it were he and not Bethie who had had the accident.

'Over in Vietnam,' said their father, 'when a guy came back from the hospital, and if there wasn't much going on, we'd have a little party. Some beer; somebody'd get out a guitar. We were celebrating the one that got lucky, I suppose, the one who'd got another chance.' His eyes stayed on the road, his knuckles white on the steering wheel.

Clare fiddled with the hem of her seersucker dress, but Bethie just said, 'Can we have pizza for tea tonight?' She blew the blonde bangs out of her eyes. 'I'll have a beer too, if you like.' Somehow it was very funny.

It was only a short drive, and they were back already, turning into the concrete driveway shaded by willow trees. Their father exhaled. 'Pizza it'll be then.'

Lou said, 'Somebody ought to tell Mum.' And was promptly told to shut up.

Later, when Bethie was told that she wouldn't be able to row again, she shrugged and said, 'I was getting sick of those 5 a.m. starts anyway.'

The sound of breaking glass echoes in Clare's reverie. Looking up, she sees a kid further along in the park; he is holding a baseball bat at his side and staring red-faced at one of the miners' cottages across the road. In one of them there is a window with a jagged hole in it. The kid runs off to a group of people over by the fortress. Clare wonders, If you could step back and change time, what would I alter?

'Pardon?' She looks at her sister blankly. They are sitting side by side at a picnic bench.

Lou repeats her question, dark glasses fixed on a distant object.

'*What* is Tupulo doing?'

Tupulo, wearing his Viking helmet, is doing t'ai chi on the grass by the road. It is a mock version, with many curly bits and extravagant foot shakings. Clare bursts out laughing. Lou crosses her legs, eyes hidden behind Ray-Bans. She takes a swig from the thermos of spirulina that she mixed for herself back at the house, and focuses on a pert leafy tree. She always thought small towns brought out the worst in people. The afternoon is very bright, and cheery with bird song.

'So what else do you do for fun in this place?'

Tupulo has taken off the Viking helmet and gone to annoy some picnickers: he has a game where he pretends to be a DOC officer, warning visitors of huge native earthworms.

'Well,' ventures Clare, 'you've probably seen it.' Lou never did have much sense of humour. 'There's the new picture theatre.' Clare thinks. Whatever do they do? Mostly they seem to be working. 'We sit around the fire, I suppose, listening to music. We're into Brahms at the moment, because he's so stirring. Summer will be good. We can sit on the beach, and go for bush walks.'

'I thought Tupulo was against anything remotely like physical exercise.'

'He has his moments.'

'I'm sure he does.' Lou often sounds like their mother – the version of their mother that Clare mostly remembers. The other version is the bright and breezy style, which Lou can also adopt at will.

'So what happened to that American guy you were seeing?'

'Nothing happened,' says Clare, looking back across the road, the broken window giving the little blue cottage a forlorn look, its roofing iron shimmering in the sun: there is obviously nobody at home over there. 'It just petered out, that's all.'

'Right.' It's irritating, the way Clare doesn't share personal details. Surely this would be a chance for them to trade secrets. Something obviously went wrong with the American guy – why bother coming home otherwise? Lou considers it a failure on her sister's part to have returned to New Zealand, and especially to this horrible little town. She's running away from something. But typical Clare, she won't talk about it. Lou wants a cigarette – smoking doesn't go with her otherwise pristine diet, although the irony doesn't seem to bother her – but she won't smoke in front of Clare. Clare would give Lou that *look* of hers.

'So how's business?' asks Clare.

'Ah,' says Lou, 'that's partly why I'm over here this weekend –'

Clare thought there had to be a good reason. Lou starts to fade if she's away from the city for more than a few hours.

'This Asian crisis,' she sighs, rubbing her forehead. 'I've lost quite a bit of money on the stockmarket –'

'Really?' Clare didn't think people seriously invested money in shares any more.

'Normally it would be okay, I'd just ride it out, and eventually they'd go back up again. Only thing is, there was somebody else's money involved as well, and they're expecting it back fairly soon –'

'So you mean you've been investing in shares for other people?'

'Sort of,' agrees Lou, thinking if you called it gambling you'd have hit it on the nail. 'It's just that I need to pay back this other party, and –' she gives a little cough, simulating embarrassment – 'I was wondering if you couldn't lend me the sum, as a temporary loan –?'

Clare is absently looking for Tupulo: the park is starting to pall, and she'd like to go. 'Sure,' she says. 'How much do you need?'

'Four thousand.' Lou hopes that by saying it quickly it won't sound so much.

But Clare hesitates for only a few moments. 'That shouldn't be a problem.'

'God, thanks,' Lou gushes. 'And I'll be good for it! You'll have it back before you even start missing it.'

'Hey ho,' cries Tupulo, appearing from between clapping trees. He flops down onto the rug at Clare's feet. He is puffing, and has obviously been enjoying himself. 'Hell I'm good,' he boasts, 'I'm a pro. You should have seen those people's faces: they really believed me!' He cranes to look up at Lou. 'I could have been a professional actor, you know.'

'I'm sure you could have been, Tupulo,' says Lou sweetly, 'but what a clever decision you made in becoming a doctor.'

Actually, Lou intends repaying Clare her money just as soon as she wins big at the Sky City Casino. The story about the stockmarket is, after all, partly true. Louise did lose some money on the stockmarket, but the hidden agenda is that she has a mission: to play her numbers on the roulette wheel. It's not often she succumbs to her superstitions, but Lou has been having the most amazing dreams, filled with numbers. She is standing in a lush green paddock and the numbers are floating down to her on little fluffy clouds. She's had several of these dreams already, and each time she wakes up she writes the numbers down. There is no doubt about it: she is destined to play the roulette wheel. She told Bob about the dreams, and he thinks Louise should be playing the numbers on Lotto, but Lou thinks Lotto is purely for suckers.

And the Lucky Night, she has decided, is tonight: Tuesday the 13th.

Dressed in her lucky lycra black minidress – lucky because she always gets laid when she wears it – Lou chooses a quiet $50 table, and starts betting. She has $4000 worth of chips in tidy piles beneath her hands, and her notebook to one side with the numbers written inside. All around her is the racket of fruit machines and rock music; the huge room is like a warehouse with its modern metal architecture and high ceiling stud – there is an air of anonymity that enhances Louise's anticipation. A little grey man seated to her right checks his own notebook, making calculations with a tiny pencil; he looks as if he's been in the casino all day.

I'm not like you buddy, thinks Lou, I've got Lady Luck on my side. I'm in then I'm out.

She places chips on several numbers, and the wheel begins to spin.

June 1983
Terry teases me, that I'm in love with a lunatic. Which one, I say.

Asi the Madman, wearing a huge sky-blue turban, was hanging about outside again. The peacock that he always had with him, a thin leather lead tied around its neck and the other end tied to Asi's ankle, was scratching nonchalantly in the dust for beetles. The bird seemed unperturbed by the shouting. Asi knew three words in English, and, without ever coming inside, hurled them relentlessly at the clinic walls: 'Aspro – bad *head*, bad *head!*' The first time Bethie had seen him she had given him two aspirin. Franco had laughed. Asi had run off, delighted, the peacock loping along behind him, its long tail dragging in the dust.

Today he squatted against the clinic wall in the sun, muttering loudly to himself in Pushtu.

'What's he saying?' Beth asked the Turkoman.

'He's talking about Azra'il, the angel of death.'

Beth came over to the bed, sat down in the chair.

'Azra'il, he lives in the Sixth Heaven. He's said to be so huge he can toss the earth in his hands just like a child can toss a ball. His body is covered with thousands, millions, of eyes. Every man, woman, child, every animal and insect in the world has a certain lifespan that is decided before they are born – and when Azra'il blinks one of his eyes, a human soul dies.'

Asi's mutterings were becoming louder, staccato. 'What's he saying now?'

The Turkoman shook his head on the pillow. 'I think perhaps now he is listing all the curries he has ever eaten, or would like to eat, before Azra'il blinks his eye.'

They looked at each other and smiled at such simplicity.

It's true what they say about climate affecting the emotions, thinks Clare. There is nothing like a foggy evening – still wet from the rain, a fog brooding over water, and a town turning on its lights against a backdrop of black hills – to make one feel melancholy.

Clare is on her way back from a friend's house, brooding, driving slowly along Parawai Road, the thickened river on her right, when she sees a baby up ahead. It's just like the night she found Grunt. She pulls the car over to the side of the road, skidding into gravel, thinking she must have imagined it. Yet it is still there: a toddler, pale and ghost-like in the beam of the headlights, teetering in the middle of the road. It can't be real: it's more like a projection from her own mind, perhaps some deep subliminal urge to reproduce. Surely not. Yet Clare isn't the kind of person to have hallucinations, and especially not of babies.

She gets out of the car, and approaches cautiously. The toddler is clutching a plastic drinking bottle to its chest. It's wearing a grimy jumpsuit: real enough. Clare is aware of the sound of a car's engine in the distance. She picks up the baby, and steps over to the pavement. The child smells of milk and rusk.

'I very nearly ran you over,' she says to the baby, who studies her impassively. Not even crying.

There are babies whom she occasionally sees at the hospital; if they are not crying when they come in, Clare knows they will burst into screams as soon as she touches them. Sheila, on reception, laughs about this – it's become an office joke – and allocates the babies to another doctor: Alex is good with them, even Tupulo, but not Clare. 'They can read your mind,' says Sheila. 'Those babies just know that the first thing you're gonna do is stick a needle in them.' 'Then why don't they do the same with the others?' asks Clare, peeved. 'You've got the touch,' laughs Tupulo, 'the anti-baby touch.'

Tupulo often talks about babies, how he can see a future with babies in it. He would like to be able to give birth and nurture babies himself – a thought Clare finds a little disturbing. Clare saw him once with a baby – the mother was sitting in the examining room, and he'd come out to get something, vaccine perhaps. He'd swung the baby up and down in the air until it had chuckled and gurgled in delight. Clare wouldn't ever risk doing that to somebody else's baby. What if you dropped it?

But this baby. It just looks at her. Clare finds herself suddenly grateful, blessed even. It's certainly an unusual situation. 'Well,' she says, giving it a little jiggle, 'look at you – going for a walk, eh.' They could be old mates. She looks round for the mother, any mother, but there is nobody on the street, although the houses all have lights on. People will be inside making their dinners, watching the news, having showers. Obviously nobody has missed a small toddler.

'Which house do you live in?'

Knowing practically nothing about babies, she thinks the toddler will be able to point out his house – the jumpsuit has blue rabbits on it, so it's fair to assume the male gender – but he just looks at her. He seems so trusting she could be his auntie, his neighbour. A pale role. Clare looks around at the equally impassive house fronts, and sighs. She imagines the baby tucked up warm and snug back at her place, in a basket next to Grunt by the fire – yes, Grunt has his own basket now, and new red collar. It would be so easy, wouldn't it. To take this baby. To just – walk away. She would look after him so well: wash his jumpsuits (this one is so filthy), feed him mashed pumpkin and scoop spoonfuls of avocado into his mouth, wash his face with soft flannels, make sure he never got out onto the road . . .

Clare walks quickly up the nearest path. The house is snot-green, mouldy, an architectural disaster of concrete block and fibrolite board. She knocks on the door, though it is already ajar. From within comes the sounds of a television gameshow, the banging of pots, and scales played poorly on a violin. The small hallway is a litter of discarded muddy sportsclothes and shoes. Clare knocks more loudly, and finally footsteps approach. A solidly built woman appears. She is wearing a plastic barbecue apron and pink slippers.

'Is this your baby?'

The woman takes him from Clare with barely a glance, and bawls over her shoulder, 'Who left that door open again?' She looks back at Clare. 'Thanks –' And shuts the door.

Clare walks back down the path and stands by her car. The headlights are still on, cutting a swathe through the darkness. Further along the street a lamp casts a muddy-orange pool of light across the road. Babies aren't like stray dogs, she thinks, of course not. She's not a baby kind of person anyway. Babies are for other people.

Still, the ability to do the occasional good deed is what separates us from the beast, she thinks, driving back to the Brightly house.

The Pinnacles is the highest point in the valley. Because it was summer and because Bethie's friends had all gone away for weeks and weeks and there was nothing at all to do, Bethie decided she would climb up to the Pinnacles and spend the night in the hut. Clare was enthusiastic: she had never been up there, but could see the rocky outcrop from her bedroom window. Louise, who was fourteen, turned away, disinterested; she had recently discovered cosmetics, and spent hours in her room experimenting with the subtleties of eye shadow and blusher. If their mother had stayed, Lou would have been her favourite.

The summer had been dry: the manuka were pale with dust from the gravel roads, and a fire warning was in place. 'No Harolds this time,' joked Clare, sitting in the passenger seat, pale in her terrycloth shorts.

'We're grown-up now,' said Bethie.

On the track and once they'd got up the steep bits, hauling themselves up by tree roots, Bethie strode ahead, her legs still strong from rowing and thighs solid. Clare followed behind, her eyes on Bethie's pack. She had had no idea it would be so tough. 'Bethie,' she called, 'wait on – I've got to rest.'

Her sister came back with tight lips, a line between her eyebrows, while Clare, red-faced, heaved off the pack and slumped to the ground. She found her water bottle, and a chocolate bar. Bethie remained standing, glaring down at her.

'I want to keep going, Clare,' she said, her words spitting out small and stony. 'You can't just stop.'

'But I'm stuffed,' she gasped. Clare drank deeply from her bottle, and poured some water over her face. It was only eleven o'clock. 'This is a mountain, for Christsake, it's not a training session on the river.' Wrong thing to say, but too late.

A tear of sweat rolled down the side of Beth's face. 'I *know* that.'

Clare glanced up. Bethie's lips were pale, but she shook the hair out of her eyes impatiently.

'Come on, I want to keep going. You can rest in another hour's time.'

'But I want to rest now.'

'Don't be such a baby. It'll be good for you: toughen you up.'

Clare struggled her pack back onto her shoulders, afraid that Bethie would leave her behind, though their father had repeatedly warned them about staying together. She trudged on, the pulse thumping in her ears and bright flashes of light zapping across her eyes. Clare wanted to cry and whine. She was a baby? All right then, she *was*. But if she'd known it was going to be like this, she would never have come. No wonder Bethie's friends all went away in the holidays, if this was what she did with them. They had all taken off to escape her. This was no fun, *no fun at all*.

Bethie stopped. 'What did you say?'

The track was flat again, rocky underfoot. Already they were fairly high; occasional gaps in the bush afforded glimpses of the canopy below. The trees too were changing, becoming shorter and stunted in their growth.

Clare pressed her chin against her breastbone and scuffed at a stone. 'I didn't say anything.'

Bethie stared at her younger sister, as if ready to hit her, but then she turned side-on, squinting at the scrub. They were both panting, the sun beating down on their heads.

'I'm losing my fitness,' she muttered.

The bush ticked around them, and a solitary bird sang in the endless blue sky.

'You're right,' said Bethie finally, and swung her pack to the ground. 'Gotta look after the weaker member of the group –' She could have been recalling a tramper's instruction booklet. She sat and leaned against the pack, her knees tucked up, her left hand resting on the ground. The forearm was still bandaged, with a gauze outer. The fingers of that hand were yellow and curled, as if they belonged to a much older person; Bethie had started physio to help her regain their use.

Clare sat down a little way off, shy now. There were times when Bethie became a stranger. 'How's your arm feeling?' she asked tentatively.

Bethie looked at her as if she'd forgotten Clare was there, then glanced down at her arm. 'It's okay,' she shrugged. She took Clare's water bottle and drank down a mouthful, her adam's apple moving in a pale throat. 'Hey, that was some smash-up, eh – going through the door. Did I make the six o'clock news?' The old Bethie was back.

'No, but they had you on the ads. They called you the Ramming Machine and said you could break any kind of plate-glass door – even bullet-proof glass.'

'Yeah, I could hire myself out, eh. Beth Purefoy, professional glass breaker.'

'Glass breaker *extraordinaire*.'

'One crash, and your door will be smashed.'

'Parties are extra.'

'But all occasions catered for.'

'Bring your own glass.'

'And we'll have a smashing good party.'

'Showing at a cinema near you.'

Bethie picked up a twig and snapped it in half against the ground. 'I'm gonna take up cycling. I can fit it in with college.'

'Really? That's great.'

This was the first time since the accident that Bethie had talked about what she was going to do next. Their father had been assiduously avoiding the subject, waiting for Bethie to come up with the answer in her own sweet time – he didn't need to push her, because she pushed herself enough; and the girls had followed his cue. Their father knew Bethie the best of all; knew her better than he'd known their mother, he sometimes said. ('You think you know somebody,' he said once, and they knew who he was talking about: Marty eating his poached egg, methodically polishing the plate with a piece of white buttered bread, then pushing it away with a morose look as if you could lay the blame on a yolk-smeared plate.)

'I'll have to lose a little weight,' said Bethie, flexing a leg, 'but that shouldn't be too hard. No more pizzas, eh –' She got up, throwing a wink to Clare. 'Come on, sis, our muscles'll seize up if we sit here too long.'

There were no trampers in the Pinnacles hut, but it smelt of urine and stale bread, so Bethie and Clare decided to sleep outside on the kauri dam. They watched the sun set, and ate dried fruit, the rush of water over rocks sounding below their feet and the bush darkening around them. It was like being on a bridge, sitting on the wide cool planks.

Clare accidentally pushed a book over the edge, and watched it plummet down into water, bouncing off rocks. 'Oh no.'

'You brought a *book* with you?'

'My French teacher gave it to me.' It was a copy of Camus's *L'Étranger*. Her teacher seemed to be labouring under the idea that Clare was capable of understanding it. But so far she had only read the first sentence: '*Aujourd'hui, maman est morte*.' The loss of the book didn't seem such a dreadful thing after all; in fact she felt quite cheerful about it.

'What if I roll off in the night?' asked Clare recklessly, peering over the side.

Bethie was getting into her sleeping bag, hair falling over her face. 'Then the water will carry you down the mountain and it'll save you having to walk out tomorrow. Goodnight.'

'Bethie –' Clare felt very small inside her bag, even though she was sixteen, lean and tall.

'What?'

'I'm sorry I was so slow.'

'You weren't slow.' You could barely hear anything but falling water. 'I'm sorry I called you a baby.' There was a water-riddled pause. 'You're not a baby, you're a brat.'

Clare kicked out, and there came an 'ow' from Bethie's bag, and a giggle. Clare lay back and looked at stars. We're very high here, she thought, we are nearly at the highest point in the valley. Funny that she still felt just as slight as when she was in the town. I am a wraith, she thought, or perhaps just some kind of shade. Nightshade, lampshade, desert shade, in the shade. Would it be enough simply to long for sunlight? Darkness came, and from the water below, a damp coldness. Clare lay shivering in her insulated bag as if the cold had permanently entered her marrow.

NINE

At the age of thirty-six, Clare thinks that she ought to have outgrown her irrational fears. However, she is driving to work one morning through the rain when she feels a sudden sharp pricking sensation on her back and immediately thinks of katipo spiders. The shirt she's wearing was hanging in the laundry this morning – and the laundry window was open. It is possible that a katipo crept in through the window, scuttled over the washing machine and somehow threw itself onto her shirt with the specific intention of biting her.

Oh God, she groans. Now that she's thought of it, she has to look and check or she might be dead before she gets to work.

She pulls the car over onto gravel, gets out and whips off her shirt. At least she's wearing that quite presentable brown lace bra. She peers into the shirt, shakes it out, unbuttons all the buttons, cranes over her shoulder to see her back. A horn tooting sends her hurriedly back into the car, where she puts the shirt on again. She sits clutching the steering wheel for a few moments. She is going mad, she can feel it. There is a kink in her brain that's been waiting to happen; a tiny black hole, like a dormant virus, will start stretching open and swallow her whole. Rain drums reassuringly on the windscreen. *Katipos, huh.* Wait till she tells Tupulo. In fact, she will ring Tupulo before she starts her rounds, and tell him – it is his day off, he will still be having his breakfast and reading the paper.

Clare drives on, hoping vaguely that none of her patients saw her odd behaviour. Yet, no matter how much she tries to suppress it, she can't help wondering: would you develop natural immunity if a katipo bit you only the once? Would it be like getting a measles shot? And how long would you have before you'd need the vaccine?

When Clare gets to the hospital she asks Marion about antivenom for katipos.

'We've got some in the fridge, do you need it?'

'Ah no, that's all right,' she says, and hurries off.

Tupulo, on the phone, laughs and laughs. 'Though personally,' he says, 'you've got it all wrong. What you really need to be afraid of, Clare – apart from your sister, that is – is runaway trucks –'

Clare leans back in the chair, safe inside her office while the rain drums outside, and indulges in a little swivelling. 'Runaway trucks?'

'That's right.' Tupulo drops his voice, even though Clare knows he is alone in the house. 'At any moment a runaway truck could come crashing into our lounge. Sometimes –' Clare has to strain to hear him, and stops swivelling – 'sometimes I say a prayer before I go to sleep – Dear Godot, please don't let a runaway truck crash into the house tonight while I'm asleep, I'll be good, I promise – but *bang*, there it is, a mutherfucker of a truck, in our lounge, like it's drawn up a chair to watch some TV –'

'Tupulo?' There are times when she can't tell if he's being serious or not.

'Yes?'

'The likelihood of that happening is probably a million to one.'

There is a breathing pause at the other end of the phone. Clare imagines him looking at his foot, perhaps studying a speck on the wall.

'You *see*,' he says, 'it happens.'

There was a day when she and Marcus were walking down to her deli for lunch and she was narrating the story of Marta, because it was supposed to be amusing to share anecdotes with lovers. Clare, however, was teetering on the edge of telling him not only Marta's story but also her own patch of childhood silence. She hadn't told anybody before, though she supposed that it was common knowledge back home. The child who wouldn't talk. Suddenly Marcus stopped in front of a shoe store. The shoes behind the glass were poised as if ready for a ball.

'That woman,' he concluded, 'is probably just subnormal.'

Clare felt a contraction in her chest. Marcus's profile was sharp, flint-like. She could have been having a heart attack, but he hadn't noticed a thing. The display of shoes seemed contrived now, as she stood with Marcus, their palms growing sweaty together.

'It's corny, I know, but I have this fantasy,' he said, studying his shoes, 'of working as a shoe salesman.' Clare, in her relief that she had not confided in him, found the idea very funny.

'We could play that role,' she said finally.

They entered the store and walked around slowly, studying the shoes. There was a particular pair that Marcus liked: red, patent-leather, knee-length boots, with black laces. It took him a long time to lace Clare into them, he in the supplicant's position at her feet, Christ tending the feet of the Apostles, his dark head bowed over the task. Let this moment be captured, thought Clare, like a Dutch still life, or a Cartier-Bresson photograph. While the real shoe salesman was busy elsewhere, Marcus lifted her skirt and edged his hands higher up her bare leg, fondling her thigh. Clare blushed for their boldness.

'Go on,' said Marcus, slapping her right calf, 'try them out.'

Clare walked around the shop: awkwardly, teetering-tottering; she wasn't used to wearing such high heels, and the leather squeaked the way a leather sofa does when you sit on it. She felt self-conscious, yet possessed as well; it was like putting on another personality. Was that all it took, a change in footwear?

'How d'they feel, honey?' Marcus was solicitous, as if they were a married couple choosing a pair of boaters.

'I feel so sleazy,' she grinned. 'Like a slut.'

'Slut is good.' He was gesturing for the salesman's attention. 'We'll take them.'

While Marcus was at the counter buying the boots, a movement in another part of the room caught her eye. A snake was slithering across the floor of the shoe store. It was about a foot long, speckled brown, like the egg of a dotterel. She opened her mouth to say something, but no sound came out. Clare had never seen a real snake before, not even in a zoo. Transfixed, she watched as it disappeared beneath a set of wall shelves. Ought she to tell somebody? The shoe salesman would want to know. But her throat seemed to have taken on a will of its own, and it refused to say anything.

Back outside on the pavement, even though it was summer, a fog had begun to lower over the city buildings. Clare felt disoriented by the sight of the snake; the day seemed somehow changed. She ought to tell Marcus, but he probably wouldn't believe her.

A snake in a shoe store? It wasn't possible. It must have been her imagination.

Clare is out the back of the house burning a heap of flax leaves just for the hell of it. The leaves are dry and they burn very well. She pulls them off the bushes that line the side of the property, using a lot of force, for they are hard to pull out; and when they refuse to budge she gets to work with the clippers. It is a dismal day, but she is sweating. Clare heaves off her old blue sweater and works in her singlet. Her gumboots are muddy from tramping back and forth between the flax bushes and the fire, and this has already created a pathway in the grass, practically a highway, which she hopes will grow back all right; later there will also be a big round burnt patch on the gravel where the fire has been. She hopes that the mowing boy doesn't turn up today – he could be acting as the Brightlys' spy. He's supposed to take care of the garden too, but the beds are starting to acquire a bedraggled look; Clare would do it herself except she can't tell the difference between weeds and flowers.

She stands watching the flames, and feeds the fire more flax leaves, which she crunches in half before throwing in. Smoke is billowing steadily into the sky, and a breeze at ground level shifts the flames from one side to another. Clare is forced to hop about so that she doesn't get in the way of the flames, or get smoke in her face. Finally she ties a handkerchief round her nose, looking like a desperado.

That time she and Bethie were feeding the fire and whooping, playing at Red Indians, Bethie had stripped off to her white training bra and had smeared clay across her chest and cheeks. Clare was too shy to do that, but was longing to. They could do things like this now: when their mother had been around, they couldn't have fires, because the smoke got in the house.

Louise crept out from somewhere. The first they knew was a small disparaging voice: 'You two are so disgusting, getting dirty all the time.' Playing at mother, when they all knew that that was Bethie's job. Lou was standing there in a white pinafore dress with her hair plaited down her back, looking very clean and holding a Barbie to her skinny chest.

'Hey Lou, what's with the Barbie?'

Louise looked down at the doll in horror: she must have run out without realising she was holding it. The Barbies were kept in the attic room, and Lou liked to creep upstairs and play muttered games with the thin dolls and their car and the pink deckchairs. There was a plywood dolls' house that their mother had assembled from a kitset; she'd painted the windowsills green, the sloping roof red. It was the perfect little house, open on one side for playing, except if you placed this side against the wall there was an air of privacy, of a secret life going on within. Lou rearranged the Barbies inside the house: here they are having a party, here they are in bed asleep. There was a Ken doll who lived permanently downstairs, or took the Barbies out dancing – his role being much more limited. But it was a matter of embarrassment to her: she was thirteen, yet couldn't seem to wean herself from their pristine perfection. She was like a drug addict who wants to give it up but doesn't know how.

Bethie, amused, persisted. 'How old are you again? Let me see . . . thirteen. Hey, you'll be able to graduate to Cabbage Patch dolls soon.' She laughed.

Louise's ears had turned red. She struck a pose. 'For *your* information,' she said scathingly, 'I came down here to get *rid* of it.' And she tossed it defiantly into the fire.

Clare and Beth were stunned. The doll landed in the middle of the flames, and its bleached plastic hair immediately caught fire, though its small pale face remained serene. It was like the end of childhood. Beth leapt forward. She grabbed the Barbie out of the fire and threw it onto the grass. Its hair was still burning, but Bethie stomped on it, puffing with dismay. She picked up the doll, and smeared clean its face with her finger, then handed it back to Lou.

'You should look after your Barbies,' Beth said brusquely. 'They'll be worth something one day.' Lou, white-faced, ran away.

When Lou had gone she held out her hand. There was a flaming red burn mark. 'Barbie's baptism by fire,' she said wryly, 'and mine.' As ever, Clare looked at Bethie and saw a hero.

You only get one soulmate, Clare mutters out loud, chucking flax leaves willy-nilly. Have I had mine? *If only I could talk to Bethie now.* Then she notices Tupulo framed in the upstairs window. A whorl of smoke lifts into her face, and when she waves it away, with eyes blinking and stinging, like a vanishing trick he has gone. Smoke stains the sky. The flax bushes edging the lawn wave their pointy fingers and shiver with light.

Bethie's bandage had been off for some time, and she sported her scar like a trophy. She'd hold up her arm, acting the show-off, especially to boys and to Lou; and to solicitous people who didn't know about the accident she would make up stories that became more and more ludicrous as the whim took her. When she picked up Clare from her summer job at the bakery, Beth told Murray the red-haired baker that she'd been gored by a bull. Clare, blushing and smiling, crept out with a backward wave. 'See you tomorrow,' Murray called anxiously.

That summer everybody except themselves seemed to be in a state of slow motion. It could have been the heat. But Clare, cycling round the country roads with Bethie, felt as if at last she was out in front. She was no longer the one who lagged behind, clumping about awkwardly, not knowing what was going on, always in the wrong place. She, like Bethie, could fly.

Cycling south, wire fences and grassy ditches flashing past, sun shining down from a hot blue sky, the bramble hedges trimmed to starchy moustaches, and the air redolent with hay and cow manure and flowering privet. When Clare had had enough she would turn for home, while Bethie became a receding dot. Then Clare would feel the town pulling her back – the prodigal daughter, the one who had nearly, but not quite, escaped. Though it was a relief as well, to slip back: who knows where those empty miles might have led her. The town was her terra firma, her defining universe, after all. She went back to her microscope and her homework projects, while Bethie would be gone till nightfall.

There was a midsummer's dance at the school hall for the seniors and past pupils that Bethie decided she wanted to go to. 'But you don't dance,' complained Lou, who desperately wanted to go but at fourteen was too young.

'Who cares,' shrugged Beth.

Clare wore a pale blue silk dress like a petticoat with shoestring straps. Lou, lifting the dress out of the carrybag, used one of their mother's old phrases. 'It's daring . . . but, you'll turn heads.' (Clare had glanced up from her school books. 'It'll do fine,' she said.)

Bethie had dressed in their father's black suit and slicked back her short hair with gel. When she walked into the dance, people stared. A boy immediately asked her to dance, but she refused, and joined a group of her old schoolfriends by the bar instead. Clare, wandering through the crowd, was dimly aware of Bethie's laughter and how loud and jolly the group sounded; they would be cracking jokes, swapping gossip. Clare spotted various friends of her own, but they were busy dancing. The band was playing disco covers, and a glitter ball hung from the ceiling, revolving slowly. Everybody seemed a little drunk, crazed even.

Clare, creeping about trying to look jolly, was thinking she should go back home – Lou and their father were watching a movie – when she bumped into the O'Brien boy. He was standing at the edge of the dancers, swaying, his eyes fixed on the ceiling. Clare stood heavily on his foot, and he nearly toppled over. She grabbed his elbow.

Clare had secretly adored the O'Brien boy from a distance for months. He was, in her opinion, the perfect boy. 'Hello,' she shouted.

He looked at her frowning, in a pouting sort of way, a lock of brown hair falling across his forehead. The O'Brien family, their mother used to say, is Old Money.

'Hello – Gerald.' For that was his name. He and Clare were in the same year at school, though different classes. He continued to frown, as if he were in a foreign country. He obviously didn't recognise her. But then, she was wearing make-up, a little eye shadow. 'Clare,' she said firmly, willing herself not to baulk, 'Clare Purefoy.' It could have been the name of a soap. 'D'you want to dance?'

Finally he responded: there was a faint smile, a shrug. He pointed to a girl already dancing, a girl with blue hair and a black mini-dress. 'That's my girlfriend,' he shouted. 'If I dance with another girl, she'll kill me.' He gave Clare one last glance. 'Sorry.'

She went away again, a lanky girl in a revealing powder-blue dress.

The glitter ball wheeled above their heads as Clare wandered about. People seemed to be laughing now, and staring at her; at a distance she was aware of Bethie standing with her friends. Nothing had changed, even after all that cycling. Wasn't this just what it had always been? Her, and them, with Bethie somewhere in the distance cracking jokes. Then her friend Diane turned up. 'Oh my *God*,' she squealed, 'what are you *wearing!*'

Clare glanced down, as if her dress had changed into a frogsuit, a nightie, a black bra and knickers . . . no, it was still the same improbably blue dress. Had she forgotten to wear something important, like underwear?

'What's wrong with it?'

'But it's –' Diane twittered behind her hand.

A brick-shaped girl, a sixth former with short thick hair, approached, holding a glass of fizzy soda. She had eyes that took everything in and spat it out again in a way you hadn't considered before: she was the spokesperson for the herd, the Voice of the Majority. Her eyes moved swiftly over Clare, over and around, up and down, back and forth, and you knew there was a summation about to be pronounced. Clare chewed her lip, getting lipstick on her teeth.

'Jeez Purefoy, you can see your tits.' The prefect moved on.

Diane giggled suddenly. 'Where did you get that dress?' she asked, but even Clare realised it was a rhetorical question.

There were times when she suspected herself to be autistic. She had even been reading up on autism, after she and Lou met Mrs Habgood on the street. Clare and Lou were standing outside the bakery, holding hands. 'You poor girls,' Mrs Habgood muttered: avoiding the girls was out of the question. 'How are you getting along these days?'

It was Clare's role to speak, although she was reluctant; there were many times when she would have preferred to return to her earlier haven of muteness. 'We're getting along fine, thank you.' And because the woman's eyes were so persistent, she felt she had to add something: 'Like a house that's been set alight, thank you.'

'*Clare*,' Mrs Habgood whinnied, trying to make light of an embarrassing situation, 'you're such a dark horse.' The very words her mother had used once about a boy in the town: *everybody thought he was such a dark horse, wouldn't speak, unco-operative; then one day they took him to the doctor's and discovered he was autistic.* As if it were a crime uncovered. Clare regretted her explicit memory, all those interwoven threads in her head that ultimately confused. Through her reading, at least, she had discovered that she was possibly quite normal.

Not that it helped at the dance. For there she was, dream-like, in a room crammed with people, most of whom she knew, in one form or another; and she was wearing a see-through dress. It was a kind of anxiety dream, from which you usually awoke in relief, except that this was no dream. Diane was still giggling inanely, her eyes bulging, while people milled all around them and the glitter ball sprinkled its sharp distorting lights over faces and dresses alike.

'That dress,' giggled Diane, 'oh, Clare.'

Clare wished herself back in the science lab, snug behind a bunsen burner. It didn't help that across the room she saw Gerald O'Brien dancing with several other girls. The blue-haired girl didn't seem to be bothered at all.

Thankfully, Diane's attention was drawn away by the announcement of a girls' request dance. 'Look at him,' she hissed, 'that O'Brien boy, he thinks he's so shithot. I think I'll ask him for a dance.'

Clare walked casually towards the door, arms swinging and chin in the air, as if she was just going to the toilets. Once through the outer doors, she made a break for it, lifting her skirt and sprinting along the pavement for home, knees bouncing, the air hard and fresh against her face. Thank God for quiet backstreets and the proximity of home.

It was only later that she remembered a couple in the shadows around the side of the hall – it was only a glimpse, a fleeting glance, and she could've been wrong – of a girl in a short black dress and somebody in a dark suit. Dark Suit had a hand on the girl's neck, and they were kissing. Was that so unusual? Clare didn't think so, except that her memory kept bringing it back to her like a photograph: *This is what you saw, make of it what you will, this is one more image to confuse and mislead you.* And in only two years' time people would be saying to her, The world's your oyster.

TEN

THE TURKOMAN was back on his feet, hobbling about with care – there was obviously still pain, though he would never admit to it – and Beth knew that any day now he would be well enough to leave.

'I've got something I'd like to show you,' she said that morning. He followed her across the gravel compound to the tree. Its leafy branches waved over their heads and cast dappled light across their upturned faces. Fleshy orange blossoms were dotted among the shiny leaves. She often sat out there, in the shade of the tree.

'Rather ancient tree,' he said, betraying a faint British accent.

'Yes,' said Bethie, 'but what is it?'

'It is the pomegranate.' He gave a slow smile. 'My wife's family they grew some of these trees, along with apricots, plum and walnut. We had a very large orchard – gone now, of course.' He looked down at her with a coy twist of his head; a faint breeze fingered the tassled black and white scarf across his shoulders. His look was indefinable. At such moments Beth thought she would never get to know these people. 'My wife, using the fruits from this tree, can make a very tasty jelly.' He laughed. 'Next time I come to Kabul, if there is fruit, I will bring her recipe.'

'I wish I could go with you,' said Beth. She'd been imagining this moment – blurting out her deepest desire, and he impulsively siding with it. *Yes*, he would say, *why not?* 'If you must go, I'd like to go with you.'

He studied her darkly for several moments. Her reflection in his eyes was very small and insubstantial. 'You and I –' he began, his voice leaden with hesitation.

'Don't worry,' she said quickly, 'it was just one of those crazy ideas.' Madcap Beth Purefoy, what a card.

'Not that crazy.' The Turkoman smiled sadly, a world lost between them. He touched his fingers lightly, regretfully, to her hot cheek. 'A good idea, only, not possible.'

'Not in this life, at any rate,' said Beth.

Clare is jogging in the early evening – up the hill beyond her house, the cemetery in the distance spread out like a tablecloth among the foothills – when she passes a man on a mountain bike: lycra bike pants, expensive helmet. Bethie could pass bikes when she was running; she had an extra gear she could switch into, which is how Clare thinks athletes are different from ordinary people, the way they can push up into faster gears.

Clare keeps running, unaware that the man is now struggling to pass her in turn: it is a bit of a hill, after all, and Clare runs up it several times a week. He manages to pass Clare, his thigh muscles pumping, but then, without being aware of him, she puts on another spurt and passes him again.

Then she notices him over her shoulder, and gives a small smile of recognition: a fellow fitness nut. But the man slams off his bike in the middle of the road. 'You fucken bitch,' he shouts.

Clare is so surprised that she trawls to a stop, her mouth falling open.

The man storms past her, pushing his bike and cursing the whole time at the asphalt.

Clare looks at her feet. Puffing hard, she squeezes a hand into her side. *Did I miss something? Jesus.* Feeling suddenly weak, sugars racing through her leg muscles, she sits down on the kerb, all shaking knees, and has an 'American' thought: *Thank God he didn't have a gun.*

She and Marcus might have run together; they might have run in the Golden Gate Park, despite the muggers – and no matter what they said about cleaning up the city, there were still muggers – but there never seemed to be enough time. So they worked out instead, in his apartment, in the large room with its two high windows which flooded the space with light. Clare, on the exercycle, was near the windows and facing Marcus who was benchpressing weights. The only sound, apart from the outside street noise, was the whirr of the bike and the metallic crunch of the weights going up and down.

Marcus was completely focused: his biceps extended and contracted; she could see the tension in his belly and leg muscles; his dark hair was wet and lines of sweat were running down his temple. It was obviously hard work, but he kept doing it. There was a dogged quality about him, about his will to succeed, and that he would reach his goal no matter how much effort it took. Clare admired that, as she considers herself lazy. She had only done two kilometres on the exercycle, for example, but she was going to stop – her thighs were starting to hurt.

She was standing at the window, looking down into the street, when Marcus's voice sounded suddenly in the quiet room and she realised that he had stopped with his weights. 'That fellow, Wiseman –' He was looking up at her intently. 'What's his beef?'

Clare turned, frowning. 'How d'you mean?'

'Wiseman, you work with him. He keeps looking at me, like I'm shit. What's up with him?'

'I hadn't noticed. Maybe he fancies you.'

Marcus blinked deeply, then forced out a smile. He flexed his fingers on the bar above his head. 'Yeah, maybe that's it.'

When she turned back to the window he stared for a moment at her back, as if reading something there.

The riddle is *still* how to make yourself impregnable, as tall as a stone tower and just as tough. Even as a kid Clare realised she didn't want to be in a position of vulnerability again. *It doesn't suit me*, she joked to herself (a barren little joke that fell onto sandy ground). One way, she thought back then, was to be like somebody else.

As the summer progressed, Clare and Bethie seemed to grow

apart, rather than closer. When she wasn't working at her summer job, Beth was cycling all the time – training, competing – just like the rowing, except on a bike. 'Attagirl,' said Dad. She was dieting too, to become lighter, to go faster. In fact Bethie seemed to miss most of their mealtimes these days. All the lost meals, pondered Clare, helping their father with the cooking.

Pondering, she had realised, wasn't the best attitude to adopt. Except that she hadn't adopted it: it had adopted her. Bugger. She wanted rather to be lively, a go-getter, a girl who would leap swiftly into any sort of interesting situation, a girl who could mix it with the best of them, who could climb mountains and jump into rushing gushing streams, a girl who could party all night and flop down onto the carpet doing dead ant impersonations. A card, a character, a hoot, a girl who . . . *bugger*.

Which idea about yourself was the real one? she wondered. The realisation had already visited her that you could try on different personalities, like clothes; that it could be simply a matter of switching over.

So Clare started hanging round with Shelley and Maxie, or S&M, as they liked to call themselves. 'You're so lucky,' they said in their high-pitched voices, 'you can go out whenever you like. Your Dad trusts you, eh.' It wasn't something S&M took for granted. 'You wanna go to a party?' one of them asked. On her way out of the house Clare barely glanced at two of Lou's Barbies that had been tied to the legs of a chair, gagged, for the last week. Would Ken *ever* rescue them?

They gate-crashed a party in a dark sidestreet late that night. There were people lying around on the front lawn: Clare tripped over a body but it only groaned. Inside there was heavy metal playing, and more bodies in corners; people were dancing, and some long-haired guys were sitting along the back wall on kitchen chairs, watching. The kitchen bench was littered with empty bottles. Still they managed to find some cask wine. S&M disappeared, and Clare, left on her own among strangers, found herself talking to somebody called Pete who had bumfluff on his chin and jeans hanging off his hips.

'I feel sick,' said Pete, 'can you just help me out to my car?'

THE INVADER WHO BELIEVES IN NOTHING

It seemed a long way down the concrete driveway, with Pete's arm wrapped firmly round her waist and the heavy beat of the music pushing at their backs. This is living, thought Clare, this is what non-pondering people do . . . A plastic gnome was head-first in a bed of turned earth, and she looked at it with fond amusement, Pete heavy against her shoulder. This is just the beginning, thought Clare, of my exciting new life, the 'new me'.

They tumbled into the back seat of a vehicle parked over the kerb, and it was only a moment before he was fumbling inside her top, trying to get past the wired cups of her bra. Then he got his finger up inside her and was pushing roughly, at the same time tugging at his jeans. 'Come on baby,' he hissed, 'give me a hand here –'

Clare didn't know what to do. Should she carry on? She hardly knew this man, and she could tell his jeans weren't exactly clean. She had a feeling of having lost something, and didn't know how to get it back again. She wanted to open her mouth and spit something out – something mean and callous, like they might say on TV. When she needed them most, words defeated her.

'I want to get out,' she gasped.

'You – cockteaser.'

He was pushing her down on the seat now, and she was trying to get back up, her thin legs foundering – it wasn't what she would call a struggle, but she realised that it might look like that from outside. Which was when the knock at the window came (none too soon): it was S&M, their faces pale against the glass, tapping on the window and opening the door, their squeaky voices never so desirable.

'We have to go now, Clare, come on, our ride's here.'

And walking down the street, Clare in between them and shaking, with S&M rabbiting on: 'We *thought* you were in trouble – we just made that up about a ride – that guy, he was just too much!' She felt nothing, just numb.

Clare scuffed along mainstreet, then turned left at Fenton. If that was what other people called living, then they could keep it.

But there were decisions to be made. Clare had come to the end of her sixth form year. People kept asking awkward questions. What are you going to do? What do you want to be? As if she wasn't being something in her own right already. Hazel was going teaching, Diane was going nursing. How did they know? How could they be so sure? Clare realised that, eventually, she would have to come up with something sensible as well.

There had been the incident at the bakery.

It was like time stood still while you served behind the glass counter with the other girl, and half the town's population seemed to come in for their pies, their tank loaves, their Sally Lunns. A woman had a heart attack on the floor one afternoon – the cynical might say it was a fitting place to have it, the root of the evil so to speak – and Murray had leapt over to the phone in one giant step and rung for an ambulance. Then he'd rushed back and tried loosening the woman's clothing – she was lying on the lino, gasping and turning purple – but he was so nervous that his hands were shaking.

Clare, pressed against the wall, feeling very much the child with so many older people milling about not knowing what to do and bleating at each other, stepped out from behind the counter and bent down to the woman. She calmly undid the scarf around her neck, then proceeded to unbutton her coat. 'Just relax,' she whispered, 'the ambulance is on its way.' She took hold of a papery hand and gave it an awkward rub – reminded of Bethie, unfortunately, but this was so much easier because there was no blood, no gaping revelations, all was contained. 'You'll be fine –'

When it was all over Murray had sat her on the stool out the back and given her a cup of tea. 'You're bloody brilliant,' he muttered, 'I couldn't have done that.' Trixie squinted jealously from the counter. 'Jeez, I really thought that old lady was going to cark it in my shop! In my very shop –' He couldn't get over it, and had to ring his wife next to tell her, then have a tipple of whisky when he thought the girls weren't looking. Later it became a bit of a joke: 'Life and death among the Sally Lunns, eh?'

When she'd tried to tell the story to Bethie who was propped up on the couch, remote in hand, she quipped, 'What happened? Didn't she like the sliced bread? Sounds like blackmail to me.' There were times when Clare didn't understand Bethie's humour.

'If I'd been a doctor I would've known what to do,' said Clare. 'I could do something about all of these things that seem to be flying out of control.'

'If you were a doctor, Clare,' said Bethie, 'I'd be seriously worried about you!'

'So,' she thought, crossing yet another yawning afternoon-empty street, listening to the sound her shoes made on the asphalt pavement and ignoring the hoon boys who were passing in a souped-up car and tooting, 'so, that's what I shall be.' Given the good grades in science and biology, it was the most natural thing to do after all. If I were a doctor, thought Clare, then people will look at me with respect. I will mean something. I will be somebody. And if I carry on being a pondering sort of girl, then at least I will be in the right profession for it.

Everything, finally, would feel natural, and Clare, more than anything, wanted to feel 'natural'. Also, she would be in charge. Yes, *she* would get to put her finger up people's orifices, and not the other way round.

In the winter there were the Family Outings to Miranda, just across the firth, that ochre-coloured sea that separated one mainland from another and provided safe waters for migrating birds. Miranda was famous for being the place where godwits took off for the long haul to Siberia. Aside from the flocks of grit-coloured birds, there was a stretch of barren coast, white with shells. The hot pools. A long straight – the road bisecting flat paddocks that were prone to flooding – where local farm boys gunned their motorbikes or their V8 Vauxhall Vivas on eternally long Friday nights. Nothing else. Except for the birds, and you couldn't take much notice of them, really, just being part of the landscape the way they were. And at night the dark land was desolate with stars.

They bought fish 'n' chips at the shop in Kaiaua, and sat at a bench overlooking another barren part of white-shelled beach and muddy firth. Their father was surprisingly cheerful, like he'd won an unexpected bet on the horses.

'I shall soon be making a little change to our lives,' he said, chomping on soggy chips.

Bethie looked up sharply. The other two had not noticed anything. She was, at any rate, their spokesperson, and they happily left that responsibility to her. 'What kind of change, Dad?'

Gulls wheeled, landed, shuffled closer, intimidated each other, wheeled again, and there was much loud squawking. In the distance a scrawny kid stood throwing stones at the water.

'Weeell.' He felt the need to draw it out.

Bethie was still looking. And the waters of the firth lapped mercilessly. 'Yes?'

'Well,' he had decided to come right out with it, 'there's a certain lady who I've been seeing, a friend, you might say, who I'd like to introduce to you girls . . .'

There were far too many chips; they lay in a congealed pile with the little packets of tomato sauce extinguished in the folds of the newspaper.

'Like a girlfriend, you mean?' wondered Lou, thinking of Ken and the Barbies.

Bethie threw a chip violently at a seagull, as if she might mash its head in. 'Don't you think that's a *little* early, *Dad*.' She could be very scathing with her emphases, Clare noticed.

But their father was made of similar stuff, it seemed. 'Hey hey,' he said, 'was it *my* fault that things turned out the way they did? That *certain* things happened –' He was leaning across the top of the smelly and tattooed bench, addressing Bethie solely. 'Life goes on, you know, Bethie. Life goes on.'

So it did. But at least you could be sure of some things. They drove back down the road to the hot pools. The girls walked past the pool of steaming grey water to the concrete changing rooms. Lou was anxious about catching athlete's foot, and had brought a pair of jandals; Clare was barefooted and pale. Beth didn't care: dumping her things on the slat bench, she stripped to nude and tugged on the stupid togs. The others watched, fascinated.

'We've only just got used to *this* – you'd think –' she hissed, hissing to herself as much as to them, to the walls, to the poxy swimsuit, 'he'd wait a *little* fucking longer. I mean, what if she comes *back*? It *is* possible, she could come back – and he'd have some –' she shuddered, 'some *lady*-friend –'

Bethie was out of the dank changing room before the other two even had time to consider their underwear. They heard the splash and looked at each other: *Last one in's a rotten pig.* But still Lou dawdled, fingering a ratty towel, tea-coloured. 'Tell me again, Clare, how it happened.'

Clare had actually taken herself off to one of the open-sided cubicles for privacy (fat chance), not liking the way Lou looked at her breasts: slight, but nevertheless present. She repeated the story of their mother's departure, which Clare herself liked to think of as a kind of fairytale.

'First of all some things got broken –'

'What kind of things?'

'Oh, things; a jam jar, plates, a cup. And there are days when Mother is away for a long time, each time when she goes out. We wonder if she hasn't got lost in a forest, whether she hasn't driven off to the supermarket and got lost on the way back. We wonder and wonder, but nothing happens, so Bethie makes tea. Scrambled eggs, 'cause she can't make anything else.'

Lou perked up. 'And she's got a bit missing, just like that girl in the forest whose hands get cut off, then they grow back again –'

'Exactly. And there are the shouting voices, often late at night, when they think you're asleep.'

'Aren't you? Asleep?'

'Not always. And then, one day, Mother felt she had to, er, run away . . .' Clare paused. How stupid it all sounded. 'Because there was something important she had to do, somewhere else, but she'll still be our mother, and in her note she said she'd write to us –' Running out of steam.

'You read the note?' Their father had torn it up before Lou had had a chance. Clare nodded.

'Was there an address?'

It is only now, years later, while tidying Marty's basement, that Clare has discovered the letters, in a chocolate box with a pile of innocuous fat puppies on the lid.

'*Dear Louise, thanks for your sweet letter, how's my baby girl? I was glad to hear from you, I was a bit shy about writing as I didn't know whether you girls would want to hear from your Mum, after what she'd done. I hope to make it up to you all one day. And you say that I'm not to write to the house, well, that's all right. This can be our little secret, just you and me.*' There were a few mundane details about Queensland, about the florist shop she was working at and hoped one day to buy, and then she signed off: '*But I am – Allways – Your loving Mum.*'

Back then, Lou sat forlorn in her own cubicle, the thin towel dangling from her hands.

When they came out of the changing rooms, Clare expected to see Bethie floating starfish-like in the steaming water. It was early, and they were the only ones there. Above them the sky was a gilded blue, and bare-limbed willows waved in the distance beyond the concrete enclosure of the pool. But Bethie was swimming lengths, and when they called out to her to stop, she either didn't hear or was taking no notice. Clare had never seen anybody swim lengths in this pool before; kids played and shiacked, adults floated about, soaked. Bethie had become a streaking arrow, some kind of machine. It was a little frightening. Clare wanted to cry out – *Stop* – but was unable. And in fact they all assumed that Bethie would herself know how to stop: it never occurred to them that they should tell her.

Lou, looking like an old lady in her white stippled bathing cap, was already stepping carefully down the large concrete steps and into the water.

'Last one in's a rotten pig,' she fluted over her shoulder.

Clare, leaping for the water, had to agree.

If it was bad enough that their father had a 'ladyfriend', it was worse that she was called Mrs Kray.

'Couldn't he have picked somebody with a normal name,' Bethie wondered bitterly, 'like Brown. Jones. Smith. Mrs Jane Smith.' She could have gone on, but instead slumped further into the couch and started picking sullenly at her trackpants.

They were supposed to be on their best behaviour, but so far it looked as if Beth would not co-operate, and Louise had disappeared altogether – though undoubtedly her eye would be glued to a convenient keyhole or her nose pressed against window glass. Louise had already made her statement about the visit: the Barbies were attached to the trellis outside the front door – in flight position, limbs poised, running away from home. All of them had their hair tightly plaited, as if there might be strenuous adventures ahead of them for which they were already prepared. One even had a small pink suitcase. They all wore jumpsuits or leggings: no glamorous ballgowns here, no flimsy shiny swimsuits designed for lying on tropical beaches.

Clare didn't like to think that the success or failure of this first meeting would rest on her narrow shoulders. She sat with knees together and ran her chapped fingers along the cool denim of her flared skirt, wondering why God hadn't given her the tapering fingers of a poet instead of the hands of a peasant, a worker.

The name *Mrs Kray* was setting off unfortunate associations in her mind. Crayfish, most obviously, slithering around the bottom of a tank in that swanky Auckland restaurant. Crayfish, all orange claws and tentacles, lifted in white plastic boxes from fishing boats; crayfish being boiled in a big pot and the sound of their dying screams; a boy on the beach smashing a rock down on top of . . . Clare quivered, at the thought of Mrs Kray.

Their father had picked up Mrs Kray to have afternoon tea at their house, and they came in noisily from the garage. There was a plate of pikelets on the kitchen bench, from the bakery, as Bethie had refused to make them. Mrs Kray was dressed in a straight wool dress, brown, and wore brogues. She had a thin mouth, which gave the impression that she didn't like to waste time on smiling, and her short brown hair was the texture of fence lichen. She stood in front of them, very upright, and the picture would have been grim were it not for the cardboard clown's head she was holding in her arms.

'Girls,' said their father, 'I want you to meet Mrs Kray.'

Mrs Kray twitched her lips somewhat, and put the clown's head on the coffee table in front of them. 'I brought you girls a present. It's full of sweeties. I make them myself, in my spare time, to sell at the craft shop. You can call me Mary.'

Normally Bethie could be relied upon to provide a quip to break the tension, but she was transfixed by the clown's head. 'I feel a bit —' Clare muttered. She stood up and staggered out of the room, the denim skirt flapping round her calves like ship's rigging. They all listened to the sound of Clare vomiting onto the kitchen floor.

'At least she made it to the kitchen,' commented Bethie.

'I always have that effect on people,' said Mrs Kray drily. Their father gave an embarrassed snigger. Beth looked up in surprise: the arid-looking Mrs Kray, sitting on the edge of the armchair and squinting at the curtains, had cracked a joke. Perhaps there was hope after all.

'Excuse me,' said Bethie, shaking off her earlier rebellion, 'I'll go and check on Clare.'

Bethie found her sister curled up on her bed, the poster of Saturn and its moons behind her head. 'What's up?'

Clare's profile was pale and sweaty. 'What if you're right,' she whispered.

Bethie sat on the side of the bed. 'About what?'

'If we have Mrs Kray,' whispered Clare, 'then our mother won't come back, will she. And, I know she's in Australia, but what if she hears about it?'

A bird was singing beyond the window. Bethie's eyes glinted. 'I hope she does.'

Clare was only just getting started. 'What if, what if all time . . . the world . . . ends here?'

'Mrs Kray is hardly the Antichrist, Clare.' Bethie grinned; it was so much easier to console others.

Clare's eyes widened, as if she hadn't reasoned that far, but it made perfect sense: of course Mrs Kray is the Antichrist, we are all doomed!

'Now get up, Clare, for goodness sake, you're not leaving me to make small-talk all by myself.'

These days Mrs Kray is fired up over the hospital and its deliberate downgrading. She has been writing letters stating the town's case –

THE INVADER WHO BELIEVES IN NOTHING

to newspapers, to the minister of health, to the prime minister – and has started collecting signatures for a petition.

'I'm not being altruistic,' she tells Clare. 'It's an entirely selfish prompting on my part. I want a hospital within spitting distance of my house so I'll be able to get a wheelchair without having to go to Auckland for it.'

'Personally,' says Clare, 'I think you might have more luck turning one of your concrete creations into a bomb and persuading the government that way.' Mrs Kray's most recent enterprise is the making of concrete garden ornaments. There are several dotted about her garden: cats, small pigs, a dwarf holding an axe, a nude wearing a fig leaf.

'I could fancy myself as a terrorist.'

'Just don't tell anybody you got the idea from me.'

Mrs Kray ponders the leafy wisteria vine that weaves its way through the fretwork of her back veranda. 'What do you think about a march to Parliament?'

'Won't do any good, not these days.' Clare nurses a cold glass of homemade lemonade against her temple. 'Money makes the world go round,' she mutters. She's been learning this ever since she got back to New Zealand.

'Have another piece of cake, Clare.'

'And at this rate, it won't be a wheelchair you'll be needing when you're old but a pacemaker,' Clare comments drily.

'Tush,' says Mrs Kray, 'butter is good for you.'

'That Mrs Kray,' says Tupulo to Clare a few days later, 'has been marching up and down outside the hospital all day with a picket, for God's sake. How '60s is that! Robeson took it upon himself to go out and tell her to piss off, told her that she was making a nuisance of herself, but that was like a red rag. She started calling out slogans while he was still dithering about on the steps. She's making Robeson's life a living hell.'

As it is a red wine afternoon, they clink their glasses together to toast the intrepid Mrs Kray.

'I may loan her my Viking's helmet.'

'I don't think that's a good idea,' mutters Clare. 'You don't want the authorities thinking she's a complete loony.'

Tupulo regroups. 'All right then, I'll just have to wear it myself.'

'While you're protesting?'

'Very possibly.'

ELEVEN

CLARE FINDS that there is a welcome sense of stability in social rituals. Like a married couple, she and Tupulo have been invited to a dinner party.

'I thoroughly intend to live for ever,' declaims Tupulo, resplendent in his king suit. Clare, and all the other guests around the dinner table, laugh. Clare's friend, Marion, has thrown the party to celebrate her husband's birthday. Everybody is dressed up, the cutlery is silver, and on the table there are two large flat bowls of water with creamy magnolia flowers floating in them.

'And how d'you intend to do that, Tup?' asks Malcolm, turning his wine glass by its golden stem. 'Cryonics?'

But Tupulo simply taps the side of his nose. 'That's for me to know, and you to find out.' More laughter, as this phrase is one of Tupulo's pet hates.

'Come on,' cries Marion, silver earrings clinking, 'spill the beans.'

Tupulo leans forward conspiratorially. 'If I told you lot the secret of eternal life, then I'd have to put up with you all for ever, and I'm not that stupid!' Anthea giggles. There may not be much substance in what he says, thinks Clare, but there is something in Tupulo's manner of speech that makes people simply fall over laughing. It is one of his many qualities that she admires. As he often says himself, he could've been a stand-up comedian. For his next birthday party he plans to do a stand-up routine for his guests.

'I vote,' Brett says coolly, 'that we throw Tupulo into the pool for being such an arsehole.'

'That's *Mister* Arsehole to you, buddy!' Tupulo plunks the end of his fork onto the table in mock umbrage. 'But I object,' he adds. 'How exactly have I been an arsehole?'

'For starting an interesting idea at a dinner party, and then not revealing the guts of it. It's like telling us all a joke but withholding the punchline.'

'You would say that,' defends Tupulo, 'being a shrink.'

Marion leaps to Brett's defence. 'He's a social worker. And, besides, his occupation's got nothing to do with it – Brett's right, I vote we throw Tupulo in the pool.'

Malcolm, a paediatrician with exquisite dress sense, turns to Clare, who is on his left. 'The time has come, m'dear, for you to put in a good word for this unfortunate fellow.' Everyone always listens to Clare.

'I don't think you should throw him in the pool,' mediates Clare, 'because he's wearing his best suit.'

Tupulo grabs Clare's hand across the table and presses it to his lips. 'The voice of Reason!'

'Okay Clare.' Brett is already scraping back his chair. 'We'll just have to take his suit off him first. But only 'cause you've said so.'

The men are derobing Tupulo, and Tupulo is kicking and protesting and fighting them off as best he can without actually hurting anybody (which considering his size is rather difficult), and then as Tupulo is carried past the table in his shirt and underwear and out onto the patio, the women continue an earlier conversation.

'The thing is,' says Marion, leaning over to Clare, 'there are rumours about the hospital closing, and if it does, we're all stuffed.'

'Not at all,' says Clare. 'You're talking about services, doctors and nursing staff like yourself – the town's not going to lose that. No, the actual building is a shambles though – the back wing is derelict, empty; there is no purpose-built operating theatre . . . I'd like to see a brand-new hospital in its place, something decent to work in –'

'Yeah, right. As if we'd ever get funding for that here.'

There is a delicate pause. Janine, who is staying at Clare's for the weekend, says, 'We're short of good staff at Middlemore. You could all get jobs there. It's only an hour's drive, too. You could even commute.'

'Exactly,' says Clare, now hoping to change the subject. 'Did you know the locals call the place "bro-repairs". Geddit?'

'My husband's in a wheelchair,' comments Anthea, 'and our house is specially fitted out for him. We wouldn't want to move, and I wouldn't want to work a 16-hour shift, then have to drive for more than an hour to get home again.'

There comes the sound of a whale-like splash from outside, and a gurgled cry of '*You – bastards –*'

'What about you, Clare? What are you going to do when your time's up?'

Clare raises her eyes to the ceiling, considering. 'Do you know,' she begins, 'I thought I'd –' They are all looking at her, waiting to hear her answer, but then she realises that she has no idea. She has been putting off thinking about her future, her career, and this is very unlike her: until recently Clare has had everything planned out in advance, it has been only a matter of stepping into the squares.

Beyond, there is a roar, followed by two loud splashes. Then a third.

Janine, with barely a glance at Clare, asks drily, 'Is he really a doctor –?'

'Oh yes,' laughs Marion, 'house surgeon.'

'God help us,' says Janine, and they all laugh.

Then Tupulo bursts into song – the Toreador's song from *Carmen* – as Clare knew he would at some stage in the evening. He can't help himself, he would sing at the hospital if it wasn't for the patients. Clare leans her elbow over the back of the chair to see what they're up to.

'Won't it be cold?' she wonders, shivering involuntarily. It is, after all, barely spring.

'Nope,' says Marion, 'the pool's heated.'

Louise, who has driven over from the city to have lunch with Clare and Tupulo, reclines on the couch.

'Where were you the day Princess Di died?'

'How should I know?' Then Tupulo thinks. 'No, I remember, I was mourning Mother Teresa.'

'. . . Clare?'

'Um,' Clare pushes down the plunger and watches flakes of coffee wash downwards. 'I don't know. Probably in theatre.'

Lou is disgusted; one part of her is deeply sentimental, and she loved Princess Diana – loves her even more now that she is tragically dead, crushed in a French tunnel. 'You two are hopeless,' she says. 'I would've thought that living in this boring place you'd be a little more interested in The World Out There.'

'Well,' says Tupulo, 'we're not all quite so preoccupied with trivial media culture as you are, Louise.'

'That's rich coming from you, the master of the trivial himself.'

Tupulo isn't so easily insulted. He leans back in the armchair with squeaking piety and links his thick fingers over his diaphragm, raising his eyes to the ceiling. 'Actually, it is true that I have developed the pursuit of the trivial almost to the level of an art form. The other day, *par exemple*, I held a custard square balancing competition in the hospital reception area.' He slides a grin towards Clare, who is also grinning into her cup of coffee. 'It was a huge success, if I say so myself. The winner – because although I did quite well myself, being the organiser, in all modesty I had to allow somebody else to win – but the winner managed to balance twenty-three custard squares on his forehead. Isn't that remarkable? I wouldn't have thought it possible, but then they are very sticky –'

They all inhale. Except Grunt, who snores on beneath the couch.

'Well,' Louise looks at Clare, 'that really is something.'

Lou had planned to stay the night, but now she decides to return to the city that afternoon. There is a lunacy at work here, she thinks, that I don't understand and don't want to either. Something about small rural towns makes people go stupid in the head.

To shift Tupulo's domination of the conversation, she asks Clare how 'good old Mrs Kray' has been keeping.

However, Tupulo must dominate. 'Mrs Kray,' he booms, so that their neighbour beyond the flax bushes – Ken Gillman, hard at work among his beetroots – will be wondering what's up now, 'Mrs Kray is the Real Oil. Mrs Kray has a Heart of Gold, she is a veritable Masterpiece of Kiwi Ingenuity –'

He might go on, except that Clare butts in to explain. 'Mrs Kray is helping to save the hospital.'

Lou widens her eyes. 'It needs saving?' Lou thinks the hospital is a dinosaur and ought to be turned into a designer shopping mall with a theatre-restaurant featuring a Basil Fawlty lookalike – and they already have their Fool, she thinks, smiling at Tupulo. She went to such an evening recently, and thought it was a hoot. It would fit in nicely with the old hotel's Agatha Christie weekends.

'Hell no,' says Tupulo, smiling tightly back at Lou, 'they could scrap the hospital and when people have accidents they could just bleed to death.'

Louise sighs. 'Must you be so dramatic about everything?'

'Yes.'

'More coffee?' offers Clare.

'No thanks.' Lou is really pissed off now. To think: she could be sitting in her favourite café having a cup of proper coffee instead of listening to this drivel. 'If you want to save your boring old hospital –' she is getting ready to leave, as fast as politeness will allow – 'all you have to do is set up a trust fund, for Christsake, run by local business people, and get the locals to donate to it.'

Clare sees Lou out to her car. 'Lou, I was wondering if you'd made up with Marty?'

Lou opens the car door, slides on her sunglasses. 'We talk.'

'Yes?'

'That's enough for now.'

She returns to find Tupulo feverishly pacing the lounge. He raises his bushy eyebrows meaningfully at Clare. 'So your sister has her intelligent moments after all, even if they are unintentional . . .'

'D'you think the trust idea would work?'

'Why not? It's worth a try.'

'I'm going to ring Mrs Kray.'

'Excellent, yes, do that. Hook that Kray on the line!'

It's been raining again. On and on, as if a switch up above has got stuck. Clare, when she gets to work in the morning, finds that the cafeteria at the back of the hospital has flooded. The women who normally make the sandwiches and filled rolls are busy wielding mops and buckets against this invasion.

Alex, too, has come down, to buy something for later. 'Ye gods,' he exclaims, 'if this keeps up, next thing the town'll be cut off from civilisation as we know it.' He has already told her that there are about seven days of the year when the helicopter can't fly in. If the river also spills over its banks, then they really will be cut off.

Walking back along the echoing corridor, Clare glances outside to see the rear lawn awash and a brown rat calmly paddling away through the water, deserting ship.

August 1983
Rob's birthday party. I left them to it, no heart for celebrations.

Bethie was standing beneath the pomegranate tree, a cup of green tea between her hands, watching as the sun set behind the mountains, heavy clouds in the distance changing from purple to azure. Also from that direction, and as if to mock the exquisite beauty of the sky, came the intermittent popping of gunfire from the front. *Jungly*, fighting. Always the fighting. The original name for the country was Yagistan, Land of the Out-of-Control. There were days when Bethie seemed to see in her mind a long line of wars, stretching back through history like a rope of uneven knots. *And as for those who have fled or been driven from their homes or been hurt in My cause, or fought or been killed, I will erase their sins from them and introduce them to gardens beneath which rivers flow as a reward from the presence of God.*

She turned up her face to the tree. There were tiny red orbs forming among the leaves. It was a shame that the Turkoman wasn't around any more to see them. He will be among his friends, in the reed city. Unless he got diverted along the way, caught up in other skirmishes in the mountains. The small fighting the giant. But somehow Bethie didn't think so. The Turkoman had his own battle to fight.

Angry voices sounded from the clinic. The truck carrying their medical supplies had been held up somewhere, perhaps even bombed by a Soviet gunship, nobody knew yet, only that it hadn't arrived. Rob was going nuts.

There was a tension pervading the city that seemed to infect all of them. Earlier in the day, when she'd gone down to the market with Franco to buy some naan and eggs, a man was running along the wide dusty street by the river firing a Kalashnikov into the air. He could have been celebrating a wedding or a birth in the family, had it not been for the hard, manic look on his face. Several men tackled the shooter, bringing him to the ground, then one of them started throttling him. There was news too that some hostages had been taken south of Kabul. Any day, thought Bethie, it could all end for them here. They existed in such a flimsy bubble that at times their situation seemed outlandishly ridiculous.

Above her head the glossy leaves of the pomegranate tree fluttered in the hot breeze, just as it had for decades already.

In her mind she followed the Turkoman as he waded through reeds as tall as men, spreading them before him like swimming through water. She could have gone, could just have followed him – he wouldn't have turned her back. She used to be so impulsive – headstrong, said Mr Bow in fifth form English – back in safe little New Zealand. Here, impulsiveness could get you blown up, maybe worse.

'A penny for them –' Terry hung a cool arm over Beth's shoulders, her eyes glistening brown as a snake. 'You've been out here for ages.'

Beth gave a guilty laugh. 'Where else am I going to get a little shade?'

'True.' Terry unhooked herself from Beth and leaned on the treetrunk, lighting a cigarette. She seemed unmoved by the heat. Leaves rustled conspiratorially above them. 'You're distant, these days. Since that mountain guy left.'

'Terry, have you been in love until you'd had enough?'

'How d'you mean?'

Beyond their patch of shade, the compound was hazy with light.

'Sometimes I feel like I don't get a chance to try it out properly. Love. It goes away too soon.'

'Hey kid, there's plenty of time yet.' She grimaced and blew smoke out the side of her mouth like a corny actor, making Beth laugh. 'And you've still got me. I'm not going anywhere.'

'Yeah, worse luck.'

Clare is walking home in the twilight when she turns up the hill and into Vernon Street. Up ahead is the choleric figure of the Marshall boy, lean and lanky, pushing his matt-black bicycle along the middle of the empty street. He could be going to her house – the lawns certainly need doing – and Clare is about to call out to him, when something flies out from a bush and hits the boy in the side of his face.

He stops pushing his bike and puts a hand gingerly to his cheek, to discover blood on his fingertips. Raucous giggling comes from the bushes. There is a gully on that side of the street, with a carefully tended bank which Clare admires whenever she comes this way. There is crashing now, the sound of bodies racing through undergrowth. Then, as if the perpetrator has made safe his escape, the word '*dickhead*' comes echoing up to the road.

The Marshall boy winces finally, and his right shoulder jerks up a fraction. Clare, coming up to him, is in professional mode – indeed, has put aside all thought about the silly lawns. 'Let me see that –'

The boy jumps, on seeing her, and grips the handlebars of his bike more tightly. Pity softens her dislike for the boy. He has sustained a superficial cut to his left temple; a line of blood is trailing down towards his chin. A sharp-edged stone lies on the road nearby. It could have hit him in the eye.

'Come back to the house and I'll clean it up for you.'

But he shrugs away from her, pushing the bike forward.

'No thanks,' he mutters, 'I'm fine.'

Clare, standing in the middle of the road, watches as he swings a leg over the bike and cycles rapidly away. It looks as if the Marshall boy, too, has his Marise Walker. Though that's unfair, considering Marise has cancer and is facing a mastectomy at Waikato. Such knowledge seems to neutralise the past.

More happily, Clare finds herself also reminded of Oliver.

TWELVE

With the coming of summer – another summer – life seemed to lurch into a higher gear again. Birds made more noise, cicadas crawled up out of the earth, early-morning frosts became an unpleasant memory, the heat pushed people out into their back gardens, and the town was infiltrated by mountain-climbing tourists and cars filled with holiday families passing through to more interesting seaside locations. A new life breathed along the streets that had been barren during winter. The café on Mary Street reopened, with 'an exciting new menu', and shopowners looked less depressed. Even the hills behind the town looked cheerful.

Clare, who was starting at the School of Medicine in February and was to live at a university hostel, mooned about, thinking she might never return to the town again. It gave everything a soft bleached look, although that may have been the heat. She biked around the quiet streets visiting old haunts: sat on the shelly beach at the promontory with her chin on her knees; cycled slowly along the straight – land flat as guilt on either side; visited the pond where she used to catch tadpoles; and skulked around the haunted house that she and Bethie used to visit – she'd put her foot through rotten boards and skinned her ankle and they'd told stories to terrify each other.

For old time's sake, Clare indulged in one last experiment in the garden shed at the back of the section. But something went wrong – she must have mixed the chemicals together in the wrong order – for there was an explosion which blew out the cobwebby window.

When the smoke cleared a little, there was a lanky boy standing framed in the doorway, flax leaves waving behind his rust-coloured head.

'Do you know,' he said, 'I'm no arsonist, but for years I've been wanting to blow something up. I was planning to have a go at it this summer. You've beaten me to it.'

Clare, coughing and spluttering, got herself out into the fresh air. 'Sorry. It wasn't intentional.'

'It never is.' The boy grinned.

They sat down on the grass. Oliver was staying next door for a fortnight, a nephew from the city. He and his brother Sid, an engineering student, were flatting together in Auckland. Oliver was training to be a social worker.

'I'm no further with my experiment,' said Clare, squinting at the smoking corrugated-iron roof of the shed, 'but I must admit, it felt good, blowing up our shed.'

'You have brown gunk in your hair,' said Oliver, biting his lip. 'Do you mind?' Quite naturally he proceeded to pick it out for her.

Clare submitted to this grooming, only her neck betraying a faint blush, and leaned back with her palms in the damp grass as if she were another type of girl altogether, the kind of girl who was used to strange boys turning up and picking gunk out of her hair. She remembered to breathe.

'If you like,' she said, in her fey mood, 'I could help you blow something up.'

They grinned at each other, the summer air blowing warm between them. Sulphurous fumes riffled over the neighbour's hedge.

By the time she was twenty Bethie had graduated as a nurse and was working at the local hospital. She was still living at home, and seemed to have no ambition to go any further afield than the town.

One night during dinner there was a phone call for Beth. She stood stork-like on one leg, her left foot tucked into the right knee. It was an invite from her old rowing squad to a party in Auckland. She sat down again and tucked a bang of hair behind an ear. 'I'm not going,' she said.

Marty kept his eyes on his plate. 'It'll do you good to have a break from work. Let your hair down a bit.'

Bethie looked at him across the round Formica table, her face leaf-brown from the weather, and she could have been looking at a stranger. She was suddenly furious. 'Okay,' she said, 'you want me to party, I'll bloody well party till I drop –' She pushed away from the table, holding her bad arm to her side, though there was no need – the days of pain and of being careful not to knock it were long past – and left the room, slamming the hallway door behind her.

Their father blinked at the wall behind Clare's head. 'What did I say?'

It was a loud party in a white fake-Spanish house in Remuera. By the time Bethie arrived there were already people spilling out onto the back terrace, and Roxy Music was blasting from the speakers. She wandered through the crowded living room among her old friends. Jean gave her a quick hug, trying not to look at Bethie's arm, that scar, but nevertheless her eyes were drawn to it; she was celebrating her recent placing in the Commonwealth Games team. There were lithe young men in the kitchen, boasting about how many bananas they could eat in one sitting, how many miles they had clocked up in training.

'So where are you guys training now?' She could be one of the boys, one of the team, again – at least it seemed that way, though she suspected the feeling wouldn't last. There was barely room for a pause.

'Bethie, what you doing these days, mate?'

'I'm cycling,' she said. Though she wasn't, not any more, but you had to say something. She might have gone on, except her old bravura was starting to fail her.

'Good on you,' they said, echoing each other and bowing their heads over their tinnies. After all, there but for the grace of God. But they were the unscathed, and the future was out there just waiting to be conquered, so it wasn't long before they were turning back to their comparisons.

In a corner of the main room, standing about in front of the flickering television set, Bethie joined a group that included Jean and

Thompson and Geoff. They were sharing a house in the Waikato, and being paid to train at Karapiro. I could have been on that squad, thought Bethie, turning a can of beer in her hands and finding that it wasn't half strong enough. 'It's driving me mad,' complained Thompson, 'living in the country. There's no nightlife. And poxy Geoff snores.'

'I always liked the training,' said Bethie. She had lived for her training. And for being part of the team. These days there was mostly the feeling of being on the outer. She shouldn't have come to this party, it'd been too long.

'You snore, you mean,' said Geoff, as if Beth hadn't spoken and maybe she hadn't. 'And talk about nightlife, what d'you think you're doing now?'

'Yeah well, a girl needs a break from that endless bloody training.'

In another part of the room somebody had started doing what looked to be a Muldoon impersonation, and the others drifted over. Beth was left with the television set. She sat down, suddenly exhausted, and discovered a brooding figure at the other end of the couch.

Feet up and chin on knees, she sat hunched, with dark hair that hung long and straight, hiding the face. She was sipping from a small bottle of vodka. 'In my opinion, rowing has to be the most boring sport in the world . . . you may as well sit on a bus, then at least you can watch the scenery –' A pale face, illuminated by the light from the screen, glanced over at Bethie. 'Actually, I think golf may be worse. It looks so ridiculous – chasing a tiny ball about with a metal stick. At least rowing has some visual sense of the heroic about it. But then, isn't *all* sport ultimately pointless –?'

'Terry,' exclaimed Beth, finally recognising her. 'What are you doing here?'

Terry grinned impishly and pushed some hair behind her ear. 'Gate-crashing, of course. My flat's just down the road. I wouldn't have expected you to be hanging round with the jockstraps.'

It was Bethie's turn to grin. 'I used to be one of the jockstraps myself – remember?'

'How could I have forgotten.'

And it seemed that an old mutual admiration was remembered by both of them: Bethie in the school gym or in the athletics events, out-distancing everybody, while Terry lingered in the shade with her long, long hair gleaming down to the small of her back. Had they always been aware of each other? Then they'd both been at nursing college, but in different classes, and had lost sight of each other.

'And you were one of the swots . . . Where are you working?'

'Greenlane. You?'

'I'm back at home.'

'So I'd heard, on the grapevine.'

'No shit.'

'Well, there has been some shit, and other unmentionables – I'm pretty adept with the old rubber gloves these days too –' And she held up her middle finger to the room in general. People were forming themselves into a conga line. A can of beer went sailing out an open window. The noise was suddenly unbearable.

'You wanna get out of here?' said Beth.

Terry uncurled her legs, giving them a stretch. 'Sure thing, Purefoy.'

They went to the Domain, because Terry wanted to break into the Wintergarden. 'This is my going-away present to myself,' she explained, 'coming in here.' She suggested using the crowbar from Beth's car for the purpose, was going to break a hole in the wooden trellis that fenced in the garden. But Bethie searched the periphery until she found a hole anyway, round to one side where it was shadowy with hedging.

It was late, and they sat on concrete steps, staring down into the long black goldfish pool at their feet, the city humming in the distance. The lily pads were shimmering with water. Terry's hair formed a dark puddle on the concrete step behind her.

'Do you believe in fate?' said Terry. 'I had a boyfriend once who was always going on about destiny and all that, how nothing is coincidental. I'm not so sure myself. I reckon it's just God, or whatever, rolling his dice. Only sometimes, if you think about it, you can roll it yourself – that's when things start working, I reckon. Know what I mean?'

Bethie wasn't so sure. 'I don't like to think about stuff like that,' she said.

Terry was leaning back on her elbows. 'Why not?'

She shrugged. 'I prefer to just get on with it. Thinking about God's dice isn't going to change anything.' Unconsciously she rubbed a hand over her scarred arm, which had started to ache, probably from the cool air coming off the pond.

Terry glanced at the arm, then away, frowning: the accident that had been the talk of the town. There were things in her own past that would've been chewed over, been public knowledge. She and Bethie were small-town girls. 'I'm going to Afghanistan in a few weeks' time –'

A fragile sliver of moon was balanced in the west.

'Afghanistan? Why?'

It was Terry's turn to shrug. 'There's a war on, and they need people to help. And besides, it's a long way from here, that's why.'

'What's it like there?'

'I dunno – dry, hot. It'll be an adventure, something different than stitching up the drunks on a Saturday night.' Terry linked her long fingers together over her ribs, and contemplated the young moon. 'Why don't you come too –?'

It seemed such a small and unlikely beginning, but Bethie, casting only a thin shadow, found that she had stumbled upon a new passion.

If only the past was always rosy, thinks Clare. She can't help harking back to that awful day with Marcus in the Golden Gate Park.

Early autumn, and the bare branches of the trees were nearly black against a pale sky. There was still thick dew in places, even though it was 10.30 a.m. Small notices stuck at intervals in the grass announced the banning of group sports, to allow the grass to regenerate. A girl, wearing a white wedding dress beneath an army greatcoat, was sitting on a stool and playing something gloomy on a cello. Albernoni, thought Clare.

Marcus had stopped in the middle of the walkway, hands shoved into the pockets of his black jeans.

'But why should you want to go anywhere?' He addressed the stained sky. 'Why shouldn't you just stay in town that week? *What* is the point in *skiing*?'

Clare lifted her chin out of her silk scarf. 'Marcus,' she said evenly, 'it's only for a few days. Tracey's organised everything. You could come too.'

'To go skiing, at Tahoe?' His tone exceeded scathing. 'I've already told you, I loathe skiing.'

A thought occurred to Clare. 'Do you even know how?'

There was a vein pulsing in the side of his neck. 'It's got nothing to do with skiing.'

'*What* then?'

'The point is – I don't want you to go. I want you to stay with me.'

'If you came with us,' Clare said slowly, 'then you would still be with me.' She opened her palms to him. 'It's just a holiday, for God's sake.'

'I *don't* want to share you with a bunch of fucking doctors and nurses.'

'*You're* a fucking doctor.'

'I can't believe it, Clare, that you're willing to put these stupid people ahead of me. We've got something going here.'

'And one little trip isn't going to make any difference. I want to see the mountains. I've been in this city for ages, and I never get the chance to go sightseeing –'

'*Sightseeing* –' His face was nearly as black as his jeans. 'Sightseeing. What d'you think you are? A fucking tourist? *Jesus.*' He started walking away.

Clare was incredulous. 'Don't walk away from me,' she cried. Then shouted: '*You bastard* –'

Her words soaked ineffectually into the air. Marcus didn't turn around. She gave a sudden sob, then turned sharply on her heel and walked the other way.

September 1983
Wonder if I'll go back home, after this. Terry's been talking about touring through Europe, doing the kind of OE that everybody else does. Me, I'm divided.

When Beth went into the storeroom that they used as a living room, Terry was sitting on a beanbag listening to the BBC World Service. There was a man droning on about beekeeping in the Midlands. Beth slumped down into the vinyl armchair. *Beekeeping is practised in all spheres of life, from the centre of large cities to the heart of the countryside* . . . It seemed suddenly so funny that she burst out laughing.

Terry looked up. 'What's so funny?'

Where colonies of honey bees are brought into a garden, the first decision must be where they shall be sited –

'But, *that*.' She was helpless.

'Shuttup.'

Beth stopped laughing. 'What?'

'I'm listening to it, for Christsake.'

'Sorry. It's just that it's so . . . unreal.'

'That's rich coming from you.'

A needle's pause. 'Pardon?'

Terry's eyes were narrowed and bloodshot as if she'd been smoking hash. Was she stoned already, so early in the evening? Mostly she smoked before going to bed, to help herself sleep, she said. 'Unreal, that's what you're becoming. All this hanging about reading the fucking Koran and –'

'Don't call it that. I think you should apologise.'

'Like hell I will. You can throw off at what's on the radio, but nobody's allowed to criticise your precious book. It's like you're brainwashing yourself. And that man, Muhammad, he had dozens of wives. Some prophet – he was a fucking sex maniac. How can you even read that shit? You always have to be the best, do the most, do everything better than everybody else, think you're so staunch, so untouchable, and this dust is driving me nuts, dirt everywhere, even gets in my knickers. I'm sick of it. Sick of it all. Sick of –'

Beth looked at her hands, her face burning. She focused her gaze on a crushed blue Gauloise packet on the floor, one of Franco's, like a sad fragment of sky. When she next looked up Terry's face was pink, her lips ashen.

She floundered up out of the beanbag. 'Sorry,' she muttered, 'sorry.'

'But I'm not going to the mountains,' Marcus stated baldly, nevertheless capitulating. 'You ought to see some of the coast. We'll go to the coast.'

Clare got up to turn down the central heating and open a window. She could barely breathe. Along with the cool air came the traffic noise; it seemed exaggerated, almost deafening. The white voile curtains she had put up two months ago shifted uneasily in the breeze, while something small and dark shifted correspondingly in her belly. She shut the window again. That was fine if he wanted to go to the coast, there was nothing wrong with that. As long as they were together, and happy. Marcus was right, why waste her precious time going off with people she didn't even particularly care about.

So they rented a car, a convertible – as if to recapture the already-spent summer – and drove out of the city. They headed north on the 101 into Marin County, then turned off onto the coastal highway. There were lush valleys, where the hippies had settled in the '60s seeking an idyllic way of life, then the coast road winding along tall cliffs. Marcus lit a cigarette off the car lighter, his hair flashing back in the wind. Several times she wanted to stop, but he just wanted to drive. Then Clare cried out suddenly, 'Hey look, that beach, let's stop there.'

White sand, surf, the water glazed silvery grey . . . 'I could be back home,' she exclaimed, except for the wind that came off the land smelling of eucalyptus. He looked away. He didn't understand the magnetic pull of 'home'. Smoking again, he threw down his cigarette and pressed it into the sand with the metal toe of his boot.

'Come on,' cried Clare, grabbing at his arm. But he remained intractable.

She ran off without him.

The beach was long, and she ran and ran, her hair blowing in the wind, rocketing along, until it seemed she was a mere black dot in the universe. You couldn't help but laugh. 'We are so small,' she shouted at the pellucid sky, a single seabird wheeling high above, unassailable. Slowing to a jog then, breathing hard, she began to feel a little ridiculous. A family group, in winter woollies, were looking at her. This was California, for God's sake, the place where anything could happen. Playing the Kiwi sheila, woman abroad, she waved at them, laughing. Then looked back for Marcus.

He was still in the same spot – veritably a small black dot: a tiny tear in the fabric of the day. She jogged back slowly towards him. As she got closer she saw that his face was hidden behind his Nikon, and he was photographing her. She put out her arms like an aeroplane and zoomed towards him. He lowered the camera.

'Did you get that?' she panted. 'Me as a plane?'

'No,' he said evenly, 'I was only photographing you in the distance.'

'Well that should be useful,' she laughed, 'you won't even get my face in properly. I'll be all blurred.'

He considered this, even taking off his dark glasses and squinting at the sky, 'Oh I don't think so. It's all automatic. Though you were a long way away.' And then, 'If I were a professional photographer, exhibiting, I would make a series and call it something like "Woman Coming Into View". Maybe I would make it a collage – cut you into bits, then stick you back together again.'

'Nice.'

'I might do it anyway. As a kind of portrait of our time together.'

'You make it sound temporary.'

'Not at all,' he grimaced. 'Though how permanent do you want it –?'

Clare found she couldn't answer that question, so the idea was left hanging.

But Marcus remained pleased with the idea of his photographs, and the day improved after that. Except that he added, on their way back to the car, 'Actually, you looked like a giraffe.'

'God is a virus,' states Clare, tilting her ruby glass to the light.

It is deep into a Sunday afternoon and Clare and Tupulo are on a red-wine binge – neither of them on call, and it is just as well their patients can't see the pair of them now, thinks Clare. Warm sunlight sharks across the carpet, while a puka waves large green hands outside the window. Winter is making a final bid, and beyond their snug sunny spot the town is being heckled by chill gusts; the sky is ominous with the cloud formation known as mares' tails. Down south it is known to bring snow.

Tupulo leans back in the leather armchair, the skin of which makes a lot of noise whenever he moves, which is the way Tupulo likes it (he is a Pirate King, among creaking sails). '*Ha*,' he says.

'Yes, God is a virus, and *Judas* –' Clare leans forward, knees akimbo and her wine tilting precariously towards the carpet – 'Judas is the Antichrist – penicillin.' It sounds rather original at the moment, though Clare suspects it'll sound silly later, when she's sober.

'Ah *ha*,' exclaims Tupulo. 'But this is fantastic. What about the Apostles?'

Clare empties her glass which Tupulo promptly refills. 'The Apostles help Jesus, so they are the antibodies.'

Tupulo plays around with the idea. 'So, when our friend Mr McGrath meets God, it is a duel to the death. God wants to take over his system, invade his lymph nodes, alter his white-blood cell count, but Mr McGrath fights God's invasion and goes to see his doctor and the good man –'

'Or woman –'

'Or woman sticks a shot of penicillin up his bum and tells him to go home, get some rest.'

'Exactly,' says Clare. 'But God isn't that easily shaken off. He can return – in another form.'

'The virus mutates,' yells Tupulo, almost slathering around the mouth, 'and narrowly avoids getting done in by Judas –'

'And he calls in the Apostles to help in the good fight –'

'You mean, she –'

Clare gives a wry smile. 'Touché. So it's God or Mr McGrath.'

'Which is when I see Mr McGrath at the hospital, nearly dead from pneumonia.' Tupulo sobers fractionally. But manages to regroup. 'A flaw,' he exclaims, 'in this tinpot theory of yours.'

'What?' Clare pretends surprise.

'If God is a virus, and if God is fighting for supreme control of the physical system, and if we assume that God is good, then that implies that the body is bad.'

Clare mulls, creating a beet-red whirlpool that swirls up to the lip of her glass and just as obediently recedes. 'Well yes, and isn't that what orthodox Christianity is all about? If one could only control the body, that unpredictable beast, then sin is eliminated, or at least kept to a minimum – cajoled, persuaded, transmogrified into something better. Something higher. Into goodness.' She takes a mouthful of wine, the inside of her cheeks roughen with tannin. 'I believe it all goes back to a basic fear – because of an understandable ignorance – of the workings of the human body. Which is why formal religion has taken a hammering in this century. Everybody knows so much about the body, about what happens inside here –' she thumps her chest with the flat of her hand, spilling a few bloody drops onto her jeans, '– that we don't need mumbo-jumbo any more to soothe our fears. Call me old-fashioned, but there is no mystery any more. You can even see heart surgery performed on television, for Christsake. A woman gives birth on the Internet.'

Tupulo twists his mouth. 'You're so brainy, Clare.' He gives a short laugh. 'But transmogrified? Now, that is *too* much for our Day Off.'

Clare can only grin. 'Look it up if you don't know what it means.'

'I know what it means,' puffs Tupulo, 'it's what happens to moggies when they fall off a cliff. In the same manner as lemmings. And did you know, by the way, that that is a myth about lemmings being compelled to leap off cliffs –'

'We all need our myths,' decides Clare, 'even lemmings. How is McGrath, anyway?'

'He's bloody sick. We saw him only just in time.' With much creaking of sails Tupulo pushes himself up out of the chair. 'I'm opening another bottle.' Then, calling from the kitchen, 'But I look on the bright side. If it had been the weekend and McGrath had had to go to Waikato, he might've lost the battle altogether.'

Asi the Madman was back, shaking his wrist at them, his bracelet of metal shards jangling. Beth looked up from her patient: she was plucking pale maggots out of a leg wound with a pair of tweezers. Without the Turkoman, she couldn't understand what Asi was on about. The sound washed over her like a moaning song.

THE INVADER WHO BELIEVES IN NOTHING

'D'you think he's putting a hex on us?'

Terry, walking past the window, said, 'What I'd like to know is where he got that peacock from.'

Asi squatted at the side of the dusty street. He and his peacock watched mournfully as an armoured tank was driven past by mujahedin. He waved his bracelet at them, then started reciting loudly in Pushtu. Like a neighbour playing loud music, it went on and on, the metal bracelet picking up the rhythm. Every now and then the peacock would let loose a falsetto cry of grief in accompaniment.

There was a poor orphan boy who was struggling to look after his widowed mother. They had one cow, a small cow. Each day the boy must go out into the fields to gather hay for the cow. One day, in the borderlands, he meets a snake who demands the boy's mother in marriage. The snake says he will strike and kill the boy if he does not do as he demands. The boy at first forgets to tell his mother. The next day he goes to a different place to cut hay, but still he meets the snake, who again demands to marry the mother. The mother accepts the offer, and all the snakes and scorpions arrive with the groom for the wedding. Nine months later the mother gives birth to the snake's child, Mar Cuceh, the 'snake chick'.

The snake then says to the mother, 'When can I eat that son of yours?' And the mother says, 'Any day.' So the snake tells the mother that the next day he will get in the ghee jar and wait for the boy. 'Don't make him anything to eat with his bread' – *for the boy could not eat dry bread* – *'then go and make yourself busy at something. When he calls out to you, tell him your hands are full. Tell him to take the cup and get the ghee from the jar to eat it with his bread. Then when he puts in his hand I'll strike and kill him.*

However, Mar Cuceh, playing in the alley, hears this plan. So the next day when the boy calls out to his mother, Mar Cuceh says, 'I will get the ghee for you. My father is waiting there in the jar for you –' The boy eats his bread and goes out to play.

Then the snake tells the mother that the next day he will get into the water skin. 'This time you make something to eat with the bread, but don't fill the water glass, so he'll have to get the water himself.' But once again, Mar Cuceh hears the plan, and when the boy calls out to his mother and she replies, 'My hands are full', Mar Cuceh fetches the water himself.

Finally, the snake decides to strike the boy while he is outside. The mother tells him to bring a handful of wood, so she can bake some bread. The boy goes out to the field and chops thorn, ties up a bundle and puts it on his back. Mar Cuceh, who has gone with his stepbrother, sees that his father's neck is showing in the bundle of wood. 'Brother,' he says, 'your load has come loose, put it down, don't move yet –' The snake stretches out his neck to strike the boy, but Mar Cuceh strikes a match to the thorns and sets it alight. The snake is burnt, turned to charcoal. Mar Cuceh, the snake chick, tells the boy that it is the mother who is to blame, and the boy goes back to the house and kills her.

Asi would have continued with his story, but somebody had started to pelt him with stones. He got up, waving his thin arms about like propellers, and with the peacock in tow, ran off down the street.

October 1983
The invader who believes in nothing.

There had been a spate of vomiting at the San Fran hospital – a bug going round, people off sick.

Clare was on duty the night of Brown & Wiseman's anniversary. They may not have been living together but they had been 'an item' for the last two years. Even some of the female staff envied their longevity. 'What's your secret, Brown?' Bonnie wanted to know, her auburn bangs hidden beneath her nurse's surgical cap.

'Honey,' said Brown, 'you are the last person I would tell.' General hilarity. Brown, at the time, was holding a jelly donut – a large box of them stood open in the staffroom. Clare even, not normally a donut fan, couldn't resist, and she reached out for one with white icing dribbled over the top like snow.

Marcus suddenly appeared at her elbow and put his hand over

hers. 'No, not that one.' He guided her to a cinnamon-coated one, his lips at her ear, and whispered, 'Apple,' so sensually that there was simply no question.

She took it, as Wiseman himself lifted out the snowy one – and Clare remembered that only because she had wanted it, the donut that incongruously reminded her of Mount Egmont. She watched Wiseman bite into it, then she turned her head to say something to Marcus. He too was watching Wiseman, a look of rapt anticipation, almost hunger, on his face. Clare looked away. It was as if she had for a moment glimpsed the true nature of his soul, and been repulsed. For a split second she had to wonder, what do I really know about this man?

When both Brown and Wiseman got sick, Clare knew instantly that Marcus had caused it.

She went round to Wiseman's apartment. When the neighbour opened the door, the sound of his vomiting could be clearly heard in the thin hallway with its art deco-framed prints.

'Are you all right?' she called through the bathroom door.

'No, I am *not* all right.' The door swung open, and Wiseman stood swaying in a stained bathrobe, his normally dark skin a sallow shade of mauve. 'Get me to the fucking hospital, Clare.'

She drew blood for the lab herself. Brown, who wasn't quite so bad, came in so that Clare could take blood from him as well. Arsenic was found in both samples.

It came out during the next few days that Marcus had probably been poisoning people for months, with doses mild enough to cause discomfort or illness but not to kill.

Clare took the pair of shining red boots that they had bought together, caught a ferry one day, and threw them into the sea. She had the lock on her door changed. It didn't seem enough to protect her, but then, she couldn't think of anything else to do. As it was, she had opened her door to the enemy long ago.

PART THREE

City of Reeds

THIRTEEN

ONE MORNING, near dawn, Clare wakes from another of her recurring dreams about the earthworm. It is just as huge and soft as always, but in this dream it is travelling snake-like across a field of grass. It slithers bulkily on, while she follows at a distance behind to see what it will do; then it comes to the local river. Without a pause it continues straight into the water and disappears from sight. Even though she stands on the bank, peering into the murky clay-coloured waters, there is no sign of it.

She wakes feeling disoriented and empty, with Tupulo nevertheless breathing reassuringly beside her, and because it is much too early for her to be awake, Clare turns her head back into an uneasy sleep.

This is not a dream: there is so much blood that Clare's shoes are wet with it and she has to be careful not to slip. The arms and the front of her surgical gown are running red, and the house surgeon is looking distinctly queasy. Blood is even brimming over the sides of the abdominal incision. There has been an urgent call over the intercom for Alex Mather, but so far there's no sign of him. Clare has got large sponges inside the cavity but they aren't soaking up the blood fast enough. She pulls them out and throws them into the bucket by the table. All the while the anaesthetist is furiously hand-pumping transfusions into the patient. She is looking into the heart of a torrential flood.

When Mather comes in, prepped, his eyes goggle above the face mask when he sees the mess. 'Ruptured spleen –?'

Clare is frantically searching for the source of the bleeding. 'I don't know.' Could it be the liver – a liver tumour? Groping wrist-deep in the blood, she blindly finds the porta hepatis and squeezes off the blood supply to the liver. It makes no difference.

'Blood pressure 50,' says the anaesthetist.

There is barely time, but a thought does insinuate itself: *This is the moment I have been dreading.*

To find the source of the problem, Clare must staunch the flow of blood. She presses the aorta shut – closing off the entire abdominal blood supply – and after the suction has cleared the blood she can now see that the bleeding is coming from an area near the entrance to the spleen. She stops the localised bleeding by packing the area with large sponges.

'I've seen something like this before,' mutters Clare. Once before, in San Francisco, but she was an observer then. 'Put your hand here, on the aorta.'

Mather leans forward, frowning. 'What is it?'

'I think the spleen's ruptured near its hilum –'

'BP dropping.'

'Put in more blood.'

Clare glances at Mather. 'I'm going to lift the spleen, bring it up to have a look at it – I want you to cut it –'

He nods, and picks up the long scissors. Clare slides in her left hand, draws the spleen forward and downward, and Mather makes the incision.

'She's needing hardly any anaesthetic . . . oh hell, BP zero. We're losing her –'

Then it becomes clear that the bleeding is not out of the spleen itself but from a place in its feeding artery. Clare has only read about what she is looking at now.

'Oh shit.'

The anaesthetist interrupts: 'Lost the pulse.'

'What the –?' Mather's lips are puckered.

'Cardiac arrest –'

She and Mather are both looking down at a gaping hole in the artery; the deluge has slowed now to a trickle. 'Aneurysm of the splenic artery,' sighs Clare, putting a soft arterial clamp on it. Blood had been pumping into the abdominal cavity with every beat of the woman's heart.

It takes only a moment to put a stitch into the damaged part of the artery, tie it tightly, and the bleeding stops. Mather takes his hand off the aorta. The field is dry. The anaesthetist is looking at Clare with wide eyes.

'Keep going, for God's sake,' she snaps. 'Resuscitate the patient –'

They labour on for another twenty minutes, Clare refusing to give up, but it is over. The woman has literally bled to death. Mather lightly punches her bicep on his way out. 'Bad luck,' he mutters.

The charge nurse is at her elbow. 'The partner's waiting outside.' Is it blame Clare detects in her eyes, or sympathy?

'Why wasn't this patient brought in earlier?' Even ten minutes would have made an enormous difference. But nobody knows.

Clare turns away to discover Tupulo and the other two house surgeons standing about – they had obviously slipped in to watch. Tupulo's face is blanched. Clare gives him a look as she brushes past him: *This is real life, mate.*

'Mr Willow?'

He is sitting in the waiting area with shoulders rounded and arms lightly folded in front of his belly, as if he has a broken rib, or she had already told him the news. His hair is wispy grey, with traces of orange. The bottoms of his trousers are frayed. She sits on the chair next to him and clasps her hands together: the supplicant and the guilty party. Would a trace of all that blood somehow betray her? She even risks a glance at her shoes. Thank Christ there is no window onto the operating room; she couldn't perform if it wasn't a sanctuary. So much for the drama of theatre, she thinks bitterly.

'Mr Willow,' she says, 'your wife was in a very bad way when she arrived.' How to explain, to put it into lay terms, the abdominal cavity brimming with blood . . . 'I'm very sorry. It all happened very quickly –' Would it ever be possible, to save all the innocent people?

He looks up, skin the colour of putty, his washed-out eyes blinking once, then fixing on Clare blankly. 'It was only a matter of time,' he mutters, 'before the luck catches up with you.'

She has no idea what he is talking about, and is reluctant to pursue it. She catches herself thinking that he is like a harbinger – though, if pressed, she would have no idea of what; and feels immediately guilty about thinking such a thing at this moment, when she ought to be completely focused on sympathy.

Clare ploughs on. 'Mr Willow, can you tell me about the events leading up to your wife's arrival at the hospital? She must have been feeling noticeably unwell for some time . . .'

He looks at the floor. His hands, linked together, are venous and dry.

'I wasn't there.'

'But surely she must've said something? There must have been warning signs.'

'Not that I'm aware of.' Mr Willow gets up without any explanation and starts to walk away.

'But, Mr Willow –?' She runs after him. 'But, you'll want to know what happened.'

Willow barely pauses. 'On the contrary, I don't –'

Clare is left standing in the middle of the draughty corridor feeling cheated. She was just about to launch into a layman's account of what happened: 'Haemorrhaging from a site near the spleen.' Everybody wants explanations – what went wrong, a catalogue of details – except, apparently, Mr Willow.

Shit.

He's obviously in shock. She will have to try ringing him later.

Clare doesn't know what to do next, so she goes back to the fracture clinic – which is what she was doing before the emergency, and what else can she do? – to whatever patients are still waiting there. But it isn't long before Robeson calls her to his office.

'You are a first-rate surgeon, Clare, but you do understand that this is just a small community hospital, don't you?'

'Yes.'

'Then why wasn't Mrs Willow stabilised and transferred to Waikato?'

Clare frowns. This is a conversation that seems vastly irrelevant. 'Mrs Willow arrived at the emergency room with hardly any blood pressure and a pulse rate that was almost twice the norm. Her abdomen was bloated. The management decision was entirely clear-cut – she needed immediate surgery. There was no time to stabilise and transfer her *anywhere*.'

'But you didn't know what was happening. The team at Waikato would have identified the problem immediately.'

'They certainly wouldn't have done that, unless they were psychic. And besides, the woman would have been dead by the time she arrived.' What Clare would really like to know is how Mrs Willow managed to get into such bad shape before an ambulance was even called.

Robeson turns to the window, unappeased, while Clare, equally dissatisfied, slips away.

That night Clare has her other recurrent dream. She has been cast adrift in a wooden dinghy. In this version of the dream there is sand instead of water – miles of it, as far as her eye can see – but it's not static, there is a swell, the sand mimicking the movement of water while retaining none of its other properties. Her anxiety is somehow to keep the sand out of the dinghy: to stop herself from sinking.

The dream is terrifying, and waking into darkness, she has to get up and make herself a cup of tea. She gets down the antique teapot that Louise gave her for her birthday, but she is shaking so badly that it slips out of her hands and drops onto the lino. The spout breaks off with a crack.

October 1983
Terry and I discovered a French school, locked up and abandoned. Among the rubble there were rose bushes, valiantly flowering. I put a white rose behind my ear. Ooh la la, said Terry.

They didn't realise that Bethie hadn't been eating properly until she started again. Terry came to stay for a weekend and the two of them ate everything in sight. On the Sunday there was to be a picnic, and Mrs Kray had taken over the kitchen. She spent the morning roasting chicken legs, making potato salad and coleslaw, and putting things in whatever small plastic containers she could find. She had even brought along her own Tupperware. 'And it's just as well,' she said to Lou, who was watching from the end of the bench, coolly angular, 'because I must say your kitchen is not adequately equipped for picnics.' Lou was watching every move Mrs Kray made: her scissor-like bending into the oven to retrieve the drumsticks, her finicky long-fingered method of slicing cabbage, the way she shook her head at the weather beyond the window, lichen hair twitching. It was a familiar scene.

Bethie, her hair all blown about, came in from the garage, followed by Terry, and looked at Lou. Bethie wrenched off her tracksuit top. She and Terry had been jogging — for miles, by the look of them.

'Lou, I want to talk to you, in private,' she said. Mrs Kray pretended not to have noticed anything.

Clare was already waiting in Bethie's room, over by the window and fiddling with the hanging model of the planets. 'This model's all wrong,' she muttered. 'Pluto is where Jupiter is supposed to be, and vice versa.' Nobody took any notice. One day soon Clare would be taking her meagre suitcases — packed and waiting in the cupboard — and getting on the bus to Auckland. Disconcertingly, she seemed to have become invisible, as if she had already gone.

Terry flopped onto the bed and put her hands behind her head, while Lou perched on the edge of the stool and started sucking a piece of her hair.

'I've got an announcement to make,' said Bethie. 'I'm going to Afghanistan with Terry, to work for the Red Cross.'

Clare left the planets alone. The house seemed to have gone very quiet.

Lou looked aghast. 'Where?'

'I've already told Dad, last night, and he's cool.'

So that was what the raised voices were about, thought Clare; they had woken her at midnight, and her first thought was that their mother had come back. What kind of a gap would Bethie leave behind, she wondered. What kind of a gap would she herself leave? (Perhaps only a dent in the bed.) And would it be easier or harder than losing a mother?

'How long will you be gone?'

'I don't know. As long as it takes, I guess.' She looked at Terry, who was nodding. Louise looked at Terry as well, with pale-faced loathing: the interloper in their midst.

'Is that it?' asked Clare. Lou was already heading for the door, lips tight.

'By the way, Lou,' said Bethie, as she brushed past, 'I wouldn't get too attached to the old Kray if I were you –'

That brought Lou to a stop. 'Why not?'

Bethie shrugged, to make it look like nothing. 'You just don't know how long she'll be around, that's all.'

'I'll bet she'll be around for longer than you're going to be!' She slammed out of the room, crying and narrowly avoiding Mrs Kray who was doing up her shoelace in the hallway.

So it was left to their father to convince Bethie not to go to Afghanistan. He had to get a little drunk to do this, for on the one hand he believed in personal choice and in taking the hard options – he'd done it himself – but this was his daughter and she was only twenty and it was such a long way to go – and for what? Some bloody lost cause – and she could still have a brilliant sporting career ahead of her if she just put her mind to it.

The television was going, though neither of them was watching it. Mrs Kray was supposed to have come over but he had put her off. Bethie was lying lengthwise on the couch, facing away from him; Marty sat in his armchair, still in his paint-spattered dungarees with his legs under the pine coffee table. He tilted his glass to one side, and the golden liquid tipped, wave-like and precarious, nearly reaching the lip; then he righted the glass and angled it the other way. Finally, he took a deep breath.

'I don't want you going.'

Silence. Bethie was well known for her stubbornness.

'It's not right,' he said. 'The ACC didn't give you all that money so you could rush off overseas on some hairbrained scheme. You were going to use it for your cycling.'

Bethie was concentrating on the screen. 'I changed my mind about the cycling ages ago, way before this.'

Clare, sprawled full-length along the hall carpet with her face against the bottom of the closed hall door, dust getting up her nose, could barely hear the exchange and she wished they'd mute the television.

'Fer Christsake, Bethie –'

It didn't help that Marty remembered his own father's admonition when he announced he was off to Vietnam: *For Christsake man you've got a young family to look after, they don't need you over there.* How things came around, inexorably, and in a way that you hardly expected. He had to have another go. 'And Terry, her parents won't want her going over there. Neither of you have thought this thing through. Let her go, if she's got to –'

Marty stared morosely at the moon of whisky captured in his glass. 'There was a time, when you were little, when you'd run and run, just for the sake of it, away down the street – your mother, she'd have to run out after you, catch up with you, catch you by your clothes just to stop you. Wilful. Always were.' He lifted the glass to his lips, paused as if about to change his mind, then closed his eyes and swallowed a large mouthful. 'Still are,' he added. 'But for God's sake, this is different. There's a war going on over there. You haven't any idea what you're letting yourself in for, love.' And he looked at her finally, from beneath bushy eyebrows.

Bethie blushed under this onslaught, but was nevertheless firm. 'And you did? Going to Vietnam?'

Marty looked at his stockinged feet. 'That was different.' Or was it? He had gone over there on a whim: there was an ad in the paper calling for short-term service engagements. It was as simple as that.

'Oh?' The word was a small tight balloon suspended in the air between them.

'Look –' he was trying very hard to be patient – 'you don't have to go, nobody's holding a gun to your head. What's the big attraction, anyway, with this place?'

There was a long pause. Then Bethie said something that Clare had to strain seriously to hear. 'I don't know.' She was struggling to explain. 'It's just . . . something I have to do.'

He ought to have fought it, except that of the three of them she was his daughter – in looks, in thought – and he couldn't have given a decent reason himself for going to Vietnam that time, except that he had to do it, and he thought that he was the better man for it. Though, obviously, not hard enough – not hard enough to assert himself in the here and now.

Then Bethie must have got up and walked across the room, because the hall door opened and she stepped deftly over Clare as if her sister always rested in that exact position on the hall floor, with hands folded across her chest. Bethie went into the bathroom and shut the door.

'Aw, Jeez,' muttered their father, refilling his glass. 'Jesus . . . Christ.'

Their father came back from Vietnam in 1968 determined to put the experience behind him. Don't wear your uniform on the street, they told him, though they said nothing about the protests and anti-war sentiment: why should he want to, anyway? At Whenuapai he changed into clothes Pat had brought with her, and left the uniform behind on a chair. He'd taken up house painting. It was easy, stirring up the cans of viscous paint, being outside on a ladder or scaffolding, giving old woodwork a fresh appearance; easier than thinking about things that had happened, men who had been killed. It was easier to put it behind him.

That summer Pat was pregnant with Louise and they took a camping trip, the four of them, to a southern lake. He spent the days walking round the shore, leaving his footprints in the anaemic gritty sands, or staggering through muggy bush. And there was the swimming. You could swim out deep, then dive beneath the cool waters and enter a dim opaque world, a netherworld, with its own distinct kind of silence, as if nothing else could exist (not even family). There was in fact only yourself, making movements through the water, the sound of your heart banging away in your ears, reminding you that you were well and truly alive. It was a little odd, but it wouldn't last for ever, and there was no one to see and call you a drongo, so – so what?

And then there was the day when they watched the marathon runners go by up on the winding road. Pat, with Clare dangling from one hand, found it amusing, and was grinning at the men in their skimpy shorts. But he found the sight of the runners disturbing. It reminded him of drill and men in training for war. He was turning away, going to go back to the chalet, when Pat suddenly said, 'Where's Bethie?' Five years old, and a child who was constantly ducking off. Pat could barely keep track of the kid.

'Marty,' she shrieked, pointing.

Bethie was far along the road, running along beside a thin, brick-coloured man in a blue tanktop. *Jeez*. Marty took off, running along too, keeping a steady pace and passing the runners who turned red faces to see what was happening. He caught her by the shoulder, and pulled her over to one side. A little kid in pigtails and seersucker shorts.

'Wait on, Bethie –' He had to bend over her, jagged breath catching in his throat, while feet continued pounding past. 'Where're you going, love?'

Her eyes were ingenuously blue. 'I'm just running, Dad.' She turned to see where her companion had got to, as if she would run off again, despite her tiny panting chest. 'Running the race.'

'Jeez girl, wait a few years, eh –'

He hoisted her onto his shoulders, and they walked back, against the stream of people, with Bethie's fingers tangled in his hair, hanging on as if to a horse's mane.

Six-thirty a.m. and her first cup of coffee. Clare hasn't slept well, but spent the night going over and over Mrs Willow's operation. Could she have done something more – anything? It had been up to her to save Mrs Willow, and she had failed. In the worst possible way. She would like to talk to Tupulo about it, but he went to Waikato yesterday with Mather.

She turns on CNN to discover a report about the latest fighting in Afghanistan. The fundamentalist Taliban party, based in Kabul, have been bombed by the Americans; foreign journalists are not allowed in – although one has obviously slipped in to film for CNN. There is footage of some boys searching along a dusty street for firewood, and then kids in a hospital with bandaged limbs from having stepped on landmines. She turns off the television.

Clare finds it hard to understand a country that goes from one war, one extreme, into another. It's as if they're not really living unless their country is in a constant state of flux, which is also a contradiction. She wonders about the aid workers and whether they will have to evacuate. Clare has a vested interest: she gives money to the International Red Cross, specifically for their work in Afghanistan. During an interview on CNN with Queen Noor, Larry King thought that it was difficult to define 'peace', that peace meant different things to different people. But surely, thinks Clare – lacing up her Nikes – peace simply means the absence of war.

She puts on a load of washing and sets off for a jog, noticing on her way out that the lawn is verging on meadow. She must ring that boy, is aware that she has been putting it off. She jogs down the concrete, leaf-varnished steps of Jacob's Ladder, then heads towards the river. There is a glow about the tops – the sun just making itself known above the lumpy hills. Then she goes up the hill and turns into a leafy avenue, the town cemetery high up to her right.

With the warmer weather, Tupulo has been threatening another trip to Auckland. Clare is hoping that he'll want to take a couple of buddies instead of her: there is digging she could do in the back garden. Clare has a yearning to do something simple and uncomplicated like digging, turning over dark earth, with no other consequence than perhaps dislodging the odd earthworm. And it would save the Marshall boy a job.

'Morning, Doctor Purefoy!'

A hand waves to her from across the street – Mr Smith, appendectomy – and she waves back, red-faced and puffing now. Just as well she's running and doesn't have to stop. The solid wooden houses flash past, as fast as they're ever going to get. Tupulo calls them 'old ladies' houses'. She jogs along her father's street, and turns right up a steeper road, from where she happens to spot the water tower far below. Even in the distance it seems ominous. She looks away quickly.

She heads back home, to shower and change. Some mornings Clare circumnavigates the entire town, and it takes her only twenty minutes.

Clare gets back to find the laundry and kitchen floors awash with grey, sudsy water. *Oh no.* She wades through the water to the laundry tub, which is overflowing, and plunges in her arm up to the elbow, pulling out Tupulo's Hawaiian shirt, balled-up.

Clare fetches the squeegie mop, and bucket. She remembers a day when their mother had left something in the laundry tub and the washing machine overflowed. She had simply opened the back door and it had flowed out, as mysteriously as a snake, the house being on a slight lean. Pat stood wiping her hands together. 'I always knew your father's poor building skills would be useful some day.'

Clare wades over to the back door and thinks, I must be practical. What would I normally do? She turns slightly – to look out at the heavy oaks, turning away from the water just as she would like to turn away from all responsibility – for she has just realised the distinction she has made. There is the idea of her old self, the one that fetched the mop and bucket from the broom cupboard in the laundry. And there is the contrasting reality: it is still herself – there are no foreign invaders – but she is vacillating on the doorstep of the house, and there is an urge deep within her gut simply to walk away. *Walk away from the problem, let somebody else deal with it.*

Mrs Kray arrives a few minutes later to discover Clare at the back door, her forehead leaning against the doorjamb and the kitchen floor flooded beyond her.

FOURTEEN

THERE *WAS* a time of innocence, when anything seemed possible, when there was a sense of safety in one's own youth. Like living in a permeable bubble. And Oliver, more than any of them, seemed to encapsulate that feeling.

Oliver said afterwards that it was Clare's idea, and Clare's alone – as if that could absolve him from calamity, though at some earlier stage he must have encouraged her – but they ended up by the estuary making a raft out of two empty oil drums and planks of wood that they had found on the beach. It looked like somebody else's washed-up effort. All they had to do was reassemble it, using a roll of twine fetched from the garage. The day was hot, though the sky was blanketed with cloud.

Clare was hunched over, mute in her concentration, stringing boards together with lengths of twine until her fingers turned pink. She'd abandoned her sandshoes for the moment and her toes were squelchy with mangrove mud. This ship, this vessel, would bear them – she and Oliver, her first boyfriend – away to a mythical land – not quite of unicorns, but perhaps a land of peaches and 'deliquescent quinces'. Stepping back, however, the effect was a little diminishing – more twine! She couldn't remember a time when she'd been so frivolous with something from home.

'What's that?' queried Oliver, catching her mutter. Clare straightened, pushed back vagrant hair from her happy, sweaty face, and left a smear of salty mud in exchange. It might have been awkward otherwise.

'I feel like a kid,' she said, 'when really, I should be putting aside childish things.'

'There's nothing wrong with that,' said Oliver, 'I'm a great believer in childish things.' He had a way of making almost anything seem natural. 'Besides, what else would we do?'

He had a point.

Not far away, Kopu Bridge loomed. Clare and Oliver were barely aware of the traffic leaving and entering the town, until a gang of kids on bikes went over. They stopped at one of the leeways on the old-fashioned bridge, poised with their bikes, and pointed. One of them yelled: '*Wankers!*' They biked on, their laughter slinging arrow-like into the torpid air.

Clare straightened. 'What did they say?'

'Porkers,' said Oliver, not meeting her eye. 'They were pointing at the pigs, way over there.'

'Oh,' she said, 'I didn't think they were talking to us.'

Clare extracted a raspberry bun (yesterday's bakery leftovers) from a brown paper bag, and handed it to Oliver. She pulled out one for herself, and contemplated it, standing leggy among the spiky roots of mangroves. There was a sound of frogs from the paddock behind them.

'Just think, this will probably be the last time I ever make a raft,' she said.

'You might make one with your children.'

'Children?' Clare considered the smear of pink icing. 'Children are much too far in the future to even think about.'

Oliver found that idea rather funny. 'Children,' he said, 'whether you like them or not, are always in the future.'

'I don't really think they're in mine.'

'But Clare, you can't possibly know that.'

She could offer no response to his enthusiasm.

Incredibly enough the raft not only floated, but held the both of them as well. Clare shrieked as they bobbed away from the bank, paddling with the oars from Oliver's auntie's house – one each. 'If I lose these,' shouted Oliver, though he needn't have: it was quiet on the water, 'I'll be in deep shit.'

The waters of the estuary, although muddy (and who knows what might be lurking), were broad enough to give an impression of adventure.

'We're on the Amazon!' shouted Oliver.

Clare, grinning, was too delighted even to speak. She couldn't believe she was sailing along, now going beneath the bridge, which suddenly roared as a truck passed overhead, and heading towards the seas of the firth. The land on either side seemed more interesting, not as flat as it did from the road, and the sky was a huge white pudding bowl above their heads. Clare dipped her paddle in the water; and, with Oliver kneeling beside her, they gained a perfect rhythm. I'm so happy, she thought, I could burst. If there were music playing it would be 'L'Apres-Midi d'un Faun'.

'We are explorers, travelling into the heart of darkness!'

'No, not the darkness,' cried Clare. 'We are sailing to the island of our outlawed dreams.'

Oliver looked at her in surprise — that sharp-nosed profile, but softened now by the light, and gleaming with sweat; blonde-streaked hair slashing across her mouth — and was nearly blinded by the light flashing off the chopping waters. Or was it —? Beyond Clare's head Oliver caught a glimpse of a body lying on the far grassy banks of the estuary: a black and white cow, hoofs in the air.

It was the sight of the cow that he later claimed caused him to lose his balance — but with Oliver's sudden shift, the precarious balance of the raft itself shifted, and they were both tumbled into the water. All he could think of was the dead cow, and it took a moment to realise that he had cramp in his legs.

'Help —' gasped Oliver, before his mouth sank below the surface of the water.

Clare, her legs struggling with long pants and sandshoes, grabbed Oliver's hair. He came up spluttering. She deftly flicked him onto his back — he was remarkably light and pliable — and wedging her hand beneath his chin, kicking and struggling against the current, she grabbed onto the raft. Neither of them had ever considered the possibility of calamity! It didn't help that Oliver was coughing and crying at the same time.

'Shut up,' she said through gritted teeth, 'I have to concentrate.'

Eventually Clare got the raft over to the bank, and she half carried, half dragged him out, sloshing through the mud. And thank God she'd put her sandshoes back on earlier; she hated now the thought of bare feet sinking into all that smelly mud and whatever might be sunk within it. Then she was dragging Oliver through reeds. They collapsed onto grass, gasping. Clare, on her back, felt her lungs would burst, and there were bright spots in the sky.

At last Oliver turned bloodshot eyes to her. 'Clare,' he whispered, 'you saved my life.'

She hadn't even started her career in medicine, and here she was saving people. Her pants were very uncomfortable, and there was some mud in her shoes; altogether she felt rather pragmatic. 'Yes,' she said, with a sigh, 'and I think you can buy me a thickshake when we get back.'

'Clare, will you marry me?'

But the thought of constantly rescuing Oliver from misfortune wasn't very appealing.

That summer it got so hot and they were all lying about feeling so bored that they decided to drive out to the Kauaeranga Valley. Mrs Kray's minivan was pressed into service, and there was Oliver too, looking rather pink after too much biking around the town with Clare. Clare's hair had lightened to the colour of hay, giving her an insubstantial look, as if she might blow away at any minute.

'Clare's in *lurv*,' teased Lou, and got chased out of the house for her trouble.

Once in the valley, Mrs Kray parked on a gravel layby, and they walked through bush that smelt like a longdrop to find the river. It was such a contrast, between dim shadowy bush and coming out onto the high bank that overlooked the river glittering with light, that it was something of a shock – though a pleasurable one: a haven found, a destination achieved. They got down, with much scrabbling and sliding on damp clay and hanging onto exposed roots, and slithered over piles of smooth grey rocks.

There was the gushing river – which they had to wade across, stepping from stone to stone. Clare slipped halfway on a slimy green stone and banged her knee. Then they reached the bend in the river, where the water rested, deceptively calm: a deep jade pool. A rock cliff faced the pool, straggly with ferns.

'You couldn't find a more peaceful spot,' said Mrs Kray, promptly turning on her transistor radio to the talkback show, 'while the sun's out, that is.' Disaster was lurking, never far away. The talkback was chewing over the gun debate: a man had shot his wife, then turned the gun on himself.

Mrs Kray spread out all kinds of food on the rug, fanning it out as if to tempt in wild creatures: she opened Tupperware containers to reveal boiled eggs, chicken wings, potato salad, small whole beetroots 'from my garden'. Their father lay on his own rug, propped up on an elbow, and opened a can of beer, foam escaping onto the lid.

Clare and Bethie and Oliver, already wearing their togs, leapt into icy water. Lou, sixteen years old, stood whining at the water's edge: 'Why's it so coold?' It was Oliver who came back to explain, standing knee-deep in the dark water and goose-pimpling.

'It's come down out of the mountains,' he said, pointing back over Lou's head to the brooding bushclad peaks. 'It makes no difference whether it's summer or not. Though I suppose,' he added, 'it *ought* to be warmer in summer.'

It was Bethie who solved the situation by hoisting Louise over her shoulder in a fireman's lift and calmly walking into the water, then dropping her.

'You – you –' she came up screaming, 'you – *bitch!*'

'Really, Lou: language,' muttered Mrs Kray, not very convincingly (and nobody noticed anyway).

'Look out for the eels,' cried Bethie, diving into deep water, her slick body turning azure, a graceful arrow beneath the surface, and bursting up for air. 'Grandaddy eels,' she screamed, then fell back laughing. Clare, stranded in the shallows, waited until Beth swam back towards the shore, then leaned on her midriff, pushing her under. Lou giggled in the shallows, glad that she hadn't gone out deep, for after all, there might be some truth in Bethie's teasing, *That crazy Bethie*. Oliver, having swum past the girls and reached the far side, tried to lead the way up the rock face, but Bethie caught him first and dragged him back into the water. She got up the rock, all legs and bum, then hung triumphantly, eyes glittering, above the dark, dark water while Oliver's head bobbed below like a ball.

'Look out, I'm gonna jump –'

'Do you think that's a good idea,' wondered their father, frowning.

Mrs Kray looked over her sunglasses. 'When I was a girl, we were always doing things like that . . .' Her voice dropped to wistful. 'Madcap adventures. The worst they can do is kill themselves.'

There was an enormous splash. Bethie came up screaming.

'What? What?' Clare was dog-paddling towards her.

Bethie's face a picture. 'My bikini top came off,' she cried.

Everybody laughed, though Oliver turned away, blushing to the roots of his rust-coloured hair, and then clambering up the rock face after all. They took turns, and even Lou, unable to bear the weight of being left out, gathered up her tousled hair under a bathing cap, and swam over to cling to the rock like a stick insect. 'From now on,' she muttered, 'I am only going to swim in proper swimming pools. Nice pools, with changing sheds where you can hang your towel, and where you can swim up and down in tidy lanes, with none of those pimply boys like at the Municipal who are always bombing you –'

Lou, finally balanced on a ledge of rock, put out her arms and executed a charming butterfly dive.

Only she didn't come up.

Their father stood up, shading his eyes with his hand. They were all thinking the same thing. Oliver and Bethie started diving under, looking. The water was that dark, you could hardly see, and the deeper you went the blacker it got. Oliver would dive, but he might see Lou only if she was a metre or so within range. Their father started to peel off his shirt. The day had slowed to a horribly dull heartbeat.

Then Bethie screamed. They all jumped. Lou's head had popped up beside her, bursting for air, the plastic cap awry. '*Gotcha*,' she squealed, already swimming for the pebbly beach.

Bethie fell back, breathing hard. 'You – child, you,' she laughed. 'I s'pose I deserved that.' Always the good loser. But (fair's fair) Beth would get her back later, when Lou was least expecting it.

Now even Mrs Kray was going to go in. Standing up with her swimming things, she walked off behind some twiggy bushes. Bethie and Clare swapped a look, and furtively followed, two large girls dripping onto sizzling stones. Their father might have warned Mrs Kray, except he liked a bit of a joke himself: she could take it.

Between a mat of leaves and twigs – it took a bit of focusing and jiggling to get the right angle – they spied pendulous white breasts. 'Oh my God,' hissed Bethie, slapping a hand over her mouth.

Mrs Kray's head popped up as she straightened herself with dignity. '*Excuse me.*' Her falsetto rang right across to the water where Oliver was floating like a lilo. 'But this is a private bush!'

They ran back over stones, giggling and clutching each other, and threw themselves into the water, belly-flopping. Lou breaststroked through the water towards them.

'What did you see?'

'The breasts of Mrs Kray,' said Clare solemnly.

Lou's eyes widened. 'Oh my God,' she murmured, 'how disgusting.'

Mrs Kray emerged at that moment from her bush, in complete water regalia. There was a one-piece cotton swimsuit that dated back to the fifties, blue roses on a yellow ground, complete with hip frill. On her head she wore a white plastic cap with yellow daisies. Mrs Kray tiptoed down to the water's edge, pale legs gleaming. 'Now, I don't want anybody thinking they can splash me,' she admonished, touching her big toe to the water, 'cause you can't. It is strictly forbidden. And also,' she added, submerging herself to the ankle, 'it's my van so I shall just leave you out here for the night.'

'Yeah, right,' muttered Bethie, and then to the others: 'Get ready . . . one, two three – *YAHHHHHH* –'

Mrs Kray was beset by four kids yelling and splashing her, until – standing in the same spot and hands unsuccessfully warding away water from her carefully made-up face – she ended up completely soaked. It must be said that she took it very well. 'Well,' she exclaimed, 'now that I am officially wet, I think I shall have a little dip, thank you, thank you so much.' And giving a bow, she entered the water, swimming two large circles like a ferret in a spa pool. It was just so funny that if they hadn't got out they would've drowned from laughing.

When Mrs Kray emerged, trudging up the stones between the prone, puffing bodies, she shook her arms over them, sending drips onto drying faces. 'At least you couldn't get my hair wet, you big monsters.' And she pulled off the daisy cap, hair springing back into place as if nothing had happened.

'Time for nosh,' said Mrs Kray, gleaming.

Oliver cried easily. 'It's a genetic weakness,' he murmured apologetically.

He cried when Clare brought him a pink cake after her shift at the bakery, because nobody had ever given him a cake, he said. Surely his mother, wondered Clare, but also testing, like putting your foot where you think there might be sucking mud. Oh yes, his mother had always brought home cakes (Clare sighed: Of course) ... but never like this, said Oliver sincerely. They spent hours just walking around, holding hands; he liked to nibble her ear lobes, nuzzle into the pale of her neck. Even Lou was driven to exasperation: 'How disgusting!' They lay on grass beneath the ginkgo tree in the park, leaves aflap, kissing, his mouth as soft as icing sugar, as sweet; and Clare thought the summer looked set to last for ever, green leaves reflected in Oliver's brown eyes.

Then the Swedish tourists disappeared.

Oliver knocked at the door, distraught, blinking rapidly, his thick ginger eyelashes damp. Their father let him in suspiciously. 'You've a visitor –' he called into the recesses of the house so Clare would come and rescue him from having to talk to a boy who had so obviously been crying.

'What's the matter with him?' he asked later that night at dinner.

'Nothing,' muttered Clare. 'He'd got a bee sting behind his ear, that's all. While he was on his bike. His eyes were watering in pain.' She was embarrassed, covering for him, but couldn't admit that Oliver was a boy who cried at the drop of a hat. Although she was also surprised at her own inventiveness. *This must be love.*

'Bee sting,' intoned their father, slicing into a piece of fried liver.

Clare took him to her bedroom, glancing sideways at the pink candlewick cover and the poster of Einstein, but Oliver didn't seem to notice. He had to be held, he said; so they lay on the bed and he burrowed his head into her armpit. She bit her lip so as not to laugh. 'I get so scared,' he said, 'hearing things like that happen. All I ever wanted was to make the world a kinder place. Then something like this happens. They were just two young people, like you and me, and now they're dead –'

'We don't know that,' said Clare, not knowing what words might comfort him, and not understanding why he should be so upset. What had it to do with Oliver?

It was true that the town was in shock: for such a thing to have happened on our very own doorstep! Police were scouring the bush, and the hills themselves seemed defiled. People were locking their doors at night, and their father had started taking Louise to school in the mornings. Every night the couple's bright faces looked out from the six o'clock news.

'I'm quitting social work,' said Oliver. 'I can't keep on doing it. I can't believe in it, not after this – I would be living a sham.'

Clare drew back from his embrace to look at him: you didn't just give up like that. It went against everything she had ever known. 'But you can't *quit*. You're in the middle of your course.' They could have been strangers. He could have been anybody.

'Course I can quit. I can do what I like. I'm going to switch to engineering, like Sid. It won't be so upsetting.' He pulled his chin down coyly. 'You won't ever leave me, will you, Clare?'

She felt a jolt of happiness. He relied on her: the future could be secure, after all. 'Course I won't,' she said firmly. Yet, less admissibly, there was also an opposing jolt of anxiety, to do with the possibility of entrapment – and just when she was about to break free.

An hour later when Bethie opened the door of Clare's room to borrow a stapler she found them huddled together, fast asleep. Beth shook her head.

'Babes,' she muttered, and hoped that Clare knew what she was doing.

But how secure is the present? Mr Willow is becoming something of a problem. Security – such as it is – has informed Reception, who has informed nursing staff, who has passed on a message to Dr Purefoy. For there he is again, hanging about at the front of the hospital in a brown cardigan and baggy pants, a sorry figure but one not entirely out of keeping with the dilapidated appearance of the hospital itself. He could even be the hospital mascot, if there were such a thing. His role has in fact barely altered from when he was an anxious husband, except that Mrs Willow has now been buried for several days and that ought to be an end to the matter. Clare finds his public grieving a little obscene.

She goes down the steps to talk to him, hands jammed into the pockets of her white coat (and fiddling with a chocolate wrapper she finds in there), and remembers with a stab of guilt that she has forgotten to call him.

'Is there anything I can do for you, Mr Willow?'

He looks up at the sky as if she hasn't spoken, or as if a breeze has bothered him. His eyes are no less the tone of a pale shirt that has been washed with something blue, but there is a stubborn quality now, and the stark redness around them tells Clare that he hasn't been sleeping. That makes two of them.

'Why don't you come in, Mr Willow, come in and have a chat, inside where I can get you a cup of tea, or something –?'

Clare glances round for help. She'd like to get the counsellor out here to handle this – her domain is the physical, not this. Clare would dearly like to put the incident behind her, but every time she sees Mr Willow she can't help but see all that welling blood again.

A bird falls through the sky. It catches a flying insect in its beak, and quickly rights itself.

'Come inside,' she says gently, taking Mr Willow's elbow.

He shakes her off – he is shaking, she notices.

'There comes a time when one must be held Accountable –' He has a biblical way of speaking, unnerving when it is underpinned by such fury, and Clare takes a step back from him. 'There comes a time,' he reiterates, 'for Accountability.'

Jesus. Such depth of grief. She is reminded of the days after their mother's departure with the Accountant. She had thought she was going to die. Is this how Mr Willow feels?

He leans towards her, aiming his nose at her pale unsullied neck. 'We were planning a trip,' he hisses, his breath hot and harsh against her skin, 'it was to be the trip of a Lifetime – a trip, to *California* –'

Clare blinks, surprised. It seems such a contradiction. Surely somewhere like the Caribbean would've been more appropriate?

'We had even bought the tickets,' Mr Willow says, 'the *tickets*, for Christsake –'

He sobs then, and can't help himself from clutching at Clare's shoulder.

This, at least, is something practical she can deal with. She gets her arm around his waist, and bundles him up the concrete steps, away from the unrelenting sky and into the hospital foyer.

As she hands him over to Sheila, Mr Willow throws pebbled words back over his shoulder: 'I know that there is a life after this one, and I certainly hope that we shall all meet up there – on the Other Side.' This accompanied by the statement of Sheila's thinly plucked, raised eyebrows.

FIFTEEN

IF SOMEBODY were to ask Louise, if, at thirty-four years of age, she has figured out the meaning of life, she would categorically say that she had.

'I have sold my soul to chaos,' Lou states cheerfully. She strikes a provocative pose with her cigarette, and looks like a magazine model.

She and Bob are sitting at an outside table at the Loaded Hog, among other sun-soaked tables of people glittering with expensive hairstyles. Louise has her knee pressed against Bob's right leg, and the bottle of chardonnay is finished.

'Really, Louise?' Bob is basking: in the sun, in not being at work, in having Louise's physical attentions on his somewhat robust person. 'Tell me more about this chaos theory of yours –'

Bob is a downtown psychologist whom Louise met through a dating agency, Dinner for Six, where strangers sit down to a meal together, swapping places with each course to get to know each other. Bob, admits Lou, was a lucky score.

Louise makes a brief pretence at cognitive thought – she is, after all, just winging it as usual, spinning the bull, shooting the breeze. 'It's like this, Bob –' and cigarette smoke dawdles about her ash-blonde hair then rises with nude ease into the still air. 'Look around you. Everybody thinks they're untouchable – that nothing bad can touch them – but all you've gotta do is turn on the box and you're faced with all this shit happening. The Yanks have got it to a tee: shit happens, they say, and it's the truth – but look around and you'll see that people don't really accept that, they think they're going to live happy ever after and win Lotto next week. Well I tell you it's all a load of bullshit. As soon as you accept that the world is falling to pieces, that we are surrounded by dark shifting forces, then everything clicks into place –'

The waiter approaches, but Bob shakes his head, and he recedes as easily as a shallow wave.

They go back to Bob's waterfront apartment, and Lou again admires the view over the port, with the boats and the ferries going backwards and forwards right out there on your doorstep. Bob doesn't bother with any preliminaries, but gets his cock into Louise before she changes her mind.

'Tell me again,' he breathes into her ear, 'about your theory –'

'To hell with that,' says Louise, pressed against the cushions of the Navajo-inspired couch, 'you should know, you're the fucking shrink.'

'How true,' he pants, 'how . . . *succinct*.'

Later, when they've rearranged their clothes, Bob makes a pot of coffee. Lou, on her way out, leaves one of her business cards on the table by the door. You never know, he might want to sell this place one day. It has been a successful lunch.

Not long afterwards, Clare and Tupulo take a weekend shopping expedition to Auckland. Tupulo wants to buy a pair of purple silk pyjamas; Clare thinks she might get an electric blanket. There is one folded away in the Brightlys' linen cupboard, but she doesn't know how safe it would be to use.

Clare meets Lou for lunch in High Street. After exhausting their usual topics of conversation – Lou's men, Clare's work, property values, and Tupulo – the talk comes round to Bethie.

'What I could never understand,' says Lou, 'is how Beth could waste all that money on what must have been a very uncomfortable trip – all that dust and heat and riding about on camels –'

'There weren't any camels.'

'And for what?' continues Louise. 'What was the point of it? She didn't even bring back any snaps.'

Louise's last overseas journey was to Club Med in Bali, where she spent her time lying on the beach, honing her windsurfing skills, jetskiing, and chatting up men in the bar each night. Bethie's trip to Afghanistan has to her remained one of life's mysteries.

'I can understand philanthropy, to a point –' donating to charity, for instance, was good for the image – 'but living over there?' Her nose crinkles in disgust. 'And another thing, do you think she was gay?'

Clare sits fiddling with her napkin. She considers the question in the light of Beth's diaries. 'I think they were simply very good friends. Terry was her safety net, in a way.'

'Safety net?' Oddly, Lou looks a little distressed.

Clare shrugs. 'Just guessing.'

'Well,' Lou decides, 'you'd know.' She throws down her napkin. 'Hey, gotta run.' She scrapes back her chair, eyes creasing into a smile for the attractive male waiter who is holding out the bill.

'I'll get that –' Clare protests as Lou extracts a credit card, but Lou's inner guilt prevails. She still intends to repay Clare that $4K – only, not yet. Just a shame she lost most of it on the roulette wheel.

Clare stands outside on the smelly pavement, with the racket of the city echoing in her head, sunlight flashing over office windowpanes. The Metropolis towers over the narrow street, its spire pointed bluntly at the sky. She thinks she would've liked to talk to Lou about Marcus – *You must think me a fool* – but (never mind) the moment has come and gone, and Clare chalks it up to family secrets.

Clare has just come back from work in time to see a small woman popping into the back seat of a red Morris Minor. A large man is squeezed behind the wheel, and he deftly manoeuvres the car out of the driveway, not noticing Clare as she emerges from the umbrous light of Jacob's Ladder. She doesn't think to wave: she doesn't know them. Tupulo stands on the doorstep, hands in jeans pockets.

'Who was that?'

'My parents –'

'Your what?'

Tupulo shrugs. 'Everybody has them – even me.'

'Why didn't they wait? I would've liked to have met them.'

He frowns thunderously. 'Oh, much too early for that, Clare, they'd only have expected us to get married, or something stupid like that, and you'll be going back to America soon, n'est ce pas?'

'I don't know.'

Tupulo turns and pads away into the house. She follows him to the lounge where it's obvious that he's sulking. She sits beside him on the couch and fiddles with a loose thread on the seat. 'I suppose you ought to know that, well, I was hurt in my last relationship . . .'

Tupulo turns to look at Clare with interest.

'This man I was seeing, it was pretty serious, or at least I thought it was – it's all rather sordid. I haven't told anybody here, but he turned out to be a psycho. He was poisoning people, for the fun of it.'

Tupulo, oddly, grins. 'Well, Clare.' He exhales largely, grabbing her to his chest. 'Then after that anything else will be a piece of cake.'

'Or custard square,' says Clare.

'There's hope for you yet.' He nuzzles into her hair. 'And next time I might even let you meet my olds, how's that?'

'Thanks a bundle.'

After dark there wasn't anywhere they could go except to their room, so when Beth went back to read her book she found Terry sitting on her own bed, smoking hashish. The pipe gurgled as she sucked on the mouthpiece, and Terry drew back her head, cradling the mouthful of smoke in the back of her throat. She looked up and grinned as Bethie went over to her own bed and sat with her back against the cool wall.

'Sorry,' said Terry, 'I'd smoke outside. Only Franco's being a pain.'

She put the pipe under the bed, and folded her hands lightly across her thin thighs. Beth found herself looking at Terry through a sea mist of smoke. In a country where you couldn't buy alcohol, hash was cheap enough and blocks of it could be openly bought from stalls in the bazaar. Up in the hills, she had heard, there were even fields of opium poppies, and there were heroin labs up in the Khyber.

She didn't mind Terry smoking, might smoke it herself if the stuff didn't make her feel ill. And there was the effect as well. 'I want to lose myself,' Terry had said recently. 'I want to float away for a while.' Bethie didn't like the thought of that, of emptying out inside. The idea of losing control frightened her.

An orange lizard, she noticed, was clinging to the wall near the ceiling above Terry's head.

'Back home,' said Terry, 'we'd spend all summer hols swimming in the water hole. Remember that water hole, up in the hills? Me and my brothers, we'd drive up there. I was just a kid, pigtails and Jansen swimsuit. There was a rock you could jump from. 'Member, Bethie? And all around, the bush was so green it hurt your eyes. My brothers, they used to all have motorbikes, ride on those trails through the bush. I'd ride on the back, pillion, on my oldest brother's bike. Wind in your face, green rushing past. I'd shut my eyes, and feel the wind hissing against my face and know that we were going real fast. It was great. Bumping over tree roots, into gullies and back out again; one time a tree branch hit Bruce in the chest and he nearly came off. Afterwards he pulled up his shirt and there was a big red mark, like someone had whipped him. Well, he had been, I s'pose, by the tree –'

She started to giggle, putting her head back, her eyes squeezed shut in memory. Then she was singing in a high-pitched voice, '*In my little town* . . .'

Beth couldn't stand it any longer. Putting her book down on the bed, she stood up. 'Jeez Terry, you're wasted. Come with me –' She grabbed her arm. Terry was so relaxed it took no effort at all to get her off the bed and out of the room.

'Hey Beth, curfew.'

'I don't care.'

The night air smelt of stone, and was cool on their faces. Guiding Terry firmly by the elbow, Beth walked them through the dark silent streets. Lights burned modestly behind curtains, yet it could have been a city of ghosts. She walked the usually familiar streets, not knowing exactly where she was going. Only that it was higher ground she wanted – to get up, above somehow, to achieve a sense of height.

A sky full of stars blazed above them. The stars seemed brighter in Afghanistan, as if they were closer to earth. *By the epoch, humanity is indeed at a loss, except those who have faith and do good works, and enjoin truth and justice upon one another and enjoin patience upon one another.* The fresh air seemed to sober Terry, so that she was able to walk by herself, though still with her bare arm touching Bethie's side.

They left the inhabited dwellings behind and soon reached a bombed stone building. They stood side by side and looked down into a grey bowl-like valley. Desolate and barren, it could have been a scene from the moon. In the far distance stars glittered above the jagged rim of black mountains, the Hindu Kush. Below, in a corner of the valley, the darkness was suddenly lit by flashes of red and white.

'Tracer missiles,' whispered Beth.

They were looking at the frontline of the fighting.

Terry's fingers, thin and cold, found Beth's. 'They're pretty at night.'

The sound of gunfire carried clearly across the stony valley.

'Don't you want to go home, Beth?' Terry's voice was small and low.

'No.'

'I do. I miss it, like anything. I miss all the green.' Terry took her hand back, folding her arms across her chest, shivering. 'I could go back, y'know.'

Bethie glanced at her. 'You could,' she said slowly. 'Are you going to?'

Terry inhaled evenly, then grinned. 'Nope.'

Beth felt able to breathe again, and grinned too. 'I've gotta admit, it is very green, back home.'

Their father never said anything, thinks Clare, but he must have approved of Bethie's journey.

She walks over to his house on a sun-washed Saturday morning to help him springclean before he leaves for Vietnam. Marty had served in Vietnam in an infantry company based at Nui Dat. He and fifteen others are going back for a reunion. Already he has been interviewed on the radio about the vets' forthcoming trip, and has admitted some anxiety about their return. He had had to be cajoled into it by his old mate Warren, the only one Marty had kept in touch with.

He and Clare take a tour of the garden first. He grows beans and tomatoes and potatoes in round beds edged with river stones – doesn't like the grave-like connotations of rectangular plots – and makes wooden toys to sell in the craft shop on mainstreet. 'This is the life,' he says at regular intervals. When he feels a bit tired he rings Clare and she sends Tupulo over to have a look at him. Tupulo checks his blood pressure, then they have a glass of beer. Tupulo leaves with a cheery wave and tells Clare's father that he will live till he's a hundred. Marty may not actually believe this – probably thinks Tupulo is humouring an old man – but Tupulo believes it. 'Your father,' he reports when he gets back home, 'is as fit as an ox.'

'Don't you mean as strong?'

'No, oxen are very fit. It's all those ploughs they're forced to pull. Even old oxen that have finished with the ploughing.' Perhaps it's Clare he is humouring.

'I want everything tip-top,' Marty has said several times this week, 'in case I don't come back.' He is onto this theme again. Clare is halfway up an aluminium ladder, scrubbing the side of the house. Marty has insisted on this; he has, to Clare's horror, already been up on the roof to hose it down. 'I may be retired,' he said, 'but I do still know what I'm doing.'

Clare pauses, the long-handled brush sending drips of water running down the inside of her arm and into her armpit (an unpleasant sensation).

'You have more chance of getting killed in a car accident than in an aeroplane,' she says, looking down at his freckled pate.

'I'm not worried about the *air*plane.' He considers the paint-spattered rungs of the ladder.

'Then what?'

'No, just in general.'

'You might be killed in general, you mean?'

'You know what I mean,' he huffed.

'No, I don't.'

'*You* know, I might have another heart attack, or step on an uncleared landmine or something, or a bomb might go off at the airport.' Another drip sails down into the recesses of Clare's armpit. 'Anyway, I'll just feel better if I leave everything in good shape.' Squinting over the weatherboards; unfortunately, there wasn't time to do any touching up. 'My will's with the lawyer.'

'Jeez, Dad.' She sneezes into the bucket.

'The house is freehold, it goes to you girls, I expect you'll get a good price for it when you sell. There's a few shares –'

'Dad,' says Clare, heading him off, 'how about a cuppa?'

They take their cups of tea out onto the back veranda. Clare has brought a Sally Lunn (the bakery has gone now, leaving no trace, but there is a modern version further along the street), and they eat chunks of it, bits of mushy coconut icing dropping off. Marty hands her his new passport to check, in case something vital has been left off: 'They might not let me through.'

'What's it going to be like,' she wonders, 'going back?'

'I don't know. It'll be good to catch up with some old mates. I had a couple of good Vietnamese friends, too.' He shrugs. 'If they're still there, in that same village. Might not be, you just don't know.' A rusty laugh. 'It'll be stinking hot. I'm taking that little camera you sent me last year – I'll bring back snapshots.'

Clare picks out a tealeaf from her cup. Her father is the only person she knows who still makes tea with leaves, in a pot. A blackbird hops among radishes, and the lawn is gleaming in the sun: short back and sides.

There is more clearing-up of loose ends. 'Clare –?'

'Yes?'

'There's something I've been wanting to tell you, about over there. Something I haven't told anyone. But I'd like to get it off my chest, you see, before I go.' It's no surprise that he has war secrets. The main characteristic of their father's war memories has till now been reticence. 'Only, I don't know if I can say it, out loud, like –'

'Take your time.'

Marty shifts irritably in his chair. 'Let's put it this way. I'm worried, now that I'm going back, that when I get over there, I'll – see things, that I would rather not think about – memory's such a tricky bloody thing, plays games with you.'

The blackbird is bouncing about on the lawn now, shiny black, orange beak: it's the only thing moving in the garden.

Clare turns her teacup carefully between her hands. 'You mean see things, like ghosts?'

'Not exactly.' Marty gives a little cough. 'No, that's not it, I don't think.'

'What then?'

'When I went to 'Nam I was older than most of them – just kids they were: twenty-one, twenty-two. I had a young family I'd left behind – maybe that was it, you know. I took it personally, you might say, in a way the other guys wouldn't have, not having families.' He was staring out over the lawn. 'Though you saw a lot of stuff over there that you'd rather not. Stuff, for example, that the Vietcong had done.'

Marty seems to be screwing himself up to tell her whatever is going to come next.

'I never told your mother or anybody about this, but I made some good friends while I was over there – a family, they had three kids, the little one a girl the same age as you were at the time, about three. They were kind to me, those people. I dunno why really, what with so many soldiers about . . . I was helping them with their English. The father was a schoolteacher, he had an ambition to visit New Zealand –' Marty shrugged, almost apologetically. 'Things happened over there – maybe they'd had a run-in with the Vietcong, refused to help them or something – but they killed them, that family. I was away at the time, off in the bush for a few days, I think. Somebody told me about it later. The Vietcong strung them up from the eaves of their house.'

Marty wipes his face with his hand, as if to clear sweat from his eyes, and for a moment Clare can imagine the heat over there, can smell the stench of the jungle. 'Jeez eh, Clare . . . I was such an innocent. I was sick the rest of that day.' He inhales. 'Still, you see shit like that now when you turn on the TV. Sort of.'

The day ticks on. 'You okay now?' They are a family of uneasy confidences.

'Yep. Course I'm okay.'

'And you'll be okay, going back over there?'

'Yep.' He gets up, with a grimace, and smooths down the front of his trousers. He chucks the remainder of his tea over the balustrade, among the dahlias. 'Bloody tea, can't stand the stuff.'

The trip to the airport reminds both Clare and her father of when Bethie went overseas.

That farewell had seemed jolly enough, thanks mainly to the presence of Mrs Kray. She had offered to take them all in her minivan, normally used for transporting heads filled with lollies around the countryside. The girls sat in the back: Lou, at sixteen, spent the whole trip brooding out of the window, chin in hand. 'Everybody goes away,' she muttered ominously as desolate fields of maize stubble flashed past. Terry and Beth were silently excited, their backpacks by their knees, so that you couldn't put it out of your mind where they were going. ('It's all very well being *altruistic*,' Lou had sneered the previous night. But without finishing the sentence, nobody knew what she meant.) Bethie's eyes glittered. She and Terry squeezed hands once when they hit a pothole; everybody jolted in their seats. 'Oh Lordy,' cried Mrs Kray, behind the wheel, 'whatever will I hit next?'

Clare didn't like to think, was in fact having trouble breathing and was struggling to open the window – a small sliding affair that was jammed shut – and wished that Oliver was with them. She started to chew her fingernails. Bethie going away, herself off to med school: the world was rolling over like a horse having a dust bath.

'I know. Let's sing a song,' cried Mrs Kray, with sharp-edged enthusiasm, and launched into an off-key rendition of 'When the Saints Go Marching In'.

At the airport it was Mrs Kray again who smoothed any imminent cracks, proving herself to be a very useful sort of person to take with you to an airport.

'Now I know I haven't been among the Purefoys for all that long, Beth,' she had launched into it, almost defiantly, 'but if just for one second you can pretend that I have, well that'd be just hunky-dory, because I want you to give me a big hug.'

Everyone was watching to see what Bethie would do, for surely there was a scathing remark in the offing. But instead she squeezed shut her eyes and embraced the thin wedge of Mrs Kray in arms that were still strong from rowing.

Mrs Kray straightened herself with little huffs of air, as if Beth had crushed a rib or two. 'My my,' she breathed, 'but you're a big strong girl.' They all burst out laughing then, it was that funny, and Mrs Kray puffing herself out like a starved chook. 'You take care of yourselves over there, you two. Be careful, and if you can't be careful, be good, or something like that –' She was losing the thread a little. But then she regrouped, digging about in her jacket pockets. 'There, it's a present. One each.' A silver Saint Christopher medal, identical, for each of them. 'And you wouldn't believe the trouble I had in finding them. You'd think,' her voice hovering now towards falsetto, so that Clare almost suspected Mrs Kray of being on the brink of tears, 'that people didn't believe in anything any more.'

After Beth and Terry had gone through Customs, and Lou had had to be given another dry handkerchief, they had all gone up to the lounge for a stiff drink. Even Mrs Kray had gone strangely quiet.

Lou dawdled behind, tugged at the sleeve of Clare's mohair cardigan. 'Will we ever see Bethie again?'

'Of course we will, silly.' She hated Louise at that moment, for even thinking of such a thing, but swallowed it down. She didn't want to start a fight, not at the airport.

Lou cheered somewhat. 'D'you think she'll send presents?'

'You are *such* a child,' hissed Clare, despite herself.

Now that it's Marty's turn to risk himself in the skies, Clare finds it's easy to take control. She helps him to check in his suitcase, then fetches two cups of strong tea from the self-serve café.

'Nervous?'

'Nah,' he fakes it. The last time he flew was coming back from 'Nam in '68.

'Don't drink too much on the plane,' she advises him, 'or your feet will swell up.' (And Clare ought to know: on the first leg of her return flight from San Francisco she had downed several miniatures of brandy.)

'Doctor Purefoy,' he jokes, 'that's a risk I'm prepared to take.'

They spot some other members of the group then, milling about in the distance, and her father gets up, obviously wanting to be over there and milling about with them.

'Well, this is it, Clare, wish me luck.'

'Jeez Dad.' She is embarrassed. 'Keep out of trouble, eh.'

'As if I'd be so lucky as to find any trouble.'

And rather formally – those wretched goodbyes – they shake hands.

Medical school had a firming effect on Clare. She worked so hard in the first year that at night she lay in her bed afraid that her brain might explode. It didn't. It was a help that she was living in the hostel – there was only a short walk to the school, with a dairy in between – although the noise kept her awake at night: traffic, the muffled sound of distant voices, footsteps in the corridor outside her door, the bang of the lift going up and down, a certain deep-throated dog that often barked throughout the night, and ambulance sirens going to and from the nearby hospital. She lay as if in a sarcophagus, her hands linked over her chest, her profile lit by the carpark lights that shone into her room despite the curtains, and thought that really it was all a small price to pay to be learning so much. Every day was filled with incredible new information; for example, that there are two bones in the arm that cross.

For light relief there was Janine with the wondrous mahogany hair. One night, about midnight, when Clare had just finished an assignment on the function of human cells, her desklamp shining onto the pages like a moon, Janine poked her head round the door.

'Hey, swottie,' she hissed, 'come with me.'

She led the way down the corridor to the stairs, and handed Clare a bottle of rum.

'What do I do with this?' Clare said.

'You drink it, dummy.'

They stood at the top of the stairwell. Janine shook back her hair, while Clare gagged on the rum. 'What we are going to do,' said Janine, 'is take off all our clothes and run up and down these stairs.'

Clare coughed.

'Just joking.'

Janine was a card, a character, the kind of girl that Clare still occasionally hankered after being herself. They set off down the stairs, Clare's shoes making cracking noises on the lino.

'What we are really going to do is run up and down the floor below us, knocking on people's doors –'

'But we might wake them up.'

'Yes,' Janine said. 'That is the entire point of the operation.' Then she added, as they reached the fire doors of the floor below, 'We shall also whoop a lot. Ready, steady, *go* –'

Janine raced along the corridor madly, whooping as she went, so Clare really had no choice but to join in. She did the other side, minus the whooping. Tearing back up the stairs to their own floor, puffing and red-faced, Clare had to admit that it had been fun. She looked at Janine more closely. There was something very Bethie-like about her.

'Why did you choose me?' said Clare.

Janine shrugged. 'I needed a musketeer; and besides, yours was the only light on. See ya.' Clare watched her swing down the fluorescent-lit corridor and disappear into a room on the left.

Janine would burst in as if catapulted. She came once with a white cardboard box containing a huge Black Forest cake, the top creamy with cherries and grated chocolate. 'What d'you reckon?'

Clare was sucking the end of her pencil. 'What's it for?' She thought that Janine was planning something wacky with the cake, like throwing it at somebody and probably from a height.

'It's to eat, of course, silly. Got a knife?'

Clare actually had a hunting knife, in its own leather sheath, which their father had given her way back in the misty days of her rabbit-skinning; it was useful now for cutting up apples. Janine cut two large slices of cake. There were no plates, however, so they balanced the cake on pieces of refill and ate it with wild abandon, cream and sponge getting everywhere.

'You're crazy,' said Clare admiringly.

'Thank you.' Janine bowed from the waist and cake plopped onto the floor.

Clare thought she'd be safe asking a personal question. 'When do you study?'

Sometimes from her window she would see Janine down in the carpark, just hanging about in the early evening sun; she had a skateboard that she practised on, going up and down the curvaceous driveway, jumping kerbs. There seemed to be parties, too, that Janine went off to dressed in short colourful skirts, once a purple hat with a huge white feather dangling from it. She seemed to lead such a charmed life you could easily be envious: how was it possible?

'I get up early in the morning. Sometimes four or five o'clock. My brain's fresh then, and I blat through it.'

Clare couldn't imagine blatting through any of her work. She wouldn't want to anyway: wanted to catch every tiny detail, as if it might get away from her if she wasn't vigilant. She double-checked herself, to make sure she wasn't missing anything. So far she had got straight As.

'What are you going to specialise in?' asked Janine. Clare hadn't thought that far ahead. 'Me, I'm going to do something with the brain. I really like brains.'

'Surgery?'

'Sure, why not?'

So blithe. Clare, sitting on her padded study chair, fiddled with the pencil. There were diagrams beneath her elbow revealing the inner workings of the heart. 'I might go into cardiac,' she murmured. Really she had no idea.

'My uncle's just had a heart transplant, in Oz. They cut out his old one, and just put in somebody else's. Wicked, eh.' Janine licked chocolate from her fingers. 'I teased him, I told him he'll take on the personality of his heart donor.'

'Did he believe you?'

'Would you?' But it was a rhetorical question, thankfully. 'They can even reuse people's eyes. Isn't that gross. But wouldn't it be amazing if we could do brain transplants? Imagine, a person who's braindead, getting a new brain, say from a coma patient. Only thing, you'd be a completely different person. Ah well, thems the breaks.'

That night Clare found herself dreaming of hearts. Human hearts, quite bloodless and clean, that sported eyes. A heart sailed past, and blinked deeply at her. 'What do you know?' asked the heart. 'I know enough,' said Clare in her dream. She found the hearts were intriguing, not at all terrifying; except, when she woke in the morning she felt exhausted. Must have been that cake, she reasoned, and debated locking her door against Janine. Though she knew she wouldn't.

Clare barely had time for friends, yet Janine persisted. 'I like you, Purefoy,' she said once. 'In a world that admires the superficial, you're so – *solid*. You are printed in bold type!'

Am I, she wondered. Solid? But even Bethie had coincidentally confirmed it, in a letter: 'You've come into your own, kid,' she had written. Clare had noticed no perceptible change in herself, except perhaps that other people seemed to be speaking to her more intently, as if she had a disease. How could Beth tell from such an unimaginable distance? Kabul? It sounded like an exotic breed of dog.

Lou was eighteen when her world seemed to fall apart. Bethie had come and gone. Nothing fitted together properly any more. The party, for instance. Meatloaf's 'Bat out of Hell' was blasting through a wooden house in the suburbs of Auckland. The living room was jammed with dark jumping bodies, most of which were drunk, and people were shouting along with the words of the song.

Sid had pissed off. Louise had to laugh: she and Clare, dating brothers. It had to be a joke. Though she didn't intend to go out with Sid again – once was enough: he stank of cigarette smoke, and called his car The Bitch. Lou liked a little more class in her men. She was already seeing a BCom guy who drove a red Camaro.

Clare and Oliver had been around earlier on – before the drinking match, and well before Noise Control had been called to the house (twice). Just as well, thought Lou. Not exactly Clare's scene. Was it hers? Eighteen years old, and definitely a party girl. She couldn't remember when innocence seemed to have deserted her. 'Lou's gone off the rails,' said the gossips. But what would they know? She was just having some fun. Wasn't that what the big smoke was all about?

Party girl or not, she'd had about enough of tonight's scene. Propped against a wall to stop the room from spinning, she was concentrating on a girl sitting on the couch who was wearing a silver wig. She was aware of a heaviness of black mascara on her eyelashes. Now, if she could just get herself off somewhere quiet and have a lie-down, she might avoid chucking up.

She peeled herself away from the wall, and began to negotiate her way down the hallway – around and across prone bodies, as if it was a war zone – until she found a dark bedroom. *Thank Christ*. The double bed had denim jackets lying all over it, but she made a space for herself among them and curled up for a sleep. There was a dream, something about a long hot-water pool, rather like the one at Miranda except this was in an empty building. There was some question about using it – was it illegal? Was it private property?

Lou was just about to check out the steam room, when she was woken by someone roughly pulling down her jeans.

'What the –?'

'Scream and I'll thump you –' Someone lurched out of the darkness above her. He stank of rum.

He wrenched her legs apart and pushed roughly inside her. She tried struggling, but he got hold of her arm and squeezed her back down. She considered screaming. Aside from the likelihood of getting a broken nose, the music in the next room was so loud you could feel the thump of it in your eardrums, through the tips of your fingers. Or was that her pulse? Nobody would hear, of course.

Jesus.

He shoved his hand under her blouse and twisted her nipple. It was probably imagination, but she got the impression he was grinning.

It didn't take long to be over, and Lou was alone in the room again.

Jesus.

She rolled over just in time to vomit over the side of the bed. From outside came the wail of a siren.

Oh good, she thought, just what I need next. The police.

SIXTEEN

Rob was talking with a trio of mujahedin out in the compound. Watching through the window, Bethie thought that you couldn't see more of a contrast: Rob in his rolled-up shirt sleeves and dusty chinos, and the fierce mountain fighters hung about with ammo clips, grenades and Kalashnikovs. She already knew their business. They wanted a doctor to come to their camp and train them in some basic medicine. It was easier for them to fix themselves up after a battle than to try to bring their wounded to a clinic. And easier than taking any foreign doctors with them. 'They think we're soft,' Franco had hooted. 'This guy, he went with muj into the mountains, and he fainted. Just like a girl. Give us a bad name.' Not that Bethie thought Franco would fare much better. She had seen him bring up his breakfast in the scrubroom more than once.

The group moved closer to the clinic.

'Even the wild creatures help us –'

'Is that a fact?' Rob, ever laconic, was squinting in the sunlight.

'Yes, here is a recent story – some of our comrades, they went through a valley, very high walls each side, and Soviets coming right behind, when many snakes appeared. The snakes let the mujahedin through, then turned on the enemy and destroyed them.'

'With a little help, of course, from mujahedin,' one of the men chuckled.

'God can open doors,' added another.

When Rob came back into the clinic, alone, Bethie put her hand on his arm.

'I want to go too. Into the mountains.' Thinking, still, of the black-eyed man and his reed city. Travel might bring her closer to him.

Rob shoved his hands into his trouser pockets, looked at her with his head on one side. His ginger eyebrows were paler than ever. 'Who says I'm going –'

'I can tell you are.'

He smiled, thinly. 'Nothing like a sightseeing trip, eh.'

'So?'

He looked at the floor, then up at the ceiling. 'You're aware, aren't you, that there's a bounty offered on foreigners travelling with the mujahedin? Even aid workers.'

Bethie shifted impatiently. 'You're still going.'

Rob's gaze lingered over her face. 'It's not a good idea, taking a woman.'

'I've come this far.'

'That's true,' he admitted. 'I'll think about it then.' He was walking away when he muttered, 'This God-forsaken country, eh . . .'

'Don't call it that,' said Beth. 'God is watching over the Afghans. Allaho akbar, that's what they all say, God is great.'

'Yeah,' sighed Rob, 'isn't he just.' He paused in the doorway. 'This *jihad* they're always talking about, it's supposed to be a "holy war" and I see the point about protecting your own country; but what I can't understand is the blind devotion to the cause. I mean, the Afghans, they're killing people too. How can that be holy?'

Bethie looked down at her feet, tanned and sandalled, dusty. The year could be 1383, 1783, instead of 1983. 'As far as I can see, *jihad's* all about trying to worship God. The fighting part, the Koran justifies that as a struggle to fight oppression. *Jihad's* all about getting rid of evil.'

'In this case, the Russians.'

'Yeah. It's a matter of belief, I guess. You submit yourself to God, so you're fighting in God's name, and God will protect you. Seems a fair deal to me. Doesn't that make sense to you?'

'I'm not too sure,' said Rob. 'That story about the snakes –?'

Beth grinned. 'A bit of poetic licence, I'd say.'

Lou lay on her bed, on her back, staring at the ceiling, her fine blonde hair splayed out on the pillow, damp. So far she had had three showers since waking that morning. The room, with its high sash windows, was effusive with creamy light. A train went past at the bottom of the garden. She could hear Leeanne going off to work, clacking down the hallway, and Pete in the attic room above her moving about, probably in his darkroom. Plumbing was clanking and complaining. It was an old house. There were cockroaches. Last night, coming in through the back door and through the kitchen, she had thought she was hallucinating: the kitchen bench was alive with insects. It was the sight of those rampant uncontrollable cockroaches, more than anything, that had kept her awake until 3 a.m. Repulsive. Someone had rung the landlord about getting the place fumigated, but so far nothing had happened. She ought to leave, get somewhere decent. But it was cheap here, the rooms were big, she even had her own shower, and with nine other flatmates, there was always something going on.

Louise turned her head to the shuttered windows, and blinked gritty eyes. *Bugger bugger bugger bugger*. It was amazing she even got home last night. The only part of the journey she recalled was turning into a side street and finding a huge mound of gravel looming up in front of her. Lou spun the car, just missing it. The car stalled, and she sat panting, sweat breaking out on her face. *I could've rolled the car – if I'd been going any faster – I could've* ... She had an image of herself, hanging upside down in the driver's seat, bleeding from the head. *Bugger*.

She knew it was Sid. She'd seen him in the light from the hall when he left the room. Rough trade, that was what she'd always thought of him. Ought to trust her instincts in the future. Now she's learnt the hard way. And ought to give up parties. That kind of party, at any rate. Really, she ought to go to the police.

Except she could see him in court, suited, hair slicked back. *No sir, it wasn't me. I wasn't even inside the house, I was out the front talking to the noise control guys, ask anybody* – and his blank eyes sliding over her – no, she couldn't face it. Besides, what's a fuck between friends. That's what they say, isn't it?

Lou went back to staring at the ceiling. There was a patch of mould in the shape of Australia in one corner. *Rise above it*. Isn't that what Bethie would've said? This was the kind of thing Lou might've talked to Bethie about. But she had already decided that nobody was going to know, least of all family.

There was a tentative tap on the door and Rory poked his head round.

'Hi Lou, you haven't forgotten, have you?'

She stared at him as he came in, hands in pockets, and he could've been a stranger: a chunky boy in army fatigues. What was the point of army fatigues? Rory had a penis that was shaped like a banana, and wanted to be a punk rocker. It was proving difficult, however, because he wasn't nasty enough. He also lacked the proper wardrobe and was squeamish about safety pins.

'The outdoor concert?' he added, standing mid-room.

'I'm not going to any concert.'

'What's up, Lou?'

'Nothing. Just leave me alone.'

'But I've come all this way across town, to pick you up –'

'I don't care,' she screamed, 'just get out, *get out* –'

Bastards, all of them. The slamming door echoed inside her head like a sharp pain. She rolled over into the light and squeezed her eyes shut.

Louise had developed a problem sleeping at night. And when she did sleep there were fitful dreams in which an anonymous man was stalking her with a knife. How Freudian, she thought, slipping out of bed. Down the dark hallway she went, wearing her winter boots though it was summer, and flicked on the kitchen light. Hundreds of tiny eyes blinked back at her, antennae twitching. Louise had been planning this moment during her restless nights – would she be brave enough, she asked herself over and over – until the act had taken on the significance of an initiation ritual.

If I do this, I will be cleansed.

Because of her squeamishness, she had taken the precaution of wearing a plastic barbecue apron, one that pictured a woman's torso in a flimsy nightie, which was supposed to be a joke, as it was designed to be worn by men. Louise didn't find that kind of thing funny any more. She lifted the cricket bat, and brought it down hard on the kitchen bench – again and again. She could be psychotic, crazed.

You bastards –

Martin, eyes blinking sleepily behind rimless spectacles, stood swaying in the doorway. It was as he always suspected: Louise Purefoy was mad. Tomorrow, first thing, he intended to call a house meeting to get her kicked out.

Lou let the bat fall onto the floor – the bat stained with the juice of cockroaches – and stood blindly shaking in the old kitchen. A nikau rubbed its trunk against the window. She was oblivious to Martin's exit, which was just as well: no murderer wants a witness.

Oliver happened to run into Lou outside Smith & Caughey's one afternoon. He wouldn't have recognised her – she looked quite different, her lips hard and sharp with red lipstick (she could have been wearing a mask), and there was something odd about her clothes – except that she had glanced into his passing face and he had thought she was Clare. He had been about to call out when he realised his mistake in time.

'Lou,' he cried. 'How's it going?'

'Fine.' She smiled falsely, and Oliver's old altruistic instincts were aroused. It seemed like a long time since he'd heard anything about Lou.

'Want a coffee? I'm buying.'

They sat in a coffee bar. Louise had dropped out of university and was living on the dole. She'd also been kicked out of her flat, though she wouldn't say why – just that they were a pack of wankers – and she was dossing down on a friend's couch until she found somewhere to stay.

'Y'know, Oliver,' Louise muttered, hands around her cup. 'You seem older, somehow.'

Oliver pulled back his shoulders unconsciously. 'Well, I suppose it happens to the best of us. Gotta grow up sometime, eh.'

Lou started to light a cigarette, but the match slipped from between her fingers. Oliver leaned over and did it for her, the flame flaring between them for a moment. She looked at him then, and she was the old Louise, full of bravado. 'So what d'you do for fun, Oliver?'

'Ah, well.' He frowned, trying to think. 'Not very much, I don't suppose. Clare and I go to the pictures sometimes, when she's got time. She swots a lot.'

Lou nodded sagely. 'That's a problem I don't have any more.'

When they left the coffee bar, she led him into an empty alleyway between grey blank-walled buildings. She pressed him against a wall, and got her hand down his pants. 'Lou,' he gasped, 'I –' She kissed him with an emotion much baser than lust, the lipstick smearing, silencing any protests. Grabbing up her skirt in fisted bunches, she pushed him inside her with fury, while Oliver could only cry out, paralysed against the wall which was scraping his back, his thin shoulder blades grazing against the bricks; and it didn't seem very long before Lou was crying, her face wet and salty, slicked sheen, and she was sobbing against his best seersucker tie like the world had come to an end.

'. . . Lou?'

As if remembering where she was, she took a deep breath and extricated herself, straightening her face and her clothes. A little flip-top mirror came out of her bag and the lipstick was repaired, the cheeks patted with powder.

'Thank you, Oliver,' she said primly, 'I needed that.' She looked up at the looming facades around them, as if pondering something quite deep. Though what she was really thinking was how it was time she started earning some decent money. Money, thought Louise, could save and protect you. 'In fact, I think I'll be quite all right, now.' She started to walk away.

'Er, Lou –?'

She turned back with raised eyebrows. Oliver was just as gawky as ever.

'That was phenomenal. When can I see you again?'

Oliver had dropped off. It was several weeks before Clare noticed she hadn't spoken to him recently, and then, thinking to ring, discovered that he had moved out of Sid's house.

'I dunno where he is, baby doll, he didn't leave no forwarding address. So much for blood thicker than water, eh.'

The last time she'd seen Oliver they were on their bikes and speeding down Queen Street – at a time, pre-mountain bikes, pre-bike helmets even, when hardly anybody cycled around the city. *Country hiiicks,* sang Clare, as the wind rushed at her face and reddened her ears, and she'd never felt more alive, weaving in and out among the traffic. Coming down the higher part of the hill that was Queen Street past Myers Park, Oliver was up ahead, hunched into the wind, and she was coming down fast behind him; then, without warning, a person stepped out in front of her.

She screamed, braked, knocked into the person, and went over the handlebars.

'I'm sorry, so sorry,' she gasped, getting up, glancing over herself: no scrapes on knees, no broken limbs, no cuts even, astounding – and to be confronted with a boy/man, shorter than herself but with a browned face which had a hint of the wizened about it. He was dressed in sagging dirty jeans and some kind of black sweatshirt; his hair was matted and black; his fingernails (she noticed later as he picked up her bike for her) were dirty. Some kind of a street kid/man? They were a problem for police in the city, and Clare noticed that the tumble had happened right outside Myers Park, where street kids liked to sleep. And Oliver was slowly struggling back up the hill. Clare couldn't help thinking of the scene in Beckett's novel about the girl getting knocked by a car and the loaf of bread she'd been carrying making a slow arc through the air. All of this noted in a portion of a second.

'God, I'm sorry, are you all right?' Clare, distraught, became even thinner and whiter.

The boy/man just grinned, and folded her in his arms, hugging her tightly. Then he retrieved her bike from its louche angle on the street, and handed it back to her.

Oliver came up as the boy/man wandered off. 'I thought you'd killed that guy.' And Clare, giggling, said, 'So had I.'

'He could've got hurt, the idiot, just stepping out like that.'

'He hugged me,' sniffed Clare, remounting her bicycle, though continuing down the hill more sedately.

Months had passed, when one day she came back from the lecture theatre to find Oliver leaning on the wall outside her door with folded arms and closed eyes, the image of patience. He opened his eyes and pushed himself forward when he heard her footsteps approaching.

'Hi, Clare.'

'Oliver,' she said, unlocking her door.

He sat on the bed and looked uncomfortable, while Clare sat in her chair. There wasn't a lot of choice – entertaining in the student lounge lacked privacy. He still looked the same, tousled hair caressing his forehead, but his clothes were a lot smarter: a dark shirt and dress pants.

'It's been a while,' she hesitated.

He fidgeted with his hands, still rather lumpish and red. 'There was somebody else, for a while, but it wasn't anything serious,' he said.

Did it matter only if it was serious? And Clare had thought she'd just been too busy.

'But Clare, I miss you.' He looked up with yearning eyes, although there were no tears. Had he managed to control his crying? Clare found herself looking back coolly, critically even, at the boy she had been in love with that long-ago summer. He seemed awfully, well, gauche, though outwardly he looked grown-up.

'Do you think we could start seeing each other again?'

She wanted to be kind, for the sake of the past. 'I don't think so,' she murmured. 'I'm too busy for relationships.' That was what Janine told the young men who waited outside the hostel doors for her; except Janine had gone flatting now, and perhaps she was saying something different these days.

'Ah.' Oliver didn't look too crestfallen. 'Well, if you change your mind –'

He left an address. She studied his handwriting after he'd gone – the same tiny squiggly marks that he'd made in all those letters when they were kids: Nope, didn't feel a thing. So I've put aside childish things after all, thought Clare. Nevertheless she put Oliver's address in the bottom drawer of her desk. She thought she might like to just look at it from time to time.

Most people go into real estate in a roundabout way; they might fail at one or two careers, before making the connection, or it might be the only occupation for a woman not trained in any other field after rearing children. It is not the kind of career that kids aspire to. 'What do you want to be when you grow up?' A Real Estate Agent. It doesn't sound right. But Lou was destined to sell property. Life could be like a fairytale after all, spinning straw into gold.

On the night of Clare's graduation from med school, there was a celebration dinner at a city restaurant. Clare, her friend Janine and Marty were considering the menus in a mood of quiet elation. They were hungry and already nibbling on pizza bread, when Lou arrived at the restaurant door, humming David Bowie. Other diners looked up, as if they might be seeing someone important. She plumped down at their table, ebullient, light flashing off her earrings and her silk suit swishing the colour of jade water.

'If you play that LP backwards,' said Janine, 'it really says, worship the devil.'

Louise frowned. 'Pardon?' Clare hid a smile in her wine glass.

'Guess what!' said Lou. 'You'll never believe it –' They waited, as if caught suddenly, expressions neutral. 'I've sold my first house!' She grabbed the nearby wine glass, and poured herself a big one, slurping in the wine grandly, an extravagant gesture. 'It was touch and go for a while. The vendor was blowing hot and cold, there was a badinage of phone calls, but I've pulled it off. It's a wrap.' It was an expression that Lou had recently adopted. 'And you won't believe the money I'm making!'

It was impossible to resume the previous, more sober celebration in the face of such loud news. Some sort of show had to be given.

'Well done,' said their father, raising his glass. 'It'll be the first of many, I'm sure.'

Clare was silent in her beige blouse. (Janine was always telling Clare that she ought to stick up for herself. 'But I do,' protested Clare, 'sometimes.' But how to say anything when you didn't know what kind of words might spill out?) A troubled pause was growing over the table.

Louise had been about to embark on a description of the great sale, but remembered in time the real reason for the celebration. 'Hey, and congrats, eh. A doctor in the family.' She turned to Clare. 'Success must run in the family.'

They raised their glasses, and touched them together to create a hollow ringing sound.

January 1984
Show us the straight way, the way of those You have graced, not of those on whom is Your wrath, nor of those who wander astray.

The fragile connections we make, thinks Clare, between the past and the present; the constant reminders that really come from within. The Marshall boy, for instance, reminds her not only of Oliver, but of Beth as well. His bicycle, the way he wheels around the town with a missionary-like intentness.

They bump into each other, literally, on mainstreet. Clare is bending over, shuffling through the basket of odds and ends outside the secondhand shop, looking for a joke present for Marty – he's getting back in a few days and Lou's picking him up from the airport: a good sign. Clare has already been over to the house and put out some flowers, set his mail on the table (a hunting magazine and seed catalogues). She hopes, with more than usual concern, that all went well. Then the Marshall boy lurches into her.

'Oh *God*, sorry –' He's gone beet-red.

Pitying his embarrassment, she offers to buy him a cup of coffee at the Argyle Tearooms. They sit at a booth, facing each other, and it's up to Clare to fill the void.

'Are you still at school?'

'No.' He is dismissive, as if she ought to know better.

'Working?'

He hunches a shoulder forward. 'Odd jobs.' They both smile, thinking of the Brightly residence.

'Plans for next year?'

'Maybe.' It could become excruciating, except that Clare feels quite comfortable now with this monosyllabic kid, and he doesn't seem that worried about her either. He is different from other teenagers, though she can't put a finger on it.

'University?'

A man in patched jeans and bare feet buys an egg sandwich at the counter. The Marshall boy waits until he goes to a table by the window. 'Shall I tell you something? It's private –'

'Of course.' Clare cast again in her professional role.

He hunches forward, his brimming and milky coffee spilling into the saucer. 'I want –' he blinks slowly, and drops his voice, though there isn't anybody nearby to overhear – 'I want to just, I have this idea, about lying on the ground – in different places, like the Sahara Desert – and just spending the whole night looking at the sky.' He remembers his coffee, and takes a deliberate mouthful, his lips pursing. With more confidence, he continues, 'Sometimes I do it here, but it's not the same. I want –' again the uncertain pause – 'to do it, elsewhere.'

This is the most that Clare has ever heard out of the boy, and she feels oddly privileged.

'You are a poet, then.'

He blushes, the embarrassment now for Clare. 'No way. I just want to do something different, live properly, before it's all over.'

She raises her eyebrows, but he says no more.

One evening Clare is walking down the long echoing corridor of the ground floor, whistling, ready to go home. Eyes follow her: the walls are lined with ancient framed photographs – former doctors, and group shots of nurses – when a loud crack sounds from behind her. Instantly she throws herself to the floor: *It's a gunshot*. Then she recalls where she is: a rural town in the New Zealand hinterland, where the only drug wars take place deep in the bush, not in the local hospital. At least her reflexes are still working. She gets up, dusting off her pants, and glances back down the silent corridor in time to see part of the ceiling, along with two heavy metal pipes, collapse onto the lino. Plaster dust rises majestically.

Cautiously, Clare tiptoes towards this pile of new rubble and looks up. A face peers nervously back down at her. It is one of the orderlies. He points, with a grimace. His trolley of linen has been consumed by the rubble. Two metal wheelie legs are poking up like the legs of a dead dog.

'Earthquake?' queries Clare, thinking again of San Fran.

The orderly's mouth puckers. 'I don't think we have them here.'

Clare's hands are suddenly icy cold. She puts them to her lips and breathes on them.

'Er, should I call somebody?' The man is still peering down through the jagged hole.

'Yes, do,' says Clare.

She shoves her numb hands into her coat pockets and heads for the door.

SEVENTEEN

CLARE WAS twenty-seven when she saw her mother again. She was in Cairns, on holiday with Janine, and it was such a short flight to Brisbane, she reasoned, it wouldn't take very long . . . She went. As she sat on the shuttle into the city, Clare realised that she had meant all along to visit Pat (could hardly think of her as Mother): with age, she found, came curiosity. Mostly, Clare just wanted to know *why*.

The florist shop was easy enough to find, though tucked in among several other similar-looking shops on an unremarkable street in a suburban shopping area like the ones back home. There it was, just like the photograph Pat had sent a couple of years back when she had bought the business. Clare lingered outside a tobacconist's, shuffling her feet and sweating in the heat. A woman walked past wearing a woollen cardigan. Was she mad? It must be at least 29 degrees. Clare was regretting her linen trousers.

There was a café nearby, facing the florist's and Clare slipped inside. She sat at a table in the window and tried an iced coffee. Then she discovered she was hungry, and ordered a plate of nachos. A man at a gloomier table eyed her over the lip of his white cup – it would be so easy to start talking to a strange man in a café – but she ignored him.

Clare watched as a woman came out of the florist's carrying a bucketful of white long-stemmed flowers and placed it on the pavement. The woman glanced briefly up to the sky – the shopowner's life, never seeing the sun – then re-entered the dim interior. *Mother?* Clare's heart gave a little thump. *Palpitations, must cut back the coffee.*

Eventually, when she really couldn't put it off any longer, Clare crossed the street. But now there was a customer, a stocky Greek man. Their mother, in a grey pinafore over a pink floral dress, was behind the counter arranging a bouquet of something deeply pink and petally. Was it really necessary, Clare wondered, for florists to wear floral clothes? The shop was gaudy enough: there were even Valentine's Day balloons scrolled with mottos like 'Luvs and Hugs' and 'Luv you Muchly'. Clare examined buckets of cut flowers and thought it would be quite all right to leave without introducing herself.

'These should hit the spot,' said their mother to the customer. Was that a twang? And why not: she'd been over here long enough to sound native.

'This is the first time I have ever bought flowers for a woman,' said the man.

'And I'm sure it won't be the last.' Actually their mother had a pleasant voice. Clare had forgotten. Though perhaps it was deliberately smoother for customers.

'It'll depend on what happens with these.'

Pat wrapped the bouquet in purple waxed paper, tying it with gold ribbon. She was dexterous, despite the missing thumb. 'Every woman likes to be given flowers,' she soothed.

And what a gross generalisation that was – Clare herself loathed flowers, being allergic to pollen; she'd much rather be given a book. Already she was sniffing, and her eyes were prickling. A bucket of white lilies was staring up at her, the shop was claustrophobic, and she could feel a heat rash breaking out beneath her shirt. She had forgotten how soft her mother looked.

The man finally left and Clare stepped forward.

'Hello, Mum.'

Their mother shied back like a startled rabbit. '*Clare* –?'

'The very one.' Clare hadn't meant to adopt a jocular tone. 'Thought I'd just drop by . . . see how you were getting along.'

'Goodness, what a bolt from the blue!' She had certainly adopted the vernacular. 'You're taller.'

'It's just good posture.' There was a stretch of time when Clare hunched her shoulders – there *were* breasts, and she didn't know what to make of them – but that was after their mother had left.

'Still –'

They may not have had anything more to say to each other at this point if it hadn't been for Clare's job. 'Of course,' her mother exclaimed softly. 'Louise said you'd graduated as a surgeon. Fancy, a doctor in the family!'

Clare remembered then that she was the first one in a long line of Purefoys to graduate with a university degree. But pride was quickly stabbed down by jealousy. 'You and Louise have been writing?'

'Oh yes.' Their mother was fiddling with a few cut stems on the bench. 'She comes over quite often, too. She keeps me posted on all the news. I thought you knew.'

'No. Good.' That was a well-kept secret. There seemed to be even less to say now. Clare searched in her bag for the packet of travel tissues she always carried. 'Well, I should be going.'

'But you've only just arrived.' Pat managed to look both impatient and dismayed, and Clare could place her now beside the earlier version, the one that had been at home, although the stench of flowers was confusing her, befuddling her brain. 'Stay and have some coffee, at least. I'll put the jug on. It's not every day one of my daughters turns up –'

Clare dabbed irritably at her nose with a tissue. 'I really must –' Inching now towards the door – this was a terrible mistake, coming here – all she wanted to do was get away. But she was pursued by her ex-mother.

'But you've come such a long way – here, have this –' Pat grabbed up a long-stemmed thingey (Clare had no head for names of plants, flowers) and thrust it at her. 'I know –' She was trailing behind as Clare reached the door, the street. 'You must come over tonight for dinner, meet Bill, see where we live, then we can have a proper catch-up –'

Clare looked down at the woman who was clutching her forearm, the lined eyes squinting at her, demanding, needy, and the flower insinuating itself between them. All you have to do is say yes, thought Clare, and you can get away. It was like being caught on a park bench by a garrulous tramp.

'Yes,' said Clare, 'all right.'

'Oh, that's wonderful, Clare.' And she waited while Pat scribbled the address on one of her cards – 'Daydream Flowers' – and thrust that upon her too. She wouldn't go, Clare was thinking; she would be entirely justified in not going; a certain balance would be recovered if she didn't go. But, on the other hand, it would seem childish not to, and Clare – as she reminded herself in the taxi back to the hotel – was a grown-up now.

The interior of their mother's house was like a white-out. There were billowing gauzy white curtains, white woodwork, a white carpet and white lampshades. A small egg-shaped swimming pool glittered beyond ranchsliders. Clare put on her dark glasses. Again, it was difficult for her to equate the woman with her surroundings: this wasn't the taste of the mother she had once known. Could a person change so radically in a comparatively short space of time? Clare herself didn't feel as if she had changed much: she even had an Einstein poster in her flat, though it had been joined now by a small Fomison and a Pat Hanly: bird and woman, bright and cheerful, to counter the other.

The house made more sense when the Accountant appeared from the hallway.

'Bill,' said their mother, 'this is my daughter Clare.'

They shook hands. He had meaty arms covered with short dark hairs, and a gold chain shivered in a nest of dark curly chest hair. The effect, however, was one of precision, offset by a white shirt. He was the kind of man who wouldn't like mess about the place.

'This is a good reason to celebrate,' he decided, and picked up a remote-control gadget. He pressed a button, and part of the wall opposite the windows slid down to reveal a drinks cabinet. 'What's your poison?'

Arsenic, strychnine, digitalis? As if reading Clare's mind, her mother jostled Bill. 'You shouldn't say that kind of thing to a doctor,' she joked.

'White wine, thanks.'

He opened a little fridge and brought out a sweating bottle. 'It's a great life over here,' said Bill.

Clare couldn't think of a thing to say to the Accountant. It was disconcerting enough, seeing him – so long a symbol – in the flesh. And there was a disturbing echo of Marise in his face. She took the glass of wine he proffered with a silent smile.

Thankfully, Pat and Bill exchanged a look, then Bill was saying, 'You'll have to excuse me, Clare, I've got some business calls to make before I sit down.' So it was obviously okay for him to leave them alone.

They took their drinks out to the patio, and sat in deckchairs facing the pool. There was a high fence, painted white, and concrete tubs with small palms growing in them. Overhead a Boeing ploughed noisily through the bleached blue sky, so that they had to wait for it to pass before speaking. On a low glass table there was a large plate of king prawns, and raw oysters in shells, sitting on ice. This was dinner? Clare was flattered by such seeming extravagance.

'So how is everything, back in the old country?' She sounded like a European emigrée, in exile; which, Clare supposed, she was in a way, though voluntarily. But how was everything? Clare mentally ran through a list of possible things to tell . . . Lou selling houses, but then Pat would know all about that. Their father – no. Work? How they'd had to cope without a mother for all that time?

'Everything's fine,' she said.

'Work?'

'Busy.'

Pat picked up one of the prawns. 'The seafood over here is excellent,' she sighed. 'Please –' indicating for Clare to help herself. Clare considered how she might go about eating a prawn without making a mess: she wasn't very good with food when she was nervous. Drinks tended to get spilt, canapés became self-propellant.

'When we first came over here, it was practically all we ate – scampi, and mangoes. Couldn't get enough of it. It seemed so exotic, and cheap. Especially after drab old New Zealand . . .' Pat was trying to pull the shell off her prawn. 'Sorry . . .' With a sharp tug at the tail, the prawn snapped out of her fingers. It went flying across the pool, hit a gold and black Japanese-style vase on a stand, and plopped onto the decking.

'Another one bites the dust,' muttered Pat.

Exactly what Clare herself said when she dropped something. How odd. And she'd always thought it quite an original thing to say. The vase trembled, and they watched with bated breath – would it topple? – but all was well. Pat got up and retrieved the prawn with a small titter. 'Butterfingers, that's what Bill calls me. *Puss puss –*' An outsize fluffy white cat appeared and delicately took the prawn from Pat's fingers. Did she get the cat after they decorated? Pat caught her look. They seemed to be able to interpret each other with ease. 'He was a present, from a mate of Bill's. Sort of a joke, really.' Pat grimaced, and resumed her seat. She didn't used to care for cats. 'You'll have to excuse me, I'm fine at work, I never drop a thing. But at home, or on the street –' Pat spread her palms at the impossibility of it all. She leaned forward and dipped her fingers in a large bowl of water, then took a rolled-up white towel from a pile on a plate.

'You've got good reason to be.' Clare reached for a prawn. She put it carefully on a plate, and took a serviette. Then decided that it was okay to confess to something herself: 'I'm exactly the same.'

Pat looked surprised. 'Really? But you weren't particularly clumsy as a child . . .' A pause. 'At least, I don't think you were.'

Clare grinned. 'It seems to have got worse as I've got older.'

'And with your work?'

'Fine. Otherwise, I suppose, I'd be in another profession.'

'Ha ha, yes, I see what you mean. Can't afford any slip-ups in your job.'

There was an awkward silence while Clare concentrated on peeling her prawn. She could hear the cat somewhere nearby, crunching.

'You're welcome to have a crack at the vase too, if you like.'

'Thanks.'

'I remember you got lost in the bush once.'

Clare inhaled evenly, the prawn cold between her fingers.

'Really?'

'You were quite little. We were on a picnic. I think you'd probably walked off after a moth or something – you often did – and I wasn't watching. Probably daydreaming.' Pat leaned forward for another prawn, her face hidden. 'I was a dreadful mother,' she added brightly.

It was, Clare realised, the closest Pat would come to an apology. She was tempted to shout, *Yes you were*, but instead found herself asking in a mature voice, 'Did you find me?'

Pat laughed at that, and Clare smiled.

'Oh yes. You'd fallen asleep under a tree. You were only a few yards from the picnic spot the whole time. You were never far away.'

They ate seafood amicably for a little while, then Pat said, 'I tried writing to you, several times, but I couldn't ever get the right tone.'

'That's all right,' said Clare, 'it was probably better this way, after all.'

'Here, let me give you something, before you go.' Pat dashed out of the room, returned and pushed something into Clare's hands. 'It won't make up for all the missed birthdays, but I'd like you to have it.' It was a bottle of perfume, salmon pink, in the shape of a female torso – no head, no legs, all breasts and hips – an outline of lingerie etched onto the glass. 'Put it away before Bill sees,' she hissed, enjoying the role of conspirator.

Back at the hotel, Clare walked through the foyer and, with her stern reflection in the elevator doors vaguely mocking her, dropped the perfume bottle into a rubbish bin.

So much change could squeeze your lips shut for ever. Mrs Doffelmeyer the home economics teacher shooed Clare out of class like a naughty child to wait in the draughty corridor until she learnt some manners. Clare, hands linked in front of her tunic, stood patiently, horse-like, by the wall, listening to the muffled voices of her class, buttering their muffin tins, spooning in the mixture, and the shrill instructions from Mrs Doffelmeyer. Baking, mother skills. Would anything seem normal again? Would they, as Lou put it, ever see their mother again? And how long could you keep that kind of thing a secret?

Clare stood and stood, with her eyes fixed on the high overhead windows, from which you could see only sky. The corridor stretched out to either side of her, empty like a barren field. If you could run, she thought, knowing it to be impossible. Clare swayed slightly (an unlikely reed) and tried to imagine herself somewhere else – *a desert island, the wild Alaskan tundra, collecting mollusc shells in Hawaii.*

Footsteps sounded. The principal appeared at the other end of the corridor. Clare, trying to fade into the wall, was aware of her approaching like a tiny black tornado. Very soon, she would be picked up and swept away.

'Clare Purefoy –?' It was a question. Clare nodded. 'What are you doing out here?'

Silence.

Clare dropped her chin, blushing a little even though she was nearly the same height as the principal.

'Answer me, girl. What are you doing out here?'

Clare imagined the principal's flat two-tone shoes suddenly catching on fire.

'Oh, for goodness sake,' she sighed, pushing open the classroom door.

Soon there were the two of them, trying to tower over her.

'The girl refuses to speak,' complained Mrs Doffelmeyer.

The principal turned to her. 'Is something the matter, Clare?' It was an attempt at kindness, but it became lost in irritation. 'Look, I'm too busy for this right now. Clare you come with me, we'll sort this out in my office.'

Clare followed meekly as the principal clattered ahead. She wondered if they would be able to get her talking again, for she seemed to have lost the knack, somehow.

Bethie was sitting on a mat beneath the pomegranate tree. Despite what he had said, Rob had gone into the mountains without taking her. They won't want a woman up there, he had said, no facilities. Meaning purdah – no walls to hide her behind. All those men, sitting in a dusty cave in the mountains. Actually, she didn't mind too much. There was more than enough to do at the clinic.

The tree's branches cast intricate shadows over the gravel, black against pale grey. The rust-red fruits were growing larger. Bethie was looking forward to trying them soon. A local woman had told her how to cut the hard outer layer of the pomegranate and squeeze the juice out of the fruit to make a refreshing drink.

Kneeling, she began her afternoon prayers.

Allah is most great   *Allah is most great*
Allah is most great   *Allah is most great*
I bear witness that there is no god apart from God
I bear witness that there is no god apart from God
I bear witness that Muhammad is God's messenger
I bear witness that Muhammad is God's messenger
Come to prayer
Come to prayer
Come to Salvation
Come to Salvation
God is great   *God is great*
There is no god apart from God.

Bob and Louise have been seeing each other for a few weeks now, and Bob has a recurring fantasy in which he is waking up next to Louise in the morning and rubbing his foot against her smoothly shaved leg, fondling certain parts of her while she is still asleep. He likes the way she has devoted her life to making money. He thinks they would make an interesting couple. He imagines himself making her an espresso before she gets up for her shower, proffering a plate of thinly sliced honeydew melon. They would have the occasional perfect dinner party, and laugh, as time went by, about how they met at that awful Dinner for Six evening.

Bob puts the cohabiting idea to Lou.

Louise has a sudden, pleasant vision of herself in pale buttery-yellow satin and holding a bouquet of pale yellow bud roses. 'Is this a marriage proposal, Bob?'

'That's not quite what I had in mind.'

Lou's pretty vision fades abruptly. 'Actually I have no intention of moving in with anybody.'

'But why not?' Bob spreads his hands in puzzlement. Surely he is a good catch, and he knows she likes his apartment: it's certainly more expansive than Lou's – a seedy light is throwing itself across the wooden floor now, and Bob can see that her bed is still unmade though it is late afternoon. 'We are ideally suited to each other.'

'So?' Lou is a little pink around the edges. 'Just because we get on, doesn't mean the next step is some big relationship.'

'I'm not talking about going the whole hog,' Bob reasons. 'I'm talking about sharing our lives for a while – enjoying each other.'

Lou gives a bright glassy laugh. 'For a while! Two minutes later and it's only temporary.'

'I was just trying to put it into perspective. We are dead for millions of years, after all,' he adds, a little tritely. His own fantasy is fraying at the edges.

'Is that what you tell your patients?' Lou can be scathing at times.

There is a pause. 'We call them clients,' he tells her, smoothing the material of his trousers over his spreading thighs, as if smoothing away crumbs. 'And if you were my client,' he says thoughtfully, 'I would tell you that you are afraid of commitment.' Bob has in fact segued into his professional role; it is easier than letting himself be hurt by Lou's apparent callousness.

She laughs, more deeply. 'That's a good one. But actually, if you must know, I am committed, to my work – I'm certainly not afraid of that kind of commitment – I just have no intention of ever getting myself married, fixed up, screwed down into any sort of permanent relationship –'

It is obvious to Bob that he must exit at this point, to salvage his pride, and avoid a scene: he gets enough crap at work without tolerating it on a personal level. Bob, giving his trousers one more graceful wipe, stands up and walks over to the door.

'And that,' he says, with barely a grimace, 'is exactly my point.'

Lou, after her 'meeting' with Bob, goes shopping. Lou always goes shopping when she feels off about something. She also goes shopping when she feels good, when it's her birthday, when it's Clare's birthday, when she feels fat, when she feels too blonde – shopping helps to focus her mind. For there is something bothering her about this Bob thing, and she doesn't know what it is, or whether it's worth bothering about in the first place. For after all, she said what she had wanted to say, and that's the main thing.

So Lou, with an hour free in the afternoon, walks uptown. She goes to the Keith Matheson shop, one of her favourite places in the city. She fingers a linen sundress, red roses on a light beige background ($550), and holds a full-length sleeveless black gown ($850) against her body, studying the effect in the cheval mirror.

Lou realises that she is feeling guilty, which is not a common occurrence. But she rationalises it by deciding that Bob, being a shrink, is probably using some kind of subliminal technique to make her move in with him. Making her feel that she will be missing out on something – her big chance – if she doesn't. He has probably been whispering something under his breath, like, *You will be old and alone soon.* She knows that he sometimes hypnotises his patients, why not her? She has her malleable moments.

Lou hangs the dress back on the rack and fingers several long-sleeved shirts that are folded in tissue paper and placed on shelves. She especially likes a shiny velvety look in burnt orange ($250). Bob has got another think coming. The lesson in all of this, Lou decides, freeing the shirt from its tissue paper, is not to get involved with shrinks.

An anaemic shopgirl slides up beside her. 'Would you like to try that on?'

'No,' says Lou, 'I'll just go ahead and buy it.'

And what she wants to buy next, if such a thing exists – and she recalls a shop where it just might – is a pair of orange crushed-velvet shoes to match.

April 1984
I've lost Mrs Kray's Saint Christopher's medal. Terry laughed, you'll have to stay put now, she said. Then she threw hers on my bed. 'Have mine. You're the one who believes in all that crap.' Actually, not true. How can a bit of metal protect you from harm?

Beth was sitting outside in the shade of the clinic wall, drinking tea after a hectic day's work. She'd closed her eyes for a moment and must have slept, for she was walking along a path, bare feet warm on dry earth, with tall reddish-green reeds on either side of her. She held out her hands on each side and felt reeds slap through her fingers, heard the murmur of the reeds all around her as if she had walked this path a hundred times. There was also the gentle shush of water below, lapping as if at the edges of an island. *I am going to the Garden*, she was thinking, in her dream. *It's not long now, not far.*

Among thornless lote-trees, and clustered plantains, and spreading shade, and fruit in plenty neither out of reach nor yet forbidden . . .

Then in her dream she saw a snake slither across her path. Even though she wasn't afraid of snakes – had seen enough of them since she'd been in Afghanistan to know that they were okay, just creatures, like any other creature, like the scorpions and lizards, plus there was the novelty factor – in her dream she was startled and anxious. She stopped on the path, the tall reeds hemming her in from both sides, aware that there was no way out, and watched as the snake disappeared among the stems of the reeds.

Panting, Bethie awoke to find the eyes of a wolf trained upon her.

'Oh. *Jesus.*'

She took a breath of cardamon-scented air, and shut her eyes to the sight. Opened her eyes. It was still there, as if cemented. A wolf – there was no way she could mistake it for being a mere dog, with the look of sheer yellow hunger in its eyes – mangy, its ribs obvious, one paw bleeding a little – and the stories she'd heard about wolves since coming to this country ran through her head. A baby snatched from its cradle. A mad wolf running through a village and biting twenty-eight people, infecting all of them with rabies. A man on a bicycle being bitten by a lean wolf which hung onto his ankle but was too weak even to break the skin. Travellers savaged in a mountain pass. A wolf would have to be mad, and starving, to come down into Kabul.

'Allaho akbar,' she whispered. *God is great.*

The wolf took a step forward, ducked its head. Lifted its nose to sniff the air.

Then a shot rang out. The wolf teetered, and crumpled sideways. Slumped to the ground.

Franco came out of the clinic, holding a handgun. He went over and inspected the wolf, pushed it with the toe of his boot. Then, seeing Beth, he held up the gun and blew into it, Western-style, joking. 'A wolf,' he said, '*incroyable*. You'd think they'd have more sense.'

The gunshot had brought people from all directions, shouting and waving their hands about. Bethie got up and calmly went inside. Franco may have pulled the trigger, but Allah had saved her from the wolf.

EIGHTEEN

Lou ONCE said: 'Clare and Bethie are the clever ones, so I'm not even going to bother competing with them. I decided long ago I'd just devote myself to the god of money.' By twenty-four Louise owned her own house, a modest bungalow in Hillsborough, a few doors down the road from the Baptist church. 'That way,' she liked to joke, 'I can hear the singing on a Sunday morning while I'm still in bed and know that there are people in the world crazier than me.'

Ten years later and she is sitting at a white-clothed table in an expensive downtown restaurant with three men in dark suits. The sound of the wharves rises up to the windows, where it's met by a Vivaldi flute concerto. Cutlery has been pushed aside and there are papers laid out on the table. Lou shows the men where to sign, marking the places with tiny crosses with her slim golden wand of a pen that the men find a little awkward to use: a delicate instrument that is nevertheless weighty with gold. She is still in residential sales, though she likes to make the occasional foray into commercial.

When the deal is done, Lou signals the waiter and he brings to the table a huge silver platter that is brimming with oysters, glistening grey in the bottom halves of their shells. Not so long ago these oysters would have been cogitating the wash of briny tide. There is champagne as well, because it's a big deal and Lou is going to get piles of money from it for the part she has played; and they raise their shimmering glasses over the plate of oysters and clink them together as if they have all discovered the secret of immortality.

'To future success,' toasts one of the men.

Lou would have said 'To money', except that always sounds so tactless. Neither would it sit so well with her feminine image – that pen, that lace-edged white blouse beneath her suit jacket – so instead she smiles and says, 'To new friends.'

Old friends can be okay too.

Later that afternoon she finds Sid outside the office. He is looking at the Jervois Road villa in the window (five bedrooms, three bathrooms, study, pool), bending towards the glass and squinting as if he is seeing something he doesn't like. Lou leans against the doorjamb, framed by glass.

'That's way out of your price range, mate.'

Sid straightens, caught out. 'Jesus – *Lou*. What're you doing here?'

'This happens to be my place of work.'

She watches him take out a packet of cigarettes and light one. Imagine, if she had got pregnant to Sid that night (what a laugh). How that time seems like a century ago. But, what would it feel like, picking that old scab? He's still got it, that certain tight-arsed *je ne sais quoi* that the men Lou usually dates lack. Briefly, Lou wonders what has become of Oliver. Probably farming asparagus, or something.

'What're you doing these days?'

He shrugs. 'You know, on the hustle, usual thing.'

'Selling used cars then?' It is Lou's idea of a joke.

Sid doesn't find it funny. 'Come off it. Nah, I'm in the air-conditioning industry.'

'You look busy.'

'Just come from a meeting. I've finished for the day.' They look at each other for a moment. 'Say, I've just had an idea –'

He is still transparent. 'I don't do drugs any more.'

'Not even for old times' sake?'

'We didn't have any old times, Sid.'

'That's not how I remember it.'

She can feel the heat coming off him, his dark eyes boring into her. My God, the bare-faced arrogance of the man. Though Lou has to admit it, he's improved with age. Even his suit is well-cut and expensive. Well well, we all grow up some time.

'I'll let the desk know I'm going out.'

She takes him back to her place so at least she can be comfortable. And besides, she can't face whatever hovel Sid is living in at the moment, though he claims to have bought his own house out in the hills of West Auckland. That fits, thinks Lou: a Westie. He has a bag of dope in his pocket and starts rolling joints as soon as he gets in the room. Lou swings her jacket over a chair.

'You're a bad bad boy,' she says, sitting opposite him on the white couch, the glass coffee table between them. 'But then, you always were, weren't you, Sid.'

Sid, handing her a joint, is still looking round, taking it all in. 'You've done pretty good, Louise.' He looks at everything: the wall-to-ceiling windows overlooking the harbour; the black shiny bar from behind which Lou has taken a bottle of chardonnay; even her shoes, which are black, a low heel and very classy. There is a big white futon over in the far corner: you can just see it behind a white paper screen. He flicks a flame from his lighter.

'You Purefoy girls,' mutters Sid. 'You've done all right. I saw that sister of yours a while back, what was her name –'

'Clare.' Lou doesn't want to talk about Clare.

'Yeah, that's the one, I saw her in the newspaper. She'd been given some award or other, for doctors.' Sid considers this for a while, letting pale smoke seep from between his lips. 'But you were always the looker, baby.'

'Don't call me baby.' She hands him the joint.

Sid grins minimally. He calls every good-looking woman baby, in spite of these sensitive times. 'Sure, if you don't want me to, Lou, I won't.' Has she gone frigid in her old age? That'd be his luck, just when he thought he was in with a chance. His dope, after all. He inhales religiously, then washes it down with a mouthful of plonk. 'Not a bad drop.' It could've been the '80s all over again.

Louise has taken off her shoes and put her stockinged feet up on the coffee table. Sid, passing the joint across, sits back, considering her soles, then slips off his own shoes and slides his feet beneath the table. 'How about I give you a foot massage, Lou?'

Lou inhales smoke. Her face is tingling pleasantly. 'Yep, you were the original Bad Boy,' she says, 'no mucking round with you, eh Sid. Why is it, do you think, that women like bastards?'

He takes it as a compliment. 'Cause it's more exciting, babe. I mean who wants a milksop, a lapdog, a whipping boy?'

'I bet you don't believe in the sensitive new age guy either.'

'What the fuck's that when it's at home?'

'Exactly my point. You're an original, Sid.' She is mulling over her glass of wine, and the atmosphere seems to be getting a little uncomfortable, though Sid thinks it could be the dope making him paranoid. She flashes him a look, some hair falling out of her bun. Sid restrains the urge to lean over and unpin it for her; the hair is making him lose his attention.

'Yep, the original smash and grab artist,' says Lou.

He washes down another mouthful of wine, like it's water. 'What's that supposed to mean?'

'You know what it means.'

'Buggered if I do –'

'Jesus, Sid, do I have to fucking spell it out? You *arsehole*.'

There, she's finally said it, and boy does it feel good.

Sid actually looks hurt. 'Well, that's nice.' He refills his glass. 'One little incident, and you're gonna hold it against me for the rest of my life?'

'I could've done you for a dog's dinner.'

Sid, vaguely chastened, remembers a mate of his who'd got into serious shit over a girl and the poor bastard hadn't even done anything. A bloke wasn't safe these days. He turns the wine glass between his fingers.

'Sorry, mate,' he mutters, 'must've been out of it that night, eh. Will you forgive me?'

Lou is taken aback. She never thought he'd admit it, let alone apologise. Actually, it's all starting to seem rather ridiculous: she can't be bothered with all that grudge-match stuff. 'Fuck it,' she says. 'You're forgiven.'

Sid savours the moment. 'Good on ya, babe.'

'Don't call me babe.'

'Just think, if I hadn't been such a jerk, what might've happened –

you and me, we'd have made a good team –' That look again, dark and hot, making the soles of her feet tingle.

'Yeah? What would've happened, Sid?'

He gets up, unsteadily, and comes around the glass coffee table to sit beside her. 'I could show you a good time, Lou.' He pushes a piece of hair behind her ear, fingertip lingering on the nice earring, gold. Sid appreciates a woman who has class. 'We could make up for past mistakes, eh –'

She grabs his tie and hauls him in close, kissing him hard on the lips. They could be rocking in an unstable boat. 'Let's relive old times,' Lou hisses into his mouth. 'Except this time, *I'll* be on top.'

The next day is Sunday, and Louise is dressed in Levi's and white T-shirt when she opens the door to Clare.

'I just need to get a glass of water,' Clare mutters, 'before we go.'

'Wait here, I'll get it for you.'

But Clare is used to getting things for herself, and squeezes past Lou who seems keen to go. The apartment is a mess, but its white walls and furnishings remind Clare of their mother's house. Louise's second passion in life (after selling property) is collecting antique teapots, and there are dozens of them lined up in formation on the shelves of a glass bookcase, their spouts all turned to the left, as if saluting a distant Major Teapot. There are empty wine bottles on the coffee table and a man's suit jacket lies throttled on the floor. Clare gets her water and doesn't say anything, not even when she spots Sid's profile at the foot of the bed.

Outside, the light is too harsh. Lou, squinting, dons dark glasses.

'Wasn't that Sid – ?'

'Ran into him yesterday.'

'But Lou,' says Clare, eyes flashing, 'he *raped* you.' An early and impulsive confidence, given in a moment of weakness, Lou has regretted it ever since. Trust Clare to bring it up now.

'That was years ago, for God's sake,' says Lou. 'Things change.' She gets into the passenger seat of the car, ignoring Clare's prim lips.

Clare puts the car into reverse. She can't think of a thing to say to that. It is as if the fabric of the day has been wrenched apart a fraction, and something black and viscous has been allowed to peep through. Lou's lack of morals makes Clare long to be snug and safe again in her little town on the edge of the firth.

Bethie had gone to the bazaar with Franco one afternoon. Walking past a ramshackle tea house near the river, she spotted through the window a man who looked just like the Turkoman sitting with a group of mujahedin. While Franco was busy at a nearby stall buying some okra, she went over and knocked on the dusty window. The man looked up, his eyes bloodshot and vacant, as if he was stoned. Then, with a stirring of recognition, he walked outside to meet her.

They spoke together for several minutes, the man gripping Beth's elbow. Then Franco, approaching from the stall, saw them break apart. The Turk seemed to stumble a little as he re-entered the dark smoky interior of the tea house. Beth's face, when Franco joined her, was impossible to read.

'Hey Beth, what's that guy doing back in Kabul?'
She attempted a shrug. 'Fuck knows.'

May 1984
City of reeds destroyed. No safe haven.

Clare doesn't know what to make of this latest diary entry. She's on her way to work, walking, hoping to clear away the feeling of disorientation that's come upon her – as if too much information has been punched into her brain. Emerging from the bottom of Jacob's Ladder, the sky barks down at her, lurid yellow as if before a storm. She is blinking and struggling to get her sunglasses out of her pack when the Marshall boy cruises past crow-like on his black bicycle, pedalling awkwardly in heavy boots.

He spots her, looks away. Looks again, confused, and nearly runs over a matted cocker spaniel that has stopped to relieve itself in the middle of the road. He swerves just in time, and with head down cycles rapidly away.

We all have our moments of weakness, mulls Louise. One of her listings is a large Victorian villa in St Mary's Bay that sits high above the street and endures in pale shades of opulence. The owners are away in France for two weeks, and one night Lou decides to visit. It's late enough for the garden to be in darkness, and Lou can let herself in unnoticed through the back door. The neighbour's television set flickers fluorescent through the roman blinds. She steps quickly across the silent kitchen (German appliances, slate floor, granite bench) and punches in the numbers which deactivate the burglar alarm.

Going through to the large lounge-cum-dining room, she eases off her Reeboks and prostrates herself lengthwise on the deep cream cushions of the sofa. Ah, luxury. She really ought not to be in here.

There is a phone on a wooden inlaid table by her head, and she lifts the receiver. 'Send a crate of champagne – no, make that two crates – ha ha –' She lets the receiver dangle in her hand, lets the line buzz. This place: this is exactly the kind of place Lou wants to have one day. Everything just so. A few expensive pieces, but not too many, a few modern artworks on the walls, a wine cellar . . . Life could end tomorrow, sighs Lou, and these people would have *lived*.

She puts back the receiver and pads down the hall to the master bedroom. She stands at the foot of the bed with its cream satin cover, then turns her back on it, and falls. *Ahhh*. Like splashing into a heap of feathers. She stares up at the midnight-blue canopy studded with gold stars, and wiggles her stockinged feet. I could dig this, she sighs, I definitely could.

There is another phone beside the bed. It's very much against her own professional standards – not to mention the company's standards – and it would mean her job if anybody found out; but it's just too much of a temptation. She slides over the sea of satin, and dials Sid's number.

'I could blackmail you, y'know,' comments Sid, cruising round the dark house behind Louise – she won't risk any lights – a bottle of scotch dangling from his hand.

'How's that?'

'I could tell your boss what you're up to – having guests.' He catches at her waist in the hallway but she ducks free.

'I've saved the best for last.'

'Holy Cow,' sneezes Sid. He is allergic to woollen carpets. The bathroom – the only room in the house which is out of keeping with the villa style – is the size of the master bedroom, and has mirrors that glimmer from the light of a single white candle: Lou has plucked it out of a wrought-iron candelabra, intending to replace it later. In the middle of the room is a round spa bath made of black marble. 'Look at this motherfucker,' admires Sid, leaning forward on the balls of his feet to assess its depth. 'You could throw a party in this sucker.'

Lou is putting in the plug, turning on the gold-plated taps; she even eases two fat white towels out of a long thin cupboard built into the wall beside the handbasin – may as well be hung for a sheep. 'And that's exactly what we are going to do.'

Sid smirks across the bath at her. 'You are the woman of my dreams,' he says, taking a suck at the bottle before passing it to Lou.

Later Lou is meditative, thinks fleetingly of Clare and the hospital, Bethie. 'Sometimes I feel like I should be doing something – well, more with my life. Maybe something more worthwhile. What I do . . . there are times when I wonder if it's not a little lacking in deeper meaning. What d'you think, Sid. Is there more to life than this –?'

Sid too is in a mellow mood. 'Sure,' he says, 'I just can't think of it right now.'

It was just another dusty day in Kabul, a dry wind racketing round the streets and making your eyes sore. If anything, the city seemed quieter than usual. Or it might have been the numb feeling in her head since the Turkoman's words outside the tea house that made the day seem muffled.

Beth and Terry had the day off and were wandering along a road flanked by market stalls. There were wooden carts selling racks of cigarettes, mangoes, tomatoes, bananas. Dark-bearded men with hooked noses sat in little booths or tents among their wares. There was a stall where Terry considered buying a knotted rug to take back home. They sat down with the turbaned vendor and had a cup of

CITY OF REEDS

green tea. He sported one of the clinic's wooden legs, which stuck out to one side while the good leg remained tucked beneath him. 'You have husbands?' he wanted to know; and when Terry laughed and shook her head, he said, 'I have two sons, very good boys, strong, you come and meet them –'

It took some persuasion to get away from the rug vendor and his plans. They wandered further, desultorily, and bought a paper cone of fried sweets from a confectioner's stall. A group of small boys was following them, calling out 'Inglistan –'.

'How can they tell we're foreign when we're wearing all this shit?' said Terry, tugging at the shawl which covered her head. Bethie was inside her burqa, shrouded as if in a cloud. She glanced at Terry, trying to focus on the sunny day, being with her friend.

'Could be because your shawl keeps falling off, and you're wearing sandshoes.'

Terry paused, tugging the muslin shawl back over her hair. She had trouble with keeping covered; scarves just seemed to fall off her, slide sideways. 'These things are hopeless,' she said. Then, 'Ugh, what's that horrible smell?'

They were passing a ditch filled with sewage. Other women pulled their shawls over their faces.

'This has to be the most dismal hole of a place you could ever find,' said Terry, squinting up at the hillsides dotted with stone-coloured shacks. In the distance a single tower block rose into the bleached sky; nearby was a turquoise minaret, its paint flaking. A heavy armoured vehicle rolled past, driven by mujahedin.

Bethie looked round, as if noticing it all for the first time. 'It has a simple charm.'

'Yeah, right.' They both laughed. 'What I wouldn't give for a great big bath.'

'Don't.'

'With lashings of deliciously scented bubbles!'

'Shut up.'

'Actually I'd settle for just a decent hot shower.'

They passed a queue of people, mostly women in burqas, waiting for a bus. Up ahead was an intersection of wide potholed roads, with an armoured tank sitting guard. 'You know Rob said we should take a week off, get out of Kabul for a few days –'

'Yeah, he said the same thing to me too, just this morning. I'd really like to get away for a while – this place is starting to get to me –'

'What do you think of Peshawar?'

'Why don't we head over to Turkey?'

Terry's eyes lit up. 'That's a brilliant idea. We could soak in one of those Turkish baths.'

'Yeah, and maybe it's not so dusty over there. I'd give anything to feel properly clean for a while.'

The bus pulled up and a man, striding purposefully towards the queue, came into Bethie's focus. His eyes were instantly noticeable – glowing, almost on fire – and his glare was fixed on Terry as if he would burn a hole through her head. A fundamentalist, for sure.

Tripping? Beth wondered briefly. They ought to get back to the clinic.

Then she saw that the man was carrying a Kalashnikov partly concealed beneath his shawl. In a war-torn city, it wasn't unusual – everybody thought it was brave to kill, she was thinking. Then the man lifted the gun and pointed it straight at them.

She grabbed Terry's arm.

'Foreign devils,' the man screamed. And opened fire.

Bethie threw herself beneath a cart, her face just inches from the stamping back hoofs of a spooked donkey. She slid out the other side and peered back, through a fallen pile of cabbages. The man had been wrestled onto the ground by several other men, who were busy punching him wherever they could get a fist in, and then a knife flashed. The air was rent with the wailing of women and children from within the bus.

Bethie staggered back. There were three casualties. Two Afghan women were down – Bethie lifted their burqas for a quick peep. 'Excuse me,' she muttered, 'excuse me.' It didn't seem too bad: one had been hit in the leg, the other in the side.

And then there was Terry.

She had broken free of her shawls – her face, legs and arms were uncovered, and the T-shirt she wore underneath was revealed: 'Jesus saves stamps' – but it was only what Beth had suspected as she'd run back: she was quite dead.

Blood was seeping into the dust. There was a single drop of blood on her smooth, tanned cheek. Beth wiped it away with her finger. She took one of Terry's hands, bending over it as if she might be able to breathe the life back into her. But all she could do was offer a futile squeeze. Time was cut off at the knees.

'Oh jeez,' she muttered over Terry's hand.

Then she turned to the group of onlookers. '*Red Cross*,' she cried harshly, her voice cracking, 'get help, quick.'

Three men ran off in different directions, shouting and gesticulating.

PART FOUR

Closure

NINETEEN

WHAT HAPPENS is that Lou rings in the middle of the night and says she has a very important meeting the next day and can't possibly pick up their father.

'No matter.' Tupulo articulates carefully into the receiver. 'I'm not doing anything, I'll get your old man –' He lies back on the couch and links his hands over his ribs, staring at rugby on the television.

Tupulo has been having odd moods lately, thinks Clare; he has been taking time off work for no apparent reason, has been drinking beer, has not mentioned hamburgers for at least a week, has stopped reading *Penthouse* at dawn, and has even been sleeping in the spare room so that Clare can't use the Internet late at night. Just yesterday she saw him trailing Mather with the other house surgeons, doing ward rounds, wearing a surgical mask. Could Tupulo be undergoing some mysterious crisis? When he remains silent she asks, 'Are you feeling all right?'

'If the All Blacks lose the fifth game,' he mutters darkly, 'it'll be the end of New Zealand society as we know it.'

In the end he and Clare go to the airport together.

When her father walks out of Customs, Clare barely recognises him. He is wearing a silver vinyl windcheater.

'Dad!'

He looks modest. 'I couldn't resist it.'

'You look like the uncle of Superman,' says Clare.

'That's the kind of thing Tupulo would say.'

They both look around.

'Where's Lou?'

'Where's Tupulo?' says Clare.

He had been standing just behind her shoulder not very long ago, giving off heat, and whispering into her ear a catalogue of inventions for the people coming off the flight: 'There goes Monica Lewinsky, disguised as a lover of poodles' – 'Now that man is suffering from severe constipation!' – And then, morosely, 'Grog's Own Country.' But Tupulo is nowhere to be seen.

'So how was your trip?'

'It was bloody hot,' says their father, scanning the crowd. 'Glad to be home.'

The other men from his group are coming out now, and they all pat each other on the back and shake hands, bidding each other farewell. 'We should do this again,' comments one. Marty is squinting and nodding, but when he turns back to Clare he says, 'You won't catch me going back there again. Once is enough. Well twice, if you count the first time. It's all very well, revisiting the past, but I'd rather keep my eyes on the future. Let's get going, eh Clare –'

Except that Tupulo has the car keys.

The airport is crowded with milling people. They go up the escalator and check the top floor: the bar, the Jean Batten café, the bookshop. Marty keeps bumping into people – their bags, their shoulders – and muttering apologies. They travel down a steep narrow escalator. The carpark is visible on their left, fanning out in the distance and lit by orange lamps. Clare is beginning to think they will never find him, that she and her father will be forced to wander this intermediate place for ever.

The crowd in the hall below is thinning now; planes are boarding. Then Clare sees Tupulo, standing in the midst of all that shifting human traffic, as if rooted to the lino. She catches up with him first, angry words forming in her mind: *Where have you been!* Marty is trailing behind, apologising to a woman in a pink suit and helping to retrieve her scattered hand luggage. Then she notices that Tupulo's eyes are staring and there's a faint sweat on his forehead and upper lip.

He turns a bereaved face to her. 'Clare,' he murmurs, 'I don't think I'm feeling very well –' Before he collapses onto the slippery floor.

CLOSURE

There is a long night of wondering how it will swing for Tupulo.

Picking himself up off the floor, he had muttered, 'Those damned Tequila Sunrises, get me every time.' Then he had walked calmly, albeit unsteadily, through the voluminous grey carpark, jingling the car keys. When they reached the VW, he had somehow levered himself into the back seat. 'Take me home,' he had said, at his most imperious.

Clare and her father exchanged a silent look.

Tupulo was unconscious by the time they got back to the town. Clare had driven straight to the hospital, and was kicking herself: *Why didn't I take him to Middlemore?* But she'd thought he was all right, just running a high fever, that it couldn't be anything serious; and he'd said, hadn't he: Just get me home! Who was she to argue? She should have argued. For here he was now, unconscious and on an IV. She had been sucked in by the rock-face of his health: Tupulo never got sick, while she herself nursed a succession of colds and petty ailments. *Shit*.

Clare helped Mather get Tupulo's clothes off. She gasped: his trunk and legs were covered in red weals, like some sort of insect bites. Clare pulled the lamp down closer. AIDS? An allergic reaction? She straightened, releasing her held breath.

'For goodness' sake,' muttered Alex, the shadows beneath his eyes a deep shade of mauve.

'Are you thinking what I'm thinking?'

'I can hazard a guess, Clare.' He was nodding, almost with a little grin. 'Chickenpox.'

Mather looks after Tupulo, while Clare is persuaded to wait outside. Couldn't even put in the IV line herself, she was shaking that much. She tries to calm down by reminding herself, This is a man I have known for only a couple of months. But it doesn't work. Mostly she is suffering from a feeling of helpless dislocation. Here I am, she thinks, on the Other Side, just like the relatives of my patients – like Mr Willow – and Tupulo himself has been cast in the role of patient! It is almost more than she can bear. She sinks into one of the hard plastic chairs. *Jeez, is this what people have to wait on out here?*

Tupulo is very sick. Complications from chickenpox are serious in an adult. What if he –? What if – ? All of the medical scenarios pass through her mind like speeding cruise missiles. She knows exactly what steps she would go through in such a case.

Clare tells herself to shut up.

Eventually dawn begins to colour the big sash window at the far end of the corridor.

When Sheila comes on duty she brings Clare a cup of sweet milky coffee. 'It's a funny old world, eh,' she murmurs, trying to sound cheerful, and backs away again as if it is Clare who is contagious. Clare looks at Sheila's retreating back. Of course, they all love Tupulo. Will they blame her if he –? Can't even say it.

Bugger Mather. She wants to be in there, to see what's going on. But it is her last burst of energy. Clare slumps, balancing the cup precariously on her thigh and between her two useless hands.

Dear God, let Tupulo be strong enough, and I'll – I'll be a much better person than I am right now, more patient, more caring – and I shall do the right thing by Tupulo, if that is possible.

When Clare gets back from the hospital later that day she cleans all the windows in the house.

It's a little difficult, as it seems to have got dark early, but she gets out the big square torch from the laundry cupboard so she can check the streaking when she's outside. She sprays and wipes until her arm hurts. Grunt sits on top of the sofa, following her movements with round anxious eyes and trembling from time to time. It appears that Grunt is missing Tupulo too.

Then, standing in the middle of the lounge with wrinkled hands and scrunched-up paper towels at her feet, Clare listens to the absence of Tupulo that is dominating the house. It is a large booming sound that, after a while, she realises must simply be her pulse sounding in her ears. She read once about a soundproof room in which somebody had heard their own blood coursing through their veins. Clare had always thought that was fanciful until now.

Ignoring Grunt's look of silent supplication, she grabs her coat and goes out, running down the slimy steps of Jacob's Ladder, ignoring how dark and creepy the stairway looks, fringed by oak trees. Below, the houses are cosy with lights. She walks until she gets to Harry's Bar, where she orders an Irish whisky, and sits. A rugby league game is playing on the television overhead, the sound turned down, and she stares at the tiny men running and tumbling, over and over again. Is there a point to this game? Tupulo could have told her, if he'd been here. Tupulo would like to be watching this.

Two men, at the other end of the bar, are making jokey remarks about her, as if she were a reflection in a shop window. They look like farmers, flushed and fifty, having a night on the town, and seem oblivious to the fact she looks as lonely as an Edward Hopper painting. 'What we need is a lady to spice things up round here,' says one. But the barman shuts them up. 'That's our doc,' he tells them, and leaning over describes to the men how Clare stitched up his leg a month ago after he fell over a bluff along the coast. He is already preparing her a second, unasked-for Irish whisky, on the house.

If Tupulo dies, thinks Clare, will I be able to endure it? No. He can't die: I won't allow it.

Staff think it's a great joke: Tupulo's room, which is overflowing with cards, flowers, chocolates, soft toys and fruit baskets. 'If I'd known I was going to be treated like royalty,' he says from the bed, 'then I would've got sick a long time ago!'

'King Tupulo,' says Clare, fingering the card on a fruit basket. 'Hope you get better soon, all the best, your friends at the Light Opera.' There is even a toy penguin from Al's Takeaways. Is this the kind of thing people send to men in hospital?

'I had no idea you were such a big wheel in this town.'

'Wheel 'em an' deal 'em,' murmurs Tupulo, still very weak.

'But why didn't you *tell* anybody?'

He looks sheepish. 'I was embarrassed.'

'But whatever for?'

Tupulo puffs out his chest, rather unsuccessfully as he's lying on his back. 'Grown men don't get chickenpox.'

Clare sits on the side of the bed, and cudgels a grape into her mouth. 'And especially not men who think they are infallible.' You wouldn't believe this man is a doctor, she thinks.

'Exactly,' whispers Tupulo. His infallibility has been sorely put to the test, and he is feeling all quivery inside.

'This has to be the most irresponsible thing you have ever done!'

He grins weakly. 'You haven't known me for very long.'

'And you're in the shit with Robeson.'

'What are they giving me?' he asks quietly, shooting intrepid sideways glances at the IV line and bag. Tupulo has never had a line, though he's had plenty of recent practice of putting them into other people.

'Never you mind,' says Clare firmly.

Tupulo rolls his eyes. 'Oh sweet Jesus,' he moans, 'who would ever have thought I'd end up in a hospital bed being pumped full of drugs like a helpless baby!'

Clare can't help laughing after all, and feeds him a grape. 'I thought I should ring your parents, and let them know about you.'

'My parents?' Tupulo frowns, thinking. 'No, they're away. Touring Alaska, or some such frivolity.'

'Anyone else you'd like me to call?'

'No, no.' He widens his eyes as she gets up. 'You're not *going*, are you?'

Clare shrugs. 'Sorry, I'll be back – catch you later.'

Tupulo rolls his head towards the bright opaque window. 'Not if I don't catch you first,' he mutters, completely wretched.

Because their father doesn't want Tupulo to miss anything, he tells the story of his Vietnam trip at Tupulo's bedside. Clare is perched on the edge of the bed, while Marty sits on the chair and hands his glossy photographs to Tupulo who then hands them to Clare.

There are many shots of older men who look like tourists posed in front of army buildings or tropical bush. 'Here's the boys outside the old barracks at Nui Dat. All the infantry companies were based there. I was amazed to see most of it's still standing. This is Jack, with the fella who saved his leg when he stepped on that mine.' Jack towers over a slightly built Vietnamese man wearing a sarong. Both of them are smiling largely.

'He's a doctor?' asks Clare.

'No no, picked the leg up out of the field, brought it back.'

Tupulo frowns out the window.

Marty also has presents. He has already decided that Clare and Tupulo will marry and live happily ever after and make up for all his mistakes, and this is his way of blessing the couple. For Clare there is a brooch in the shape of a palm tree. Tupulo gets a small box made out of transparent shell. There is also a bottle of duty-free brandy.

When Clare's father leaves the room to get a cup of coffee, Tupulo starts rolling his head about on the pillow and looking miserable. 'Just think, Clare,' he hisses, 'no nasty contraceptives for you any more –'

Clare has been wondering when this subject will surface. Tupulo could well have been rendered sterile from the infection. She has decided that she's okay not having children: she does not ache with maternal yearnings. Tupulo, however, is a different story. He often talks about starting a family, and she teases him about how he'll have to get a rural practice. 'Kids and cities are not incompatible, Purefoy,' he said once, with incipient disgust.

'It's much too soon to be worrying about that,' says Clare, giving his hand a squeeze, 'I'm sure you'll be fine.'

Tupulo raises his eyebrows, then turns his head into the pillow again. He is already mourning his lost lineage, all those tiny future Tupulos.

'You should wait until they do a sperm count,' she adds, then tries for a joke: 'That's the time to get depressed.'

It generally works for Tupulo. 'You're right,' he mutters, 'it's a waste of time getting depressed now. I'll save it up for when I know for certain, then I can get really depressed. In fact, let's throw a party, so the dump will be even rougher –'

'You're lucky to be alive, y'know.'

'Is that the kind of patronising salvo you give your patients –?'

'Fuck you.'

Their father returns with his paper cup of coffee, and pauses in the doorway. His silver jacket catches the light beguilingly. Walking along mainstreet, in a town of cow cockies, he stands out like an American visitor off a cruise ship.

'Have I missed something?'

Clare recalls Mrs Kray's last birthday party. A bevy of small children had appeared, clutching drooping flowers and teetering across the lawn to where she sat resplendent in purple sundress, and later Marty was heard to remark that so far the gods had not blessed him with any grandchildren. Clare had been surprised to see him go over to the children, who were running about and soiling themselves with cake, and pat two or three of them on their shiny heads, murmuring and bestowing Pope-like benedictions. Lou appeared at her elbow. 'Gawd,' she hissed, 'don't tell me the old man's getting clucky.' And with a small rocky laugh: 'You'd better give him some babies, Clare –' the ice clinking in her vodka and orange – 'cause I sure as hell won't be.' Clare seems to be surrounded by maternal men.

'No,' she says to Marty, 'you haven't missed a thing.'

Tupulo, still holding his box of shell, closes his eyes like a languishing prima donna.

At any moment God could come along and knock you over. A simple blow to the temple, a jab to the kidneys. Beth, curled tightly on the bed at Dean's Hotel, red-eyed from lack of sleep, stared at the finely cracked wall and did not register the call of the mullahs at dawn. She seemed unable to interpret sound any more, could not eat, could not sleep. There was only this painful moment of time that she existed within, like a bubble made of glass. If you moved too suddenly – stretched out an arm, a leg – the walls might splinter. Best to keep as still as possible.

Franco knocked on the door and came in with a glass of tea. He stood, hesitating for a moment, then sat on the twin bed. 'Beth, you have to take something. A little tea.'

She turned over carefully, to face him. 'Why?'

'Because you must be strong, to go home.'

An echo of the old Bethie surfaced for a moment, like a face floating up to the surface of a dark pond. 'I'll make you a deal –'

Franco brightened. 'Yes?'

'I'll drink your tea, I'll even eat some food, but in exchange I want to go back to Kabul.' This reverse journey that she was being forced to make had an element of farce about it. 'Let me stay here, in Peshawar even – just don't send me back.'

He sighed, looking down into the moon of green tea. 'You know, Beth, I cannot do that. It has been decided. All arranged. You must go home.'

She rolled back to face the wall.

'Just for a while,' he said, trying to keep the pleading out of his voice, 'then come back. We will all be here, you'll see. Very soon. Think of it –' he rolled his grey eyes to the ceiling and the slowly revolving fan, seeking inspiration – 'think of it as a holiday. *En vacance.*'

Beth closed her eyes. There was something she was trying to remember. A prayer. Such a small, simple thing. Surely you'd think she could remember it. How did it begin? If only she could remember, it might help to ease the roaring in her head. But, search as she might, there were only blank spaces there. She had thought she'd discovered her city of reeds, but unlike the Turkoman she had found hers in faith, in belief – so much more reliable than the physical. But she was wrong. Just as the Turkoman had been wrong. No Terry. No safe haven.

Franco put the glass of tea down on the floor beside the bed, and left the room.

TWENTY

THE HOUSE is eerie at night with only herself knocking about inside it. And it doesn't help that a high taunting wind has come up. There are creaks that Clare hasn't noticed before, and unidentifiable rustlings. The Brightly house has an alarm, but she doesn't know how to use it. She wraps a blanket tightly around herself and does a round of the house, checking windows and locks. All is secure. Unlike her own interior, which is welling with formless anxieties.

She closes the door of the spare room, which is in darkness, and also the bathroom door: the bathroom has a long opaque window which looks out onto the black and gesticulating garden. Then she pulls down the roman blinds in the kitchen and turns on an extra light. Better. She tucks herself into a corner of the couch and listens to Grunt's snoring, the fire flickering only a few inches away from his nose. She picks up a medical journal and tries to concentrate on the latest developments in heart surgery, but the wind is making such human wailing noises that she puts aside the journal and huddles deeper into her blanket.

It's just a bit of a storm . . . *I used to live by myself, not that long ago . . . there's nothing to worry about.* But how to sleep? *I'm just transferring my anxiety about Tupulo onto the house, the night.*

She feels better then, and picks up the television remote. She tries CNN first, but there is only more futile munching over of the American president and his mistresses.

Then Grunt jerks out of sleep and looks around the room.

'All right, boy?' says Clare, grateful at least for doggy company.

Grunt, ignoring her, gets up and trots over to the bathroom door, holding up his pushed-in snout and making a growly noise in his throat. Clare gets up and follows, reluctantly. Perhaps Grunt wants a drink: he likes to drink out of the bottom of the shower, an indulgence which Tupulo has encouraged.

She opens the door and there, framed in the long thin window, is the silhouette of a man. He is trying to peer through the glass and into the house.

Clare freezes. From the lounge clear words jump out at her from the television: 'Is this really the kind of man we want running the country?'

Grunt gives a throttled bark, then hides behind Clare's legs.

Clare flicks on the light, and the figure disappears from the window. *Fuck, fuck* – what to do? Call the police? But they are always so busy. And this is the kind of thing they are busy with. And then what? The prowler will have gone. Perhaps not. But it's very likely. Probably just a potential burglar, a peeping tom. Do nothing? And risk getting broken into. She is, after all, alone. (You can't count Grunt, who is now shivering with fear.)

So Clare rings her neighbour, Ken Gillman, one house up the hill, whose telephone number Dr Brightly left on the fridge. He appears at her front door in about three minutes, and is armed with a shotgun. Clare, holding the terrified Grunt in her arms, lets him in warily. It is times like this, she thinks, that you really find out who your neighbours are.

Ken catches her look. 'It's plastic,' he explains. 'I am metaphysically against firearms. But there are times when a show of strength can come in handy.'

'Like now,' says Clare.

'Exactly.' Ken straightens himself somewhat and takes a large torch from beneath his arm. 'Lead the way.'

Clare shows him the bathroom, and then the back door. Ken, torch wavering, heads beyond the pool of light on the lawn and is lost in the black of the garden for what seems an awfully long time. Clare – and probably Grunt, if it could be known – are imagining all sorts of horrible things: Ken getting knocked on the back of the head, Ken getting a large hunting knife stuck into his solar plexus, then kicked into the vege patch, his toy gun broken in half, Ken . . .

Ken reappears, breathing heavily. 'I couldn't see anybody,' he pants, 'but there are footprints in the soil outside the bathroom window.' He could be addressing Doctor Watson. 'And I found this –' He holds out a posy of red flowers wrapped in clear cellophane.

Clare takes them dubiously. 'Outside the bathroom?'

'No.' Ken ducks his head. 'Just out there, on the barbecue –' It is illuminated by the outdoor light.

'What are these, these flowers?'

'Pelargoniums,' states Ken, making to leave, 'usually known as geraniums. Quite harmless.'

Perhaps it was the Marshall boy, creeping round at night, too ashamed to come and see her because he has completely given up on the lawns, the garden. That's what it will be. The Marshall boy.

She leaves the flowers on the kitchen bench, and goes to bed – curled up tight beneath the duvet, with Grunt at the bottom of the bed, snoring again, and a chair under the door handle, just to feel safe. How could anybody ever feel safe, Clare wonders, in our houses built on sand. In the end it all comes down to a matter of attitude, of belief.

So it is during the time of Tupulo's dangerous illness, as he lies in the hospital, that Mr Willow gets in while the woman is unguarded. Thus thinks Clare sitting on the couch with her hands folded tightly in her lap while Mr Willow paces up and down in front of her, territorially. After all the precautions, he had simply walked in through the back door – the door that she had neglected to lock once Ken had left. It was as if he had anticipated Ken and his toy gun, using the flowers as a decoy.

'Everything is breaking down. One is never safe from life's woes . . . I'm not saying it's your fault. But you see, there is always a beginning,' he says, 'and an end. Don't worry, I'm not going to go all religious on you – I am not a religious man, maybe that's been my problem. If I'd had religion, then we wouldn't be here now, would we, you and I –' He pauses in his pacing, and glances over the stiff figure of Clare. 'The earth turns on its axle and everything changes, just like it has always been doing. People in the Renaissance understood it.'

How dangerous is he, she is wondering. He doesn't appear armed, and he's older than I am, undoubtedly less fit as well . . . I shall try it, why not? Everything is fine here, under control . . . this is not another Dr Mellows, a crazed patient taking to the doctor with a mallet . . . This kind of thing used to happen regularly at San Fran. People blowing their tops: you just stay calm, let it wash over you. So, I shall just get up and phone the police. I refuse to sit here and listen to a madman, raving on now about his trip and saving money.

Clare stands up, calmly walks over to the telephone, and dials one-one-one.

Mr Willow watches in disbelief. 'You don't have to do that,' he says, little wrinkles appearing at the bridge of his nose. 'I'm not going to hurt you: how can I?' He opens his palms to her, an improbable supplicant.

'Police,' says Clare, and gives them her address. 'It's an emergency.'

Willow gives a sigh, and resumes pacing.

'Of course,' he mutters, 'it's always an emergency with you people. My wife was an emergency, wasn't she, bustled in like she was and her guts heaving with blood. Yet you couldn't save her, could you.' Again he pauses. 'You did try, didn't you –?'

Clare remains by the telephone. If she has to, she will hit him with it, even though it's only plastic, a flimsy modern instrument more like a toy. 'Of course I tried,' she says, pissed off now, 'that's my job. I try to save lives, when I can. But your wife, Mr Willow, was already in very bad shape when I saw her –'

'Don't you think I know that?' Pacing again, he gives Tupulo's footstool a little kick on his way past it. 'Don't you think I knew that. When I called the ambulance. All day it had been going on, and I'd thought she was just complaining – she did that sometimes, just to punish me, going on and on – why should it be anything serious, no more than any other time – why bother the ambulance people, they've got enough to do, what with the drunk drivers killing each other on the roads – one old woman – because she's always ill. There's no getting around that.'

Finally he sits on the couch, his hands between his knees. '*Requiescat in pace*, that's the phrase, isn't it? That's all very well for the one who's gone. But there's no peace for the buggers who're left behind.'

Clare, too, sits. She is listening for the siren, for the police car to draw up outside and relieve her of Mr Willow.

'You're grieving,' she says, 'it's only natural – it's part of the process, to be angry.'

He doesn't seem to hear her. 'And what happens now?' He puts his face in his hands as the siren rings its approach. 'What will happen to all that money we saved?'

Mr Willow, broods Clare.

A policewoman visits the next morning and Clare must go over the whole incident again. She has had only a few hours sleep, despite taking a sleeping pill, and finds that the sequence of events is becoming a little confused in her mind. Did he leave the flowers before or after he knocked on her bedroom door? The police want her to press charges. The man is unhinged, the policewoman implies, without actually going so far as to use such a word; he could be dangerous, he ought to be sent for a psychiatric evaluation. It is unusual for a man, a stranger, to simply walk into one's house, she says, especially into the house of a surgeon. There *was* that case of Dr Mellows.

Clare, however, doesn't want to press charges, would feel too much of a heel. 'I'm confident he won't do it again,' she says. 'It was a one-off.'

The policewoman moves her shoulders within her tunic jacket, unable to restrain her doubts. It may be a rural town, but she has seen things to turn your stomach. 'We would all like to think that,' she replies.

'Besides,' adds Clare, 'he didn't hurt me.'

The conversation can go no further, and Clare is left alone again.

CLOSURE

Her main concern at the moment is keeping Tupulo in the dark: he would rant, rave, then fret. And in his present condition, Clare doesn't want him doing any of those things. It *is* possible – *isn't it* – that word won't get around the town. Unconsciously, Clare crosses her fingers behind her back.

She heads for the bathroom – she has put a sheet over the window, just until Tupulo gets back, feebly pinned it up with thumbtacks, as if it would keep out anything larger than moths – and vomits her breakfast into the toilet bowl.

Still in her blue bathrobe, Clare turns on CNN and catches the news that there is talk of a possible ceasefire in Afghanistan. Hospital footage is shown, and a dark-bearded doctor is interviewed. He says they are very short of medical supplies, can barely cope. When asked about how much longer they can go on, he begins to weep.

Clare rings Lou with the vague idea that she would like to talk about Mr Willow's intrusion; she needs to talk to someone, and Lou seems the best option. But there is only the answer service. She listens to all of it. Louise sounds clipped and polite on the phone, like a school principal. Business, thinks Clare, and hangs up without leaving a message.

There was a day when Clare really had to talk to Lou about Bethie or she would have burst. Twenty years old and wandering the sun-shafted city streets as if she was on a planet from *Lost in Space*. Dr Smith would appear at any moment, being silly, and she would have to rescue him from some large, ugly space monster. There were, however, only lunchtime shoppers and office workers enjoying the sun while they ate their sandwiches. She leaned over Grafton Bridge, thinking how people sometimes jumped off here; and she herself, a small sad speck on the earth's surface, was mesmerised by the motorway traffic below.

Clare walked on, and caught the bus over to Ponsonby.

At Louise's flat, Clare found the back door open and just walked in – she had been having trouble lately with simple procedures like knocking and waiting. The door was open, so she went through it.

Thankfully the harsh glittering light remained outside, so her eyes could have a rest. Clare took off the dark glasses she had taken to wearing. Inside the house, in the wooden-floored hallway, it was dim, pleasantly cool. A pink light shone from the glass above the front door.

There were sounds coming from Lou's bedroom. Clare stepped forward, knowing those sounds, of course: she watched TV, after all, down in the student lounge; there was a certain soap opera she liked to watch in the afternoons. And besides, she was no virgin; she had done it that once with Oliver, though that had been a silent affair. The bedroom door was open too. And there were Lou and a man, making sounds together, puffing and snorting beneath the white sheet. A bare foot protruded. There was much thrashing about, as if there was a large fish under there that the two of them were trying to hold down.

Clare ought to go – leave the house, and go away – but she *really* wanted to talk to Lou. At that moment, there was nobody else she could talk to. Janine would be all right, but Lou was her sister. There were things in common, things that didn't need explaining. She needed to talk about what went on when Louise last saw Bethie. Clare knew she ought to have brought it up ages ago, but somehow hadn't been able to until today.

Now there was an unforeseen hitch. Gruntings and snoutings, puffs and sighs, much rolling about with legs.

Clare, leaning on the doorjamb of Lou's room, turned to look at the panes of opaque coloured glass around the front door. There was a clotted triangle of dust in the corner of the hallway. Perhaps she could go into the kitchen and bang some things around. Or retrace her footsteps and knock loudly on the back door – nobody need ever know she'd already been inside. Like a ghost, yes. She ought just to go. But when she glanced back into the bedroom, there was Oliver's face peering at her over Louise's bare shoulder.

Clare left then, blindly, fumbling to get the dark glasses onto her face. She ran along the hot bleached street, back the way she had come, and was just in time to catch a Downtown bus, from where she felt herself to be at a great height, overlooking the streets and passersby, as if she was a foreigner. Clare blinked and shook her head as if she had something stuck in there. Although it was a relief once again to be out of the sun. The hottest summer on record, it was said. The city was sweating. Clare didn't do very well in heat: she burned instead of tanning and her armpits got soggy. A tall muttering woman with a nest of white hair sat across from her.

Louise and Oliver?

It didn't make sense. But then she had just seen it with her own eyes. Oliver... After all, she wasn't actually seeing Oliver any more: they had drifted apart. She didn't have time to have boyfriends... Louise? Really, what did it matter? Except that it was so inexplicable. Maybe she truly was a foreigner in her own country.

Later, over the phone, Lou had begged her forgiveness. There's nothing to forgive, said Clare, standing on one foot in the hostel corridor with the other foot tucked into her knee; and Lou had sounded relieved. It wasn't a matter of forgiveness, Clare had realised, as she replaced the receiver in its cradle. More, she had absolutely nothing in common with her younger sister.

'I fell from grace a long time ago,' thought Bethie.

It was the winter of her twenty-second year on the planet. *You've got your whole life ahead of you*, Marty had told her. Yet as she walked the streets of Auckland, it seemed as if even the blue-black asphalt was mocking her with its slick winking presence. She wandered aimlessly along Princes Street while trees leaned dark naked boughs over her head. Her arm ached from so much cold and damp. A cold wind blew leaves along the wet gutters, and the rain seemed extraordinary. If only they could have a small portion of this rain in Kabul, thought Bethie, they would think themselves kings. Water actually gushed down the gutters, heading for lower ground, heading for the sea, wasted.

Everywhere she looked there was evidence of waste. Too much of everything.

She sat in a café with a cup of milky coffee in front of her, while affluent people came and went; and like a betrayed lover she searched the day's newspaper, her fingers becoming soiled from the ink, looking for news of Kabul. Any scrap, something! But, incredibly enough, there was nothing. Nothing at all. She knew there were battles being waged over there, Afghans still being killed and made homeless – the 'Soviet Vietnam' – but where was the news of it? It was as if she had stepped off the page of one book only to find herself in another, totally different kind of story altogether.

And just as Afghanistan seemed to be invisible to the Western world, a fear was growing in Bethie that she too was becoming invisible, fading away. Even her tan seemed fake, like something she'd picked up going through the metal detector at Customs. She had taken to checking her hands, holding them up against the light, as if she might be turning transparent.

Bethie went to visit Clare. She thought that if she could talk it over, she might make herself seem real again.

She burst into Clare's room at the hostel, realising at the moment the door swung open that Clare might well be in class, or wherever else they went at med school. But no, she was there in her clean, cell-like room that reminded Bethie of her own room with its whitewashed walls back in Kabul. That fractional moment of hesitation chilled Beth even further.

She eased herself onto the bed, exhaling noisily, congested with a head cold. There was an unaccountable numbness in her legs that may or may not have been pain.

'Hi Bethie.' Clare's focus had sharpened since Beth had been away. Her hair, too –

'What have you done to your hair, Clare? Have you had it styled?'

Clare giggled. 'Janine cut some off –' she made a chopping gesture at her shoulder – 'here. Then we put a rinse through it.'

Bethie squinted. 'No wonder you looked different.'

Her hair was pale orange, for Christsake. She ought to have noticed when they first met, when they'd all got together at the house the night after she got back, Marty beaming and Lou opening bottles of fizzing champagne, Clare passing round a plate of sausage rolls. Bethie squeezed shut her eyes. The world seemed to be spinning, but had left her standing to one side.

Clare didn't seem to notice anything. Perhaps she just assumed the cold. 'Dad nearly had a fit.' She giggled again. 'He thought I'd have orange hair for the rest of my life. At least it wasn't blue, I told him: that was what Janine wanted to put in. But I told her I'd get kicked off the ward if I had blue hair.'

Bethie licked her lips, without managing to moisten them. Clare seemed so happy that it seemed abnormal, induced. To quell her anxiety about herself more than anything, to assuage the fear that she was hallucinating, she asked, 'You're not on drugs, are you, Clare?'

'Bethie! All I've done is colour my hair.'

'Sorry . . . my mistake.' Of course. In this country drugs were illegal while alcohol was not. 'Was thinking of something else.'

She was so tired.

It was only a few days ago that Marty had picked her up from the airport and driven her back to their hometown. 'You'll need to be debriefed,' he had said, driving through the night. How odd it sounded, like having someone come and pull down your briefs, or something: *da-brief*. But then maybe it was a kind of stripping down. Bethie didn't know. If it was that – and she suspected it was – she didn't want to be stripped down, didn't want anything taken away from her.

She had nodded into her wan reflection in the window, a dark landscape flashing past. 'Something's already been arranged, I think.'

It was hard not to let it alone. 'I was debriefed when I got back from 'Nam.'

'You were in the Army,' said Bethie, trying not to snap at him, when he only meant well.

'Same difference. They even do it these days in advertising!' He found the very idea amusing. 'I heard a chap talking about it on the telly the other night. After a big job, they'll go and have a debriefing session. Funny old world, eh.'

She was longing mostly for her bed, though when she finally got there she couldn't sleep. It didn't take long before restlessness, the quiet, and Marty's constant reminders – *You should make contact with them*, he kept repeating – drove her to leave after only two days.

So she was at a small hotel up the top of Queen Street, but the streetlights, police sirens and noise of buses going up the hill kept her awake into the early hours. Lou was disgusted. 'You must stay with me,' she'd said, but her flat contained no privacy. Bethie tried going there, thought she could crash on Lou's couch, but had fallen into a room containing a group of red laughing faces drinking cask wine. Impossible to stay with Louise.

'You carry on, with whatever you were doing when I came in –'

'Study,' said Clare, flicking up a glossy page, 'for next week's test. The spinal column.'

'Yes. Don't let me disturb you, I'll just have a little rest. Think I'm still jetlagged.'

Clare frowned. 'Yeah, I think you probably still are.' She watched as Bethie lay down and put an arm over her eyes. 'The cold won't be helping either,' she trailed off, wishing herself qualified already – for surely, if she were a proper doctor, and not just a student, she could help with whatever it was that so obviously ailed Bethie.

'I hope you've remembered to pay the Sky bill, Purefoy!'

As soon as he gets home Tupulo takes over the couch, is back in control of the television remote, and has become a rather demanding patient. Clare lasts the weekend, but is relieved when she has to return to work.

'Haven't you got anybody who could come and look after you for a few days? Family?'

'I don't need looking after,' huffs Tupulo.

Mrs Kray offers to stand in. She is, admits Clare, an expert in the soup department, and even comes complete with blender.

'I am forsaking hamburgers!' exclaims Tupulo.

'Al will go out of business.'

But Tupulo, calling himself one of 'death's escapees', persists. He has decided to go vegetarian, in the interests of living on for ever. He makes Mrs Kray fetch a packet of tofu and a bottle of powdered spirulina from the health food shop. It lasts all of one day.

'How can people *drink* this shit!' he exclaims hoarsely, holding up the glass of viscous green liquid to the light. 'This has to be the most revolting hoax and snowjob the dietary world has ever swallowed!' He tips it down the insinkerator. 'Goodbye, you putrid stuff. Mrs Kray –!' His pathetic bellow barely carries out to the vege patch where Mrs Kray is collecting fodder for her soups. Tupulo stands in the back doorway, pyjamas aquiver. 'Mrs Kray,' he declaims weakly, 'you are to take this revolting stuff back to the health shop *at once*. Tell them –' he thinks – 'tell them that their Product is – faulty! No, tell them it is Worse Than Useless, and if they won't refund your money (*my* money) tell them I intend to expose this pathetic sham (this grass powder), tell them I'm taking them to *Fair Go* –'

Mrs Kray flapping a bunch of silverbeet before her and threatening to ring Clare, ushers Tupulo back to his couch.

'I am a prisoner,' Tupulo sighs, coughing phlegmatically. 'A prisoner in my own house.'

Clare likes to consider miracles from time to time. They do happen, that's for sure, and there's no point in trying to explain them away. Tupulo, for example, has quite a good sperm count and is ecstatic. And the Marshall boy has pulled through. In fact, the Marshall boy goes some way towards assuaging Clare's guilt about Mrs Willow.

She was at home, on call, when the paramedic rang. A firearm injury, he said, a 'scoop and run'. She was out the door and backing her car down the drive in a matter of moments.

Clare had seen quite a few attempted suicides in San Fran, but it still gave her a shock, especially when she realised who it was. Marion, who had a son a similar age, had turned white when she'd seen the boy, covered in blood, lifted from the ambulance.

'It's a friggin war zone tonight,' muttered the paramedic.

It was clear what she had to do. With Mrs Willow firmly in mind, Clare rang Waikato. 'Put me through to Intensive Care. I want a helicopter retrieval.' Then she had got him stabilised – he had lost a lot of blood; she had made sure the airway was safe, put clean soaks on the wound, and given him fluids and blood, all the while avoiding the sight of his face. His arm, where she put in the line, was very pale and smooth, as if it rarely saw the light.

Clare imagined the boy waking up in a few hours time, not to any bleak paradise, but to the limbo of his normal life – except that it wouldn't be so normal for a while. All things considered, he really ought to be dead. He was probably saved by the fact that he'd been found so quickly. And because somehow the gun must have slipped.

While the helicopter crew were preparing the boy's transfer, Clare went out to talk to the parents. They both stood when they saw Clare approaching. Mrs Marshall was dressed in floral cotton and sensible shoes and looked every bit the old-fashioned ideal of a Countrywoman; Mr Marshall was red-faced and built like a bull. Clare was impressed once again that not everybody's offspring was an imprint of themselves.

'What happened?' Clare asked.

Mr Marshall glanced down at his wife, then cleared his throat. 'We heard the shot. A big bang. He'd taken my .22. I found him under the loquat tree.'

Mrs Marshall, unable to control herself any longer, blinked widely and tears sprang out. 'We don't know why he would do such a thing to himself. He'd broken up with his girlfriend, but –'

'Don't go on, Mum.' Mr Marshall frowned.

Clare motioned for them to sit down. She had a lot of things to explain.

'It's early days. It doesn't look as if the shot has hit anything major, but I can't tell for certain. It looks like the gun must've slipped when it went off.'

'Oh God,' wept the mother.

Later, leaving them, and looking back at the couple sitting talking quietly, holding hands, Clare had an intense feeling of *déjà vu*. They were the lucky ones, so far.

Sirens wailed in the distance, while Bethie sat at the hotel window gazing out over the night sky. Quite near was the dome of a cathedral, floodlit, so that it looked like a stranded moon.

There was so much noise that disturbed her at night that she sat wrapped in a blanket for hours at the window with its lower sash raised, the cool night air touching her hair, staring at the dome. It reminded her of the mosques – those pale blue buildings shimmering in the heat – though this dome was different, more womanly in shape. Yet it was solid in the centre of so much noise and metal and glass architecture; it retained a degree of beauty amidst the ugliness, the hard lines and sharp reflecting surfaces of the city canyon. There were fireworks one night, and Bethie lifted her knees up to her chin and hugged her legs, thrown back to Afghanistan and the sound of popping gunfire, *jungly*, imagining herself home again. *Home*, she laughed bitterly.

And what was ahead? She could see no further than the barren plains of work and marriage. Everything seemed so impossible. Impossible to go forward, impossible to go back. Voices raged in her head, then died off into futile arguments, only to circle again, like wolves. Until she just kept coming back to a single thought: *I've done everything I want to do.*

She made one last-ditch attempt to talk to somebody; and because of circumstances it turned out to be Louise – Clare was unreachable by phone, their father was away for a few days down south – so Bethie walked over to Lou's flat in Ponsonby. Louise was still in bed when Bethie knocked on the front door of the peeling villa, and she appeared wearing a red silk dressing gown.

'Bethie,' she groaned, 'what time is it?'

'I don't know,' admitted Beth, already regretting her visit.

They went into the gloomy kitchen, where Louise busied herself with making coffee. A man – nude, except for a red beret covering his shaven head – walked through the kitchen on his way to the bathroom and didn't even notice Beth sitting at the table in the corner. So she was invisible, after all. 'Was that a friend of yours?'

Lou looked up from the kettle with red, puffy eyes. 'No,' she said, 'I don't know who that was.'

Bethie tried for a joke, to cast a little light. 'That's what's wrong with the world,' she said. 'There's not enough nude men wandering about in it –'

Lou was too hungover even to laugh politely. Beth stared at the wall. There was a picture sellotaped there of a woman in Victorian dress, with wings, flying through the air over a city.

'So . . .' Louise placed a cup of coffee on the table and sat opposite Beth so that now the picture was right above Lou's head. 'What've you been up to?'

Bethie found that very funny – the picture, Lou's oblivious head, *what have you been up to* – and spluttered into her coffee.

'What?' muttered Lou. 'What?'

'Nothing.' She had located some of her 'old self' again. Old self, new self, past self, past-useby-date-self-life. 'I passed a park on the way here,' she said, remembering with a sudden jolt of energy, 'let's go to the park.'

'Come on, Beth, we're adults now.'

'Which is exactly why I want to go to the park. Go on, get some clothes on, or better still – no, come like that, come on, we have to hurry – we may grow up completely, any minute now – it may already be too late!'

Beth grabbed Lou's arm and dragged her out the door and onto the street. She was still in her red silk dressing gown and protesting madly. But then they were running down the dilapidated hill with the city distantly glimmering and winking and framed between wooden houses, past dark-eyed windows, Lou's bare feet slapping and watching to avoid broken glass, and Bethie holding her hand now with hair careering back on the wind of their velocity. She could have been back with Terry, sailing above a dry city landscape – until they skidded to a halt at the park.

'Beth Purefoy,' Lou gasped, squeezing a hand into her waist, 'you're a fucking madwoman . . .'

'Yes,' breathed Bethie, 'thank Christ, eh.' She leapt a chain hanging between wooden posts. 'Bags the big swing!'

And she sailed on the swing, feet in the air while Lou's dressing gown was like a red flag flapping with each downswing, heads back and laughing into the blue blue sky as if nothing could ever hurt them again. Lou, getting into the mood of it, opened her mouth as her swing plummeted downwards, and screamed. Bethie grinned at her new buddy, the sky.

There was a roundabout. They took turns pushing, their faces blurring – until they thought they'd be ill. Finally Lou *was* ill, leaning into the bushes, a white hand clinging onto the metal post of the climbing frame. 'Oh man,' she heaved, 'I've gotta go home.'

They walked back sedately. 'That was fun though, wasn't it,' said Beth, feeling her cold again.

'Yep,' admitted Lou, 'that was fun, I suppose.' But thinking that she'd rather be having fun in bed with Stuart any time of the day, and wondering if he'd still be there when she got back or whether he might've buggered off to uni yet. 'And,' added Louise out loud, 'my coffee'll be cold.'

Bethie snatched only a glance, but couldn't help seeing their mother in Lou's profile. They paused outside the house, and Beth laid a hand on the warm roof of Lou's new second-hand car. She was remembering their mother taking them for picnics at the old tower, the paddock of grass swaying in the breeze, how clean and secure that felt. A simple idea came to her.

'I can't sleep at the hotel,' said Beth. 'This afternoon, could you drive me back home?' She thought of how Marty was away for a few days, and how quiet the house would be. The deep skittery feeling inside her seemed to subside a little.

Louise was surprised, but didn't have to think about it for too long. After all, she hadn't done much for Beth since she'd got back. 'I haven't got anything on – why not?'

So it came down to this: a silent tower in the night. Opening the wooden door at the side with a crowbar, she shone her torch onto a set of steps that wound up into darkness. She started to climb. If she'd been more sentimental she might have imagined muted singing coming from above, angels or whatnot, but all she heard was an old-man wind shuffling about outside. And so much junk in her head. 'A penny for your thoughts,' she muttered out loud, finding comfort in the sound of her own voice. The metal banister of the stairway was rough and possibly rusty, and bit into the palm of her hand. In the torchlight she found another door, this one with a bolt which simply slid across. Just as well: she was running low on energy. Then she was outside, thank God. She stood breathing in the fresh cool night air. Stars glittered impossibly bright above her.

'Imagine if it was icy up here.' Like the mountains of the Hindu Kush. *Jungly, jungly.* Beth Purefoy, always the daredevil, that crazy Purefoy. And the words of the Turkoman echoed in the dark air, getting mixed up with images of Terry's face, *my wife her family reeds washed with blood*, as if Terry and the destroyed city had merged into being one and the same thing.

Only one regret: that the sky was not blue. But she couldn't get up during the day, too many people around, even in this small town, interfering. So, 2 a.m. and the sky a dirty black.

She walked the circle of the metal deck.

It wasn't all that high; but high enough – and at least it was *quiet*. She thought she could hear a fountain playing. It could be a garden, with running water, *thornless lote-trees* and she still didn't know what they were, but she could sense it behind her eyelids, that paradise, like a place that might not be very far away after all. Ah no, it was the river.

While all around lay the small town, sleeping – a few lights, speckled – and how precarious it seemed, how flimsy. One puff, and you'd blow it away. She grinned and cried out at her own largeness, filled up with it like a new discovery, for it was finally hers: '*Ha!*' For the lights too were so pretty, and the stars high above as well, making up for the lack of blue – but anyway, if you closed your eyes, there it was, all blue, as much blue as you could wish for.

Beth flung her arms wide, and cried out again – '*Ha!*' – then she fell into space.

TWENTY-ONE

W<small>HERE HER</small> mind would once have been occupied with practical thoughts – what to cook for tea, the state of her patients, going to the movies – Clare now catches herself thinking rather odd sorts of things. In the course of an afternoon, doing endoscopies, she thinks about:
- how snails would go about mating
- how they have a lifespan of twelve years, and what they do with that time
- cruising in the Concord, everybody sitting very neatly, strapped in like mental patients
- the Concord being snapped in half like a baguette
- all the people falling out but floating down like skydivers
- herself as a jet of smoke behind a jet
- what if Tupulo grew a beard, and what that would feel like
- kissing a hedgehog
- picking up a debilitating virus
- and spending months lying in bed
- Camille dying romantically of TB, the room filled with white camellias
- lying for months in her bed
- how there is nothing romantic about TB
- the anonymous caller who reported Beth's fall

On her way to the supermarket that evening, in the car, Clare nearly side-swipes a blue Toyota. The car toots its horn, but it's an afterthought and the sound is drenched by the rain that's tumbling from the sky. I'm lucky, thinks Clare, that the man hasn't followed me: imagines herself pulling up at a stop sign, the blue Toyota idling beside her and the driver punching her through the open window.

Clare winds up her window, just in case.

When the Marshall boy is transferred back from Waikato, Clare goes to check on him. He is lying with his fingers knitted on the pastel blue coverlet, his neck swathed with white bandage and protected by a neck brace. His eyes are closed and the eyelids are a translucent shade of yellow. She swallows down a feeling of hopeless nausea. If only she'd known, and been able to stop him.

'How are you feeling?'

He looks up, as if from a great distance, then flicks his eyebrows up and down.

'Your vocal cords weren't hit,' Clare tells him, 'but you won't be able to speak for a couple of days. Might have a bit of a sore throat too.'

That elicits a small smile.

'Is your neck giving you much pain?'

He moves his hand, as if to say 'A little'.

She stands by the bed looking down at him, and he has the same stark look on his face that she saw the day of the bike incident.

'If it gets too bad, the nurse can give you something more . . .'

He was so lucky, she thinks, that the pellets missed the internal carotid and the spinal column, and just penetrated soft tissue. There are so many structures in the neck that could have been hit. She wonders if he appreciates what a close call he's had, but then he must know that. Or perhaps he isn't very impressed at being dragged back from the abyss. And what would he have seen, at the edge? Would he have seen the same kind of thing Bethie saw? Clare feels certain that the Marshall boy must have discovered something important in his brush with death. She very much wants to know what it is. She would also like to know why he did it – but that's an impossible question right now, perhaps always.

Clare squeezes out a smile. 'See you tomorrow? Rest now.'
The boy blinks, dark-eyed and mute.

She thinks back to that day Beth visited her at the hostel. If only she had helped her, if only she'd known what lay ahead, she could have, might have – if only she'd been psychic, or simply hung onto Bethie and never let her go . . .

Clare rings Lou. It's 11.30 p.m. but Louise sounds alert.

'The last time you saw Beth, at your house –' She can hear Lou's careful breathing on the other end. 'What was she like? Was she depressed?'

'We've been over this before, Clare.'

'I know. But I just want to hear it again.'

A sigh. 'I didn't notice anything out of the ordinary – she seemed a bit low, and kind of mixed-up about something, taking me off to the park like that –'

Clare's hand on the receiver is sweating and she swaps it over, wiping her palm on her jeans leg. 'Yes?'

'I was only a kid, Clare.'

'How did she get back to the town, d'you think?'

There is a slight pause. 'She didn't say.'

'But –'

'Yes?'

'Didn't you try and keep her at your flat?'

'You saw her the day before – why didn't *you*?'

Clare swallows, painfully. There's nothing she can say to that.

'Look, Clare, I don't want to go over all this shit again – Beth was a lost soul, that's all there is to it –'

Clare can't picture her sister for a moment, can hear only darkness breathing.

'Goodnight, Clare.'

She slowly replaces the receiver. Turning, she sees her reflection in the black glass of the french door. That person looks pale and thin, a hand held to her mouth as if she might start to cry. The real Clare, however, takes a deep breath and folds her arms across her ribs.

It is a small town, but Clare keeps seeing Mr Willow: the other day in the supermarket, in a tweed overcoat, intently studying a packet of noodles; hanging about outside the new cinema, as if waiting for somebody; lined up lugubriously in the queue at the library. He could be following her, except that he's in these places before she gets to them. And he makes a point of avoiding her: doesn't meet her gaze, shrinks into his coat defensively, or simply leaves as soon as he sees her. Then Clare feels shunned. She'd like to think he could acknowledge her, but is relieved as well that he doesn't. What would she do? Nod, smile, say how d'you do? He is, after all, the man who walked uninvited into her house.

There has been more evidence coming out about Mr Willow. The policewoman rings to tell Clare that he is turning out to be rather an odd fellow. A few years back he stood trial for impersonating a nurse. For a year he had worked at a city hospital, and nobody had been any the wiser until he had had to re-register and his ruse was uncovered. But then he had escaped a conviction on the grounds of being emotionally disturbed, and spent some time at Kingseat. He wasn't even legally married to Mrs Willow. Her name was Haslett. And does Clare consider Mrs Willow's (or rather, Miss Haslett's) death to be in any way suspicious?

Clare doesn't think so. Only that the condition must have been apparent for some time before it came to a head. A matter of negligence perhaps – and how to prove that?

The policewoman also wants to warn Clare: to keep her house locked, leave the outside lights on. Just in case. Clare, getting off the telephone, is oddly shaken, as though she has stepped off an aeroplane into a strange and unexpected country. As if it isn't bad enough already, she thinks.

The problem is that the family are so grateful they have given her a gift: a large ceramic chicken. 'To keep your bread in,' explains Mrs Marshall cheerfully, pressing it upon her. Clare doesn't want to accept it – the boy, though secure now, may try to take his life again, for after all his parents can't be with him twenty-four hours of the day, and won't they then regret giving her this gift? But she can't refuse it either. It also seems inappropriate. It is much too optimistic an object, considering that a boy's life was nearly lost.

She tries reasoning with them, blushing a little in her embarrassment. 'Mrs Marshall,' says Clare, her head lowered over the chicken that is already weighing heavily on her palms, 'I appreciate the thought, but I didn't do anything – it was the team at Waikato who saved him.'

Mrs Marshall resolutely refuses to listen to her. 'We insist,' she says. 'He wouldn't have made it to the big hospital if it wasn't for you. And all the care you've taken since – well, it's the least we can do to express our thanks.'

'Besides,' adds Mr Marshall, his backside jutting in unlikely jeans, 'I get a discount.'

Clare can only shuffle and smile politely and thank them. It is obvious that as far as the Marshalls are concerned God has given them a reprieve, a second chance, and they are going to make the most of it.

'He was mowing my lawns, you know,' Clare adds. 'At the Brightly place.'

They light up. 'Oh yairs, the Brightlys.'

It isn't that noticeable, but Clare is getting quieter, is speaking less, and avoiding situations in which she might have to converse unnecessarily.

So far her slide towards muteness has barely been registered by those around her. At work she has even started writing notes to people. There are, of course, many situations when she must speak – during operations, for example, when requesting instruments or more blood; also before and after such procedures, when she must speak with relatives – but on the whole, she keeps it to a minimum. She is perfecting the art of the monosyllabic. And it is a blissful relief when she can go into theatre and sink into the blank spaces of her mind; it is the only time these days when she feels at peace. Nobody can hassle you. Cocooned in the operating theatre, for a brief time at least, she feels that nothing can touch her, that the outside world is held at bay and she is in control.

Words have become both meaningless and overly weighty, like small boulders tied in raffia sacks. Clare would like to escape into total silence. Perhaps she will head off to Tibet and join a monastery.

The ceramic chicken sits accusingly on the mantelpiece, a jogging reminder of her own inadequacies. One night if she lights a fire, it might accidentally fall off its perch and get knocked into the flames.

Tupulo leans over and confides in a whisper to Mrs Kray, 'I'm going to whisk Clare off to Club Med.' He is whispering because Clare has been very odd lately, especially after getting that crockery chicken, though she nodded when Tupulo said you shouldn't look up the bum of a gift horse – or in this case, a gift chook. She keeps moving it round the house, and can't seem to decide where to put it. Yesterday he found it in the shower. 'I'm going to organise it all, and then we will be winging away –' He flies his flattened hand through the air. They are sitting on Mrs Kray's back veranda, and Tupulo is tucked up beneath a mohair blanket on the deckchair. 'All I have to do is fix her down for a date – she's been a little obtuse lately – and look out Noumea, here we come –'

Mrs Kray cuts a piece of lemon ginger cake for Tupulo.

'My favourite,' he sighs, mournfully rolling his eyes and thinking about Clare, who appears to be lingering in the dark interior of Mrs Kray's house for some unknown reason. He leans over again to whisper, 'What do you think she's doing in there?'

The practical Mrs Kray goes to have a look. She finds Clare in the front lounge, playing with the wooden Noah's Ark set that Mrs Kray keeps in pride of place on a table beneath the bay window. Her grandfather made the set, and she considers it to be a very unusual family heirloom. Clare, crouched at table level, is walking a wooden sheep up the ramp of the Ark. She has also grouped the animals in an uneven line, ready to board the vessel, although not in pairs.

Mrs Kray reports back to Tupulo. 'She's playing with the Ark.'

'Ah, good,' says Tupulo. 'Did you know that they found what they think is the real Ark a few years ago, stuck up on a hill in the Middle East.'

'Perhaps Clare would like some cake,' ventures Mrs Kray, frowning.

'I should think so,' decides Tupulo, frowning too.

When they come to leave the house, and even though it is only a few metres to the car, Clare silently stops Tupulo before he steps outside and winds his scarf around his neck, pulls the wool beanie onto his head, then brushes his lips with a slight kiss. Tupulo has – temporarily at least – resigned himself to such ministrations.

The boy is soon talking hoarsely, and eating normal though mashed foods. She comes in while he is having his lunch, sitting up and looking quite bright. Clare sits on the end of the bed and checks his file, feels his pulse.

'Missing your steak?' she jokes.

'I'm vegetarian,' he grimaces. The voice isn't too bad, he is recovering nicely. He will need physio, but Clare expects the neck to heal very well and the boy to regain the full use of his throat.

'I'll look at your neck,' she says, 'all right?'

He nods and puts his fork down beside the mashed potato.

She carefully unwinds the bandage until the wound is revealed. Still no sign of infection: good. Clare fingers the pale skin below his ear. 'Tender?' He nods. 'You're going to have a scar,' she warns.

'That's cool,' mutters the boy.

How cool, she wonders, that constant reminder; or will it become like a gang badge? An emblem of masculinity, like a soldier might sport a war trophy. She puts the bandage back in place. Her fingers mutter over his skin.

She is still at his shoulder when she asks the question that has been running over and over in her mind and which she had promised herself she wouldn't ask him: 'Why did you do it?' It comes out muted, even though the small ward is unusually empty, sunlight playing over the polished lino floor and the three other beds like starched lozenges.

The boy shrugs, his eyes flash up at her. 'I dunno,' he says, then looks down at his dinner tray with its congealing mass of potato and pile of soggy carrot.

Clare thinks there isn't any more, and sucking back the taste of disappointment that's in her mouth, prepares to move on. The boy speaks again, without looking up. His voice is husky.

'Everything important that's happened, seems to be in the past – and the future is too . . .' He moves his hand, unable to find the words.

Clare swallows, and feels pain in her own throat. She inhales a steady breath of air, nods: 'Yes, I can see that.'

The boy, as she leaves the ward, glances thoughtfully over her narrow shoulders, then rests his head back against the stark white pillow.

This is Lou's past. A New Year's Eve when Clare was still training to be a surgeon, and Lou arrived at the door of her flat to take her out partying. 'You can't sit around at home on New Year's Eve,' Lou exclaimed, dragging her to the door, 'I won't allow it. Only very boring people do that, and fundamentalist Christians. Let's boogie.' Outside was a car parked halfway up the grass kerb and full of people singing 'Ninety-five bottles of beer on the wall . . .' Clare reluctantly squeezed herself into the back seat beside a young man wearing a stocking over his head, his features mashed beneath, grinning insanely. A bottle of something was being passed round, but Clare shook her head.

The party was already spilling out onto the front lawn, and as they pulled up outside a man sailed out of an open window and landed face-down in a dark leafy bush. He remained where he was, and Clare, trailing along behind the others, automatically reached out for his wrist to check his pulse. The man turned his head and vomited over her shoes.

'Oh no,' breathed Clare, stepping back quickly.

She didn't know what to do, so took off her shoes and left them under another bush. It was lucky she was wearing her old sandshoes. This was one of those small catastrophes she might make into a joke to tell Janine later. Barefoot, she entered the house.

CLOSURE

Lou was already in the centre of the party, teasing off her coat like she was a stripper, one bare shoulder at a time, to much whooping and clapping. She is obviously well known here, thought Clare, leaning against the doorjamb, people shoving past as if she were a piece of seaweed in a roughly tossed ocean. Finally Lou got her coat off – to reveal a mock nurse's outfit: a strapless white mini-dress which showed her cleavage, suspenders, white stockings, white high heels. As people clapped and wolf-whistled, she plunked a nurse's hat on her head and started gyrating round the room. How ironic, thought Clare, remembering that Louise had once wanted to be a nurse. She also remembered a med school party where one of the guys in her class had dressed up like that – but was funny. She smiled, thinking of the great hairy legs encased in white stockings.

Behind Clare, two men were having a muttered conversation.

'Fifty bucks if you score the nurse tonight?'

'Okay, I'm game. But what if we both do it?'

'Then the deal's off, fuck-knuckle.' A dull underhand laughter.

Whatever were they talking about? Janine ought to be here; she would be able to make sense of all this – but Janine had gone home for the summer break. Where Clare ought to be, except that she had a holiday job at the hospital. What would she do back home anyway? Lie around in the sun and read trashy novels. Clare couldn't face anything that wasn't work. Lou waltzed past, mouthing the words of the beating music, and tried to grab Clare on the way. But Clare deftly avoided the clutching hand. She didn't want to be pulled into that hellish mass of bodies. The doorjamb was solid like a lifebuoy.

What size tsunami would it take, Clare then wondered, to demolish this whole house and all its occupants (including herself, that's only fair)? Ten metres would probably do it quite nicely. She imagined water sweeping in through the windows, that wall with the three plaster ducks tumbling down onto the heads of the revellers, the house that seemed so solid a moment ago now a matchbox wreck.

Revel, considered Clare, to revel. She seemed incapable of it at the best of times.

She pushed her way out of the house with its deafening music. The unknown man was still prone in the bush, and appeared to be snoring. Stars were faintly apparent beyond the city glow. Clare turned left on the street and walked away, unaware of the police car pulling up outside the party behind her, her feet slapping along the asphalt pavement like pale guppies in the semi-darkness.

And this is the present. In Lou's latest letter from their mother there is also a postcard from Tahiti, a picture of a school of white pointers floating in a turquoise sea. The legend reads, 'Un banc de requins du large.' A school of deepsea sharks. Louise turns the card over and over, admiring her blood-red fingernails against the turquoise. *Well, if that's what they have in Tahiti, I think I'll give it a miss.*

'*PS*', writes their mother, '*show this picture to Clare as well.*' But Lou has no intention of doing any such thing. Her maternal correspondence – no matter how ridiculous – is private, and always has been.

After digesting the usual contents of this latest letter – Bob's minor illnesses, the shop, the price of prawns – Lou finds that she has to go out. It's either that or sit around contemplating slashing her wrists. She can't be bothered ringing anybody – it's late and she must go out *straight away* – so she puts on her tight black skirt (thank God for lycra) and walks uptown to Stamp, her favourite club at the moment. Lou has found that she can walk into this place on a busy night after 10, and nobody will take any notice of her being alone. Also she went to school with one of the women who works behind the bar.

But Melanie isn't working tonight, and Lou, wedging herself onto a bar stool, orders a margarita from a young man with silver spiked hair who doesn't look old enough to be serving alcohol. She crosses her legs as he shakes and pours, very seriously, then barely looks at her as he takes her money. Hey, is she invisible? When he returns with her change she says, 'I haven't seen you here before –' actually, she has to shout, the music's that loud, some sort of hip hop with no discernible lyrics – 'what's your name?' There was a time when she could pick up barboys simply by adjusting her bra strap.

The young man leans over and speaks quite softly, making a joke of it but also serious at the same time: 'My name's way out of your league –'

CLOSURE

He goes off to serve somebody else and Lou takes a mouthful of her drink. Her face has gone hot.

Not far away, a wall of young people is jumping up and down to the beat of the music. To give herself a focus, Lou studies the dancers. There are young women wearing army fatigues, others with nose rings or tattoos on their biceps. A boy bounces past, his shaven head pale blue under the club lights. Ten years ago this would've been a punk scene: today it's average. Beyond and above the dancers is a huge screen with a single image being played and replayed on it: footage of the President's mistress, big and soft in a pastel cardigan, walking into court. Then she is rewound like a cartoon doll, and is walking again, that sly smile and dark American-beauty-queen hair. Years from now, she will be compared to Marilyn Monroe. Lou finds that a depressing thought.

Why did she even start coming to this club? Jesus, bring back the simple days of disco.

Lou swallows the rest of her margarita, and waves her glass at a different bartender to fetch her another. When did she suddenly get old? She's only thirty-four, but she feels ancient among all these kids. All because of that up-himself dickhead behind the bar who is probably gay. *I could buy and sell you any day of the week, mate.*

Her drink arrives, she pays for it, the barperson leaves her alone. She ought to have rung Bob, not come out alone. But if Mel had been here, everything would have been different, she would've had fun.

She ought to settle down, take up Bob's offer. Like trying on a dress, Lou imagines first Bob moving into her apartment – where to put his African totem collection? – then herself moving into his apartment . . . then, buying an apartment together. In fact, she has just listed a beauty . . . The second drink is easing down and making her feel a little better. Since when did some kid put her down like that and get away with it? *Fuck you*, she mouths at his back.

There is a man near the door, leaning against a pillar watching the dancers, who looks about eighteen. Lou slides off the bar stool, loses her right shoe – black suede, chunky high heel – recovers it, muttering, 'Come on, baby, let's rob a cradle –'

She could do it too, she could. A kid like that, all they're interested in is sex, it doesn't even matter all that much who it's with, as long as it's free. But halfway across the room, Lou has a vision of herself. She is in professional mode. Dressed in her black silk suit and white lycra top, she is waiting in the marble vestibule of the Maxwell Road property, folder held between her hands, demure, patient, while the client peruses the bedrooms. Normally she would follow them about, point out all the salient features, but this client is a private person, likes to make his own judgements. He is also worth a hellova lot of money round town. Lou sold him an investment apartment only a few months ago. So Lou waits in the vestibule, barely moving. There are times when she gets a gut feeling about a deal; it is like the feeling she gets when her gold-link chain clinks against bone. The feeling she gets when she's about to make a lot of money.

'I've got to get home,' she thinks urgently. If it's going to happen he'll call tonight, and Lou has (remarkably) left her cellphone at the apartment. The boy smiles as she walks past him; already sober, she throws him a wink.

Next time, she thinks. Or then again, maybe not.

There is no doubt in her mind: Mr Willow is hanging around inside the hospital. Clare has just come out of surgery (a straightforward appendectomy), has just cleaned herself up and is heading down the corridor to speak to the teenager's mother, when she glances at the orderly pushing the laundry trolley towards her from the opposite direction and recognises the world-weary features of Mr Willow.

The man must be mad. This hospital is too small for him to pull off such a stunt, and especially at his age. He is obviously trying to taunt her. How dare he! Is she to be subjected to such attentions, in her place of *work*? Normal people simply don't behave like that – barging in where it ought to be sacrosanct – pretending to be someone else.

Mr Willow is breaking the rules.

This is what it feels like to be invaded from within, again.

Clare has stopped in the middle of the corridor and watches in disbelief as the orderly and his trolley disappear into the laundry room, and in one breath realises not only how stuffy she sounds but also how defenceless. *Have I become so vulnerable?* Yet, if she can't be safe here, in her hospital (and when was it ever hers?), then where can she feel truly secure. Will they need security guards here too? And she remembers something that makes her laugh, rather hysterically: *my profession has offered me shelter.* Yeah, right. How could she have been so naive?

Clare hurries off to alert the front desk. Halfway along the corridor, however, she slows. Isn't this just what he wants her to do? To panic? Clare refuses to panic, for anyone. She continues more sedately, spacing out the words in her head: *Sheila, call the police.*

A minor panic spreads through the building nevertheless, like a bomb scare. The hospital is systematically searched, but no trace of Mr Willow is found.

Then all the orderlies are gathered together on the scruffy grass outside the cafeteria. They are a small motley band, and seem irritated to be called away from their various duties about the hospital. All those dirty jobs, thinks Clare with distaste, now that Mr Willow has tainted their lot – all those mundane folding lifting cleaning jobs; though normally she thinks of the orderlies (if she thinks of them at all) with respect: rather them than I, she usually thinks. Actually, Clare knows them all by name, except for a soft-shouldered man with grey hair tied back in a ponytail who nevertheless looks familiar.

She steps up to him. 'Are you new?'

He nods, halfheartedly. 'Since last week.'

Clare looks over her shoulder at Sheila, who confirms this. There is a muffled pause. 'Did I pass you, by any chance, in the corridor half an hour ago?'

'Yep,' says the orderly. 'Doctor Purefoy,' he adds. He even has the advantage of knowing her name. *Bugger.*

'Thank you,' she mutters. 'False alarm. Sorry.'

On the day he is due to go home, she finds the Marshall boy sitting, dressed, on the side of his bed. It's odd seeing him in jeans, boots, black T-shirt, looking like a visitor, except for the bandage. She sits beside him, and keeps her hands linked tightly together. She wants to wish him luck, but it seems the wrong thing to say. She wants to, hell, she just wants to say something, for Christsake. *It can't get much worse than this.* And there were so many things she had wanted to talk to the boy about. She wants to fly up and away; yet the past clutches vengefully at her heels, keeping her down.

Sensing her frustration, the boy speaks quietly. 'I heard that nurse saying you've got laryngitis,' he says, then gives her a frank glance. 'My personal motto has always been, never tell anybody the whole truth.'

It's as if they're temporarily transparent to each other.

There is a murmuring inside her head, as if she hears the movement of reeds. This is wrong, Clare is thinking, this is so unethical, unprofessional – *I am completely losing it.* Yet increasingly each day she has the feeling that she is trapped inside a huge glass jar, and she can't stop herself from leaning close to the boy and brushing her lips gently against his, so that for a moment at least nothing seems to matter any more.

The Marshall boy closes his eyes, and kisses her back.

TWENTY-TWO

CLARE DOESN'T get very much interesting mail. There are overseas medical journals, *NZ Doctor*, occasionally a postcard from Brown & Wiseman, and the odd book she orders from Amazon. So when Tupulo extracts the large brown envelope from the letterbox he brings it to Clare as she sits drinking coffee by the french doors and reading Saturday's *Herald*, and stands over her while she opens it.

There is a 4x5 black and white photograph: a group shot of medical staff at the entrance of a hospital. Clare shakes the envelope, but no letter or note of explanation falls out. Tupulo is disappointed, and pads away, coughing. She puts the photograph on the newspaper and cradles her mug between her hands, enjoying the sun. Perhaps it's an old photo from her intern days that somebody has sent as a joke. She peers at the shot again: no, that's not Auckland Hospital. And there are no familiar faces among the group.

Then it springs out at her: a tiny face, lurid slab-like cheeks beneath curly dark hair (a wig?), hands linked in front of the uniform, the chin turned slightly to the left. And that smile: a little askance, as if he had been caught unawares, both smug and uncertain.

The devil in our midst. The face of anarchy.

The jolt of the past causes her to spill coffee onto her jeans. She'll have to get them off and wash them before it stains. But still Clare sits, poring over the image, damp heat soaking into her skin. Why has he sent her this picture? Maybe he is proud of what he did. Is it a warning? He must know that the police have told her about him – so why follow up with this photograph? What is she supposed to do with it? Frame it and put it on her wall?

Willow peers out at her as if he had looked into the future and seen Clare Purefoy studying the photograph over her morning coffee. As if he knew what lay in the future.

Silly, she thinks, you are being silly. For some perverted reason, he is trying to intimidate you. No, she thinks, he is staking his claim. But, to what?

Clare throws it down in disgust. Is there no end to the man's intimidation?

'Tupulo,' she calls, more a gasp. No reply.

Clare thinks about taking the photograph outside to the barbecue and setting it alight. Mr Willow's earlier incarnation would buckle and blacken, and be engulfed in flames. Would some small part of Mr Willow, on the other side of town, silently scream? *Silly*, thinks Clare. Her heart gives a thump. Too much coffee, too much –

She has to do what those self-help books tell people: confront your fear or, in this case, your *doppelgänger*. She needs to put this younger, more cunning version of Mr Willow into perspective, so that he will shrink back to being simply a figure among the crowd. She knows all of this, intellectually, but Clare instead finds herself paralysed between a photograph and a hard place.

The problem is that nothing seems to make sense any more. Several days later Clare wakes in the morning with gritty eyes, and states to the air, 'Chaos is only a fingertip away.'

Tupulo rolls over with a moist snorting noise. 'What –?'

Clare can barely repeat the phrase, indeed, has no idea where it has come from. It is not the kind of thing she normally says: it's too, too Slavic. No wonder she doesn't want to talk. You don't know what might slip out from between the neural transmitters and the aberrant lips. You don't know when your defences are going to slip either. She hadn't even been aware that she had defences. The body as moat, the mind as fortress.

Tupulo rolls over, blinking awake. 'Shall we have waffles for breakfast?'

Clare, lying on her back with her blunt fingers linked over her ribs, continues to stare silently at the ceiling.

There is a muttered conference going on in the kitchen. Mrs Kray has been caught in mid-stride, holding a metal pot of cold soup against her waist, while Tupulo harangues her at close range, practically spitting into the poor woman's ear.

'She hasn't got up. You can see what time it is –' Tupulo holds his wrist in front of their faces so that they can both examine his Rolex. It is 9.35. 'She always gets up,' he hisses. 'She gets up, she makes coffee, she goes to work, always the same. Oh, and has a shower. She has a shower first. She gets up and has a shower.'

Mrs Kray looks at Tupulo, surprised at his obvious distress.

He snouts even closer to her ear, hissing hotly. 'I think it's a *woman* problem. The other night, she sat up in bed, covered in sweat, and said we should have babies.' As much as Tupulo would like babies around the house, he knows that Clare is not maternal – it is all very confusing.

Mrs Kray, for her part, is finding it difficult to reconcile the man she is seeing right before her – only three inches away in fact – with the young surgeon who works so efficiently and cheerfully at the hospital. Has the world turned upside-down?

'Have you tried talking to her, Tupulo?'

He shrugs miserably into his dressing gown. 'Of course! I even offered her waffles. Clare loves waffles,' he adds sadly.

Mrs Kray hands Tupulo the pot of cold soup, and heads with determination to the bedroom. Clare is still in the same position, lying on her back, her eyes fixed on the ceiling. Mrs Kray sits on the side of the bed. She takes one of Clare's hands, unlatching it from its partner, and holds it between her own, rubbing it. Despite the duvet cover, Clare is cold. Tupulo is hovering anxiously in the doorway.

'Make coffee,' Mrs Kray says over her shoulder.

'So, Clare –' Mrs Kray treads carefully, as if among butterfly mines. 'We've known each other for a long time now, Clare,' she says, straining to be diplomatic, 'I know you would tell me if there was anything the matter, wouldn't you – Clare?'

Clare shuts her eyes. There are muffled bangs from the kitchen. Something falls on the floor, shattering loudly; then there's a muttered curse. Mrs Kray shakes her head.

She tries a different tack. 'When I was a child, I held my breath for as long as I could, because I didn't want to milk the cow. I was sick of getting up every morning in the dark, and sick of the ugly stink of cows' udders. So I held my breath because I thought it would go away if I could hold on for long enough.' Clare opens her eyes again. 'What happened was that my mother slapped my cheek, and I took a big breath, then I went out and milked that damn cow again.' She sighs. 'You must tell me what's the matter, Clare, 'cause Tupulo's going nuts, and that's not a pleasant sight.'

As if to illustrate this point, there is another smash from the kitchen. Mrs Kray holds up her chin, as if to sniff the air, or to listen to a distant sound of wailing.

Clare, too, seems aware now of Tupulo's distress. She is like the hospital: when it stops functioning, all is affected; she is a structure that other people rely upon. In a very low voice she says, 'Everything is falling apart.' Her eyes are exceptionally blue at this moment, practically azure, but then, like switching off a light, she shuts them again.

Back in the kitchen Tupulo has managed to make some coffee, although the bench and floor look desecrated. He pours an unsteady cup from the espresso machine.

'In my opinion,' says Mrs Kray, folding her arms across her bony chest, 'that girl just needs a holiday.'

'Exactly,' spits out Tupulo, 'exactly what I've been saying myself. All she ever does is work. Look, we even have the tickets –' He rushes into the lounge to get the travel voucher, as if Mrs Kray has demanded proof. 'You see, Noumea –'

But Mrs Kray has her head on one side, and is staring thoughtfully through the open laundry door. The brightly coloured ceramic chicken is sitting on the washing machine. Then Mrs Kray's hair seems to twitch with sudden inspiration.

'Isn't that the chicken that the Marshalls gave Clare?'

'Not exactly Clare's style, is it –'

'Did you know,' Mrs Kray says slowly, remembering that Tupulo is still on sick leave, 'that the boy walked into the sea yesterday –?'

So Mrs Kray brings the Marshall boy to visit Clare.

When Mrs Kray shuts the bedroom door behind him, the boy at first hangs about, not knowing where to look. Clare doesn't seem aware of his presence, though her eyes are open. He sticks his hands in his pockets, and paces up and down a little. He touches his fingers lightly to his bandaged neck, and snuffles, wipes his nose with the back of his hand: he's caught a bit of a chill. There is a picture on the wall that catches his eye – a Fomison oil painting of a jester, monochrome, grainy, almost bestial in its simplicity. The boy is greatly disturbed by this painting. Such bad luck, he thinks, this kind of picture. Like all his bad thoughts illustrated for anybody to see. He grabs a Hawaiian shirt that is crumpled on the floor, and drapes it over the painting to hide it.

This has brought him round to the other side of the bed; and, feeling rather tired now, he lies alongside Clare, crossing his Doc Martens over the edge, and links his fingers beneath his head. He sighs. Actually, it's way easier this way, because he doesn't have to look at her any more. 'What am I supposed to say to her?' he had asked Mrs Kray, who hadn't known herself, all of them blundering about like moths near a lightbulb. It's a bit like he's lying on his own bed at home looking at the ceiling, so it's a smooth jump to feeling like he's talking to himself.

'Shit, eh,' he begins. 'This makes me think of when I was in the hospital, and I woke up and everything was white, and I thought, Fuck, I'm up in the sky.

'But then it came to me, slowly, that I wasn't, and especially when that fat woman brought me a tray of food. She didn't even know about me, and there she was putting a tray of food at the end of my bed – she was giving them to everybody I suppose, her job, eh – on that table thing that wheels up and down the bed. I thought, maybe it's her first day on the job or something. But what was I supposed to do with it? I couldn't even swallow. But I could smell it, real clearly:

there was roasted meat, beans, custard. What was I supposed to do with that shit? So I knew I was somewhere I hadn't ever planned to be. That kind of threw me. That you think you've got it all planned, all sorted out into little boxes – This is what I'm gonna do, this is where I'm gonna go – but you end up somewhere so radically different, that it's – ah, I dunno how to say it – I felt all odd, like I was being pulled in two directions, like nothing meant anything any more. Like, well, I guess like I had no meaning even. Like I'd just been erased. But I'd already felt like that, *before*, so how was this different? *Before*, it was something I hated, that I couldn't accept – like I was being pulled in every direction, and I wanted to fight it, I wanted to do something about it, and there seemed only one thing to do. But in the hospital, it was just a big emptiness, and that was okay for a while. I could just lie back and forget about stuff, all that other shit.

'So, the second time, what I did, I figured if I got away with it a second time, then it was meant to be, and if I didn't – if I lost, you know if I got fucking *saved* again – then I'd accept it and give myself up completely to living, forget all that shit about meaning. I'd finally accept that life is just an illusion and the only truth is that you've gotta keep moving.

'But I had to test it, you see, and that tray of food and the fat woman walking away again and the room filled with light like somebody had flicked on strobe lights, I knew I had to test it again.

'So I was swimming, in all my clothes, though I'd taken off my boots – I left them on the beach, all neat like you're supposed to leave boots – and it was like I'd been swimming for fucking ages when it all went real calm. Inside my head, I mean. Outside, the sea and all that shit, well it was really rough, and with just about every wave I was swallowing great chunks of water, and you know how disgusting that is, swallowing sea water? Well, it is, man. I mean, Doctor Purefoy.

'So, there I was, and I rolled over onto my back and the sky – you should've seen it, it was beautiful, so pearly grey like I'd never seen it before, you couldn't have painted it, even if you'd been a great painter, Van Gogh or somebody, it was that good – and I thought, This is great, this is the whole meaning of everything, I'm ready now, take me now, take me, take –'

The boy's voice petered out. It was very quiet in the room, yet he could barely hear Clare's breathing, so he had to keep going to fill up the battering embarrassment of silence.

'That was when this fishing boat comes along. I dunno how they saw me, in all that grey rolling water, but they did. And they dragged me on board, even though I was real pissed off, *really*, at the time. Honest, you wouldn't fucking believe it . . . and my boots, when I went back to get them, somebody had fucking nicked my boots . . . so, here I am.'

He clicks his fingers, and points in the air, as if aiming a gun at an old adversary.

'Gotcha!'

Clare makes a noise in her throat, and the boy turns his head, his black eyebrows raised, to see that Clare's face is crumpling. He's confused at first – and for a moment feels a worm of fear in his gut – but then he sees what she's doing and it's not long before he starts too.

From the other side of the closed door, where Mrs Kray and Tupulo are pressed against the wood, there comes the inexplicable sound of mirth.

TWENTY-THREE

A HIP-HIGH PICKET fence defines the boundaries of this wooden villa on its corner site. At the back of the house narrow wooden steps lead down to a thriving vegetable garden. Smoke lifts up from an oil drum in the rear corner. Clare is reminded of Marty's horticultural efforts. She finds herself admiring the procession of beans, the huge leaves of courgette plants, shiny clumps of silverbeet, and finds that her nervousness has dissipated.

In the midst of all this finery is Mr Willow. In his grey cardigan (which she now notices has the elbows out), his back to her, he potters about the tomatoes, fiddling with something. Shoulders hunched, head bowed, he could be any elderly fellow among his vegies. She can even see the dandruff sprinkled over the collar of his navy shirt, though that may be her imagination.

'Mr Willow,' she calls softly.

He looks up blindly for the source of the voice. Clare stands by the fence, one hand on the faded gate. She has no intention of entering Mr Willow's territory (and has no need to).

He does a minute double-take. His fingers are tangled up with string.

'Mr Willow,' Clare says more firmly, 'I have something for you.'

Finally he musters the wherewithal to make his way towards her. His eyes, though, shift from side to side, unable to meet her frankly curious gaze.

'This is yours, I believe.'

She holds out the 4x5 group photograph. His own, younger face, stares up puppet-like at the indolent sky. He takes it and stands subdued, as if expecting a telling-off. But all Clare says is, 'Goodbye,' and turns on her heel.

As she is walking around the corner, and about to lose Mr Willow from her sight, she notices a movement in her peripheral vision – a gun? a stone? – and glancing up sharply she sees Mr Willow, back to her once more, drop the photograph into the smouldering oil drum.

It has become apparent to Clare what she must do. It can't be put off any longer. As she walks along quickly, a breeze soothes her hot face. She would jog, only the backpack is too awkward.

Lou, following her sister at a cool distance, wonders where Clare can be off to in such a distracted state. She'd been mooching about all morning, cleaning things and not saying very much, until Lou thought she'd go crazy. And after Mrs Kray had practically begged Louise to come and talk to Clare, babbling about people hurting themselves and other nonsense – something about a mute boy – that Lou didn't understand. But what good had that done, rushing over here? Clare had said barely a word to her, then she'd taken a backpack and gone out.

So she had followed her. It was easy. Clare never looked back. Lou had waited, smoking a cigarette, in the oak-leafed shadows of Jacob's Ladder, while Clare went into the neighbour's house, then came out again with a strained look on her face. What the hell was going on? Lou couldn't help but recall Bethie that day. Had her other sister gone nuts now too? Surely not. But then, think about it . . .

Clare walks along at a clipping pace, and at one stage Lou has to jog to keep her in sight. Then Clare hesitates, and turns into the familiar gravel road at the edge of town that they all prefer to avoid.

Clare stands at the farm gate, trying to put off entering the paddock. Her old feeling of revulsion for the thing rises like nausea: she wants to run away, anything. Grass waves and shiffles, like the surface of water, and the tower rises up out of it.

The tower itself looks smaller up close, quite innocuous, a relic. Is it tall enough? It's several metres, maybe fifteen – but how would you know, how to be sure, that it was tall enough? You might be left a cripple, in a wheelchair: worse, surely, than just living. Surely a gun would be more reliable. But then (thinking of the Marshall boy) perhaps not. You had to be determined, to kill yourself. Really determined. Bethie would have been. But would she have known, how tall the tower? Perhaps if you dived, head first. That might help. But would you be thinking straight, about such a thing? The coroner's report – only last night she'd had the courage to look at it, and all this time it had been in Marty's rolltop desk, under sixteen years of Telecom receipts – had discussed head injuries.

You would have to be brave. Could Clare ever be that brave?

A movement in the dark shadow of the puriri trees catches her attention. An orange heifer comes out into the sunlight and wanders away down the paddock.

Clare climbs over the gate and wades slowly through the grass towards the base of the tower. From down here, yes, it's tall. Towering, in fact. But she needs to know exactly how tall.

The door around the side is, of course, locked. There's a chain and padlock. Would anybody ever come here, for maintenance? Clare doesn't think so. She eases her backpack off her shoulders and gets out the boltcutters she has borrowed from Ken Gillman. She takes off the padlock. The door, though stiff, yields to her shoulder.

Inside it's gloomy, musty. Clare hangs by the door, psyching herself to go on. She gets the hip flask of brandy out of her pack (again, prepared) and drinks a stinging mouthful. She feels like she'll be swamped by restless spirits if she goes in, or at the very least, large hairy spiders.

There's a dusty metal staircase curling up into the gloom. A large pipe, like a curled vine, lies abandoned on the concrete floor. Light comes through the odd window, though not very much of it. The sound of her feet on the metal staircase is so loud that she keeps looking over her shoulder. The whole place has started groaning and whingeing. She thinks of Tupulo and Grunt back at the house, and wishes she were there with them. A large thick cobweb falls against her face and she screams, brushing hysterically at air. By the time she reaches the top she is puffing with fear. This door has a slide bolt

CLOSURE

on the inside – as if to keep out intruders – and it opens with relative ease.

The light is dazzling. Clare steps out onto a round metal platform that skirts the central column. She looks down to the grass, holding on tightly to the metal railing, and is swept with vertigo. Inhaling, she focuses on the heifer which is grazing innocuously below, a plastic farmyard toy. But she's so dizzy that she sits, cross-legged, on the metal: definitely high enough.

She takes out the hip flask again and has a swig. Then she gets out the plumbline and tape measure (also from her helpful though frankly curious neighbour) and takes quite some time dropping the line over the side, then hauling it back up and laboriously measuring it. Clare ends up in a tangle of string, fingers shaking, and the back of her neck burning in the sun. An orange that she'd brought just in case she got hungry rolls out of the pack and falls over the side. *Damn. Old butterfingers Purefoy.* She's near tears now, when she figures out the height. Twenty-three metres. The tower is twenty-three metres tall.

Tall enough. High enough that there would be no pain, no lying injured in a dark silent field, but instant. Lou was wrong: not a lost soul. Beth knew exactly what she was doing. Nobody could have saved her.

Clare slumps, more relieved than she could have imagined, the sun beating rudely down upon her. She thinks that she ought to burn something, symbolically, and scatter ashes, but she has neglected that side of things.

'What are you doing, Clare?'

Lou stands in the open doorway, looking down at Clare in disbelief. 'You nearly killed me with an orange. Have you gone completely mad?'

Clare puts away the tape measure, then starts to wind up the plumbline, but is only making the tangled mess worse.

'Here. I'll do that.' Louise sits down on the deck, and deftly untangles the line, shaking her head. Clare leans back against the tower, and takes another mouthful of brandy – she's feeling definitely light-headed – then passes the silver flask to Lou. 'You're full of surprises, I must say, Clare.' Her tone is that of a scolding mother, and Clare feels suitably chastised. It's not long before the plumbline is neatly wound up again on its reel. I could've been fishing, thinks Clare, and a small giggle escapes her.

Lou doesn't even bother asking. She too leans against the brick and lights a cigarette, squinting at the blue. 'It'd be a nice spot, if it wasn't for –'

'Bethie,' Clare finishes firmly. She is already thinking about the return journey out of the tower. It'll be easier, she decides, going back down. And she can send Lou first, in case of spiders.

Louise drinks deeply from the flask. 'You're on the wrong side, though.'

Clare looks up, startled. 'What? Sorry?'

Lou is looking straight ahead, and blows out smoke. She finishes the brandy in one mouthful, and hands the flask politely back to Clare. Her eyes are the yellow of a churned-up sea.

'Wrong side, Clare. Bethie jumped around there – I would've too. If you push off hard, the ground's lower. It slopes away quite quickly. You must remember that. From when we used to play here, as kids –'

Clare can hardly take it in. Her hands have gone numb. Marty had never told them where exactly, he was the only one who had spoken to the police – they had never known. Had never wanted to know, Clare realises now.

'How do you know this?'

'I was here,' Lou says simply. She wipes her fingers slowly across her forehead, the burning cigarette between them. Turn it, thinks Clare, and you'd have a brand, the mark of Cain. 'Well, down there –' Louise leans forward. 'Among the trees.'

Clare is seized by a sudden desire to tip Lou over the side: her hands even twitch with the impulse. But then it is gone, leaving her depleted.

'I brought her over here, to the town, in my car – I never told you that, drove over with the radio blaring the whole way and Bethie silent as a rock. We were staying at the house, just the two of us; I kept thinking this is what it must be like with Beth and Clare, bosom buddies, we could get drunk together and swap secrets, have a midnight snack – but it wasn't like that. She just sat there, like I didn't exist, like . . . Afterwards, I didn't know what I was doing, I drove back to the city, can't even remember doing it – later, couldn't tell anybody, couldn't tell –

'I followed her that night. Don't ask me why. It was dark, really dark.' She gives a small laugh, her lips sucking in on themselves, as if she might cry, but doesn't. 'And windy. A lot of noise . . . what's that phrase?' She turns glassy eyes on Clare.

'Sound and fury.'

'Yes,' Lou agrees. 'And before I really knew what she was doing, she's –'

'Falling.' Twenty-three metres, she thinks. *Damn.*

'And I ran –'

Suddenly Clare realises. 'You made the call that night, you were the one who –'

'I didn't know what else to do,' Lou cries.

The Marshall boy on the stretcher flashes through her mind. 'She might still have been alive –'

Lou has gone pale. 'Come off it, Clare –'

Clare can't help herself but is on her feet and screaming. She grabs Lou by the shirt and drags her up too. 'She meant the world to me! You had the chance, *the one person who* –' Beside herself, she is smacking Lou about the chest and head with useless hands. 'You stupid bitch, why didn't you just shout out, stop her, do something, *anything,* you could have –'

Lou tries to fend her off in the narrow space, backing away from her sister's furious eyes, her mouth opening and shutting as if she can't get enough oxygen.

Then Clare's foot catches on the backpack and they tumble. Clare screams. In a microsecond, spinning, she feels space, sees too much light all around her, sees the ground fly up beneath them. Lou grabs for her.

Whump. They land heavily side by side on the floor of the metal platform, breath driving out of them. They didn't go over the side at all, they haven't gone anywhere. They look at each other, realising what has happened, and laugh hysterically. Lou buries her face in Clare's shoulder, the hair smelling of oranges, while Clare blinks up at banks of deep white cloud.

'Oh my God,' she pants.

Lou is quietly sobbing into Clare's hair, the breath hot against her neck. 'I'm not a bad person,' she whispers, 'am I Clare? Am I –?'

Clare puts her arms around her younger sister, and just like a mother draws Lou's head down onto her chest, rubs circles over her heaving back. '*There, there now.*' The sky is a painted ceiling above them. While down below an orange heifer continues to graze.

NOTES FOR THE LEAVE-TAKING

FINALLY THERE comes a day of leave-taking. Clare sets out from the steps of the hospital in Mackay Street, passing the small sign on the shed – Miscellaneous Dangerous Substances – and she still doesn't know what that is. Walking past the white church with its green turret, the pub right across the street, the Salutation Hotel, its front door facing the corner. Everything is in its place, a proper symmetry maintained. While the hills are scrubby with sunlight and the gorse is yellow with flower, she walks up Karaka Road. Goes past her father's house with its solid processions of vegetables, the exuberance of beans, the sound of cricket playing from within, and a sense of neighbours leaning over the fence.

Along the Terrace, past the white house sitting secure on the hill, while their old street dips darkly, she crosses the bridge over the rocky creek and there is the metal gate of her childhood. Wrought iron, painted black, rusted now in places though still a presentable gate, a gate you can tell just by looking will swing open easily, with only a small effort of bending at the waist, unlatching, pushing back. Bethie swinging on it with pigtails, the screech of the gate going in and out. Louise running through, hair flying, feet tapping along the concrete path. 'Mum Mum, Bethie's got my dolly!' Their mother standing at the gate, arms folded in pink mohair cardigan, waiting for the postie on his creaking bike with the peppertree – *that awful old thing* –

looming in the front corner. 'Morning, Mrs Purefoy, no love letters today.' Her outside laugh carrying on the frigid air. 'Never mind, perhaps tomorrow.' Turning back to the house, back to the dishes, the vacuuming, the smearing of Windowlene onto thin panes of glass. Their father pushing his way through the gate after a day's work. You might wait there for him, in the summer when it was still light, hanging off the gate like it might support you for ever, in cotton shorts and broderie anglais blouse, ends of your hair still scorched from the last experiment, bending too far over the burner. 'That child!'

The swing in the peppertree is still intact. You'd think that the present owners who appear childless would take it down, though perhaps there are grandchildren, or the hope of future children, who might upend the tyre to get rid of the accumulated rainwater and mosquito larvae and rotting leaves, and lever themselves up onto it with bare feet and push off. Bethie, legs hooked around the rope and sitting on the top of the tyre, being pushed by Clare, and yodelling. Until she couldn't go any higher, but still she shouted to be pushed. *Keep going, keep pushing.* Wanting to get higher, higher. Until her head brushed among the branches, the feathery leaves of the tree. They would collect the seeds, and crush them between stones, the smell of pepper stinging their eyes. 'Let's make a stink bomb, a love potion, a poisonous vehicle for destruction. Gunpowder! That's made from pepper.' But in the end, nothing more violent than a flea lotion for the dog that sent him bounding off to the muddy banks of the creek to rub and roll himself clean again. And Clare's solitary experiments involving a bunsen burner and sulphur crystals. Spinning gold out of lead, a child's alchemy. Collecting leaves for Mrs Buckett's goat, who would gobble and gobble, its beard wagging, until you had nothing left, then it would butt you when you turned to go. A mottled goat, with yellow eyes. The time it got loose in their vege garden, the scent of fresh lettuces luring it on, a dream of sweet pansies and blackberry bushes, and their mother had come out carrying the rifle. 'Just let me catch that creature – !' Would she have shot it? Clare will of course never know, feels fortunate not to know. The goat, with a sudden intelligence, had scarpered back through the hole it had made in the fence, disappearing with a hairy waggle of tail and flick of muddy hooves.

Walking the deadend block that is Mill Street, a black pig basking behind a cross-bar gate, with the bush on her left, the hills here too close to be visible any more, and the town far below, Clare catches a sweet scent on the air. Eleven years old and walking along that bush track in sandshoes, shorts, in the languid heat of a summer holiday afternoon, the air redolent with the scent of manuka. You could go on for ever, it is so blissful being by yourself – even though you know that your cousin Roxanne is up ahead with the others and may at any moment backtrack to find you. *Stay together in the bush, there's safety in a group, watch out for Clare she's always tripping over things, have you got the bandages?* 'You're always so quiet, why don't you *say* something –' R's pertinent nose, poking into Clare's thoughts, always so quick with a taunt. 'Go on, say something *inneresting.*' The cousin waiting, but all you can do is stare at the formation of fern that is etched on the trunk of a mamuku. Leaning into the side of your face, as if to share a special secret: 'You're such a *hick*,' hissing so knowledgeably, 'a country *hick.*'

So you linger behind, and further behind, until their voices are meaningless high-pitched echoes, the squeaking of bats in the canopy, and the bush can enfold you with kind fingers, and you breathe in the smell of flowering flax in the heat and your legs have never felt so long and buoyant. Growing up, though you're barely aware of it.

Past Mrs Kray's house with the lilies etched in the glass of the front door, and hollyhocks towering by the fence, pink petal edges fluttering in the breeze, the scent of scones, a woman's perfume, remembering the year she won the best garden competition and the prize a 'cut and blow' at Maison Sheree. Looking back down Mount Pleasant Street to the toffee-coloured firth below, the Toyota factory that employs Mrs Kray and many others like her, the new mall with its playing-field carpark.

'You have to grow up somewhere,' said Janine, raising her nose to the smell of crushed onion weed, Bruce Springsteen twanging away in the background about his home town. Clare walks past the school, where aeons ago she trotted about in her roman sandals and scathed knees, where the caretaker worked in the distance with his weedeater and the smell of onion weed hung heavily on a summer's breeze. Games beneath the oak trees, elastics and skipping: *how many times did you kiss? was it sloppy or wet? how many children will you have? one-two-three-four* – And boys brutal with motorised toy cars. Containing the savages of man and promoting the gentle: wasn't that, once, why she went into medicine? Clare kicks a stone beneath the wire fence and into the school yard, empty with asphalt. Yet is it possible? She wonders with slight anxiety, is that even a wise thing to be doing? For if you contain the savage, aren't you really containing passion, life? Wouldn't it be boring, just having the gentle? A cool breeze smelling of mudflats assaults her face, and she walks on, drawing her cardigan across her chest.

Then back down to the flat and along Parawai Road, the river as looping and muddy as ever. Across the river a lumpy paddock complete with farmer and his herd of black and white cattle, the racecourse and the noise of the traffic from the main road, *passing through*. There was a boy who hired a white suit for the high school disco and imitated John Travolta, but later in the evening was found in a cow paddock disturbing the flock of Jerseys. The Holy Trinity church, small and white on flat grass, with its peaked red roof, where ALL ARE WELCOME, and a cabbage tree leans into a stark blue sky. There is Bethie: they were running early one morning, a weekend morning when Beth was back from nursing college and it must have been winter, for there was fog. River fog, hanging fat and heavy round the lamp-posts and the trunks of trees. You had to be careful else you'd run into somebody walking along Parawai Road, looming up at the last moment. Car headlamps coming out of the fog like ghosts. Fog so thick your hair was wet, your face was wet and the musty-attic smell of it was in your throat. 'I'm not very sporty,' Clare gasped by the time the sludgy river appeared to their left. 'Rubbish,' said Bethie, her profile lean and focused, 'everybody's sporty, it's just that some people don't know it. It's the nature of being an animal. To run, to compete.' But we are not animals, thought Clare meekly – heretical to disagree with Bethie, even in the privacy of her own mind. Even later, dissecting a cadaver, everything laid out inside the cavity, so different from frogs, rabbits, even sheep. 'And here is Miss Pancreas 1986,' joked Dr Jackson. And then, later again, operating on live patients: you can cut them open, sew them up, take bits out, put bits in – but still, they get up afterwards and sing and dance. I am not an animal, thinks Clare, at least, most of the time I am not. So they keep running, running, until Clare can't keep up any more. She turns off at Fenton Street, while Bethie doesn't even notice and continues running, for ever onward. Did she have anything in her mind, while she ran?

In Heale Street there is the baby, in another dirty jumpsuit, plopped in the grass by the rotary. The woman is hanging out the washing with thick red arms (a checked shirt, a yellow sheet) except she wouldn't recognise Clare anyway, though the baby might offer her a sly wink. But Clare lifts her chin and keeps walking. The baby sticks its fist in its mouth and drools over a clump of snatched grass. Onion weed flowering in the ditches, she passes the bottom of Jacob's Ladder and its one hundred and twenty-three steps. From down here it looks dingy, uninviting, a place to risk your reputation or the welfare of your body.

She walks past the old hotel. She and Oliver, on a bright afternoon, though the room was cold, cave-like because of the dark wallpaper, navy blue with white dots. They had one of the cheaper rooms so the bathroom was down the hall, and Clare wondered how she would get to it, later, without anybody seeing her, the town alive with ears and eyes – how to conduct your life, without it being chewed over by acquaintances: *Clare was that you I saw at the old hotel and who was that young man you were with?* Right across the road a car dealership. 'Pull down the blind, Oliver.' Clare had bought condoms from the machine in the med school toilets weeks ago, making plans (where to do it, what town to do it in, when to do it), until the old hotel had seemed the only place possible for such an act, offering the right kind of ambience and anonymity; yet still it was like having sex with your cousin. Kissing cousins. 'Sid says there might be some blood,' said Oliver with apprehension. Oliver might faint if exposed to blood. And so Sid intruded, all angles and small brutalities. 'You've talked to him about *this?*' Clare by contrast lying pale and thin, a series of bumps beneath the sheet, that meagre body that Mrs Kray during the holidays took pains to fatten up. A smell of fried eggs sneaked into the room. 'No, course not.' Oliver was blinking and shedding clothes, a nineteen-year-old virgin. 'Just in, well, general terms. That's all.'

'I could have told you about that,' said Clare, peeling back the sheet for Oliver to get in, equally pallid – 'What a pair!' – his skin nearly blue with fright and erection quivering. There was a wall heater, sitting low and malevolent, but neither of them wanted to turn it on while the sun was so insistent beyond the sash window, glaring orange through the blind. Oliver getting a headache from the wallpaper. The hotel hall, when she got to it, was musty and dark with more antique flowers on the carpet. On the way back Clare turned into another small shabby room – 'Oh, sorry!' – yet it was not a man in the room, but empty wetsuits lying along the carpet by the bed. *Gawd.*

Passing a bird-of-paradise flower – its red neck, high pointy tuft of orange and dark purple, the sharp, sharp beak. Looking as if about to pounce. Lou, when she first saw one, thought it really was a bird peering out from between broad taro-like leaves. A brooch in the shape of a bird, in blue enamel with a silver eye, that Clare had come across by accident in Lou's singlet drawer. Lou bending back one of Clare's fingers: *Give it to me or I'll break your finger.* Where had she learned such a technique? Chinese burns in the playground. A mother's brooch among underwear.

CLOSURE

Clare turns into mainstreet. The legend sprayed onto the pavement: *NO Dogs Rollerblades Skateboards Bicycles*. People screw up their eyes at her, Doctor Purefoy: old Mr Lincoln raises his trilby, hand purple with broken veins, the legacy of high blood pressure, Mary Maxwell saying, Gidday Clare whatcha up to? She smiles back, but doesn't stop. Nobody will reach out and stop her today. Going past BIN INN, John Round and Son's printing shop, the Argyle Tearooms advertising their Big Breakfast which includes fried bread and black pudding, the place where the Walker family's bakery used to be with its ovens out the back, the Sally Army Centre with its sign reading 'This is a CH—CH. What's missing?' and somebody has filled in the gap with the word 'alcohol'.

Going past the doctor's surgery. The time she'd asked to go on the pill. Doctor Fleming was laconic, sitting largely behind his desk, and said, 'Are you quite sure about this?' But there was no lecture to follow, and Clare, already studying to be a doctor, looked at everything with interest – the way he scribbled on his notepad (no computers yet), the cabinets, the examining table, the few instruments that were visible. 'What do you do,' she wondered out loud, 'if you want to be a doctor, but you're squeamish, say, about giving people injections?' Her legs very thin and pale in denim shorts, the bike parked outside against the clinic's brick wall like she was still a kid. Dr Fleming looked over the desk at her with indulgence. 'Oh, you soon get used to that. I used to think of it as sticking a needle into an apple.' Apples, thought Clare, rotted, went brown, as soon as you cut into them. 'It's all in the mind,' he said, adding a Biro flourish to the pad, his pen lingering over the page for a moment. 'Like anything, you just decide that you're going to like it, and you do.' And he offered her a lazy smile. 'It's that easy.' He stood up, and placed his hand on her shoulder while she made her way towards the door. Oh my God, thought Clare back outside, propping up her bike and suddenly lost in the sunlight, he thought I was talking about sex! Her cheeks going bright red. Later she heard that Dr Fleming had left his practice and the town because he'd given drugs to a young girl in exchange for sex. His marriage had broken up, it was said, as if this was enough explanation. He had large soft hands, remembered Clare, although cold that day on the back of her shoulder.

She walks past Junction Hotel where the Friday night band is called Rox Ya Sox Off, and the mustard-yellow Backpackers' Hotel. The young Frenchman who had fallen over a bluff on his way up to Table Mountain. His friend, an anxious Dutch boy, had run back down the track for help; the pair had hooked up at the Backpackers' Hotel. It could've been me, he grinned. Quite. He was very beautiful, that Frenchman with his broken leg. When it was over, pulling off the rinsed rubber gloves in the prep room, aware of the snapping noise they made, it was as if God had snapped his fingers. God not on high, but lurking about just behind your shoulder, ready to push. Three young backpackers sitting in the sun on the hotel step. A head pokes out of a bottom window: 'Gidday Doctor Purefoy, got time for a cuppa?' Joyce Miller, her hair still in curlers and minus her tonsils, who runs the place. Rumour has it that she tries out the young German men, though why German and not other nationalities? There is no sense in gossip. There was that German in San Fran, he'd come to the ER with a cut head and they had discussed the merits of various movies while she had put in some stitches, then he offered his erect penis to her like a tasty morsel. 'I'm sorry,' she'd said, with a deprecating laugh, 'I'm spoken for –' He tucked his penis back under the sheet with a matter-of-fact pat. 'Never mind, it was worth a try.' Wasn't it always? Clare imagines what would happen if she had done something similar to a man – if she exposed a breast, say – but then men are visual creatures, she thinks, easily seduced by sight alone. Brown & Wiseman had laughed. 'You get all the good ones,' said Brown, rolling his eyes. Not true, she knows now, thinking of Marcus. Her time in San Fran like living on a fault line. That dream where she is caught in a quake, the bay house in Marina caving forward with a sickening wrench, and Brown's mother appears holding a pot of coffee, only the face is that of her own mother. Clare decides not to take any notice of her dreams any more. Bethie's secondhand book of dream interpretation that she found in Marty's basement and offered to Tupulo: *If you dream of falling water it means your wife has always hated you.* For days afterwards the sound of Tupulo's dense laughter issuing from the toilet, and rolling apart one morning bathed in oily sweat, Tupulo always erect at early hours, he declaimed: 'Dream of an avalanche, your wife is having an affair with a politician!'

And another time in the Valley, with Bethie vaulting through the air, arms and legs flapping and wheeling, it only takes a second but it slows down to a lifetime, Bethie against all that blue (so blue), bum sticking out, and her madcap grin – '*What a character!*' – before being swallowed by the river. Another time when they'd both lain in the long grass down by the reserve in the heat of a summer's day, hidden from sight by the waving grass as high as your hip, and she'd had her hands linked behind her head and you'd stroked the fine fine hair. *Will I ever get some too?* Course, said Bethie, and you'd been relieved, cause Bethie always knew, cause Bethie was up ahead, had been there before. And another day when you'd found the girl crying on the back doorstep. She was huddled sobbing, all knees, hair over her face. There was nobody home, except Clare, and she wasn't equipped for sobbing girls. What to do? She'd retreated to the kitchen – *All right, I'll make her some Milo* – and put water in the kettle. But when she'd next looked (creeping Miss Mouse) Bethie was there, crouched over the girl, one hand on the girl's head, one hand on the girl's knee, and the sobbing had turned into muffled noises against Bethie's shoulder. Clare had withdrawn just as quietly. Milo wouldn't be needed after all, and wouldn't she *ever* grow up?

When she turns into the gravel driveway from Jacob's Ladder, Clare finds Tupulo is hovering about, waiting for her on the doorstep with the suitcases lined up neatly in the sun, and Grunt too sitting like an inconspicuous dog-shaped case.

'Are you ready?' he calls.

The sun makes Clare squint, and Tupulo for a moment looms

largely, with the darkness of the house behind him. But then he steps forward and she can see him clearly.

'Yes,' she says, 'ready.'

ALSO BY PENGUIN

RECONNAISSANCE
Kapka Kassabova

A powerful and sensual début novel.

Nadejda is backpacking around New Zealand, in the surreal haze of summer. Her encounters are comic and revealing – and often sexual. But Nadejda's tour is a deep and personal one; it is a journey into memory and family myth.

Faded memories of happy times conflict with more disturbing pictures as her determination to uncover the truth is diffused with an immigrant's yearning to belong and a young woman's longing for love. And who is the mystery narrator who 'talks' to Nadejda as her travels lead her to him?

Set against the turmoil of present-day Bulgaria and the sweet simplicity of her new country, *Reconnaissance* is a grand, sweeping novel of family secrets, dislocation and ultimate reconciliation.

Winner of the Best First Book category in the South-East Asia and South Pacific region of the 2000 Commonwealth Writers Prize, and finalist in the 1999 Montana New Zealand Book Awards.

Classical *Music*

JOY COWLEY

We dive together and come up, our clothes floating around us. The water is surprisingly warm and it occurs to me that this is the first time we've been in the sea together since her near-drowning incident.

Delia and Bea, sisters, but never close. Delia lives a glamorous life in New York and Bea lives thousands of miles away in New Zealand, looking after elderly parents and playing the role of dutiful daughter. Delia and Bea both long for the warmth and intimacy of sisterhood, but it always eludes them.

When Delia rushes home for their father's funeral there is an opportunity to spend some time together, but Delia and Bea move in orbit around each other, both recalling grievances and hurts, neither prepared to admit their need for each other. But as the day of the funeral passes, memories are unlocked: memories of their mother and her passion for music, memories of their father and memories of a magical summer and a man they had all loved.

Joy Cowley is one of New Zealand's most loved children's writers. She is also famous all over North America for her wonderful children's readers. *Classical Music* is her second adult novel.

THE CURATIVE
Charlotte Randall

The narrator of this compelling and unusual novel is an inmate of Bedlam, the London mental asylum. He is living chained to a wall in unspeakably horrible conditions, yet he is witty, urbane and seemingly sane. He reflects on freedom, on love and on love lost, and on the fleeting nature of happiness.

As this beautifully constructed story unfolds we learn about the bizarre treatments he has endured under the asylum's curative regimen, his life before Bedlam, and the answers to the critical questions: *Why is this man here? What has he done?*

This novel deftly explores the devious in human affairs and the intricacies of language to create a brilliant and utterly memorable book.

Charlotte Randall's first novel, *Dead Sea Fruit* (1995), won both the Reed Fiction Award and Best First Book in the South-East Asia and South Pacific region of the Commonwealth Writers Prize.